First published in 2015 by Aloejimmy Publishing

A CIP catalogue record for this book is available from the British Library

ISBN 978-0-9926276-2-1

Aloejimmy Publishing

www.aloejimmy.com

Cover design illustrated by Emma Morrissey BA

www.emzportraitscrafts.wordpress.com

My thanks to

Penny Legg for her continued support and for the character of Salty Sam, James Reeves for editing the manuscript, Emma Morrissey for her great cover design, Shirley Kersey of Bournemouth Library for information about the funicular railway, Robert Painton for tales of skullduggery in Southampton Docks, Jeremy Moulton for his enthusiasm for my idea of a crooked councilor, Joe Croll Yellow Dog Jazz Club, Southampton Archives Department, The George Hotel Ashford where the idea for this book was born, Bobby Parsons for his memories of the Portswood Hotel, Treena Westwood for her suggestions about locations.

I have mentioned everyone I can remember who helped with the production of this book. If I have missed anyone then do please accept my sincere apologies.

Born To Be Evil

James Marsh

Aloejimmy Publishing

Chapter One

1941. The height of the blitz over the port of Southampton. With bombs raining down from the skies overhead, the plaintive cry of a newborn baby is still audible above the racket. Coming from a small house in Empress Road down near the docks it heralded the arrival of one Thomas Nevan Littlejohn. His mother, a middle aged lady who had experienced a troubled and very difficult life, now lay with her new son on a rickety bed. She tried to be happy to see him. But this war had been raging for over two years and though hardships were felt everywhere, in this neighborhood they seemed to be trebled. So the new arrival would have to make the best of things as did everyone else around him.

Mr. Littlejohn worked as a stevedore in the docks so was exempt from military service. His job was too important. Any ships that managed to make it through, evading the torpedoes of the German U Boats, had to be unloaded quickly. Ready then to sail again and bring much needed supplies to the country's starving people, a noble occupation that should have stood him in good stead. But this was a man who cared for no-one but himself. Even his wife and children came second to his wants and needs. He was in a perfect place to operate a black market racket on street corners and the dubious houses in this part of Southampton.

1

Ever alert for police presence he was as ruthless a character as many more well known gangsters from both this country and across the Atlantic. Leading a gang of like-minded men, all of whom worked in the docks, they too were as ruthless and greedy as Mr. Littlejohn. Stolen goods from ships holds went into their store room, the small back bedroom of the Littlejohn home, number 34 Empress Road.

Having a bedroom unavailable for the families use caused considerable inconvenience as they already had six young children. Four girls and two boys slept in the one single bed, three of the girls at the top end and the younger girl with her two brothers at the bottom. Undressing in the same room had become a simple routine so that none of them were embarrassed to see each other in this state, especially as they all shared the same tin bath once a week.

What did upset them however were the constant visits of the ARP wardens, the Home Guard and police, all of whom suspected their father of black market activity. At such a time, with food and other essentials in such short supply, this was a very serious crime and anyone caught would face a long prison sentence. Albert David Littlejohn was already known to the police who were keen to put him behind bars, where he richly deserved to be, but of course they needed proof.

So at least twice a week the Littlejohn home was raided and that back bedroom was searched thoroughly. To counteract this, a network of spies was put in place to tip him off about every raid before it actually happened. Albert Littlejohn then took appropriate action.

Stolen contraband was moved out of the small bedroom and distributed into the beds of the children and also that of his wife, the long suffering Ida Littlejohn. Not only was she involved in his criminal activities, she acted as a decoy. Transformed into a bedridden invalid on each of these raids, she even managed to garner sympathy from the police, ARP wardens and Home

Guard, who would bring little treats for her such as sweets or items of food.

It has to be said that Ida was a very good actress. She really did appear frail and ill. Her eldest daughter Maggie always did the makeup that made her mother look white and sickly. So much so that although the raiding parties felt sorry for her they, none-the-less, kept their distance from her bed; which was just as well because she was never alone. Tucked around her were bottles of whisky, brandy and gin, as well as the tins of food and dry goods that were in such huge demand at all of the local shops. Real nylon stockings were also secreted around Ida Littlejohn, while under her nightdress were clothes originally destined for some of the most well known and expensive shops in London. All strictly rationed of course, only those with both the required number of coupons and money to pay for them would have been able to enjoy the clothes, food and alcohol that the supposedly sickly Ida was tucked up in bed with.

In the children's room, carefully placed inside the mattress were small toys, watches, and various items that simply could not be purchased during these dark days such as ball bearings. Everything fetched a good price. Coupons of course were not required for these more dubious transactions. Black marketers these gang members may have been but they, along with many others all around Great Britain, were known more commonly as Spivs.

The small back bedroom was always the main source of suspicion and Albert knew this. So a transformation was necessary. Before a raid a double bed would be brought in whereupon one of his gang members would entertain a girl in the Littlejohn house. They were encountered plying their sex trade on the Southampton Streets so this was just another job for whichever girl was chosen. Always well paid they certainly didn't object but this came with a stern warning to keep their mouths shut or else. Hard and tough they may have been

3

because their trade was dangerous enough, but this threat went home so neither girl ever dared to disobey.

Told simply to strip completely and get into the bed, the Littlejohn gang member would then do the same thing. When the door burst open and the police charged in it was always to find this lodger in bed with his girlfriend and about to enjoy her body. They were ordered out of bed and made to stand naked in the room. Both of them started to protest at this intrusion into their private world. The girls were simply wonderful at this, every one of them made an attempt to cover themselves with their hands while shouting at whichever raiding party was currently in the room.

"Having a good look are you, you bleeding perverts?"

Her makeshift partner on the other hand simply stood his ground, making no attempt to cover his own nakedness, while uttering threats. As it was always a different gang member playing the part of outraged lodger the raiding parties simply never suspected the connection of these men with the black market activities. None of them wanted anything to do with men who threatened the sort of violence that came their way.

"Can't a bloke have a shag without you bastards bursting in? Get the fuck out of here before I gets me mates round to sort the bloody lot of you out. And we ain't particular about what happens to bastards like you."

They were fully prepared to carry this out as could be seen from the vicious looking knuckledusters that adorned their fist. If used in a fight these could cause very serious injury.

The police of course would not be threatened in this way. Knuckledusters were illegal so a fight always ensued with the gang member eventually dragged from the house in handcuffs and thrown, still naked, into the back of a Black Maria. The sentence was always the same when the court case came up with a Littlejohn gang member spending the next few weeks in prison. The object of all this was to disrupt the search of the house and each time it was successful.

4

To the police this was highly frustrating. Before the war Albert Littlejohn operated an even bigger racket involving many more men. Working in Southampton docks they watched as cigarettes, alcohol and other goods were loaded onto the backs of lorries. These items, although destined for various parts of the British Isles, could easily be sold on if intercepted first.

This was where contacts in other towns and cities came into play. Information was sent out with a description of the lorries and their registration numbers. The rest was simple. Catch up, wait for the driver to stop at a roadside café then simply steal it along with the load it was carrying. This was mostly achieved with no-one getting hurt.

Sometimes the drivers simply pulled into a lay by in order to rest and have something to eat and drink. On such occasions the pursuing gangsters crept stealthily up to the cab before throwing open the door. These unfortunate and completely innocent drivers were then beaten up and left unconscious in a ditch somewhere while the lorry was driven away.

Some of them ended up in hospital with very nasty injuries. On one occasion, however, a driver who was young and much stronger than the gangsters had anticipated gave a very good account of himself. The crooks were actually getting the worst of things before a gunshot rang out. The young driver reeled back and looked down in shock at the red stain that was quickly covering the front of his white shirt. Slumping to the ground, he was dead before his body hit it.

The drive back to Southampton in the stolen lorry was a worrying one for the gunman. His boss Albert Littlejohn had a very nasty temper. When informed about the lorry drivers murder, the tough young hoodlum had no idea what would happen to him. With a flourishing empire at this time, all stolen cargoes were delivered to a disused, crumbling warehouse at the back of the Littlejohn household. A dangerous old building that no-one, not even the local boys went anywhere near. So contraband could be stored without anyone even becoming suspicious.

The operation was carried out at night with complete precision. It had to be. Lorries turning up continuously in a small street like this would stand out a mile, quickly arising suspicion amongst the neighbours. Cargoes were transferred into cars that could come off the main road then use the small cut way by the side of this old warehouse.

Always watching them unload was the man they all feared so much, Albert Littlejohn himself. A thief and a thug who never trusted anyone, any transgressions were always swiftly dealt with. Albert himself would lead at least three of his most trusted henchmen and make sure the offender was very badly beaten up, but never killed. Littlejohn never went that far. So how was he going to react to the fact his gang had now committed murder?

The news had filtered back to Southampton by the time the gang members arrived and predictably Littlejohn was waiting. He had them dragged into the office in the corner of the building and demanded to know what had happened.

"The bloody young fool was fighting back boss," the eldest of these toughs tried to justify their actions. "He was young and bloody strong too. You can see the boys have all got marks on them. Well there was only one way we could stop him so I shot the bleeder."

Glowering at this man Albert snarled back.

"And now the police are going to be out in force looking for the young blokes killers ain't they? Are you sure no-one saw any of you?"

"Yes boss, we pick a lonely spot to hijack the lorry if it dont stop at a café like as always. There wasn't as much as a cow in a field to see what happened."

Dismissing them Albert turned to his closest friend George (the cosh) Harcourt. Large and bruising, his main contribution to life seemed to be to provide the main muscle for this gang. Many unfortunate men had fallen foul of him over the years and

6

been lucky to escape with their lives. He wasn't called the Cosh for nothing. He favoured this weapon above anything else.

"What do you think George?"

"I believe them boss, they was all scared of what you would do about it. I know most of them. If shooting that driver was the only way to stop him then that's why they did it."

"Yeah I suppose your right but we may have to lay low for a bit. The heats going to be on now ain't it? They can trace the lorry from Southampton Docks and it won't to too hard digging deeper and finding out about this racket we've got going."

George rubbed his chin as he pondered this.

"Hold on a minute boss. I don't think we should stop. We cover our tracks very well, both in the docks and on all our hijacking jobs. No-one knows we use this warehouse. No I say let's go on as we are. This may work in our favour."

"How the bloody hell can it?" Albert snarled. "We've killed a bloke and that's gonna stir up the bloody fuzz."

"Yeah, but it's also going to send a message to anymore have-a-go drivers. They'll know soon enough about this killing and it won't take them long to figure out why it happened."

A slow smile crept across the face of Albert as he reasoned this out. His second in command was right. Between them they headed a large and very crooked organization. Everyone was expected to tow the gang's line. The men in Southampton docks helped with the loading of lorries and so were able to give details of these to Albert. He passed the information to George (the Cosh) who then detailed gang members in whatever area any particular lorry was travelling and ordered the hi-jacking.

No-one had stepped out of line or gotten greedy and tried helping themselves to the spoils of this crime for a very simple reason. The Cosh was well known, as was the reason for this nickname. With very little conscience and many would say no soul as well, he had been known to beat a man to within an inch of his life with that deadly cosh. Sometimes for reasons as

7

simple as the unfortunate person saying something insulting about him in a pub.

In this organization though his contribution and the way he went about his business, keeping various gang members in line, was worth its weight in gold to Albert Littlejohn.

"As usual you're right mate. I didn't want things going this way but blimey this will give us a reputation won't it?"

"Yeah it will, but let's not forget the police will get to know soon enough about this murder and then things will start to pop. They'll step up their inquiries. We need to make sure they don't drop on us. We want drivers to be scared, but not so much that they go running to the law."

"No that's right but they will know we mean business and will use guns if necessary."

George Harcourt was still pondering the consequences, specifically how much more they would be scrutinized going forward.

"That's the idea boss and I'm sure it will work. Our boys know to hide the fact they've got a bloody sight more money than anyone around them, which is why no-one in the docks is looking at us over all these lorry hi-jacks. I know you keep a lot back from your old lady and all. How you do it has always been a mystery to me."

"My Ida is a good girl and a bloody good mother to all our kids. But she doesn't know how much money I've really got. Don't get me wrong, she and the kids are well provided for and she knows some of the money I give her doesn't come out of my wage packet. That's all though, there's no way I want her to find out about my other house or the little raver who lives there. That's the perks of this racket George, and blimey we want some fun don't we?"

Ida Littlejohn was indeed a good mother and looked after her six children very well. None of them went without shoes or proper clothing and all were fed and kept clean. Well most of the time anyway. Her two sons managed to regularly come back from playing either covered in dirt or soaking wet from swimming in the rivers or staying out in the rain.

On bath night however, always a Friday when the tin bath that was kept in the back garden was brought into the back kitchen of the house in Empress Road, they did their best to disappear. They never managed to get away with it. The eldest daughter of the family, Maggie always made sure they ended up in the bath. Mrs. Littlejohn was glad of her daughters help in matters like this and grateful too that she managed to stay happy, even though their small house afforded very little privacy to a girl of her age.

Two of her neighbours were frequent visitors. Not only were they on friendly terms with this woman, but very curious about her and her family.

How, for instance, were her children properly dressed when all the others in the area relied on charitable institutions for clothing? True her husband had a very good job in the docks but there were times when the work simply dried up, so how did the Littlejohn's survive so easily at times like this? Ida knew they wanted her to reveal her secrets but if either of them found out the news would be all over the neighbourhood in no time at all

Little snippets of information would have to suffice and this was exactly what she fed them, stopping just short of the truth. Her husband had another job outside of usual work hours.

"It's a lot for him to take on," she would say. "But he's that good a dad he wants to make sure me and the kids don't go without."

Though this seemed to pacify her gossipy friends she did wonder what these two busybodies would really make of her husband. Ida and Albert first met when she had been sent to live with her strict Victorian Grandmother. With a large family of ten children this had been too much of a strain for her own mother. A better life as far as food and clothing was concerned, nice dresses on home visits and even doing hand stands to show off her new knickers. The price for this, however, was sheer hard work in a very Victorian household.

The man of the house was almost worshiped because he was the breadwinner and everything revolved around him. Ida of course had to accept this as all children did, that is until she met the dashing Albert Littlejohn who lived with his family in the next street.

In this part of Southampton, taking in Newtown and Northam, many roads had very tough reputations. With the Gas works always sending out a very distinctive smell life here was a case of fight or go under. The Littlejohn family lived in Dukes Road in Bevios valley and this certainly was a place for fighting families.

Ida lived in the next road and from the first time she saw Albert it was love at first sight. Tall and handsome, many local girls also had their eye on him. But for the first time in his life Albert saw a girl who immediately set his heart strings pinging. The two of them became close and Ida was in dreamland as she walked beside him. In dark corners his arms would be around her and his lips on hers.

Love of course can overcome many difficulties and in this case it was Albert's contempt for the local police. She knew he was no saint and had met his brothers and many of his friends. All of whom had the same disliking of anyone in authority. What she didn't know was the full extent of the things her boyfriend, and the gang he ran with, got up to when she wasn't around. Shoplifting and vandalism of other people's property was a game to the Littlejohn's and their friends.

But she began to realize as time went on that there was more to Albert than she had first thought. One night at his home when the rest of the family were out he took her in his arms and after kissing her passionately started to remove her clothes. This hadn't happened before as all he had done was grope her breasts under her brassier. Now he had the blouse undone and was pulling it from her shoulders. She panicked and tried to resist

10

but he whispered in her ear and kissed her again until he felt her relax. After that not only her blouse but the rest of her clothes came off and they had full on sex on the floor of the lounge. It was the start of a real relationship between Ida and Albert and many more steamy sessions took place in various other places.

Until the day Albert turned up at Ida's grandmothers house to collect her for the day out they had planned and saw how she was being treated by this elderly Victorian woman. Ida was on her knees scrubbing the kitchen floor while her grandma shouted at her to hurry up.

"You've got all the beds to make yet and the ironing to do you lazy girl. Get a move on can't you?"

Looking at Ida, Albert made what some would call not the most romantic of marriage proposals.

"Christ mush, let's get you out of this."

They were married on Christmas Day 1927 and moved into the house in Empress Road. Here they set up home and began raising their family, which meant Ida bearing the children and seeing to their needs once they were born. Albert spent very little time at home. He was apparently always needed in the docks. In reality of course his out of hours job was running his gang and collecting large amounts of money from their illegal activities. By the time their sixth child, a boy named Charlie, was born world war two was about to be declared.

Ida kept more of an eye on her husband than he knew. She was of course aware that he was up to something and that it was probably against the law. But she tended to overlook this. The money given to her each week was more than sufficient for all the family's needs. But just where was it coming from and how much damage could it do to her and the children if the police were to arrest Albert?

She began to listen as much as she could when unfamiliar men came to her home to meet him. By the look of most of them she wouldn't ever want to get to know them. So she made sure her children were never around when these meetings took

11

place because she certainly didn't want any of them getting ideas about following in their father's footsteps. It might after all seem like a glamorous and prosperous way to live.

But was it just these activities Albert was getting up to when he was absent from their home for several nights at a time? This she was determined to investigate so started going out for an evening at the local cinema once a week, leaving her eldest daughter Maggie in charge. This became a regular routine that the Littlejohn children not only accepted without any qualms at all, but enjoyed these nights tremendously. All of them could get round their elder sister in order to stay up later than usual, and also make far more noise than their mother would ever tolerate.

Ida was careful to know which films were showing so she could always say which ones she saw. But in fact she went to a good friend who lived near the docks, her intention being to watch the men leaving and see whether her husband was amongst them. This proved more difficult than expected because there was such a steady stream of men pouring out through the dock gates and identifying just one was near impossible.

That is until the day she quite clearly saw Albert in earnest conversation with George (the cosh) Harcourt, a man she intensely disliked and was also fearful of. This was also the day when he said he would be working very late as more ships were due and they had to be unloaded as quickly as possible. Why then was he leaving with the horrible George Harcourt at the usual time?

Quick as a flash Ida put on her coat and, waving to her friend, went out into the street and quickly saw Albert, now alone, up in front of her. She followed and watched him board a number 11 Corporation tram and just as it was about to leave jumped on herself. Still keeping a good eye on her husband she rode the tram as it wound its way around the Bargate, through the town centre then up Lodge road until it reached Portswood Junction.

This wasn't an area Ida was very familiar with although she had heard of it before. Now as the tram drew to a stop just past the small Palladium Cinema she saw Albert leave his seat to get off. Discretely shuffling back she waited till the last minute before leaving the tram and kept a good distance behind her husband as she followed him into Highfield lane. This was an area of very large and expensive looking houses, the like of which Ida had never been anywhere near. Surely only very well off people could afford to live in the luxury that these houses afforded.

Albert came to a big house standing in expansive grounds. The front garden was covered with a neatly trimmed lawn and had flowers growing around the edges. A wide graveled path led up the oak paneled front door and as Ida watched Albert simply placed his hand into his trouser pocket and drew out a bunch of keys. One of these he fitted into the door lock which he opened and simply walked inside, leaving the door slightly open.

"Hey, Janice. Where are you baby? I'm back and raring to go again with you."

Almost at once a blonde girl with a striking figure, most of which could be seen through the thin negligee she was wearing, came rushing up and fell into Albert's arms. As they kissed, with a passion that certainly surprised Ida, the girls negligee fell away from her body leaving her stark naked. This was the last Ida saw of this particular scene because the big front door crashed shut. The squeals of the girl could be heard for a time after as the two made frantic love together.

Standing on the pavement outside this big house Ida was fuming. She had been suspicious of Albert for some time now, but this was far beyond anything she envisaged. *"Whose bloody house is this?"* she thought to herself *"and who the hell is that little tramp inside? Well I'll be back here soon and if I don't get some bloody answers that little whore and my husband are going to find out just what sort of a woman I really am."*

13

Just two days later Ida, in her best clothes, once again found herself sitting on a number 11 tram. Going through Lodge Road her anger was building up and even before the tram stopped just past the Palladium cinema and in front of Portswood library she knew exactly what she was going to do.

Once more she walked up Highfield lane until she came to the house she had seen Albert go into. This time though she strode up to the door and loudly banged the ornate door knocker. After a short pause the door was opened and a young woman's face peered out.

"Yeah what do you want missus? My old man said we don't buy anything at the door."

Ida simply stood on the doorstep and looked at this woman, who actually was little more than a girl. With long flowing blonde hair and a nice figure, this was easy to see as the dress clung to her body and showed off every curve, from breasts that stood out, all the way down to her slim waist. Taking in the expensive nylon stockings and the shoes on her tiny feet that must have cost at least twice as much as Albert earned for a week's work in the docks, Ida simply pushed past her before she could react and entered the house.

"Ere, you can't come in this house," the girl shouted. "I'll get my old man on to you if you don't clear orff."

Trying to pull Ida back towards the door she quickly found herself pinned against the elegant hallway wall. Ida glared at her.

"Your old man? No he ain't you bloody little tart he's my old man. I'm his wife and the mother of his kids so who the bleeding hell are you and whose house is this?"

The girl now cowered in fear. Not easily scared, but finding herself in the grip of a very angry woman and accused of having relations with her husband was outside of anything she had encountered thus far.

"It weren't my fault missus; I didn't know who Albert was before he picked me up and brought me here. It weren't my

14

idea, he was just a punter. He brought me here and I have to do what he wants or else. And I know he's got some right nasty friends as well."

"How?" Ida shouted but the girl failed to see what she meant.

"How do you know about my husband's friends?"

Realization now dawned.

"They come here at night see, and talk in the big front room. Then some of them come up to my bedroom and I have to have sex with them. And right nasty they are and all."

Ida looked at her and for the first time saw a lovely but frightened young girl so let her go.

"What's your name girl and how old are you?"

"Janice Saunders and I'm twenty one."

"I'll accept your name Janice but you certainly aren't twenty one, now how old are you? And I want the truth this time."

With tears now glistening in her eyes Janice spoke quietly.

"Fifteen missus and I need this work because my family needs the money. We ain't got no dad see so my brothers have to get jobs instead of going to school. But they don't earn enough for the whole families' needs."

"Alright Janice," Ida gently replied. "I won't harm you or stop you doing this but you be careful. Don't ever refuse the friends of my husband because I know some of them myself and they'll show you no mercy if you do. So don't say a word to him about my visit here today."

"But what will you do missus? He gives me lots of stuff as well as money, food for the kids and clothes as well. I need to keep going here for as long as I can."

"Don't worry about that. I won't tell him I've been here because I don't want him to know. This is something I'll keep to myself until something crops up where I need to throw it in his face."

Walking back to the tram stop, cunning plans were forming. Her thoughts though were also of Janice Saunders. Poor little cow, she'll only last as long as her looks do or until that bastard

15

of a husband and his creepy friends get tired of her. At least Albert gives her something that's helping her family to survive, but what a price to pay. Ida really hoped nothing nasty ever happened as she did seem like a nice kid and genuine victim here.

Ida was true to her word and kept the knowledge of the house in Highfield Lane a secret for now. Putting up with the nights when he wasn't home, knowing of course he was at the big house as she now called it. She found out who owned this house and wasn't surprised when the name of Albert Littlejohn came up. Now she would somehow get back at her scheming husband and give him as much trouble as she could. She of course looked after her own house and children, but knew someday she wanted her husband's other house for all of them to live in.

But before she could do anything about this, two things happened almost simultaneously. She fell pregnant with her seventh child and World War Two was declared.

Chapter Two

There had been unrest for months over the situation in Europe and when war was declared with Germany many young men joined up to fight for their country. But not those whose jobs were considered important enough to exempt them from military service, these became known as reserved occupations.

Among these were dock workers. The government knew that the Germans would try to sink merchant ships and in so doing attempt to starve the nation into submission. Men with expertise in loading and unloading were therefore kept back to carry on this really important job.

The British people were literally on their knees and whole families had to make do on whatever they were allowed from the shops in their area. A method of making this fair was, of course, the introduction of ration books. Money alone was not enough. Coupons were now required to buy food, clothing, and other essential items. They determined how much each family could purchase. Even children were to find this awkward situation applying to them because sweets were included in the rationing.

Adversity quickly gave rise to opportunity. Many were quick to seize upon the chance this afforded them to offer goods without requiring coupons. It meant higher prices because the people supplying them were breaking the law. Known everywhere as spivs they operated on what became known as the black market.

Albert Littlejohn was very interested in this and soon became the man to see if what you needed was either not available in the shops, or too many precious coupons had been used up. The first year of the war had split his gang operation apart as the ravages of repeated bombings took their toll on so many towns and cities. Gang members now had to make sure they avoided being called up to fight then look to the black market to survive. The lorry hijacking business was no longer viable as incoming goods were watched so closely by both the police and armed forces. Each time a ship made it past the German U boats its cargo never seemed to be enough to meet everyone's needs.

Albert had discussed this very problem with George Harcourt in his Empress Road home.

"I know we can't target the lorries any more not with the way the police are watching everything. Blimey we can't even pinch a few oranges like we used to can we?"

"No boss, but there are ways we can keep on making money so we can live as we always have done."

"OK George I'm listening. It better be good cause I can't see much of a way round this at the moment."

"Boss, we've got everything we took out of that old warehouse for a start. It was a good bloody job we did wasn't it?"

"Yeah," Albert agreed. "The army took the place over and they're using it for a food storage. We got out just in time."

"Yeah and we took everything to your big house in Highfield Lane didn't we? Well we can move stuff from there, a bit at a time, and store it here in Empress Road. From there we can operate a black market racket here in Southampton. It'll be easy pickings. Once we get started we can use our gangland contacts to get us anything we need. We'll clean up because this country is short of so many things. If we can supply some of them we'll be able to charge what we bleeding well want."

Albert was thinking this over.

"George I think you've got something here, but some of the stuff we want may be hard to get. Perishables for instance, are being kept in places like our old warehouse and watched round the clock by the Home Guard. Getting into places like that will be dangerous cause those old men are likely to shoot anyone trying to steal stuff."

"That's true Al."

George had only recently started to call Albert by the shortened version of his Christian name because the two of them were so close and both in complete control of everything they and others under them took on.

"But think for a moment," he continued. "We know that warehouse so well and can get in and out through the back of the bleeding place without those old men even finding out about it. And don't forget we know when more stuff will be going in because we, or some of our boys, will be around in the docks when it arrives."

"It sounds good George but what about when they find out stuff is going missing? They must be able to count and surely they'll realize someone has been helping themselves."

"Lenny Warren and Pat Matthews are taking care of that already. They've organized a few of our old cronies to not only do the stealing for us but cover their tracks while they do it. We can get hold of margarine a bloody sight easier than butter so our boys will be armed with this when they go in. For every packet of butter they grab they'll substitute a pack of margarine."

"I like this," Albert replied. "It's bloody devious ain't it and right up our street, so let's get things organised quickly."

"Already in hand," George assured him so the two of them set off to the Portswood Hotel, the pub on the corner of Dukes Road. In here all the men who both knew and worked with these two were to be found. Many criminal activities were planned here. The landlord was a large man whose name was Bernard Bumstock and he knew both Albert and George (the Cosh) Harcourt very well indeed.

They had been schoolboys together at Portswood Secondary Modern. None of the other boys were ever left in any doubt over who the king of the playground was. Albert ran a gang that included George Harcourt and Bernard Bumstock. Anyone trying to stand up to Albert's gang was ambushed either in the boy's toilets or on the nearby recreation ground. Victims were stripped and whipped until they cried for mercy. Then, having promised to always obey the gang in future, they were released and given their clothes back.

George Harcourt thought this treatment was too tame and said as much.

"We got to really scare the sods, just whipping them ain't good enough."

"What do you think we should do then?" Albert had wanted to know.

"Just wait for the next kid who tries to stand up to us," George sneered, "and then I'll show you."

Just two weeks later a new boy, whose name was Michael Ford, refused to hand over the dinner money his mother had given him. When making his way home he suddenly found himself surrounded.

Albert smiled at him. "You made a mistake today kid. You should have given us that money, now we are going to show you what happens to anyone who defies us."

The frightened boy was thrown to the ground and, feeling both scared and humiliated, he cowered as George Harcourt stepped forward.

"New boy's need teaching don't they so here's your punishment kid."

Producing a sock that he had filled with pennies, before anyone could stop him he started viciously striking the

20

defenseless boy on the ground. Time after time that sock was raised then came down hard on the body of his victim. This shocked everyone in the gang and it was Albert who eventually stepped in and brought this awful punishment to an end.

"That's enough George," he yelled. "We don't want to kill the kid, for Christ's sake stop."

The red mist that appeared to come over George Harcourt's face as he began this beating now slowly vanished. With reluctance he put his make-shift cosh away.

"Ok Albert, you're the boss, but we needed to teach this bleeder not to try standing up to us again, And let any others know what they'll get if they try it too."

"I agree but, blimey, the kid looks half dead we should get out of here quick."

"Right, but let's just do this one thing more."

With this George yanked Michael's trousers off. Then, hanging them from a branch of one of the nearby trees, he lit a match. With the smoke from the burning clothes rising, Albert's gang all ran off back to their homes. None of them were expecting the row that was to erupt the next day.

At morning assembly the headmistress Mrs. Cave glowered at the boy's side of the hall.

"Yesterday a new boy Michael Ford started at this school. I am aware certain initiation ceremonies take place, a practice I must say I have never agreed with. However in this case Michael Ford was very badly hurt and this morning is in hospital. He was found, badly beaten in woodland near his home. His injuries are serious and he was discovered in a state of undress. His trousers, which were new, had been taken from him and burned. I can't begin to tell you how serious this is. Every boy in this school will be spoken to by the police who will be here shortly. When we catch those responsible the punishment will be swift and hard."

In the playground at morning break Albert and his gang had been very busy. They knew if the rest of the boys decided to get

21

together and gang up on them they would not be able to fight their way out. So fear of retribution would prevent this from happening. The gang was hard and even if they did turn on them, Albert and the others would not stop until every single one of them had been caught on their own and very badly beaten up.

So today everyone listened as a message went round the playground. Say anything about us and the new kid will have company in hospital. The police were very frustrated when everyone they spoke to claimed to know nothing about the attack or have any idea who could have carried it out.

Detective Sergeant Ackerman from Portswood CID knew when he spoke to Albert and George Harcourt that these two boys at least were responsible for the beating of Michael Ford. He glowered at them both.

"I know you two did this because we know all about your gang. This time we can't get any evidence against you because the boy you hurt so much is scared of you and won't tell us who beat him. But watch it you two. We're watching you closely now and just one mistake is all you need to make and we'll have you. Your feet won't touch the ground and both of you will find yourselves in Borstal."

The memories had come flooding back to Bernard Bumstock as he saw the members of Albert's gang sat in his public bar. None of them had made another mistake so never went anywhere near Borstal. But he'd never forgotten how George Harcourt beat that kid with his homemade cosh. Blimey he earned the nick-name that day and still has it now. So just what exactly was that lot planning over there?

Albert addressed everyone sat around the table, which included Lenny Warren and Pat Mathews.

"George has told me how we can still operate in this town, and I like what he's said. We can work a black market racket, starting with the stores of stuff we already have. We'll make as much dosh from that as we can. But it won't last forever. None of us knows how long this bleeding war is going to go on. So there will be jobs for all of you and the blokes you know individually and can trust."

"How do you want us to work this?" asked Lenny. "We have some ideas already but you know how tight things are in the docks now. How do we get our hands on everything we want?"

George Harcourt answered by explaining how butter and other perishable items could be gained by raiding the stores where they were kept. But there were other ways to get stuff and when needed little conversations could be had with certain shop keepers. Other black market dealers would be approached for things like alcohol, nylon stockings and even knicker elastic. This brought loud laughter all around.

"Alright I know it's funny," said George. "But women are starting to get short of things like that and they do want it so they'll pay us to get it for them. Right then, let's get started. Lenny when are you and Pat going to make a raid on our old warehouse so we can get our hands on some butter and anything else we can grab?"

"We're going to start this Saturday and we'll hit more than one warehouse. I'll lead the raid on our old place while Pat will be getting into Eastleigh airport. That one is very big and it's guarded by the army. So we'll need men who can squeeze through very small places and then open the high windows for the rest of the raiding party. It won't be easy but everyone will be up for it."

Albert looked around the table with a smile on his face. "Good, so let's get this show on the road."

Then calling out to Bernard who was still watching from behind the bar, "get some drinks over here will you then I'll tell you want I want you to do for us."

While all this was taking place Ida Littlejohn was having a serious conversation with her eldest daughter Maggie in the small front room.

"I know your father is up to no good and is out stealing anything he and his gang can sell on. Even in peacetime what they're doing is against the law, but in wartime it's far more serious. He wants to use this house to store some of the things he gets and he will sell them to anyone who can afford to buy. I will allow him to do this because, quite frankly Maggie, with the large family we have and now the new baby money is very tight. But I don't want you or any of our children becoming involved with crime. This is never easy when your father is, for want of a better word, a crook. Don't get me wrong, I do love him. For all his faults he makes sure you are taken care of financially at least. But you must help me keep your sisters and especially your two brothers from knowing what is going on when we get police visits, as I know we will."

Maggie looked keenly at her mother.

"I can look after my three sisters alright Ma. Jean, Doris and Angela are no trouble and they'll help with watching Edwin and Charlie. But little Thomas will need more done for him won't he cause he's only a baby?"

"Yes that's true Maggie but you can leave him to me, and Charlie as well as he's only just over a year old. But Edwin is old enough to notice what's going on around him and your sisters certainly are. So you must make sure they know when we go to the clothes warehouse and buy what they need for school and best wear, they see me using coupons to do this. Also for food and everything else that is on ration. They must never say to any of their friends that we have more things than they have. Your father is supplying me with enough money to look after all of you and he will get things for us but we won't need to use our coupons."

"But how can that be Ma? Everyone knows about rationing and families can only get the amounts they've got coupons for. I know we are registered at Martins the butchers for our meat and Chandlers for groceries. But already we see queues of women outside those shops every morning on our way to school."

24

"Yes and I do the same thing Maggie, only in my case it doesn't really matter if the shop I'm queuing at runs out before I get to the counter. I moan the same as everybody else but it's all show. We must not let anyone know we have things at home, or the means to get more if we need them."

"But what will happen if anyone finds out Ma, will we get into trouble?"

"Yes, but more importantly your dad will be arrested and God knows what will happen to him after that. The government don't take too kindly to people cheating the system and punishments will be very hard indeed."

"Is daddy in danger then?" Maggie asked with a worried frown on her face. She knew he wasn't honest, nor were the men he associated with who came to visit the house. But he was her father and she loved him.

Ida was looking for some way to reassure her daughter when really she could not make any guarantees.

"Now that cities are being bombed Southampton has already been hit quite a lot. Some crooks go into bombed houses and are supposed to be looking for injured people to get them out. But some of these men are far worse than your dad because they grab anything that looks as though it will bring them money when sold. This is a despicable thing for anyone to do and it's called looting. These men are rotten to the core and just add to the distress of those whose homes have been destroyed. I know the penalty for anyone caught doing that is the death penalty."

"Oh no," Maggie gasped. "Not my Daddy, they can't do that to him can they?"

"No don't get upset. It won't ever come to that because no matter how bad some of the men who work with him are, none of them are that low. What they do is serious though and will bring a long prison sentence if any of them are caught. What I need from you is understanding. This house will be watched and raided, I'm quite sure of that, so you must get your brothers and sisters together when that happens. They must not say a word

25

about anything that goes on in this house. Young Edwin especially will be asked questions if the police or army get to him. They'll be very nice men who appear to be kind. He will think it's a game when asked about things being hidden away and gleefully show those crafty police blighters where your dad stashes things in their bed."

Maggie was still a young girl although nearly a teenager, but she had an understanding beyond her years of things such as this.

"Alright mum, I understand. I know daddy won't do anything really bad so leave the family to me. Jean and Doris are old enough to understand. I'll explain it all to them and get them working with me to keep the youngest out of the way when anything goes wrong in our house."

Ida looked fondly at her eldest daughter.

"Thank you Maggie but there's one more thing I need to ask. Some of the more expensive and hard to obtain items like cigarettes and spirits will be hidden inside the mattress. I will always be in that bed and I need to look really ill. I know your pretty good with make-up, at least you were before the war started, so I will need you."

"I know mum," Maggie interrupted. "You need to be made to look as though you've got a horrible disease or something, and I wonder why that is."

She was grinning as she said this so Ida knew her daughter had realized why she made this strange request.

"You're a good girl Maggie. I knew I could rely on you."

In the Portswood Hotel Albert had already set up the first raids on government warehouses and worked out what to do with any stolen merchandise that came into their possession. Now he crossed the bar to talk to the landlord.

"We'll need some space soon Bernard. I expect a lot of good stuff to come our way and it will need hiding."

"Yeah I know that. But where do I come in for this?"

26

"Your cellar of course, we all know about that secret room that runs off behind the beer barrels and it will suit us down to the ground. We can keep our alcohol down there as well as things like nylons. Things the army and them meddling ARP wardens are always on the lookout for."

The landlord of this old pub now shook his head.

"No Albert I ain't getting into anything like that. I may have been as bad as the rest of you when we was kids. But this is different. My missus will create hell if she was to find out we've got contraband in here. And let's not forget the coppers will arrest me quick as you like and I'll spend God knows how many years in clink. No mate, sorry, you'll have to find somewhere else."

Albert stared hard at his old friend and his reply filled Bernard with dread.

"You don't have to help us Bernard, but if you don't I won't be able to stop George from having a go at you. He's never liked you, even when we were all at school. If he doesn't like what he's hearing now he'll come and pay you a visit. And you know what he uses for a weapon."

"I know alright," Bernard replied. "I still remember when he beat the new kid with that sock full of pennies. And the poor sod he half killed with his cosh a few years ago. But I'll take a chance because my missus will kill me if I don't."

"Your right there my dear," a voice came booming out behind them. Whirling around both Bernard and Albert found themselves looking into the steely eyes of Catherine Bumstock. This lady was by no means small and had married Bernard four years ago and now set up with him as landlady. Although Bernard's name was displayed over the door of the public bar it was his domineering wife who made all of the decisions about the pub and how it was run. Most regular customers knew this and not even the strongest and most troublesome of them ever made the mistake of upsetting her.

27

The tradition in this part of Southampton was for anyone who wanted a bit of agro to simply stand up and shout, "I'll fight the strongest man here." A vicious fight would swiftly ensue with one or sometimes both men involved being very badly hurt. Knuckledusters were often used to cause horrific injuries. There was also, of course, considerable damage done to the bar.

Catherine would have none of this in her pub and on more than one occasion during one of these fights it was she who waded in with her father's old walking stick. This was wielded with devastating effect. Fights stopped very quickly once that stick was brought into play. She also possessed a great deal of knowledge of the pub trade and it was this that kept the Portswood Hotel ticking over.

Now though she glared at Albert Littlejohn and George Harcourt, who had wandered over to join them.

"And just what do you two bastards want my Bernard to do for you? Because if it's anything that will harm this pub you can both piss off. And don't you glare at me George Harcourt. I know your reputation with that cosh but you also know what I can do with my old dads stick."

Both Bernard and Albert waited with bated breath to hear how George would respond. He stood as though glued to the floor and it was obvious he was fighting to control his very volatile temper. No one spoke to him like that and got away with it. Even a woman was risking injury once that famed cosh started swinging. But Catherine Bumstock really was made of sterner stuff and matched him completely as she glared back.

This led to a few seconds of real tension before the impossible happened. George (the cosh) Harcourt suddenly roared with laughter and only when he managed to control this did he respond.

"Bloody hell Catherine, I think you mean that so I ain't going up against your stick. I've seen some of the toughest blokes from round here getting clobbered with it, so you win."

The atmosphere now eased considerably and everyone including Catherine herself laughed at this. But still the landlady made it very plain that any arrangements including the Portswood Hotel would have to be approved by her.

"I want to know exactly what you and your lot want from us Albert Littlejohn, and if I don't like it then it won't happen."

"Relax Catherine, nothing is happening yet but when we get going we'll, let's say, get hold of things we don't want anyone knowing about. Now your Bernard has told us about a secret place in your cellar and we would like to use it. We'll put a lot of our stuff there and the two of you won't go short if you work with us."

"My bloody husband says too much." Catherine glared at Bernard before softening a little. "But I suppose you and he go back a long way don't you? What you're talking about is stuff you will knock off though ain't it? So what sort of things do you want stored here?"

"Booze mostly, but you and Berny will get a share of that to sell in the bar. We also want to store nylon stockings, parachute silk when we can get any and if it's cold enough down there, meat as well."

Casting a discrete glance across the bar she made sure none of the customers drinking at the moment were taking any notice of what was being said.

"Well you and the Cosh here had better come down and see for yourselves, so follow me."

One sharp word to Bernard would suffice to get him to look after the bar. She then headed for the door that led down to the cellar of this old pub. The staircase was steep but they soon found themselves on the next level before more steps lead down to the expansive but bleak looking back garden. The downstairs room was empty except for a small bar in one corner.

"We don't use this much. Maybe when this bloody war ends we can do something with it. I think the people before us used it for music. My Bernard likes his jazz so maybe we could have jazz bands playing. But we'll see what happens."

In the corner was a small, almost concealed door, which led to another set of steep steps. With very little light it was difficult to see where they were going but soon they had nearly reached the cellar

Catherine was way ahead of them.

"Watch your step going down here. We wouldn't want either of you tough men falling and breaking your legs now would we?"

The cellar was large and very cold with rows of barrels packed against the far wall with pipes leading from them going all the way up to the pumps in the bar.

"Now you two, what I'm going to show you is not known to anyone but Bernard and me, so make sure you keep your ruddy traps shut about it."

Albert was quick to reply.

"That ain't really true Catherine. We all know this pub and have heard about the secret room. None of my men are daft enough to open their trap about it. They know what George here will do to them if they do."

With a sniff of disapproval she turned and beckoned them to follow. She went to the far wall where the barrels were set up and squeezed behind them. It was very tight, both Albert and George had a difficult time getting their large bodies past this obstacle. But once past the first two barrels the space widened and walking became easier.

Catherine stopped at a spot that on first glance appeared just the same as the rest of the wall that ran the length of the cellar. But she pushed her body against it and a fantastic thing happened before their eyes. A large part of the wall opened up to reveal a room that was certainly large enough to meet their storage needs. With a smile she beckoned them to come in, "Welcome to smugglers reach gentlemen."

30

Albert and George stared into this room that clearly dated back a very long way. They could see at once it would suit their purpose admirably and both accepted the landlady's invitation to enter. Larger and colder than the cellar it had a somewhat musty odour. There also appeared to be a door at the far end.

Catherine immediately saw this had caught their interest.

"That was the entrance door back in the days when this pub was opened in the 1850s. The building is older, and was part of Southampton estates even in the 1770's. It's believed this room was used by smugglers getting spirits and bringing it here to store before selling it on. They brought their bounty up the River Itchen and came ashore just this side of the railway tracks. Then all they had to do was cross over and make their way inside. They dumped their stuff before coming out through the cellar and enjoying a pint in the bar."

"Well Catherine we'll do pretty much the same thing and some of our stuff will come the same way as the old smugglers did. Thanks for this. We won't forget you and Bernard."

"You'd better not because if you do, we'll not only stop you from using this place but we'll keep whatever's in there at the time. And come to that, what exactly do me and my old man get out of this?"

"Hold your horses Catherine," George intervened. "We won't let you down. Albert has already told you our men will keep quiet about this place. Now what we'll give you and Bernard is spirits, especially whisky. But it's getting so scarce now you'll have to be careful who you sell it too. Keep it away from your normal stock so none of your regular customers can see it."

Catherine gave him a scornful look.

"Have you heard of the saying 'teach your grandmother to suck eggs' George Harcourt. Me and my hubby don't need telling about simple things like that. We'll make money out of anything you lot give us but we know how to do it quietly, we're not bloody amateurs."

Now it was Albert's turn to try and pacify her.

31

"We know Bernard ain't Catherine. As you rightly said we was kids together and had to find out how to survive from a very early age, but we don't know a lot about you do we?"

"I don't know how you can say that Albert Littlejohn," she shouted back at him, now getting quite worked up. "You may not know me but you do know my dad and three brothers. You ought to. You've fought against them often enough."

"Have we? What was your maiden name before you married Bernard then?"

A smile now came across her face.

"Oh he's never told you that. Well I'm not really surprised. Before we married I was Catherine Lewis and my family lived in Harefield Road."

Albert gave George a quick glance.

"The bloody Lewis boys, we had many a run in with them. They was the day's eh George?"

"Yeah but we had a right job with them sometimes. The bleeders knew how to fight alright. My cosh was always busy in any punch up but especially with that lot."

"Right then now we all seem to know who we are, I'm going to leave you two to look around down here, but one thing I want you both to know is the correct way to open the door to this room. Going outside and swinging the big door shut she pointed to a tiny brass ring set into the floor.

"You must stand right on this ring and then push against the wall, if you're standing anywhere else you can push all you ruddy well like and the door won't open. Remember that. It's done that way so that any snoopers, coppers, ARP wardens, even Home Guard won't know this room exists. Now I'm going back up. When you two are ready remember to look through the crack in the door upstairs to make sure no-one's around before you come up out of it."

Back inside the secret room Albert and George looked out through the back entrance and both liked what they were seeing. They knew this district like the back of their hands and they gazed out at the meandering River Itchen as it wound its way past Northam Bridge then round the big bend, beyond which was the widest part as it approached the Floating Bridges.

They knew they could come up the river this way. It would be quicker and more discreet even though they were only moving their things further up the same side of the river. Too many interfering official types who could stop and ask them questions by road, but who would even notice a small boat coming up the river in the darkness? They would just need to check the tides of course and time their operations around the high tide. If it was out then their boat would very quickly run aground. A perfect plan was forming.

"Right George we need to get the men together and start moving stuff here from my house in Highfield Lane."

"Yeah, then we can start planning how to do all this under cover, so let's get started shall we."

Chapter Three

After taking a good look around Albert Littlejohn and George Harcourt made their way cautiously back through the large downstairs area of the Portswood Hotel, having first peered through the large crack in the cellar door to make sure no-one was around. Going back up the stairs they came out again into the public bar. With a nod to Bernard they rejoined their other gang members who were still seated at the table.

Albert now lost no time in explaining exactly what he wanted to happen and made sure he couldn't be overheard by any of the other customers.

"Right now, the room downstairs is perfect for what we need. We can store stuff without worrying about it being found. Even if this pub gets a direct hit from a fucking German bomb it won't affect that room because it's deep down under this floor and at the back of the cellar."

"Yeah boss but if that happens the ARP wardens will stop anyone going into a bombed building don't they, so how do we get to our stuff then?"

"George and I have just been into that room and it has two entrances, one from inside the cellar and the other from the outside of the building. So it don't matter what happens to this place, we'll still be able to get in from the outside door. We get to that entrance by coming up through the railway marshalling yard and that's patrolled so we'll need to work out how to do that without anyone getting caught. But first things first, let's get all our stuff from my house in Highfield Lane and bring it down here. Then whatever we need each time we go out to sell will be brought to my family house in Empress Road."

There were nods all around but they could still foresee some difficulties.

"Ok boss, but how do we do it?" asked Lenny Warren. "The roads are all patrolled by ARP wardens and them nosy old Home Guard blokes. The police are more alert for anything like that now and all. So if a lot of us start turning up with hand carts or whatever they'll soon rumble to what we're doing."

George Harcourt had already thought of this.

"A lot of you have got small kids ain't you? Well, you'll be taking them out for nighttime walks see."

He was met with very confused looks.

"Get you wives involved and have them put false bottoms in your prams. Then we can put our stuff in there and have the kids sleeping on top. If any of you are stopped and asked what you're doing out with a pram at nighttime in the blackout, you simply say your missus can't get the kid to sleep so you're walking him or her round until they drop off. Underneath will be bottles of spirits and fags and other stuff that's on ration."

"That should work alright," said Albert. "Some of it can be moved that way but don't forget at the bottom of Highfield Lane, next to the entrance to the tram shed, is Portswood Police Station. So we'll be moving our stuff right under the noses of the coppers. But there's a lot in that house so we'll get in touch with old Percy Winkleman."

"I thought that old codger was dead," said Lenny trying to contain his laugh. "Don't tell me he still drives his horse and cart round the streets."

"No he bloody well ain't dead," exclaimed Albert. "That old codger as you call him has been doing his rag and bone job in this area for more years than even I can remember. So many people know him and give him things every time he comes onto their road. You can hear him shout 'Rag Bone' above any other noise."

"Ok boss but how the hell is he going to help us? He's not a young bloke now is he? Blimey he must be in his seventies."

"No more like eighties, but he's still as sharp an old boy as ever. My family has known him for years and he was a good friend to my dad. So he'll do anything he can to help me. Now as you know the rag and bone trade is dead at the moment. The Government has called for metal that can be melted down to be used for the war effort. They'll use it for making ammunition, guns and even tanks, so most households are chucking out saucepans, frying pans, irons and tin baths for this cause. Men like Percy collect as much as they can and take it to the handling depot down by the South Hants Hospital. So I'll have a word with him and get him to do a collection that's not going anywhere near that depot but down by the marshalling yard at Bevois park."

Before he could say anymore they were interrupted by the piercing sound of a siren telling everyone that an air raid was imminent. They needed to get into the air raid shelters without delay. Everyone in the bar dashed over to the door leading to the downstairs space as this was as good as any shelter outside. Albert, however, made for the outside door.

"Where the bloody hell are you going? The damn Germans are going to be dropping bombs all over the place any minute now." George Harcourt shouted.

"I can't help that George. I must get to my wife and kids. I don't see very much of them but that don't mean I don't care. I need to know they're all safe from this raid."

Rushing outside Albert turned into Dukes Road and ran as fast as he could. Overhead was the drone of aircraft and the crump of bombs hitting was audible. The searchlights were up and anti-aircraft guns were roaring out in defiance of these German bombers. The ground shook beneath his feet as he rushed past the small factory on the left hand side that was turning out clothing for our troops, before reaching the turning into Empress Road. The Waterloo Arms on the far corner was blacked out and the customers inside were all taking shelter in the cellar.

Racing past faster than he normally could, he made it to number 34 and gratefully put his key in the lock. Not stopping to do anything else he simply raced straight through, down the garden to the families Anderson Shelter and banged on the door.

"Ida, it's me open up."

As the door opened Albert threw himself inside and looked anxiously around.

"Are you alright, is everyone here?"

"Relax Albert," Ida reassured him. "We're all here and safe. It's very cramped but that's better than being blown up in a raid ain't it?"

She was right about that. Anderson shelters weren't exactly large and with a grown woman and seven children inside there certainly wasn't much room. With Albert there as well they were practicably sitting on each other's laps. But the children were so pleased to see their dad and all the girls made sure they gave him a big hug.

Edwin, the eldest boy, of course thought this was a silly and sissy thing to do. He wasn't going to do anything like that. But just as this thought entered his head a bomb landed close by and the whole of their shelter was rocked by the blast. Edwin flung himself into his father's arms and clung on in fear. At just under five years old he wasn't old enough to know about death, but the noise and the way the shelter shook frightened him so much.

Albert hugged his son and displayed a side to his nature that very few ever got to see. He whispered to him.

"It's alright my boy. Daddies here so no-one is going to hurt you or any of your brothers and sisters. Me and mum will see to that. We'll just have to put up with a bit more noise before this raid is over that's all."

Ida looked fondly at Albert and knew this was why she loved him and would always support him. Maggie also realised how much her dad being here meant so she too worked her way to her father's side and planted a kiss on his cheek.

"Thank you daddy, we all love you and trust you. It's really wonderful when we're all together as a family."

Ida had been busy getting her younger children washed and ready for bed when the siren sounded. She did the same as so many other mothers and had them wrapped up warm because most nights now were interrupted in this way. She needed Maggie to help get them all out of the house and down into the Anderson Shelter at the bottom of the garden.

Her sisters Jean, Doris and Angela all helped with this so the two younger boys were given the attention they needed at these dangerous times. Ida herself stayed until they were all out of the house before she went to the bottom drawer of her sideboard that acted as a cot for Thomas. He was just a few months old and needed nappies and bottles prepared before the drawer was pulled out and he was carried to the shelter.

She always briefly paused to look at him with a little sadness in her heart.

"This is such a bad time for a lovely boy like you to be born. But we will get through this. You will get the chance to grow up with your two big brothers I promise, and become a fine man just like they will."

Right now though it was Albert gazing down at his youngest son and wondering how on earth anyone could sleep peacefully with all the noise erupting outside. More bombs dropped nearby and the shelter shook with every impact so that all the children, even Maggie, crowded close to their parents. Just being near gave them a reassurance that not even one of these enemy bombs would fall on them. Misplaced maybe but it made them feel a whole lot better.

While all hell was breaking out around them Ida quietly spoke to Albert.

"Thank you for getting here to be with us, you can see how the children have settled since you came. Now we're both here they all feel safe."

"Yeah I can see that alright mush," Albert slipped his arms around her. "You know I ain't such a bad bloke. I do me best for you and the kids. Alright I ain't a saint and I steal stuff, but we need the money and this is the best way I can think of."

"I know that, it's why I support you and will help in any way I can. As long as you don't bring any danger to our house, I don't want it affecting the kids. Maggie already knows what her dad does for a living and she will help too. But Albert, none of our children must be allowed to think what you do is in any way glamorous. Our boys especially may want to be just like their dad when they get a bit older."

"Don't worry mush," said Albert, still holding Ida in as loving an embrace as he could manage. "I'll make a pact with you. Tell the girls. Say it is simply to ensure they have everything they need. I'll look out for Edwin, Charlie and little Thomas. We can get them jobs in the docks when they're old enough, or even an apprenticeship. Either way they won't follow me in running any sort of a gang."

So with bombs still falling all around them this was cemented and worked well, with just one exception. For this night though the future was just that, and no-one knew for certain what it would hold for this family.

As the wail of the siren sounded outside once again, signaling the all clear, most of the children had already settled into sleep, with only Maggie still awake. Relieved that the bombing was over and they were still alive and uninjured, she glanced over at her parents and saw them deep in conversation. Albert beckoned her over.

"Come here a moment Maggie, I need to speak to you."

She made her way to her father's side, having to carefully step over her sleeping siblings in order to do so. Albert took this opportunity to explain what would be required moving forward and for the entire duration of the hostilities.

"I know your mum has already spoken to you about what me and my boys will be getting up to Maggie. I want you to realize what we're doing is really providing a service. A lot of people need help with stuff they can't buy in the shops. Ok, it's not legal. We all know that but it's going to bring in the money we, as a family, need to get by. This house will be used as a sort of shop where our neighbours, and other people who get to know about us, can come to buy things even if they haven't got enough bloody coupons. We'll be here to serve them when they do, but we must keep a watch out for the coppers. Your mum has asked you to help by making her look really ill hasn't she?"

"Yes Dad I know. You don't want the police finding your contraband otherwise you will be in big trouble and they will arrest you. So you're gunna stash the stuff in the mattress. If mum looks really ill then they won't wanna catch whatever it is and they will keep their distance from the bed."

Albert hadn't been sure how his daughter would take this news so he was taken aback at how clued up she was and wished some of his own men were this sharp and enthusiastic when it came to planning operations.

Now Maggie burst out laughing, "Oh daddy, I think it's really funny. Don't worry I'll do my part, this is so exciting."

Soon they were back inside the house which luckily had managed to escape the bombs. Albert voiced his concerns to Ida.

"I was pleased our Maggie understands what's needed. I'm sure we can rely on her. But I am a bit worried. She was so happy about it. Blimey I hope I ain't started her on something she'll get involved with later on. She's a good girl and I don't want her living the sort of life that I have where she needs to be one step ahead of the law all the time."

"Don't you worry about our Maggie, Albert. She's still young and does see this as an adventure. But her heads screwed on the right way and I haven't any worries. She already knows right from wrong and understands that her involvement with what's happening now is purely because of the war."

The children were awake now of course and after being washed in the kitchen sink, something the boys hated, they were tucking into their favourite breakfast of toast spread thickly with beef dripping. The usual arguments having broken out about who gets to dig deep inside the bowl. Ida was sorting this out when a loud knock came at the door."

Albert was on his feet in an instant. "Who the bloody hell is that?"

The knocking was repeated and got louder.

"Ok keep your bloody hair on I'm coming."

Reaching the front door he flung it open to find George Harcourt on the front doorstep.

"George, what's up?" he asked, looking keenly at his second in command. "What's happened?"

"It's bad Al, we've lost two of our best boys in the air-raid last night."

Albert stood still in shock for a moment. "Which two and how did it happen?"

"Billy Foreman and Joe Kinslade, they was working in the big shed at 104 berth when those bloody Nazi planes came over. Most of that raid was targeted on the docks and that shed took a hit. Part of it collapsed in flames and our two were working just there, they didn't stand a chance."

"You'd better come in," said Albert, and stood aside to make room for him to enter the narrow passage that led to the family's living room. Ida had heard what was going on and though she both feared and loathed George Harcourt she knew enough to realize this was serious so she made no objection to him coming into her house.

Getting the children on their way to school, each with gas mask in tow, she took her two youngest boys upstairs so as to be out of Albert's way while he discussed this situation. She even made George a cup of tea, so grave was this situation.

Albert and George sat next to the crackling coal fire that burned in the grate. They knew this was horrible thing to happen, especially as both men had wives and children. Finally Albert broke the silence.

"I know this is going to sound like I don't care but we must face facts George. Those two were good at what they did, both for the Docks and for our organization. They'll be very badly missed. We need to find another two we can depend on to do what they did for us."

"Yeah I know that Al and I do have some blokes in mind, but what about their families? What they gonna do for money now? Billy and Joe was the breadwinners, now they ain't got no-one old enough to go out to earn them money."

"They won't go short. We'll see to that. They'll get a weekly sum from what we get off the black market. We'll tell them it's out of our wages. I don't see that they need to know any more than that."

"No I agree, but Winnie Kinslade is as sharp as a button. I think we may have trouble with her."

"In what way?" Albert demanded to know. "She'll get looked after, her kids will be alright. What kind of trouble can a woman cause us?"

"It's just a feeling Al. Joe was always saying he had to be careful she didn't find out what he got up to when he was out at night. She knew he was into something and I think she'll try and find out what it was."

Albert simply scoffed at this.

"She can nose around all she wants but I say again no woman is ever going to make trouble for us. They belong in the house doing the chores and looking after kids. No George, she won't bother us."

Ida had come down to the kitchen and overheard this particular snippet of the conversation. Her husband of course was deeply rooted in the prevailing attitudes, a society that hadn't shaken of its Victorian chains and wouldn't do so for some time yet. It was very much a man's world but Ida was ahead of her time. She accepted this was the way her husband was but still the anger built up inside her. Women wanted to be recognized for what they were and men ought to beware of this.

The next day Albert, George and the rest of their gang looked on sadly at the wrecked shed at berth 104 in Southampton Docks, acutely aware that two of their number had died inside just a few hours ago. Wreckage was strewn along the dockside and even the crane was hanging at a dangerous angle. There would be no work done today until this mess was cleared and everything repaired.

The foreman announced that all workers could begin helping with this, but none of them had the stomach for it. Not one of the gang wanted to go anywhere near where their friends had died so suddenly. So they left the docks and, under Albert's direction, took the tram to Portswood Junction before making their way to his house in Highfield Lane.

"Right, George and me will walk up and go in the front way, the rest of you lot go round the back and come in that way. I don't want the nosey neighbours round here seeing you going in."

They all laughed but obediently followed their bosses orders, and made their way round the back cutway that was used by the dustbin men, until they came to the gate of Albert's house.

Harry Small looked down the back garden. "Blimey, look at that."

The others all followed his pointing finger and saw the figure of Janice Saunders. She had some music on and was dancing around the room. The thin dress swirled around and rode up revealing her legs and the tops of her stockings.

43

"Cor blimey," exclaimed Harry with a leer on his face. "I think we all need to meet that tart don't you?"

They all agreed. Then saw Albert and George enter the room which meant the girl stopped her dancing at once.

"George, this is Janice. She stays here and looks after the house for me."

Janice stood rooted to the spot as George Harcourt stared at her. Was she expected to have sex with him? This was not a nice thought, he was a hard man and at times like this it showed. He was certainly not leering. In fact the look he gave her was the complete opposite.

George secretly had no time for women at all, his preferences lying with members of his own sex. He was a sadist and liked younger men who he could dominate. What he did with these unfortunate victims was a closely guarded secret and one that wasn't likely to come out. He frightened his boys, as he liked to call them, with violence if they so much as hinted at what he did to them. Even Albert knew very little about this, although he realized George didn't like women, so simply accepted the fact.

Janice now cowered under the hard and very unfriendly stare she was receiving. George though just turned away, having no intention of even speaking.

Albert quickly intervened.

"Right Janice, love, a lot of my friends will be coming here today so I want you to be nice to them. Go upstairs please and wait for them to come up."

"How many will there be?" Janice was alarmed. "I don't know how I will cope if it's too many."

Albert had been having a stressful day and his patience was wearing thin. Unfortunately this brought out his bad side and he grabbed the frightened girl by the throat.

"Never mind how many, they're my friends and you'll do as you're told or out you go. There'll be no more money and no more stuff your family needs. I told you when I brought you here that everything you get has to be earned."

44

Janice was crying but the fear of what Albert and especially George Harcourt would do to her if she refused made her realize she had no chance at all of getting out of this predicament.

Once they were alone downstairs George queried him. "What was that all about? That stupid girl was really frightened."

"Yeah but she knows all this luxury comes at a cost. Up till now though it's only been me who has had sex with her. Now it's gonna be most of the boys taking turns. She will be getting more money though and she happily volunteered when I suggested it so I don't know what she's complaining about."

"I can see that, but why do you want her to do it?" George really did not have the least desire to come anywhere near this young, very attractive girl for sexual gratification.

"She's young. Even though she knows anything going on in this house has to be kept a secret, if she sees what we have stored here she may not be able to keep her mouth shut. And if that should happen we would have to make sure she don't tell anyone see. You know what I mean?"

George Harcourt knew exactly what Albert meant and secretly hoped the girl would make a mistake. This would give him the chance to silence her permanently. Although his reputation was with the cosh, he had by now got himself a gun and was fully prepared to use it if and when the situation required. The sly sneer that came across his face at the prospect of shooting Janice Saunders was not a nice sight to behold.

His hatred of girls was not shared by the rest of the Littlejohn Gang. When Albert explained what he wanted from them all today this was met with universal approval.

"We'll be taking it in turns to bring the stuff up from the cellar and putting most of it in the big shed at the bottom of the garden. From there I'll get old Percy Winlkeman to drop some of it off at my house in Empress Road. This will be done gradually because I'm limited for room. Most of it will go straight into the room behind the cellar of the Portswood Hotel."

45

"How do we get it there?"

"I haven't spoken to old Percy yet, but I know he'll help. We'll see him alright and he ain't no squealer. After he stops at Empress Road he'll go on over the railway crossing at Mount Pleasant then past the Plaza cinema to the banks of the River Itchen. We'll have a boat waiting and whatever's left in old Percy's cart will be ferried up to just under the road bridge over the railway. There some of our boys will carry the stuff through the marshalling yards up to the outside door of the secret room under the pub. Let's get started, and which one of you is going first with the girl upstairs. I don't want her clocking what's going on down here."

Harry Small spoke up at once. "I'm doing that first boss. It's only fair ain't it? I saw her first."

"Yeah ok, hurry up Harry. Get on with it so the rest of us can get started down here. Make sure she doesn't get the chance to look out the window. Her room looks right over the garden and she'll have a grand stand view of what we're doing."

"Don't worry about that boss. I'll be keeping her occupied alright."

Albert led his men down to the large cellar to begin removing the merchandise his gang had managed to acquire over recent months. But upstairs Janice Saunders was waiting nervously. She knew exactly what Albert meant when he told her to be nice to his friends. Hearing heavy footsteps on the stairs she knew she needed to face whatever ordeal was in front of her.

Janice enjoyed the benefits that came with this arrangement with Albert. It was an empowering feeling knowing she didn't have to worry about her family going short, and having nice clothes that everyone else wanted but had no chance of getting. So when Albert suggested she extend the favours to other members of his gang for extra compensation she had jumped at the chance. Now though, when faced with the reality of the situation she was a little scared. One or two of the gang members seemed alright but they certainly weren't all her type,

46

she would just have to think about the ways she was benefitting from this and that cheered her up slightly.

The door of the room flew open and the large form of Harry Small stood leering at her.

"Well, you're a bit of alright ain't you? So let's see a bit more of you shall we?"

The speed with which he moved across the room took her completely by surprise and he soon had her in a tight grip. His big hands found the zip at the back of her expensive dress. Wrenching this down Harry soon had her dress off. Throwing this on the bed he looked at the cowering Janice, dressed now in equally expensive underwear of white silk brassier and matching panties, under which was a black suspender belt. These were keeping up a pair of sheer nylon stockings.

Janice was thrown on the bed and the rest of her clothes were torn off, laddering the nylon's in the process. Completely naked she tried to cover herself but Harry shouted at her.

"No you don't you little tart I want to see all you've got so keep your bloody hands down."

She was made to watch as this big loud man now stripped his own clothes off before coming to the bed, and snarling at her.

"Now girl let's see how good you are at this."

The man, now looking horrible as well as frightening in his nude state with his large stomach overlooking the lower part of his body, now fell on top on Janice and he entered her body and started having his way with her. As he thrust in and out she was screaming with the pain and humiliation.

Harry, however, enjoyed it even more because of that. He, in his ignorance, thought her screams were ones of ecstasy and so was proud of himself.

"That's the girl. I knew you'd enjoy it once we got started."

The ordeal went on for the next ten minutes until at last the big brute on top of her was spent. Standing up he quickly put his clothes back on and noticed Janice starting to do the same.

"I wouldn't bother with that girl. More of my mates will be coming up to have their fun with you."

As the door slammed shut behind him Janice buried her face in the pillow and cried. With sobs racking her body and tears running down her face she spoke quietly.

"Oh mum if you could see me now, but it's all for you and our family that I'm here. If you ever find out please forgive me."

This was as far as she got because at that moment there came more heavy footsteps on the stairs.

Down in the cellar Albert acknowledged Harry's appearance.

"Well, how did it go? Is that kid upstairs ok?"

"She's fine boss, a right little raver if ever I saw one. She's up for it alright."

Albert wasn't so sure about that but knew Janice had to be kept away from the bedroom window while they were all working down here. "Ok, whose up there with her now?"

"Billy Marshall boss and he's a right bloody stud. He can do it to a girl at least four times before he runs out of steam like. Well that may not be true but we'll find out if it is or ain't."

"We've got more important things to do down here than worry about Billy Marshalls sexual prowess," Albert reminded him. "All this stuff needs to be moved out and down to the shed at the bottom of the garden And it has to be done quietly. We don't want any nosy neighbours seeing what we're up to."

The rest of the gang were already hard at work and things were being put into piles ready for transportation to the shed. Clothes, perishable goods, cigarettes and alcohol were all ready to go up and everyone played their part with gusto, especially when they knew they would get their chance upstairs with Janice as a reward.

Albert was well pleased with how things were going until he noticed that George Harcourt was nowhere to be seen. "Where the bloody hell is George?" he shouted. "He should be down here helping with this lot.

48

"I seen him go upstairs just now," one of his men replied.

Albert wondered why. George wouldn't want anything to do with Janice so what other reason could he have for going up there? Admittedly the bathroom had an inside toilet, so he could just have gone for jimmy riddle. But if that was the case why didn't he use the small toilet down off of the hall. He was interrupted from these thoughts as one of his men announced, "Boss Percy Winkleman has just turned up with his horse and cart."

Chapter Four

Albert hurried down the long garden. The degree of privacy here was aided by the thick hedge that grew at least two feet higher than the surrounding fence, which gave this garden natural protection from prying eyes. This was why he had chosen this particular house as he knew that any activities carried on here would need this sort of privacy. Down at the back gate was old Percy Winkleman standing next to his horse, who was also far from young these days.

"Hello, you old scragger."

"Hello yourself," Percy replied with a toothy grin before turning to complete the job of fitting a nose bag for his horse. Old he may have been with a well lined face, but Percy was still as sharp as ever. He had a definite stoop, his legs were bandy and his breath wheezed in and out. He was dressed in his favourite overcoat that seemed to be almost as old as he was, at least that's what the people who knew him best always said. With trousers held together more by faith than anything else, his boots were in dire need of the services of a cobbler.

50

But the old man himself was happy with the way he looked. It made people feel sorry for him he would tell all his friends. "You'd be surprised how much stuff comes my way cause folk think I'm on my last legs."

Each time he said this he ended by giving his characteristic cackling laugh. "On me last legs? No I bloody well ain't, well not for a long time yet anyway."

Albert, of course, knew how trustworthy old Percy was, and that he, like so many before him could rely on the old rag and bone man completely.

Percy turned from ministering to his horse.

"Got to make sure Major here gets his oats, he ain't as young as he used to be. But he still does a bloody good job for me. Now then young Littlejohn, what can I do for you?"

As the father of seven children now it amused Albert to be called young. But Percy had known his father and sometimes worked with him.

"I need you and your cart Percy to move some stuff for us. It needs to be carried past the old Police Station at Portswod Junction then on down Bevios Valley to my house in Empress Road. Some of the stuff will be unloaded there and the rest I want taken down to the river by the Plaza cinema."

Percy's cackling laugh rang out loudly.

"That means Major and me will going right past the cop shop won't it? Give me a right laugh that will. You know the coppers often give me stuff for my cart cause they feel sorry for me too. Well how do we get your stuff out of sight if any of them do that then?"

Albert looked into the cart. "Look Percy, you've got a whole load of metal things in here that you're taking to the holding warehouse ain't you?"

"Yeah, down by the South Hants hospital."

"Right then, what we'll do is bury our stuff underneath. Then you go down through Portswood Junction like you always do and down Bevois Valley, but turn off into Dukes Road then onto

51

Empress Road. My misses and eldest girl will be waiting for you and they'll know what to take off your cart and into my house. Then you go on round and turn right past Mount Pleasant School and out into Bevois Valley Road again. From there you go on to unload all your metal outside the warehouse. No need to tell you to make sure no-one is around while you do that. Then Percy, get round to the Plaza cinema as quick as you can where some of my boys will be waiting by the side on the river bank. Once there they'll take over and unload all of our stuff."

"And what's in it for me Albert? You know I'll help because your dad and me was bloody good friends so his son will get anything done that's in my power to do. But I have to live as well don't I?"

"Yes of course you do Percy. I know how much my dad liked you and how much you helped him. So we'll pay for your services, not only with money, but maybe the odd bottle of scotch and some food if and when you need it."

Percy was silent for a few moments but then his thin reedy face creased up and that distinctive laugh rang out.

"Hee, this sounds right up my street Albert. Blimey it will be so good to get back to a bit of skullduggery. I ain't been able to do anything like this for years so I'm your man."

For the first time that day Albert managed a laugh.

"I knew I could rely on you Percy. Now my friend George Harcourt will be here in a minute and he'll see the first load goes into your cart. It won't be much this time because some of my men are only just getting it out the house and down here to the shed. And I'll tell George to give you a bottle of scotch to take home with you tonight."

Percy nodded his thanks.

"George Harcourt eh, is that the bastard they call The Cosh? Right little tearaway he was as a nipper and I've heard he's a bloody sight worse now."

"Yeah you're right there Percy, he is a hard case. But I need him to be so that he keeps trouble away from us. Anyone who thinks they can get the better of the Littlejohn Gang is made to think twice."

Three gang members were now approaching, keeping close to the fence so as to make sure no-one from outside could see what they were up to. Albert went up to meet them.

"Right boys, I want ten bottles of Scotch and some Gin and Brandy, as well as a hundred fags to go in Percy's cart. The rest goes in the shed."

"Ok boss, George told us to bring another bottle of scotch and 40 fags for Percy here."

The old boy was well pleased with this and helped them carefully place the contraband under some of the metal objects, the bottles in stout wooden boxes to make sure they weren't broken on route.

"We all appreciate what you're doing for us Percy and my dad will be too, even though he's been dead for more than ten years now. Off you go, and good luck to you."

"Me and old Major don't need luck, we've both been doing this sort of thing since neither of us can remember."

Albert's mind drifted back to a time just before he left home to marry Ida.

"How old is Major now? Blimey, he must be getting on a bit. I remember when you used to come round in this same cart shouting 'Rag and Bone' in our road. We used to feed him with bread and sugar lumps."

"Yeah that was a long time ago weren't it? Major is eighteen now so he ain't got many more years left. But then neither have I so we'll see who hobbles off this world first. Whatever is left of it if this war ever ends. But he ain't finished yet."

Then, jumping up onto the cart with an agility that belied his age, he took up the reins.

"Walk on Major. We've got work to do."

For a fleeting moment Albert was concerned about the explaining Percy would have to do if any ARP wardens, Home Guard or police stopped him then brushed this aside. He wouldn't say a word about us. So he turned his mind to more pressing issues, where on earth had George Harcourt disappeared too?

Upstairs in the bedroom Billy Marshall was getting dressed. When he arrived he found Janice, still naked, trying to cover herself as best she could. But the man who stood here now was the opposite of the thug who had ripped her clothes off, then caused considerable hurt as he ravaged her body.

Billy was not only younger than Harry Small but decidedly better looking. And to make things even better he was one of the few members of the Littlejohn Gang with a softer side to his nature. He could, and on many occasions had already, been just as ruthless when dealing with gang business. But he was also capable of kindly behavior when in the company of children and young women.

So he had spoken softly, taken her in his arms and kissed her gently yet passionately on her soft lips. This took Janice by surprise, they clung together and his youth and vigor raced through both of them. The effect was to make her start tearing at his clothes in an effort to get them off.

"Hey slow down a minute," he chided her. "If you rip my stuff off I won't have anything to wear when I go back downstairs will I? Take it more gently and then we can both enjoy ourselves."

Janice did just that, so that one by one each item of clothing Billy was wearing was dropped onto the floor. For the first time in her young life Janice really was able to enjoy the attentions of a man. She knew she had to give herself to Albert whenever he wanted. But that was simply a job. She acted out her part, faking it most of the time, even on the rare occasion she was able to experience some pleasure he meant absolutely nothing to her.

But this lovely boy was different in so many ways. Every part of him touching her body sent electric shock waves of sheer pleasure through her and when she climaxed the screams that came were genuine ones of pure delight.

54

She watched him dress and knew that he alone was the man she wanted to see more of. He realized this too and gave her a kiss as he was about to leave the room.

"We'll do this again as soon as we get the chance love, so keep your chin up and think of me when the next member of our gang comes up here."

Then blowing her a kiss he opened the door and went outside. Here though he was met by the commanding figure of George Harcourt.

"Hello George what do want? Are you next in there with Janice?" he asked, somewhat taken aback, but soon found out this was far from the truth.

George had noticed Billy before and as soon as he saw him knew that he wanted him. He was young and had a great body. In hot weather Billy always stripped to the waist and often wore short shorts as well. His legs were long and slim and George had all sorts of problems preventing himself from openly displaying his need for this young man.

When he knew Billy was going upstairs to make love to Janice his jealousy had boiled over. Why should she get to see him naked and touch him? So he gave instructions about the bottle of whiskey and forty cigarettes to be given to Percy Winkleman then, making sure all the men were doing their jobs properly, crept away.

Going silently upstairs he waited in the dark outside the bedroom where Janice and Billy were busily engaged. George cringed as he heard the cries of pleasure coming from the girl and his own needs came roaring to the surface. He knew exactly what he was going to do when Billy came out.

Grabbing him by the front of his shirt he quickly pushed him up against the wall.

"This is what I want boy," he snarled as his hand went down to Billy's groin.

The younger man was taken so much by surprise that he didn't immediately respond, but as realization dawned he began fighting back.

"Let me go you pervert," he shouted and tried to knee George in order to get away from him but missed his main target and only managed to hit him on the top part of his leg. This angered him so he let go of Billy's groin and, reaching inside his coat, brought out his famous cosh. Billy seeing this knew he had no chance against this man where that weapon was concerned.

"Alright you win. I'll let you do whatever you want but put that bloody cosh away."

Sneering now George did just that, then with a nod of his head indicated towards one of the empty bedrooms across the other side of the house. Walking in front as he entered this room Billy knew all of his clothes would be coming off for the second time, but this time for George's pleasure instead of the lovely Janice.

Unknown to both of them Albert noticed Billy was missing and upon being informed that he went upstairs ages ago, now had a pretty good idea where George was likely to be found. Sure enough, when he silently entered the bedroom, he was greeted by two naked men. Neither George, who was at a fever pitch of excitement, or Billy, who most certainly was not, even noticed that the door of the room had been opened.

Billy was silently cursing the man who was forcing him to do this and vowing vengeance against him at the first opportunity. Albert just shook his head as he walked back down the stairs. There was nothing he could do about George's sexual preferences. He just hoped it wouldn't cause any trouble amongst the gang.

Percy had set off with Major pulling the cart at a good, steady pace. Reaching the end of Highfield lane they made the turn into Portswood Junction. Percy glanced across at the old Victorian building that stood between the tram depot entrance

56

and the gent's toilet. This, of course, was Portswood Police Station. He smiled to himself, if only that lot knew what he had in this cart, and then started to sing as he went along.

But not for very long, a shout of "Hey Percy, wait a minute," rang out. Looking around he was alarmed by the sight of Police Constable Malcolm Nantwich waving at him and knew he had no option but to stop. So with a pull on the reins and a shout of 'Woe Major' he waited to find out what was going to happen next. As the policeman stared running towards him his thoughts were in a whirl. Surely they couldn't have found out?

The panic proved to be unfounded though for when a rather breathless PC Nantwich reached him he had a very simple request.

"Ok Percy, sorry to stop you but we've got a load of metal pots and pans that have been handed in at the station. Can you turn round and come and collect it all please?"

Relief flooded through Percy and he quickly produced that famous toothy grin.

"Sure, I'll be glad to."

Pulling on one rein to turn the cart around he shouted, "Walk on Major."

The old horse tried to do as he was told and pulled with all his might but the cart wouldn't turn. Cursing now Percy yelled "What the bleeding hell's wrong? Come on Major, get us moving."

PC Nantwich had seen what was wrong.

"Your offside wheel is caught in the tram lines Percy, Major won't be able to move you until we can free it."

This was a disaster and Percy knew it. Tram lines were an occupational hazard for carts, bicycle riders and many others. Sunk into the road and easy to forget, many a wheel had gotten stuck and even caused delays to the trams if the offending vehicle could not be moved in time. Percy's cart had just one wheel stuck but his load was heavy so freeing it wasn't going to be easy.

The policeman could see at once what was causing the problem.

"I'll have to get some of the lads to help. I'm afraid most of your load will need to come off before we can get you free."

Percy was very alarmed, if they unloaded his cart they were likely to find the boxes hidden underneath. He knew he would be in big trouble. How on earth would he be able to explain the contents? Bottles of whisky, gin, rum, and real Russian Vodka that wasn't even available to buy in this country. That just had to be contraband didn't it? He was really going to be for it now and he hated the idea of letting Albert down.

There was no time to think. Policemen came pouring out of the old station to help move his cart. Ordinarily he would have been extremely grateful but this situation was rapidly turning into a disaster.

"Right lads," said Sergeant Len Warmburst, who was preparing to direct operations. "That wheel's stuck good and proper in that tram line so let's get most of this metal off then see if we can lift it out."

Percy stayed glued to his seat, resigning himself to his fate, as more and more of the scrap metal load was lifted out and placed in the road. Down and down went the level until he knew those boxes were almost at the point where they would become visible. If he were to be arrested and locked up who on earth could he get to look after his faithful horse Major.

Just then the sergeant shouted out again.

"Righty ho lads, I think that's enough. Let's see if we can lift this side of the cart so the wheel is free. Percy, be a good chap and jump down a minute. We don't want to be lifting you as well."

Percy stood in the road and surveyed the heap of metal objects that were piled up on the surface, then silently offered up a prayer as the police contingent heaved together. The cart rocked alarmingly, and old Major gave a loud whinny and looked as though he was about to bolt.

Percy hurried up to him and threw his arms around his neck.

"Woe Major, easy now, it's only people trying to get our cart back on the road, stand easy and we'll soon be on our way."

The cart suddenly rocked again but this time it stood upright.

"There you go. The wheels back on the road so make sure you take more care in the future. It's not like you to make a mistake like that."

"No it ain't sergeant. It's this bloody war that's upsetting everyone ain't it?"

Sergeant Warmburst agreed, although it did strike him as a little odd. Percy had been around longer than any of them and was not easily frightened. But he soon shrugged off these thoughts. The job he was doing was very worthwhile so now it was time to send him on his way.

The metal that the police wanted to get rid of was brought out and added to the heap on the ground, all of which was being thrown back onto the cart. Percy's nerves were nearly shot to pieces by now, and he was going to need to pour a very large measure from the bottle he had been given before too long. If this clumsy lot managed to break through any of the boxes they would smell the spirits for a start, and Albert Littlejohn would do his bloody nut if the boxes were delivered full of smashed bottles.

He was spared any more of this by the sergeant.

"Alright Percy, up you get. You can go on your way now and thanks for collecting our stuff to take with you."

Relief flooded through the old man and he jumped back up onto his cart.

"Any time sergeant, it's all for the war effort ain't it so we have to do our bit."

Then, clicking the reins, he shouted to Major to walk on. Down through Portswood Junction they went. But once past the Broadway Cinema he pulled up and inspected his cart. None of the boxes had been broken thank goodness. He could tell straight away because there was no smell of spirits. Now though he had to move some of the metal objects that had been haphazardly thrown back to get at the two boxes he needed.

It was a heavy job and Percy wasn't anywhere near as fit as he once was, so by the time he had uncovered them he was out of breath and needed a long rest. At least the trip should be plain sailing from here he hoped.

Inside the house at number 34 Empress Road Ida was making preparations when Maggie came back from dropping off her brothers and sisters.

"You're dad said that old Percy Winkleman will be here tonight with some things he wants hidden. Are the children where they are supposed to be?"

"They're alright mum," Maggie reassured her. "They love going to Aunty Mavis' house and playing with all of her kids."

Ida smiled. "I know they do, but with her five and our six there as well it must be like a madhouse."

"They're not in the house much mum. They all rush down Dukes Road and get through the fence at the top of the road bridge over the railway lines. From there they can play near the water and Aunty Mavis's eldest, Jennifer, keeps an eye on them so it's all quite safe."

"But what about the air raids?" Ida now sounded very concerned. "What if one starts when they're all out playing at that spot, there aren't any shelters anywhere near there."

"No mum. But Jennifer knows what she's doing and if there's a raid she gets them all back home quick I can tell you. Then they all get into the Anderson shelter in Aunty Mavis's garden. How they all get in there with our lot as well is a mystery to me. But she's done it at least three times already and it works alright. And even if she don't have time to get them all together to make the dash back to Aunties' house she can get them all under the road bridge where they'll all be safe till the raid is over."

"Well I still don't like it. I suppose we've got no choice but if anything happens to any of my children because of what your father is doing then he'll need the protection of his whole bloody gang to save him from what I'll do to him."

She paused as the sound of horse's hooves was becoming audible.

"That will be old Percy Winkleman. Quick Maggie, go out and meet him and make sure none of our nosey neighbours are looking out."

Maggie did as she was told and scrutinized the windows of all houses in sight of their own. No curtains were moving, even as Percy drew up and Major stamped the ground with his hooves.

"Quick Mr. Winkleman, mum is waiting inside. So what have you brought us?"

"Hello young Maggie ain't it? Bloody hell girl you've grown since I last saw you. Proper little lady now ain't you?"

This compliment was one that Maggie might have liked to hear at any other time, but not right now, and there was urgency in her voice.

"Yes Mr. Winkleman I am Maggie, but we need to get the stuff into our house quick before anyone looks out and sees what we're doing."

"Ok girl I get you," he answered. Then, for a man of his age, he acted with a speed that took even Maggie by surprise. In next to no time three wooden boxes had been removed from the cart. With Percy taking two of them and Maggie the other they quickly took these inside Albert's house. Ida thanked the old man and offered him a cup of tea.

"No thanks Mrs. Littlejohn, I ain't got time for that. I've got to get me load of metal down to the warehouse then take the rest of your husband's stuff down to the river by the Plaza see. But thanks all the same."

In no time at all he was gone with his call of "walk on Major" echoing down the empty road.

Ida and Maggie carried the boxes upstairs to the big front bedroom where they opened them up. Bottles of spirits from the

61

first two were carefully wrapped in thick newspaper before being laid inside the mattress. The third one contained tinned food, mainly meat, soup and various vegetables. Most of the shops in this area were nearly always out of stock of things like this so Ida did what her husband had told her to and took some of these for her family's use. The rest went inside the mattress with the spirits.

Maggie shouted with excitement when she saw what else this box was hiding.

"Look mum," she exclaimed, holding up a pair of sheer nylon stockings. "You can't get any of these now because there ain't none in the shops. Where did dad get these from?"

"Never mind that," her mother replied, not sharing her daughter's enthusiasm. "We aren't supposed to know. Let's get them put away quickly they must be very safely out the way from any prying coppers."

The nylons were wrapped in newspaper and placed in one of the paper bags Ida kept for any purpose, where and when they may be needed. These were also placed inside the mattress, well away from the bottles of spirits.

"That should do it, alright Maggie go and get our kids back from Mavis's house and let's get them all ready for bed. They should be tucked up before now anyway, if they even get to stay in bed all night, what with these bloody bombing raids."

Percy, meanwhile, had reached the holding warehouse for metal objects that was situated close to the Royal South Hants Hospital. Here so many people just like him were bringing metal and adding it to the huge mound that was being given to the government in order to be melted down and used to make things needed to fight the Germans.

Some lucky folk had cars to enable them to make this journey. But for many others, pots, pans, tin baths and even metal gates and fences were carried by hand cart or wheel barrow. Southampton's residents were fed up with not only the destruction raining down from the skies above but also so many of our ships being sunk by this enemy, and they were going to extraordinary lengths to help in the fight against them.

Percy was proud of them for this, but tonight he kept Major right away from any prying eyes as he added to the pile. Throwing all the metal objects from his cart he was satisfied when it was done that no-one had been able to see inside it. Sacking was placed over the exposed boxes before, once again, urging Major to get them to their next destination.

He drove back until he re-entered Mount Pleasant Road, this time going in the opposite direction past the school, then the Old Thatched House pub, before going over Mount Pleasant Railway crossing. Then the short distance up Union Road, past the Plaza, and out across the main road before taking the little road that led down to the bank.

"Easy now Major, we have to go down to the water and meet them under the bridge. Walk slowly my old faithful friend then we will do the last job for tonight before we goes home. And you get a good helping of oats cause you've bloody well earned it."

The old horse gave a snort in answer to this, almost as if he knew. The way these two communicated with each other was a wonder to behold and it worked every time. So they cautiously made their way along. The river flowed past at a particularly fast rate at this point. Percy took no chances and pulled up well short of the water.

"Now we'll wait cause I don't know what's going to happen next."

As an almost immediate response to this, a torch suddenly started flashing. "Ok Major I guess this is it, let's go."

At a slow pace they made their way up to where the torch light was still shining and pulled up as they were greeted by a voice.

"Alright Percy stop here and we'll unload you."

Through the dark he could just make out the water and drawn up on the bank was a small boat with a powerful outboard motor. Into this, four men were now taking the remaining boxes out of Percy's cart and transferring them. When it was finished the man who had first spoken to Percy addressed him again.

"That's it all done. Thanks a lot old man, Albert will be well pleased when we tell him how good you were, arriving right on time like this."

Percy couldn't really see him but grinned in the darkness. "I bin doing jobs like this before you was born lad. And Albert knows that."

Then, with a wave of his hand, both Percy and Major headed back on up and disappeared into the night, making their way home.

"Right boys, let's get the rest in the boat and shove off before anybody sees us. Albert and George will be on the other side of the river by now waiting for us."

The speaker was Philip Burton who had worked in the docks for a great many years and was also a member of the Littlejohn gang. In some ways he was even worse than George the Cosh, carrying a gun whenever on gang duty, and it was this that had killed the young lorry driver who fought with them in the years before the war. Everyone on this side of the Itchen knew about it so no-one would argue with him. Besides, they knew he was right and their boss and his right hand man would indeed be waiting for them on the other side of this fast flowing river.

With the boxes from Percy's cart now carefully placed in the boat they climbed in and the members of Albert's gang started on their way upstream against the current. The outboard motor was only started when they were well away from the bank and with this they powered their way towards the road bridge that crossed the railway lines just around the bend from where they began.

George could see them coming. "It's all going well ain't it All, here they come now."

64

"Yes so I see," Albert replied. "And that means old Percy did his bit as I knew the old bugger would."

They both laughed as the boat came closer and finally grounded on the shingle at the river's edge. The big road bridge now hid them from any prying eyes so the boxes were taken out and placed on the ground ready to be moved into the secret store room.

This had all gone perfectly to plan, except for the fact one of the men lost his balance while climbing out of the boat. As he fell the box he was carrying was snatched away, allowing him to continue with a huge splash as he fell into the river.

Now standing dripping wet on the river bank, he looked round at the other gang members.

"Couldn't one of you bleeders have done somefink to stop me falling in?"

"Not bloody likely, we saved the spirits in the box you was carrying and all of us had a laugh seeing you fall arse over head in the water."

Seeing this had the potential to result in a fight George waded in straight away.

"Stop that you clowns, we've got work to do, and you," he now glared at the wet and bedraggled figure who had taken an unexpected bath. "You should have been more careful. You can thank your bloody stars the rest of the boys saved that box and none of the bottles were broken. Now put up with things, and help with what we've got to do now."

Albert now took over. "George is right, I don't want any of you falling out and getting rough with one another. Now pick up these boxes and follow us."

The gang moved in procession, carefully carrying the contraband spirits, and followed their leader as they crossed the mainline railway and entered the marshalling yards on the other side. Keeping to the darkest parts they nearly made a mistake by crashing into some piles of rubbish that had been left lying around.

This made a loud noise and at once a voice rang out.

"Who goes there? Advance and be recognized."

Squinting into the darkness they could make out the form of an elderly man in army uniform, he was carrying a rifle and looked as though he knew how to use it.

"I know someone's there so come out, or I start shooting."

He was a member of the Home Guard and had unslung his rifle. Now it was pointing towards the place where Albert and his boys were hiding. He began slowly walking towards them and they knew he would have to be stopped. As his footsteps grew louder George Harcourt drew out his cosh, and even more menacingly Philip Burton drew his pistol. Just a bit closer old man and you're dead he thought to himself as his finger tightened on the trigger.

Chapter Five

Cyril Smethick had been with the home Guard since its formation and was on duty in the Bevois Park marshalling yard most nights of the week. He and two more of his company were there to make sure no-one tried to steal anything from any of the trucks that were waiting to be hooked up to steam engines and transported to various parts of the country.

A veteran of the First World War he was no stranger to this type of duty. Many a German had become victim to Cyril's rifle in that conflict and he was alert enough to use it again here. The noise that had drawn his attention had come from behind a long row of trucks so he made his way there, ready to fire if he found any sign of looters.

Waiting behind these trucks were Albert Littlejohn and his boys. They were watching Cyril's advance and knew that if he kept coming he would spot them and raise the alarm.

"Come on you old bugger," George quietly whispered. "Just a bit further and I'll knock your bloody head off."

Albert knew he meant it and was quite prepared for George to deal with this situation. But looking round he was alarmed to see that Philip Burton had his gun in hand and it was pointing at the approaching Home Guard soldier. If he shot the old boy they would be in all sorts of trouble, the last thing he wanted was a major police presence in this yard investigating a shooting so he hissed at George.

"Burton's got his gun out, if he uses it all hell will break lose. Stop the silly bastard will you."

Looking around George saw at once what Albert was talking about and knew he had to act fast to stop Burton. He didn't even have time to think about it so acted out of sheer reaction. Moving quietly but with a speed that belied his age he came upon Philip Burton and with one swift movement his cosh landed on the other man's head. Burton crumpled to the ground and George caught his gun before it dropped. Then, without stopping to make sure the man he had coshed was alright, he returned to Albert's side and saw Cyril Smethick was now very much closer.

His hand once more gripped his deadly cosh but just as was preparing to spring out and hit the old man a shout pierced through the silence. From the shunters hut another man appeared and seeing Cyril in the distance he called out to him.

"Cyril, what the bloody hell are you doing? The tea's ready so come and get yours while it's hot."

"I heard something over here Ted. I'm sure we've got bloody looters in the yard."

Sighing as he realized he had to follow this up, Corporal Ted Mudpool knew this was by no means the first time old Cyril had heard something in the yard. The problem being that each time a thorough search of the yard usually revealed absolutely nothing. The only people here were the Home Guard patrol. No looters in sight and another false alarm. This was made worse by the shaded torches that slowed down the search, but blackout regulations were in force because any lights could aid enemy bombers in finding their targets.

Albert and George watched closely as the other man reached Cyril, and Albert felt the gun being pushed into his hand. His look of surprise was answered by George.

"There's two of the bastards now Al. So I'll take the old soldier and put him out of action, but you'll have to shoot that Corporal."

"I ain't never killed anyone George and I ain't starting now."

This was quite true. Albert usually always left the enforcement to George and some of his other men.

"You don't have to kill the bastard Al," George hissed back. "Just shoot him in the legs. We've got to get out of this yard without anyone seeing us so those two have to be put out of action."

Albert knew his second in command was right so gripped the gun tightly in his hand and pointed it towards the two Home Guard soldiers who were closer still to where they were crouching.

Corporal Mudpool stopped within a few feet of them. "Right Cyril what did you hear?"

"Someone crashed into the rubbish that's lying around all over the place here Corp and I believe its bloody looters."

Just then Albert had a sudden idea that he acted on straight away. Kicking out he deliberately made contact with the rubbish and it made just as much noise as it had done the first time.

"There Corp," Cyril shouted. "I told you they're in there behind them trucks."

"For Gawds sake Cyril use your brains will you. If they are looters they're the most incompetent ones you'll ever come across, making all that noise while we're standing here with rifles at the ready. Its rats Cyril that's all. Now come on, our tea is getting cold."

The two soldiers then turned and started walking back towards the shunter's hut, though old Cyril was still looking round. He wasn't as convinced as his corporal.

Albert and the rest of them remained still until the two men actually disappeared inside the small hut and the door banged shut behind them.

Then it was all action as Albert directed them.

"Right let's get going and get our gear stowed in the secret room at the Portswood Hotel. We can get in the back way once we're clear of this shunting yard."

He went over to where Philip Burton was lying motionless and looked down at him.

"Is he okay? George hit him hard I know."

"I think so boss but he's out cold so how are we gonna get him out of here?"

"Carry the useless bastard and put him under the road bridge. He can come round under there and make his own bloody way home. And I'll have a lot to say to the murdering swine if he does wake up before we go."

The other men were uneasy about just leaving one of their gang to recover on his own. Supposing he was really badly hurt, George Harcourt had hit him hard and could have caused a nasty injury. None of them ever argued with Albert because he ruled this gang with a rod of iron and would not take criticism from any of them.

But tonight, concern over their fallen comrade overrode this and together they stood around the one man who was speaking for them all.

"Look boss, we can't just leave Phil here we don't know how badly hurt he is. He might need hospital treatment and none of us can give him that."

Impatience mingled with anger as Albert took this in. He didn't want any more hold ups. Their ill gotten gains had to be moved to the door of the secret room in the cellar of the Portswood Hotel so it would be out of sight of prying eyes. But he also knew his men were right. Philip Burton was still unconscious and his breath was wheezing in and out. He did indeed look as though medical attention was going to be required.

So he relented. "Alright, get the sod up to my house and tell my misses to get Peter Smyth from his house in Dukes Road. He'll come and look at Burton for us."

"But he's been struck off for doing abortions ain't he?"

Albert was not going to have his word questioned again so replied angrily. "Yeah but he's still got more knowledge about medical stuff than any of us so two of you get him round to my house out of sight, then do what I tell you and get Peter Smyth."

Just then the air around them erupted into sound as the air raid siren let out its warning. Another raid was about to start. The night air was transformed from utter darkness by bright lines of light from the powerful search lights, probing the skies above for any signs of these enemy aircraft.

"Right that's all we bloody need, get moving all of you," Albert roared at them. Let's get this stuff up to the pub, we can shelter from the raid in the secret room. It's far enough underground to be safe from any bomb hits. You two do like I told you, you'll have to get him down to my families Anderson shelter but tell my misses to get Peter Smyth as soon as the all clear sounds."

As each gang member carried at least one box, the ground under their feet started to shake and the drone of enemy bombers could clearly be heard so they lost no time finding their way to the back of the Portswood Hotel. Albert was leading and operated the door release, then stood aside as his men hurried past him and gained the safety of this old room.

Albert hesitated and stood looking out of the door with George beside him, they both knew that Southampton High Street was under fire again and also the docks.

"How much bloody damage are those bastards going to do tonight?" Albert wondered out loud. "They're hitting the docks again and if they keep doing that we won't have any berths left

71

for the poor sods who do make it here and don't get sunk by them fucking U boats."

"Yeah and the pilots of them planes use the spire of St Michaels Church to guide them in. Hitler's told them not to bomb it for that reason. We'd be best off blowing the bloody thing up ourselves," George wryly observed.

They watched the bomb flashes as they hit the ground and both men hoped with all their hearts that none of their families were anywhere near those blasts.

"It's too close to here for my wife and kids to be in any danger tonight," Albert observed. "So they should all be ok but I don't know about yours George. Where do they go during these raids?"

"Well you know I ain't got any kids Al but my wife goes out into the big shelter in the road. Belgrave roads got lots of them see and I know she don't lose any time getting into hers."

With the whole world going mad all around them Albert thought back to just a few hours ago when he had seen what his best friend in the gang was doing to young Billy Marshall. George Harcourt was married yes, but it had long ago turned into a marriage of convenience. His wife Shirley suspected almost from the start, back in 1934 just after they were married, that her husband's sexual desires lay elsewhere.

He had made the mistake of looking longingly at the young and very handsome milkman who had taken over the round in his road. Lust was written all over his face and in his mind he was already undressing the young man. But George knew this was not going to be possible because his desire for other men had to be kept a secret.

His professional reputation as a hard case and cosh man was so important, added to this the fact that homosexuality was a criminal offence. Not that this bothered George particularly because of the way he led his life, which was hardly law abiding, but if he ever did end up in prison he wanted to make sure it was for his actions with the Littlejohn Gang and not because he was caught with his trousers down.

His wife had no such problems and she too had noticed the new young milkman. So the first time he knocked on her door to collect payment for the week's milk he was invited inside. Pleased with this because it probably meant he would get a cup of tea he was overwhelmed by Shirley Harcourt and soon his clothes were scattered all over the living room floor. He was late on the round for the rest of that day but he delivered his milk with a very big smile on his face.

Albert of course knew very little about this side of George's life, and it didn't bother him really. But he knew Billy wasn't that way so it dawned on him that George must have threatened him with the cosh to get him into that position. He was going to have to have a word with the boy to prevent any in gang fighting. If this started to interfere with gang business then it couldn't be allowed to continue. Now was not the time or place though, other matters were more pressing.

The all clear sounded before they had even joined the others inside. So Albert went in now to check that his men had stacked their boxes up against the far wall, well away from either the front or rear doors.

"That's fine boys, now let's get up to the bar and get ourselves a much needed drink. It may be after closing time but Bernard and his misses won't chuck us out just yet."

The public bar was now deserted except for Bernard and Catherine who were busy clearing up and washing glasses ready for opening time tomorrow. Though with the damage outside caused by this latest raid they both wondered how many customers were likely to be in. They knew Albert and his boys were going to be using the secret room downstairs but the bar had been crowded this evening which had kept them busy.

This time though when the raid began the regulars simply remained where they were and carried on drinking their beer. Most of these men and a few of their wives who were with them

73

had formed the opinion that if the Germans were going to blow them up then what better place for this to happen than in the bar of their favourite pub. Shelters provided a little protection for sure but no one would survive a direct hit on one.

Some of the older med had actually carried on with their game of dominoes, and Catherine had been curious as to how they could remain so calm.

"We've been through this before Cathy love. All of us were in the last war and old Robert here was on convoy duty in the Merchant Navy. A load of his mates got torpedoed and either died in the explosion or drowned when their ships sunk. All of us round this table got through that war, if they didn't get us then well they can try again if they want but none of us here gives a damn either way."

Now with the bar empty she and Bernard welcomed Albert, George and the rest of them into it and Bernard began pulling pints for them all. Catherine was relieved to have gotten through another raid unscathed so her welcome was a little warmer than usual.

"We should be alright tonight boys," Bernard told them as beer flowed into the pint glasses he held under the pumps. "Old Gerry Wilkinson the local bobby will be busy all over the place out there, so he won't be poking his nose in to catch us serving beer after hours."

"Just as well for him then," muttered George as he fetched his pint. "The way I'm feeling right now I'd cosh the old bugger and shut him up that way."

"And lose us our license, no you bloody well wouldn't George Harcourt," Catherine said in a very determined voice. "You keep that cosh of yours in your pocket while you're in this pub. Bernard and I don't want any trouble of that sort. Besides, it would only alert the coppers that you're around and they'd start keeping a watch on the Portswood Hotel because of that. Now drink up and shut up."

74

It never ceased to amuse Albert that she was the only person who could get away with talking to him like that. George meekly did as he was told and nodded to Catherine as he took his pint to a table as far away from her as he could get. A remark like that from anyone else would have resulted in George Harcourt's cosh being violently used for the second time that night. He really did not like women and was inclined to be very wary around them.

Albert was still at the bar with Catherine.

"We really have had a hard time tonight, a bloody home guard soldier nearly spotted us in that marshalling yard and one of my boys was going to shoot him. I had to get George to stop him with the cosh. I'm just going home to make sure my wife and kids are all ok and see if they've got the doctor to the stupid sod. The stuff we've brought tonight is downstairs. The spirits are in boxes stacked against the far wall. You and Bernard can have two of each from them boxes to sell here in the pub. Is that ok with you?"

"Yes it certainly is, so what have you got down there?"

"Everything you'll need, whisky, gin and some brandy. You can have 100 fags as well. They'll be more coming in the next few days and if things work out a lot more stuff after that."

Quickly finishing his pint he waved farewell to his boys and, with a nod to Bernard and his wife, went outside to make his way home. Walking down Dukes Road the darkness all around him suddenly meant more than it had ever done before. He had never really taken in the fact that without street lights or any light from the houses it really was pitch dark. In fact he couldn't even see his hand in front of his face. Having worked nights on and off in the docks for more years than he could remember darkness had become a way of life. Now though his criminal mind saw a new venture opening up before him.

The blackout conditions could certainly be turned to their advantage even more than they had already considered. No one would see them, they could do house break-ins to get some of

75

the stuff they needed. With George on the case anything would be possible. A meeting with the rest of the gang was clearly in order to discuss these possibilities, after a day at the docks and the inevitable clearing up from tonight's raids of course.

These thoughts were interrupted when he passed a house that had a radio turned up loud and the news made him stop to listen.

"Tonight's raid was concentrated on the docks and high street, much damage was caused to shops and news is coming in that an air raid shelter in Hogland's Park, opposite Edwin Jones, took a direct hit. There are thought to be no survivors. Edwin Jones was also hit and badly damaged, and so were the docks. There are reports of many casualties as well as extensive damage. The air craft factory at Woolston that was turning out the Spitfire was completely destroyed. Messages coming from management seek to reassure all that work on this aircraft will continue in other parts of Southampton."

We'll find a way to keep building them Albert said aloud feeling angry at the devastation that had been caused yet again. Little did he know that his prediction would come gloriously true as the spitfire was, indeed, put together from so many different outlets. In other factories, private garages and even garden sheds parts of this aircraft were being made.

Albert's was suddenly disturbed by a voice behind him. "Now then, what are you doing out here at this time? Don't you know it's dangerous? Some of them Nazi planes may have bombs left and they drop the bloody things anywhere just to get rid of them."

Albert turned to see a rather stout man in a blue uniform with the letters ARP written on the front of his helmet. This was an air raid warden and the letters stood for Air Raid Patrol.

"Oh sorry," Albert tried to appease him. "I was at my brother's house when the raid started and I'm going home now."

"And just where is home then?"

"Empress Road, number 34, I'm worried about my family, have any of the houses been hit do you know?"

"Not this time mate and we haven't any reports of injuries down there either so you're lucky. But get going now and get off the streets."

Albert thanked the man and quickly walked away but turning into Empress Road his thoughts were elsewhere. He was of course pleased to know none of the houses in this road had been hit and it sounded as though all of his family were alright. But he was concerned about the incident with the ARP warden. He hadn't heard him coming up from behind, even though he wore big boots. They were going to have to keep a rear guard whenever they were out in the blackout else they may be caught out with their trousers down so to speak. They didn't want to have to fight their way out of trouble unless they could really help it.

Reaching number 34 he turned his key in the lock then went inside, being greeted by Maggie who rushed up and threw her arms around him, planting a kiss on his cheek.

"Oh daddy you're alright. Mum and me was worried because you was out during that raid."

"Hey slow down young lady," he laughingly replied. "Of course I'm alright. Me and the boys were in the Portswood Hotel when them sodding planes came over. I couldn't get down here in time to be with the family so all of us sheltered in the pubs cellar. Now are all the kids and your mum ok?"

"Yes dad, they are in bed now but Doctor Smyth is here looking at that friend of yours who was hurt. Mum is with him as well, they're in the front room."

"Right, I'll go and take a look but I could murder a bacon sandwich Maggie, that's if we've even got any."

Albert quietly entered the front room, which his wife Ida kept as her show room. None of their children were allowed to play or even enter the room during the year. But at Christmas it was decorated beautifully and on Christmas morning filled with the children's presents and of course sweets, cakes, and all sorts of treats not given to them at any other time of the year.

Now though with the war on Christmas was a low key affair. Albert did his best though to make sure his family had a chicken for their special dinner, and all sorts of other goodies that came from his criminal activities.

This evening the room looked anything but a show room as Doctor Smyth worked on the still unconscious form of Philip Burton.

"This doesn't look good Mrs. Littlejohn," he said without looking up. He hadn't seen Albert come in so was still addressing Ida.

"This chap has been given a hefty blow to his head and I think this is more than I can deal with, he'll have to go to the hospital. How did this happen did you say?"

"It was as the raid began doctor," Albert jumped in before his wife had a chance to reply. "A few of us was on our way to the pub and a bloody lump of stone come down from the roof of the building we was passing and hit Phil here on the head."

"Oh Mr Littlejohn good evening, I didn't see you there. Well as I have just said this man needs more treatment than I can administer to him so I will make arrangements for him to go to hospital."

Doctor Smyth knew a lot about medicine of course and had already formed the opinion that the wound on Philip Burton's head was not caused by falling stone. He knew when someone had been hit with a weapon and now looking at Albert he realized that the falling stonework was simply an excuse, and that this was most probably the work of George Harcourt's cosh. It would however be unwise of him to voice these suspicions.

"Well Mr. Littlejohn as you know I no longer officially practice medicine but with this war on and so many people being injured in air-raids I am still able to get patients into hospital if there is any hope of saving them. So if you bear with me I will go and use my telephone and get an ambulance here as quickly as I can. This may take some time as I can't guarantee my phone will be working. If that is the case I will need to use the phone box on the corner of Dukes Road. Even then it will take time for the ambulance to get here because there are sure to be many casualties tonight that will need attention as well."

"Don't worry about that Doctor," Ida replied. "My daughter and I will watch him and wait for the ambulance. Is there anything we should do to help him in the meantime?"

"Just keep him warm and quiet Ms. Littlejohn. If he comes round you can give him a drink of water but nothing else. The Doctors at the hospital will want to know they can administer drugs if need be, so anything else inside him can interfere with that. I will be as quick as I can."

With that the Doctor hurried out into the street. Despite being struck off he still managed to maintain his car so he started the engine and headed off back towards his house in Dukes Road.

In the front room of 34 Empress Road Ida now turned her fury onto her husband.

"Stone fell onto his head from a building did it? Well Albert Littlejohn that's nonsense and we both know it. This is the work of that thug George Harcourt isn't it? It's his bloody cosh that's caused this."

Looking sheepish now, which was certainly unusual for a man of Albert's lifestyle and position, he was forced to admit it.

"He had to Ida, we were about to get caught by the bloody Home Guard in the marshaling yard. You can't see a bloody thing in this blackout and we kicked a pile of rubbish. George could have handled it by clouting the old sod but hot head Phillip here had his gun out ready to use. I had to stop him doing that because war or no war the coppers would turn this area upside down to find the killer of a Home Guard soldier and I can't have that happening at the moment can I? So George used his cosh and here we are."

"Yes here we are," his wife spat at him, "and here this member of your gang is as well and from the looks of the swelling on his head your friend George bloody Harcourt may soon be guilty of causing his death."

79

"Oh Ida he knows what he's doing that's why he's known as the cosh. That bump on Burtons head just looks bad that's all. They probably won't even keep him in hospital for long."

Just then an ambulance drew up with a screech outside their home followed by Doctor Smyth in his car who quickly hurried inside.

"This was lucky I managed to flag the ambulance down and they've got room for our patient inside so we can get this man looked at properly very soon."

After quickly checking on Phil Burton he was quite anxious.

"And not a moment too soon by the looks of him, he's gone very white and his breathing is labored it isn't a good sign."

As the ambulance roared off with Burton now inside and Ida tapping her foot in anger as she stared at her husband, Albert was at a loss to understand what had really happened. He knew and trusted George Harcourt and knew he would always do just what was needed in any situation, in this case tapping him on the head to stop him from using his gun. It couldn't be that bad, George only konked him once, he will be back home tomorrow right as rain.

What Albert didn't know was the resentment George Harcourt had harbored ever since that incident before the war when Phil Burton shot and killed a young lorry driver. Albert may have forgiven him for this because it had given their gang a lot of credibility among the criminal fraternity of Southampton and some of the surrounding towns and cities such as Portsmouth, Winchester and the seaside towns of Bournemouth, Brighton and Weymouth as well. But Harcourt had always resented this as it dented his reputation as the hard man of this gang. He used his cosh with deadly effect sometimes but until now had not actually killed anyone.

But tonight, with Burton at his mercy, he had dished out the punishment he always thought should have been given back at the time of the lorry drivers death. So it wasn't simply a tap he gave to Phil in the marshalling yard, but the most powerful hit his strong arms could deliver as his cosh crashed down. The pent up rage of the past two years gave that hit even more venom and the probable result was that Phil's skull had been fractured. George had a smug feeling of satisfaction. Take that you bastard, he had thought. No-one's gonna be bigger or have a badder reputation than me, not only in this gang but the whole of Southampton.

Had Albert known just how much George resented Burton he would be a worried man. A gangster he was but he still didn't like the idea of murder. And if Phil Burton did die then it would, in fact, be an act of murder. Ida was still very angry and was not yet done with him.

"We both know you and your grubby mates could get caught and if you do then the whole lot of you will end up in prison. And what will happen to me and our children then God alone only knows."

Stung by the criticism Albert reacted like the gangster he was, and turned on Ida.

"Just you wait a bloody minute. My gang ain't grubby mates like you're saying. There are two sides to most people and my lot ain't no different. There are some bloody good workers amongst them, and most have wives and kids just like we do. If I do end up in prison then I've made arrangements so that you and the kids will be looked after. I know I ain't much of a father and I suppose I ain't much of a man either but you and our kids come first in my life and everything I do is for all of you and no-one else."

With that he stormed out of the room and went in search of a bottle of beer and the bacon sandwich he could smell from the kitchen.

Ida stayed where she was but her thoughts now were so different from those of her husband. They came first? Well what about that poor little cow he had hidden away in that huge house in Highfield Lane? It must be worth a fortune and that girl was simply a sex slave. Just to get what she and her family need to survive she has to give herself to him whenever he felt the need. He wasn't much of a man but as his wife she was stuck with him.

Philip Burton did indeed have a fractured skull and at seven minutes past midnight, after his admission to the Borough Hospital in Southampton, he died. His wife just managed to get there in time and was at his bedside as he breathed his last. Bursting into tears she vowed vengeance against the person responsible for this. It meant she would have to go on and bring up their three children alone.

This wasn't strictly true though, as Albert had recently said to his own wife, if anything happened to him his family would be looked after. Now Mrs Burton would be added to the list of families who would be looked after financially by the Littlejohn Gang.

Funerals needed to be arranged, for the two gang members killed in the raid on the docks and now Phil Burton as well. A conference would be arranged where the families would be informed about their futures and what they could expect in the way of support from the gang.

Albert was unaware of another casualty claimed by tonight's raid. An ARP Warden patrolling in the Bevois Town district came across the body of a young woman who had been caught by a bomb blast. That she was dead was obvious and the warden reported the fact.

As he looked at her lying there, covered in fallen masonry and with blood staining her clothing from her many injuries, he thought she was not much younger than his eldest daughter. What a waste of a young life.

It may have been a German bomb that did in fact cause the death of Janice Saunders. But the very fact she was outside when it fell was down to the members of the Littlejohn Gang. After the ordeal of intercourse with most of the gang members, only one of whom had respected her and given her any pleasure, she knew she couldn't take any more of it. When the house was

82

empty she had gathered up whatever clothes and personal effects she had, and made her escape whereupon she met with her fate.

Chapter Six

The air-raid had been in full force as she ran through Portswood Junction and gained Bevois valley, happy because she knew she was getting close to her home. It was at this moment the bomb exploded and the house front she was passing came crumbling down. Janice gave a scream as she knew she couldn't escape from this, dying right there in the road, her pathetic belongings being scattered by the wind. It was a tragedy that could so easily have been avoided and one that Albert Littlejohn was going to remember for a very long time because he would have to accept that it was his fault.

He had first met Janice when she got herself a part time job in a little café down by the docks. Many of the men used this on their way to and from work. Albert, though a big rough looking man, had a certain charm about him and he quickly used it to get to know this very attractive, but vulnerable young girl.

He found out she had only left school a few months previously and he also knew that she did this to help support her mother and three brothers, her father having died of a drink related illnesses a year or two previously. George Harcourt and Albert spoke often to Janice. When serving Albert his tea one day he casually asked if she would like the chance to earn much more money than she was getting in the café, and also some other perks that she and her family would enjoy having.

"Where too mister," she had nervously asked, "and what sort of job is it?"

Albert told her about his house in Highfield Lane that he had then owned for only a few months, the proceeds coming from his many criminal activities, as for the job itself?

"I need a housekeeper see and I do have other needs like any other bloke. Make sure I get this Janice my love and I'll make your life a hell of a lot easier than it is now."

Janice came from the area by the gas works in Northam where many of the women had large families. Their husbands were looked upon as the breadwinner, who went out to work to earn money for the family's upkeep. But Janice also knew the men demanded their marital rights and frequently had intercourse that on so many occasions led to the births of more babies. They also beat their wives regularly to make sure their sexual demands were never turned down. So sex was something Janice knew about but until now had never practiced.

"I don't know Mr. Littlejohn. I ain't never done nofink like that see and my mum would have a fit if she knew I was even thinking about it."

"Well Janice for one thing your mum needn't ever know what you're doing. Just come up tomorrow evening, you don't work Thursdays do you? I'll show you my house and we'll get to know one another better like."

It was a very nervous Janice who got off the tram in Portswood junction the following evening and made her way into Highfield Lane. Coming to Albert's house she walked up the long front path and tapped meekly on the knocker. The big front door swung open and Albert beckoned her inside. Showing her around a house so big it took Janice's breath away he outlined what her duties would be.

"First of all Janice, my old woman don't know anything about this house so if you ever meet her you stay dumb about it.

85

I want you to do some cleaning to make the place look nice and well, we'll see about the next bit soon. What's the matter girl are you alright?"

Janice managed to nod at this though she was very far from alright. She was overwhelmed at the size of this house and the fact there didn't seem to be anyone actually living here. She was used to living in squalid conditions with a tin bath and a toilet that had to be shared with at least three other families. So this house was a mansion to her. And she was as nervous as she had ever been in her life so far at the reference to the next bit.

She didn't have long to wait though as she was taken upstairs and in the sumptuous big front bed room was introduced to the world of sex. Standing looking at the huge double bed she was taken by surprise as Albert started unzipping her thin cotton dress.

"What are you doing?" she cried jumping back, only to be caught by Albert's strong arms.

"Steady girl," he snarled. "I told you there was another part of this job and this is it. Now stand still and don't try to run."

She was in shock as her dress was stripped from her body exposing the crude knickers and grubby bra she had on underneath. They didn't last long though and quickly joined her dress on the floor. Now naked she watched in a little fright as Albert took his own clothes off.

Throwing her onto the bed his big hands covered her small but perfectly formed breasts and it was no time at all until he thrust himself inside her. That first time intercourse hurt her, but amazingly despite the continuing pain and embarrassment as Albert continued to thrush into her, she started enjoying the experience. She wasn't able to feel anything herself though. Albert had gone too quickly for that merely seeking his own gratification.

When it was over she lie naked trying to take in how she felt about what had just happened, not even trying to cover herself as she watched Albert getting dressed again. He went out of the room and still Janice didn't move. When Albert came back in he had some things with him.

"Alright Janice, let's see what these look like on you."

The next three quarters of an hour was the most exciting time of Janice's life so far as she was shown, and then allowed to try on, some very fashionable clothes. These included underwear from some of the biggest fashion houses in London and New York. Before she did this though Albert said she must have a bath.

"I don't want to hurt your feelings Janice. But you ain't quite as clean as you need to be to wear stuff like this so come on, let's get you in the bath."

Janice started to go downstairs but was stopped straight away.

"Hey, where do you think you're going? Didn't I just say you need a bath?"

"Yes," she replied nervously, "so I'm going to get the bath in from the back garden. Where shall we put it Mr. Littlejohn? Me and my three brothers always bath in the scullery at home."

Albert burst out laughing at this. "No Janice, we don't use a tin bath here. I know you do at home and so do my wife and kids where we live. But not in this house you don't, follow me."

She was led into a large bathroom and stood in complete shock as she took in the surroundings. There was a bath along one wall with a water heater and a tap at one end, a wash basin of matching white enamel, and to Janice's further amazement, a white toilet bowl with what looked like a gold chain to flush it. Never having seen anything like this in her life before, she started asking many questions.

"Why is the lavvy in here? It should be outside down the bottom of the garden and where is the copper? We can't heat up the water without one can we?" She thought about this a little bit more. "And that bath looks heavy, how do we carry it downstairs when it needs to be emptied?"

She was a touch put out as Albert once more burst into laughter. Eventually he answered her.

"One thing at a time Janice, now the lavvy is here because houses like this one all have what are called indoor facilities. That means you use this one inside instead of having to go outside in all sorts of weather to the bottom of the bloody garden."

He walked over to the bath.

"And this my dear is your copper, it's called a water heater and once I turn on the gas underneath hot water comes out of this pipe here. And when you've finished your bath all you do is pull out the plug and the water goes down this plughole. The water taps on this basin have a red sign on one and a blue one on the other. That means the one with the red on it runs hot water and the other one cold."

He then pulled out a tap that was under the water heater and turned on the gas.

"This makes a bit of a noise when it lights up, but don't worry about it because it ain't going to hurt you."

Lighting what was in fact the pilot light, and with the blue flame burning, he swung this back underneath the water heater. Although he had warned her Janice jumped back in fear as a big whooshing noise erupted in the bathroom.

"Hey I said it won't hurt you, come here you silly girl and watch what happens now."

Coming gingerly forward she looked in amazement as hot water started pouring from the spout of the heater and landing in the bath. When there was enough Albert used the cold tap to get the temperature just right for Janice to climb into.

"Alright your still naked, we don't have to wait for you to undress do we, into the bath with you."

This was an unbelievable luxury for this young Southampton girl. Compared to the life she had led it was almost as if she had tumbled through the looking glass into her own little wonderland. She had never, until now, experienced anything like this. The tin bath she normally used was coarse to sit on and the water was always too hot. It had to be because once she was finished with it her brothers took it in turn to use the same water for their own baths.

Now though she lay back and thought she must have gone to heaven and even more so when Albert started to wash her hair, and her young body. He touched parts of it that sent shivers of joy through her. It was a shame he never managed to do the same for her when they were having sex which is why it became a chore in the end.

Stepping out she used towels the quality of which was something from another planet. The softness caressed her entire body. Now she was taken back inside the bedroom and introduced to clothing the like of which she had only seen in black and white films at the little cinema in Portswood called the Palladium.

Dressed expertly by Albert, for the first time in her life she was introduced to a suspender belt, to keep up the nylon stockings she was about to be given. Janice had seen the huge corsets her mother and grandmother wore, so a delicate little garment like this was a sheer wonder. And the lace panties that went over them with the matching bra made her feel like a queen. The dress that completed her outfit was of cotton and satin and clung to the curves of her body, showing these off to perfection.

"You look great Janice," Albert told her, "and they'll be more of this to come, as well as food and money to help your family survive and they will be better off than the average now that's for sure. But one thing I want you to understand. I will have sex with you again, in fact whenever I'm in the mood. And sometimes other men come here to see me and then I might want you to entertain them as well, do you understand what I'm saying?"

Janice was in another world as she gazed at her reflection in the full length mirror on the door of the big wardrobe. She nodded her head in agreement but Albert knew she hadn't been listening. He decided to leave her to it for now. This conversation could always be had again at a future time. For now he was happy to have this young girl to himself.

Over the next few months Janice spent most of her time at this house. The war begun and she went occasionally to work at the cafe but this was merely for keeping up appearances. The pathetic wages she got here were more than made up for by the money Albert gave her every week. He did indeed have his way with her often and started bringing other men, who were gangsters like himself, to the house.

Each time this happened Janice had to dress in an extremely provocative manner and be paraded before them. Although she wasn't made to have sex with anyone else until that fateful final night of her life, it was the allure of this possibility that gave Albert an edge in his dealings with these men.

She put up with them leering over her because the rewards were great and her life was starting to be so much more enjoyable, until the day when Albert came up to her with a sense of urgency. This was the first time she had been made to do something that to her was very unpleasant.

"Janice, a particularly important colleague of mine is on his way here so I want you to be especially nice to him. He can do a lot for me and my gang so let's make him welcome. He comes from Bournemouth and he's well known down there, his name is Salty Sam.

At first stunned Janice then burst into a fit of giggles.

"Salty Sam?" she laughed "What is he, a pirate or somefink? Will he have a parrot on his shoulder? Oh dear I've never heard anything so daft."

She was taken completely aback by Albert's reaction. Grabbing her by the front of her expensive dress he shoved her up against the wall. Then, with his face close to hers, he snarled at her.

"Don't you dare make fun of this bloke you silly little tart. He heads a gang down in Bournemouth and he's got men who are hardly human. Life means nothing to them and they kill anyone who get's in their way. Me and my boys need some help from him so we have to keep him sweet."

Janice was shaken up badly by this. Albert had never referred to her as a tart before and in fact she had never thought of herself like that either. She didn't like the side of Mr. Littlejohn that she was seeing now. Anger she knew about, but nothing as raw and menacing as this.

Albert's eyes had flashed and his jaw was set. He showed in that moment that Janice was simply a plaything for him and anyone else he wanted to share her with, a truth that did nothing to help her confidence.

It was a fortnight later when Albert came up to the bedroom and introduced Salty Sam to Janice. She took an instant dislike to this man. He stood just inside the door and his eyes, that were like flints, seemed to probe right inside her. He was tall and slim and had a pointed chin and hooked nose. There was a scar running from the right side of his face down to the chin which did nothing to help his appearance.

"You're bloody young to be doing this ain't you girl?" he asked in a deceptively quiet voice. "I'm used to real women see. I'm known by my gang as Salty Sam the Knifeman."

This was so much more frightening, and something Albert Littlejohn had not told her about. Her legs turned to jelly as this man drew out a wicked looking knife from under his coat.

"Don't hurt me Mister," she cried, "I'll do whatever you want only don't hurt me please".

Sneering now he replied, "This knife ain't for hurting you missy I just want to have my fun with you."

Coming forward he slipped the tip of his knife inside the material of Janice's dress and with one swift movement slit it from top to bottom. She was petrified as the ruined dress dropped to the floor and she had to stand in her expensive and alluring underwear.

What happened next both surprised and disgusted her. She had to watch as this odious and frightening man stripped his own clothing off. Then, under the threat of that knife, was forced to indulge in sexual acts on his body. She had never done anything like this before and it was the worst moment of her life.

When it was finally over and Salty Sam went laughing out of the room she couldn't hold her anger, fuelled by shame, in any longer. So when Albert came in she flew at him. He had to hold her off as she shouted loudly.

"I ain't never going to do what that bastard made me do to him in here, never again I ain't."

"Hold on a minute," he said trying to fend her off but still she struggled against his strong arms and scratched his face. It took a punch to temporarily knock her senseless before he could regain control. Picking her up, he carried her into the bathroom and brought her round using cold water.

"Now stop trying to take this out on me. You knew what I wanted from you and you're being bloody well paid for it so stop snivelling and come and pick out some more clothes to replace the ones that animal ruined."

Following him back inside the bedroom as he picked up the ripped dress she watched as he opened up the wardrobe.

"Pick what you want from here Janice. There are plenty of really nice things in here including underwear. It's all just as good as the dress you've just lost. And get over this because I can promise you no-one as bad as that salty bastard is ever going to come near you again."

Only slightly mollified she waited until Albert had left the room and gone back downstairs before she did indeed select some very nice clothing. Looking at herself in the latest Paris fashion lingerie she soon forgot all about the Bournemouth gangster and started to realize just how beautiful she was. An idea formed in her mind of how she could use this beauty to make her life and that of her mother and brothers so much better, but for now she would wait and simply bide her time.

Back downstairs Albert found Salty Sam making inroads into his whisky supply but made no comment. He needed this man and didn't want to antagonise him. Instead he poured himself a generous tot and sat next to the knifeman.

"Ok you've had your fun a so now let's get down to business. I know you and your mob down there by the seaside are doing alright because you know where to get things me and my boys can't. So how much are you willing to do for us?"

Salty Sam sneered at him.

"We'll see. I'm not sure your lot are up to it. But you've made a good start by introducing me to that girl. I'll contact you when I'm in Southampton next month."

With that he had got up and abruptly left. Janice had unwillingly played a very important role in the start of what was to be a very volatile relationship between the Littlejohn's and the gang from down the coast.

Four weeks on with Albert focused on this new idea and determination to utilise the blackout to its full, he had set up another meeting. He was incensed though at Janice's disappearance. He had not seen her for a couple of days and had no idea where she had gone.

Nothing much had been taken but she had known about this meeting and how important it was to him. Although her first experience with Salty Sam had not been a pleasant one she had now had sex with nearly every other member of the gang so surely she would be willing to accommodate him more willingly this time. But where was she? He would have to bring out some of his best drinks instead.

Salty Sam was disappointed not to find Janice in the house but was tucking into Albert's supply of whisky and after several glasses started to talk business. The sneer that was never far away now made its full entry.

"My boys are so much more adaptable than your lot. We get most of what we want from our friendly local shop keepers see, and if they don't want to help us we show them why that upsets us. We've got rid of quite a few blokes who have tried to stand up to us."

"Yeah we know. You've killed a lot of people and got yourself a good reputation. But my men aren't like that. We use force when it's needed but we've only killed one bloke so far. And I don't want that to alter. Hey, where the hell are you going?" Albert shouted as Salty Sam slammed down his glass, got up and made for the door.

"I ain't doing business with a load of soft mushes. My boys do what they need and we get results. And I ain't bloody scared to use this."

He had pulled the wicked bladed knife from his pocket for Albert to see but his anger was rising and he wasn't intimidated. The memories of what Sam had done with Janice were still fresh and despite being angry that she had let him down he was concerned about her and hoped she was alright.

"Those clothes you ruined with that thing last time were worth a fortune. And you frightened the life out of the young girl. Don't mistake what I said about killing. One of my boys has already done that and the rest will do what's needed, when it's needed as well. I've got a man with me who'll match you and that bloody knife of yours anytime I ask him too. We're from this town and we run things here."

"But you can't get all you want can you and that's why you're asking for my help, so what are you gonna offer me in return?"

"Me and my men work legitimate jobs in the docks here, so we know what's coming in to this country through its greatest port. Forget London and Liverpool mate. Southampton is where most of it happens and we are right there keeping tabs on it. We know where stuff that's not even in the shops is kept, and how and when to make our move to grab some of it for ourselves. Help us get things that ain't easy and we'll cut your lot in on what we can get here, it's as simple as that so sit down again and tell me what you think of that."

Salty Sam not only regained his seat but before saying anything reached for the bottle of Bells Whisky and poured himself another generous tot. Taking a large pull at this he sneered again at Albert.

"Make sure if anything ever goes wrong and we need to fight, your boys have got the guts to step in and help. And I mean anything goes in any situation. Because make no mistake my friend, if you come in with me then we'll want you down in our town from time to time when we are taking on big jobs."

Then a smile replaced the sneer, "Ok and I want you and your number two, George Harcourt's reputation with his cosh is well known to us, to come and meet a man both of us will need. Come down to the Horse and Groom pub in East Street tomorrow night. Just the two of you, and I'll introduce you to the man who can get anything from anywhere, but at a price. Without a bloke like him you'll always be small fry so if you've got any ambition to improve on what your gang can do then he's your man."

"Sounds good to me," Albert replied. "What's this bloke's name? I may have heard of him if he's in Southampton."

"You'll find that out tomorrow, and why you don't yet know anything about him, so see you both down there."

Watching him walk down the long front path Albert heard the door of the room open again. Making sure Salty Sam had indeed left he looked round and found George Harcourt pouring himself a generous tot of whisky and he didn't look up but sounded really serious.

"Thinks a lot of himself don't he? Our boys may have to teach his lot a smart lesson and soon."

"Yeah you're right George," Albert agreed, "but don't underestimate him or his mob. Bournemouth is known as a great place for old people to retire and live a quiet life. I know the beaches are mined now and have barbed wire all over the place. That's to stop the germans coming ashore and invading us. But beneath the quiet orderly side of things down there that salty swine and his boys are cleaning up. They terrorise the local shop keepers and the pubs and demand protection money. They've

95

got girls working the streets as well as gambling and drinking rackets. They use the darkness of the blackout to rob business places and private homes and I tell you George there's a lot of bloody money down there."

"Yeah and we should be doing the same here. It's just as bloody dark in Southampton at nights now with no street lights on or nothing. And we've got areas like Bassett that's rolling in money and stuff we can sell on. I know our boys are up for this so we can broaden our activities Al."

"Yeah we will but first we'll go and meet this mystery man that Salty has told us about. The Horse and Groom eh, I haven't been in there for bloody ages, funny that cause it's so close to the docks ain't it?"

George didn't answer at first so Albert prompted him.

"Did you hear what I said George?"

It was an awkward moment for the cosh man because the pub they were talking about was a meeting place for men of his persuasion. Well known in Southampton pub circles it was famous for the stuffed grisly bears that stood just inside the door of the lounge bar.

The pub had a reputation for drunkenness, fights and robberies. But also a place where men like George could meet other men for his own reasons. George had done this on quite a few occasions now. From this pub and the one at the back of the old walls, The Juniper Berry. He had kept this secret even from Albert because he valued his reputation as a hard man.

Now he looked at his boss.

"I've been there quite a lot Al, it's a great pub and one that I like going to. So I'm looking forward to going again tomorrow night."

The next night just after yet another raid on Southampton with even more damage being done to the nearly obliterated High Street, Albert and George found their way through the darkness, going through the main arch of the Bargate and entering East Street.

96

On the right hand side of this well known street about half way down they came to the Horse and Groom. With the raid over the pub was once more getting back to as normal a nights trading as was possible in these hard times. The public bar was packed and Albert noticed how George looked nervously across at it.

They had gone into the lounge bar with the two stuffed bears overlooking proceedings. Albert wondered why George looked so apprehensive. He was actually making sure none of the men he had picked up here before were in the pub this evening. The last thing he wanted was for an obviously queer man to recognise him and try to talk to him. It didn't happen but just as he was heaving a sigh of relief a voice came from behind them.

"You got here then, so what are you drinking and before you ask I can tell you they ain't got no whisky."

The speaker was Salty Sam and after buying them both a pint of beer he indicated towards a table. "Come over and meet the man I've brought you here to see."

They went with Salty right over to the far corner of the bar where a man was sitting on his own. There wasn't much light here so it took them a little while to make him out. Albert or George were not prepared for what they were about to see.

At this table was a thin man dressed in black with a clerical collar and these two certainly didn't need to be told what he did for a living. He was obviously a vicar and they simply looked at each other and then at Salty Sam.

"Let me introduce Father Jonathon Wilkinson. But we all know him by his real name. Gentlemen meet Leroy Wort."

He looked up at them both and there was nothing clerical in the glint of his eyes or the set of his mouth. The silence around the table lengthened and became chilling. Even Albert started to feel fear. This was so strange to him and he didn't know how to handle it. The only thing he did know was that his stomach had gone into a knot and his mouth was suddenly dry.

The silence was evil too and slightly eerie because it only seemed to be in this corner. In the rest of this pub, both here in the lounge and over in the public bar there was noise and bustle.

Leroy finally broke the silence in a thin, reedy voice. "Albert Littlejohn and his right hand man George the Cosh Harcourt. I finally get to meet you both. I have kept tabs on you and your gang and I don't believe there is anything you and your boys get up that I don't know about."

"But I don't get this," said Goerge. "You're a bloody vicar so what do you know about us or anyone else for that matter?"

"Not a vicar Harcourt, I am in fact a Catholic Priest, or at least I was before they unwisely defrocked me. I practiced in my Bournemouth parish and that is how I came to know Salty here. I have always had an eye for the good things in life and I soon found this clerical collar gave me access to places that the ordinary man couldn't go. I learned about the criminal fraternity on the south coast and they knew I could help them.

Many a load of stolen goods were stored in my parish church where the police didn't even think of looking. It was excellent cover and would have still been in place today but for the unfortunate occurrence for which I was thrown out. A rather attractive altar boy stumbled on some jewelry that was hidden in the crypt and then had the nerve to make demands of me for his silence.

The little bastard had realized my liking for boys. I had taken the vow of celibacy of course but not having any sex at all is not easy. He wanted me to have sex with him and I had no choice but to give in and do it. Well I had noticed him above the other altar boys anyway. But then I was caught with him and had no excuse to offer as we were both naked at the time. So I now operate outside the church and have taken on new duties, about which the two of you are going to learn. Sit down and let's get down to business shall we?"

Gingerly they both did as this man said and took their place opposite him at the table.

"Now then boys Salty here and I know what you both do for a living and how well placed you are here in Southampton to see what is coming into the country. You know which trains carry the stuff around and can give this information to us. In fact you can effectively go back to how you were operating before the war, with the same result."

Salty then chipped in. "My boys as well as a lot more around the south coast can make raids on the trains and get a lot of what we need to make a profit from this war. But you and your lot will have to do a lot more than you are now to make your contribution. I mean house breaking, stealing cars whenever you get the chance and robbing blokes in the street under the cover of the black-out. This one thing alone is giving all of us a great chance to line our pockets."

"Salty is correct in what he says," said Leroy, "and if you do your part I will make sure you and your gang get what you need. Things like ration book coupons for petrol and clothes are fetching anything you like to ask. But first of all I want your word of honour that you won't at any time attempt to hold out on us. If you acquire goods that will make a lot of money and try to hold onto them, then you will find that Salty and his boys, who will be well backed up, will visit Southampton again and this time their visit will not be so friendly."

"We'll agree to that alright," Albert reassured him and made to stand up. He wanted to get as a far away from Leroy Wort as he could. The man radiated evil and was creepy as anything. It was nearly impossible to believe he had been a Catholic Priest.

"Sit down," he hissed, "I haven't finished yet."

Slowly Albert did as he was told and watched as Leroy produced a bible. Surely he wasn't going to deliver a sermon now? But it was only the outside cover, taken from a real bible, which bore any resemblance to that holy book. Inside Leroy kept records of all the gangs who worked through him and what their contributions to the big haul were. He made both Albert and George sign this.

99

"Now my sons you are members of my congregation or my flock as most of my boys say. You have given your word to work with us and we expect you to honour it at all times."

Once more agreeing to what was being asked of them both George and Albert made their escape.

"Keep a close watch on these two, Salty." Leroy said "I don't have a good feeling about them. They may well cause us trouble before this war is over."

"You can count on me. I will watch everything they do and one step out of line then me and my boys will act."

Outside and on their way home Albert was voicing his feelings.

"I don't like that bastard one bloody bit George but at the moment we have to go along with what he wants. He can help us get stuff that would be out of our reach otherwise. But we will keep some of the stuff we knock off for ourselves. What did he say to you just as we were leaving?"

"He wants me to come down to his place in Bournemouth with a list of all our men who work with us, both in the docks and the gang. He says he wants records of whatever we knock off as well."

"I don't like that George. So when you go down there I'll come with you."

He was surprised by the answer.

"No Al I'll go by myself cause I think I may be able to set up the chance for us to get to know a lot more about bloody Leroy Wort. I've never told you this before but my marriage is just a sham. I've been attracted to boys ever since I can remember."

"I know," said Albert. "I saw you at the Highfield House with Billy Marshall."

"Bloody hell I didn't know that," George was caught off guard and for once didn't know how to react. "Why the fuck didn't you say something?"

"Because you're a friend of long standing and I know I can always rely on you in any situation. Your sexual preferences are

100

your own affair. It will never interfere with our friendship, but I should watch young Marshall. He didn't look too pleased at what you were doing to him and he may try to get back at you some time in the future. Now what were you saying about Leroy Wort?"

Chapter Seven

Having picked their careful way up East Street and now walking towards the Bargate, Albert was determined to make George elaborate on this point. Until now he had not responded to this question but seemed deep in thought.

"Now come on, what were you telling me about Leroy Wort? What may you be able to do for us where he's concerned?"

George laughed. "One thing that's very true Al is that a bloke who only likes his own sex can tell just by looking if another bloke is the same way. Well I can anyway. That's how a lot of men like me get together. I don't suppose you even noticed how Wort was looking at me but I returned the look. So he knows I'm open to whatever he wants from me in that direction."

"I certainly didn't notice anything like that George. So I don't know what to say. Just what will Wort expect from you?"

"When you was signing his bloody Bible Al his right hand was on the table holding the book open wasn't it?"

"Yeah now you mention it that's right," Littlejohn replied.

"Well his left hand was occupied as well, underneath the table. I know that because it was on my leg. And it went up bloody high I can tell you. He wants sex from me Al and I'll give it to him. If I can get myself into his confidence by doing that I will be able to wheedle information out of him."

"That's fine George but be careful for Christ sake. He's a mean and soulless type of bloke and I don't trust the bleeder an inch. Reaching into his pocket George pulled out his trusty cosh and cradled it in his hands.

"Loads of men in this town know how well I can use this Al. But only a very few know how good I am at my other love. I'll get Wort so worked up he won't even realize what he's saying to me."

"Not at the time no," Albert warned him. "But he's sharp George and once he's alone again when you've gone, that's when he's going to know he's told you things that you shouldn't know anything about."

"It's ok Al, even if he does he won't be able to do much about it. I'll bet you anything you like that only a few blokes like Salty bloody Sam know about that side of his life. And he won't want any more of them finding out."

Albert was still not convinced.

"Once he realizes that you know too much about his life he's still likely to send one of his gunmen to finish you off so I say again George, be bloody careful."

Just then they were interrupted by a shout.

"Hey you there, where do you think you're bloody going?"

Looking up they saw what was becoming a familiar sight of another ARP Warden bearing down on them.

"Where have you two come from? Can't you see the destruction in the High Street and the fires? Where the blazes are you going?"

"Alright mate, keep your bloody hair on. We're just trying to get home ain't we?" George growled at him.

"Well go round through the parks then, there's too much damage here and we've got casualties. And get out of the way of the Civil Defense and ambulance people as well."

103

As they both went down into Palmerstone Park, in order to cut through to Bevois Valley Road, George was still seething with anger. He wasn't used to anyone speaking to him as the Warden had just done and he wrapped his hand around the cosh in his pocket.

"Bloody loud mouth, I should have belted the sod with this."

"And if anyone had seen that we would both be running from the police now wouldn't we?" Albert chided him. "Calm down George and let's get home. We've got work tomorrow and our two friends that were killed in the air-raid last week get buried in the afternoon. So we'll all be there for that."

This had the desired effect and brought George right back to the present and thinking about the men Albert was talking about. Billy Foreman and Joe Kinslade had been good gang members as well as really efficient stevedores and their loss was still being felt by everyone. Their families were of course the ones finding it hardest to come to terms with their loss as both men had children who now had to grow up without their dad.

Albert knew they had a lot to do.

"We've got to unload the remnants of that convoy that got bashed something chronic out in the Atlantic. So many ships have been sunk and a lot of good men are dead because of it. But we should get at least four in and we'll work them until all the cargo is off and in what's left of the warehouses. Those bloody German bombers are causing more and more damage in the Docks every time. Anyway we all need to be at St. Mary's Church by four-o-clock for the funerals."

"Yeah of course," George agreed, "where are they being buried after the church service?"

"Bills wife wants him put in South Stoneham cemetery but I've heard Winnie Kinslade don't want her husband buried there. She's managed to see he goes into Southampton old cemetery on the Common. It's nearer where she and the kids live see, so they'll all be able to visit the grave whenever they want. Afterwards my wife is putting on the wake at our house.

104

It's there we'll speak to Winnie and to Bills wife as well so they'll know they won't lack for money at least."

Ida Littlejohn had been busy organizing the wake for the funeral the next day. Maggie and the girls were helping her with this. The two younger boys were getting in everyone's way and also helping to clean out the bowl after their mum had finished mixing the ingredients for sponge cakes. Both were already experts at this and their fingers were extremly busy wiping the bowls clean of any leftover mixture.

Ida drummed into her girls that they must not reveal where things like butter came from. This was in such short supply, even more so when a German bomb fell on a holding warehouse full of butter that burnt for nine days afterwards.

"Your dad gets us things like butter and also paste and jam to go into sandwiches. But our neighbours, who will attend the funerals tomorrow and come back here afterwards, are to be told I use flour, margarine and golden syrup along with baking powder for the cakes. No-one must know I used butter and eggs in these. And they will ask. Women are curious about things like that and when they taste the cakes they'll know they are better than they should be. I just want them to think I'm a better cook."

Just then the door rattled as Albert pulled the key from inside the letter box with the string it was tied to. Coming into the back kitchen he took Ida in his strong arms as he always did whenever they had not been together during a raid.

"That was a bad one tonight and I think the docks have been hit badly again. I know the bloody High Street has nearly been knocked flat, how much longer can Southampton hold out?"

"They're calling this the blitz," his wife told him. "And I think they've got that right. But for now we're all getting ready for the funerals tomorrow. Will you all be there?"

"Yes of course we will. The docks are closing down so all of us can go and pay our respects to Bill and Joe. Then when we come back here for the wake I want to talk to both of their wives."

"I'm glad to hear that Albert but watch out, especially for Winnie Kinslade. She's devastated at losing her Joe and she'll want to know how much help you and your boys are going to give her to raise her family?"

"That's what I'll be telling her as well as Mrs. Foreman. They'll both be looked after proper like, their husbands was good in our gang and always did what we wanted. So their wives and kids won't have to go without now their dads are dead."

"Yes I know that but I went to school with Winnie Kinslade. Her name was then Winnie Trumble. Even in school she only wanted what she thought was rightfully hers and she ain't changed since she's grown up. She won't just settle for what she'll see as a handout. She'll only take what she thinks she's earned, so I say again watch out for her."

Albert took this in but was inclined to shrug it off. After all Winnie Kinslade was only a woman so what harm could she do to a gang like his? Before the next day was out he would get an answer to this question.

Early the next morning Albert was at work and all his boys were alongside him. There were battered ships that needed to be unloaded and a great deal of clearing up because of last night's raid. Southampton was being hit hard by the German Luftwaffe and the docks were a prime target. More of the dockside warehouses had been hit and as Albert, George and the rest helped to clear away the debris all of them were remembering that just a short time ago two of their number had met their deaths in just this situation.

But as all British people during this difficult time did, they worked their way through the mess and by lunchtime had made space for cargo that was even now being unloaded to be stored. The foreman then came up to them.

"Alright you've all done well today so get off now and go the funerals. Bill Foreman and Joe Kinslade were good workers so we'll miss both of them."

106

It was a very formal procession from Bevois Valley to St Mary's Church in Newtown. Sitting in the close packed church Albert was moved as the Reverend David Potterwaite led the service, paying a glowing tribute to both men whose bodies were laid out in coffins one behind the other, facing the altar.

"They were good men whose unstinting work rate was helping this country overcome the bad deeds of our enemies. Unselfishly they worked to unload vital cargoes for the benefit of their fellow countrymen in these dark days. May their souls go on in glory and be received by our gracious Lord in Heaven."

Moved he may have been but Albert was also thinking about how much Bill and Joe had done to help them too, by stealing whatever was needed.

Outside the church, with the coffins going onto two separate hearses, Albert put his plans into operation. It had been agreed that George and at least three of the gang members would go with Joe Kinslade's body to Southampton Old Cemetery on the Common where he was to be buried. Albert meanwhile took the rest of his gang to South Stoneham cemetery to say their final farewells to Bill Foreman.

It had started raining which added an even more somber feeling to the scene. It was then a relief when they all met up again at Albert's family home in Empress Road. The food set out on the big dining room table, borrowed from the Portswood Hotel, looked wonderful and Ida had been having trouble keeping her two young sons Edwin and Charlie from making a start on the cakes.

"No you can't start eating yet," she had chided them. "Not until everyone arrives."

This they soon did and the two groups arrived with just ten minutes between them. The women immediately scrutinized the food, as Ida had predicted. For the most part they were complimentary.

"It all looks lovely Mrs. Littlejohn," they all agreed, except old Mrs. Worksop who had lived in this district of Southampton for more years than she cared to let on. She was a chronic busybody and always wanted to poke her nose into everyone else's affairs. Looking at the sandwiches and the cakes she declared in a loud voice.

"It's alright for some ain't it? We can't get the stuff to make cakes and things like this."

Ida of course had anticipated this and saw at once the interest sharpening in most of the other ladies who were present. They too were wondering this very same thing.

"There's nothing on that table that you, or anyone else, won't be able to make Mrs. Worksop. I've had to make do and use whatever I can get for ingredients. There are no eggs in the cake and I use dripping instead of lard for the mixing. I even use parsnips in the mixture instead of sugar and here you can see how they turned out.

"Well I suppose that's true. But what about this jam and paste in the sandwiches, made that yourself too did you?"

"No, this came from the stocks I put by each week so that I can give my family a treat at Christmas. Now I will have to try and make up the difference again. Now everyone, please help yourself to the food, and tea will be coming round shortly."

Maggie and her sisters were all in the kitchen making this and with them was their youngest brother Thomas. He was in his drawer sleeping peacefully having just been fed by his mother. All four Littlejohn girls heard what their mother had just said about the food and were giggling quietly to themselves. Maggie, who was just as amused as her sisters, thought it best if no one noticed this.

"Quiet you lot, mum don't want any of them women getting a sniff of what's really in them cakes or where she gets stuff from. Let's make the tea in the big pot and take it in to them."

Edwin and Charlie were now in their element, each of them was sitting under the big table with as much food as they had been able to grab. All was going well, the ladies had reverted from suspicion of Ida to delight at the spread she had put on.

108

Each of them was holding full plates, and this was unheard of anywhere else with this war raging out of control.

Albert and his boys were certainly not drinking tea. They were in the back parlour with small glasses filled to the brim with best malt whisky.

"Here's to our fallen comrades," Albert toasted them and raised his glass. "They was good blokes and they bloody well didn't deserve to die like they did."

"Hear hear," everyone shouted in unison. "Here's to Bill and Joe."

More whisky flowed and the air was becoming blue. The spirits they were drinking made their own spirits rise. One of them was telling a joke about two men in the docks who come across a businessman who had been to a meeting and was now on his way back to his car. Unfortunately he found himself needing to use the toilet. But having no luck in finding one was relieved when these two men came into view.

"Excuse me Gentlemen but can you direct me to the urinal?"

Having no idea what he was talking about one of them scratched his head before replying. "I dunno mate, how many funnels has it got?"

The laughter that greeted this could be heard in the front room and brought Ida into the parlour to see what was going on.

"You're making this sound more like a drunken party than a funeral wake," she hissed at them. "Have some respect for the men that were buried today."

Albert answered in a way she was certainly not expecting. "We are showing respect dear, all of us are. We worked with and knew Bill and Joe, and a lot of times we went out for a drink together. When this war started all of us agreed we could be killed at any time. We work in the docks love, and the bloody Germans are trying to destroy it. We all know the risks we take every day and we've agreed that if it does happen then the rest of us who survive will make sure we have one last piss up with the poor blokes who don't."

109

Ida was only slightly mollified by this. "Well Mrs. Foreman and Winnie Kinslade are waiting to talk to you so I think it's high time you had them both in here for that. Most of the other ladies are leaving."

The rest of the gang got up and went in search of their wives who were indeed just making their way home. Only Albert and George remained in the back parlour, they were quickly joined by the two women they needed to speak to and once Ida had given them tea Winnie Kinslade opened the meeting.

"Alright Albert Littlejohn and you, George Harcourt, me and Beryl Foreman here have lost our men so what the hell are you and your gang going to do for us now? We ain't got nothink, our kids need looking after and the bloody rents got to be paid."

"Hold on a minute Mrs. Kinslade," said Albert. "You're talking as though it's our fault poor Bill and Joe got killed. But we didn't have nothing to do with it did we? It was the Germans what killed them. So calm down a minute and I'll tell you what we're gonna do."

She glared at him but was now prepared to listen to what he had to say.

"Now then, your husband's both worked with us, not only in the docks but with what we do outside. All of my boys pay in each week. By that I mean they gets their share of what we've got, money, food and sometimes clothing for all of their families, but the rest goes into a collection that we sell on and make our money that way. We have a fund for emergences like this so that if anyone gets killed their wives and kids will get their share.

We'll soon have stuff that's not even in the shops and you won't need coupons to buy it from us. We may even be able to get extra coupons as well. Now I have their money for this week in these envelopes and each week both of you will get paid out in this way."

110

Taking the envelopes both ladies opened them and Beryl Foreman gave a shout. "Blimey there's more than twenty quid here, my Joe never earned that much in the docks did he?"

"No of course he didn't Mrs. Foreman. But he knew how much he had in the fund and that he could claim anytime he needed it. Ginger Strangemore is our banker and he looks after all our finances. Now as I say, both of you ladies will get envelopes each week. The money inside will vary because like anyone else we have good weeks and bad. But I can tell you it's never gonna be less than ten quid.

Anything else you and your kids need, you simply get in touch with Ginger. I'll give you an address to do this. But one thing I must stress and that is the need for silence. Don't, for instance, start going out buying stuff that other people can't afford, and don't send your kids to school in brand new clothes. Because it won't be just the neighbours who will notice and comment on that but the bloody coppers will soon get to know about it too. Then the trail will lead them straight to us."

Both ladies nodded their heads in agreement. They knew that amounts of money like this would normally take the average working man at least three weeks to earn, so it wasn't exactly coming through legal means.

"Don't you worry about that Mr. Littlejohn," said Beryl Foreman. "Neither me or my kids will let on. We're all gonna miss Bill such a lot but at least we won't starve and, well, thanks."

With this she got up and, smiling at them all, went out the room. She was met by Ida who gave her a big hug, then left the house and made her way home.

Winnie Kinslade, however, had not moved and she now glared across at Albert.

"It's all very well you saying we're being looked after mister, but it all sounds like bloody charity to me. I ain't used to that see. Whatever me and my old man had we sodding well worked for. He did what he could for us. So I ain't going to be pushed

111

aside, if I take this money and any more that I get it'll have to be worked for.

"My wife has told me you would say that Mrs. Kinslade but I can't see how you are going to, as you say, earn it. You can't work in the docks and my gang is strictly men only. So please just take what your given and don't make trouble."

"Trouble is it?" she shouted back at him. "Well Mr. high and bloody mighty what about young boys? Have you got any of them in your gang?"

"Boys, no of course we ain't," said Albert. "What use are boys?"

Winnie now surprised him by smiling. "You and your lot were nearly caught in that marshalling yard weren't you, that was before you took all the stuff you had with you into that room at the Portswood Hotel."

Albert was startled and jumped up at this, and so did George.

"How the bleeding hell do you know about that?" they both demanded and Winnie now burst into laughter.

"Boys," she shouted, "the ones you say are no use at all. Well tell that to my three and see where it gets you. My Alan, he's the oldest, along with Barry and Michael always play under that big road bridge over the railway line. They knows that place like the back of their hands and so many times come home soaking wet cause they like to jump in the river. I wouldn't mind if the silly sods took their clothes off before they do that, but boys are boys ain't they?

They also play in that marshalling yard, even though it's now patrolled by the Home Guard. They think it's the best fun when they make a noise and that old man with the rifle comes running out of that hut to find out what's going on. They hide and watch him poking about and it's all they can do to stop laughing out loud.

Well the other night they was there as usual when they saw your lot arriving under the bridge and then the boat coming up from the Plaza. They laughed themselves silly when one of your

112

blokes fell in the water. They saw all what went on in that railway yard when you made such a bleeding row. How the lot of you weren't caught we'll never know. Once the Home Guard blokes was back in their hut my boys followed you and saw you go into that secret room They was so excited about that because all the kids round here have heard of that room but none of them knows where it is.

Well my boys do now. The air-raid began after that and Alan got himself and his two brothers back under the road bridge to shelter from the bombs. I don't have to worry about them being out in a raid cause Alan always makes sure they gets undercover somewhere. Now gentlemen did any of you see my boys or have any inkling they was there watching you?

My kids, and a lot more like them from roads round here, can act as lookouts and help with carrying things for you. They can all swim and know this river well. They can do it with their clothes on or off and swim underwater for long periods of time. They can all be a bloody good help to your gang."

"Good God Al," George exclaimed. "This sounds as though we'll have our own version of the Baker Street irregulars who Sherlock bloody Holmes used. It ain't on is it, we can't work with kids."

Albert was deep in thought and didn't answer straight away. What she said was starting to make sense.

"Hold on a minute George, Mrs. Kinslade is right. None of us saw her boys and remember we was on the lookout for anyone who might clock what we was doing. Sherlock Holmes always did alright with his gang of street urchins didn't he?

Alright Mrs. Kinslade I'm impressed, so I would like to meet all three of your boys as soon as this can be arranged."

"We can do that tomorrow. They are supposed to be at school but I can send a note to say they've got the measles."

"There's no need for that," Albert told her. "We'll be at work all day so a meeting will have to be arranged in the evening. But where can we have that, it will need some thinking about."

113

"No it won't, we can use the Anderson shelter in my back yard. No-one can see over the back fence so if you come through my house you'll be able to go down to the shelter without any prying eyes watching you. And call me Winnie. Mrs. Kinslade is far too posh."

They all laughed when the door burst open and another woman came barging in. Glaring round the room she fixed her eyes on Albert before blurting out.

"I'm Jean Burton and me and my eldest son Johnnie have just come from the South Hants Hospital. My old man Philip is in the morgue because he got a great big hit on his head and died because of it. Now I wants some answers, how did it happen, how did my old man get killed like that?"

Albert looked beyond this very angry woman and saw Ida standing behind her in the doorway of the room.

"I couldn't stop her. She came barging through the door as soon as our Maggie opened it."

"Alright Ida leave this to me please," then turning to Mrs. Burton, "calm down for a minute and I'll tell you what happened to your husband, and what we as a gang are going to do to help your family now."

"Calm down he says, my bloody hubby was killed by a member of your precious gang weren't he?"

She shifted her gaze to George Harcourt. "And we don't have to look far to know who done it do we?"

Albert stood his ground as he saw George about to react. He would never allow anyone to bad mouth him. Even women were not usually safe from his temper in these situations. Albert, of course, knew this only too well so he made sure he stood between him and Mrs. Burton.

"Keep back George," he hissed, "leave this to me."

The air in that room became electric as Albert and Mrs Burton faced each other. She quickly waded in, shouting at him.

"Oh yes a fine funeral today weren't it with two of your gang getting a good send off. But my old man's body ain't even cold

114

yet so what are you gonna do for him eh, tell me that you bastard."

Albert was losing his patience and shouted back at her.

"He was going to cock up the whole operation we was working on. If George here hadn't stopped him he would have killed a Home Guard soldier and that would have brought the coppers swarming all over us. They suspect us as it is and we need to keep one step ahead of them. But your hubby was about to blow that wide open. George had no choice but to bop him on the head with his cosh. It was only meant to knock him out so none of us knows why he died. He was a good man in many ways but in a situation like that he was too quick to use his bloody hand gun."

"Hand gun. What the hell are you talking about? Phil never had one of those things."

"I'm afraid he did," Albert said now feeling some sympathy for her. "He used it just before the war. A young lorry driver fought back when Phil and three others were trying to steal a lorry that was loaded with fags. The youngster was much stronger than any of our boys thought and he was getting the better of them. Phil stopped it by bringing out the gun you say he didn't have, and he shot and killed the young driver. It's only this war that's got in the way of the police investigation into that young man's death."

Jean Burton's mouth gaped open in shock. She stuttered as she tried to speak. "No, my Philip wasn't much of a man and even less as a father, but killing, no, he wouldn't do that.

George now interrupted, producing the gun he had taken from Phil Burton as he coshed him.

"Albert has just told you I had no choice but to stop your husband from shooting the Home Guard soldier. I admit it was me who coshed him and this is the gun I took from him as he fell. I regret he is dead and I certainly didn't mean that to happen. But I too know about the lorry driver he killed just before the war started."

115

Turning faster than George expected Jean Burton now shifted her fury onto him.

"You dammed murderer, the doctors at the hospital told me Phil had a very hard scalp and for him to suffer a fracture he must have been hit a mighty blow. And we all know how good you are with that wicked cosh. You meant it you filthy swine you killed my husband on purpose."

She tried to rush George in order to rake her nails down the side of his face. Her eyes were bulging and her mouth was twisted in hate. Surprisingly it was Winnie Kinslade who prevented this from happening. Stepping in between George and Jean, she turned the startled woman and gave her a hard slap on both sides of her face.

Jean reeled back in shock and stared at Winnie in complete confusion. Winnie now spoke kindly.

"We're all sorry to hear about your loss Mrs. Burton, but he will be given just as good a send off as my husband and Bill Foreman got today. Now I don't know anything about a Home Guard soldier being threatened with a gun, but I know Albert Littlejohn runs his gang properly and he don't like killing so whatever happened to your old man, it must have been an accident. Now why don't you listen to what Mr. Littlejohn is going to tell you about how you and your kids won't have to go without."

It was quite a speech but it did have the desired effect. Jean Burton stared at Albert.

"Alright I'm listening, so what have you got to say?"

For the second time that day he outlined how the gang would look after families of those who die, whether in gang operations or by other means for which they have no control. Jean Burrton listened and began to realise that her children would be alright. She knew her husband had been a crook who also went with other women, even paying for sex with some of them. In many ways she would now be better off.

These thoughts were suddenly and dramatically interrupted as a voice came from the doorway.

"What about my dad's gun. He's dead now so that's mine and I want it."

All eyes went to the door and fixed on the teenage boy who was standing there. He was Jean Burton's eldest son Johnnie and as she looked at him she was shocked at the determined look he was giving Albert and George.

Jean screamed and made to slap her son to get him from the room but he was too quick for her. Dodging out of her way he came right into the room and repeated his demand for his dad's gun.

Albert wasn't going to have a youngster speaking to him like this in his house, nor was he going to give a gun to a teenager, no matter if his claim was genuine. So, quickly for a man of his size, Albert grabbed Johnnie's right arm and twisted it up his back. As he screamed in pain his mother rushed to help him only to be stopped as George Harcourt barred her way.

With the cries of her boy ringing in her ear she shouted. "Get out of my way you cretin, I must help my son."

"Have some patience," said George. "Albert ain't hurting him. He's just teaching the little sod a lesson. There's no way we'll give a boy his age a bloody gun."

With a gulp Mrs. Burton stopped her mad dash as Georges words sank in, so she watched what Albert was saying to the boy.

"I'm going to let you go son, but if you start anymore trouble I'll make sure you regret it. Do you understand?"

Almost sobbing now Johnnie Burton had no choice, "yes I understand mister let me go please."

Releasing the boy Albert now revealed the gentler side of his nature as young Johnnie stood massaging his arm.

"We know your dads gun is rightfully yours son, but you've got some growing up to do before you can even think about having something that's designed to kill. You will be given it

117

when you're old enough but right now I have another job in mind for you."

"What job mister, I don't understand."

It was Winnie Kinslade who now stepped in and placed an arm around Johnnies shoulder.

"I think I know what Mr. Littlejohn has in mind Johnnie and it also concerns the other lads in this area. You know my son Alan don't you?"

"Yeah we both went to Portswood School, we was in the same class there."

"Well I want you to come and attend a meeting at my house in a couple of day's time. Your mother can come as well because we need her permission for what we want you to do. Is that agreeable to you Mrs. Burton?"

Still feeling shocked at the way things had happened so quickly Jean Burton willingly agreed.

"Yes Mrs. Kinslade I will bring my son to this meeting as and when you give us a time and date."

Everyone in the room was relieved now things seemed to have worked out satisfactorily. That is, until the door opened again and Ida Littlejohn came in. She was holding a copy of the Southampton evening newspaper the Daily Echo. Walking up to her husband and showing him the paper's front page she said, "I think you should see this."

Chapter Eight

Albert stared at the newspaper and his blood ran cold. A glaring headline shouted. 'Who is the Girl, Where Does She Come From?' It was accompanied by a photo of the face of Janice Saunders. Her body was still covered by the masonry that had fallen on her and caused her death, but her face was undamaged and showed that she seemed to be at peace. Snatching the paper from his wife Albert read the story.

"Who is this girl whose body has been found under rubble in the Bevois Town area of the town? Detective Inspector Robbins of Portswood CID is anxious for information. The girl was wearing clothes and make-up not available in this country in these present circumstances. In her purse was a great amount of money. Is she a spy for Germany? Anyone with information is asked to contact Portswood police station."

Albert swore but Ida was watching his reaction closely. "I thought you would know who this girl is, this is important isn't it?"

"Yes," he snapped then paused. "But how do you know Ida?"

"The clothes the girl has got for a start. I know who she is and the fact she worked in a grotty cafe near the docks."

Ida had of course got this information from Janice when she visited the Highfield Road house just before the war started.

"So how is it she now has things she couldn't possibly have afforded and money in her purse as well? All I needed was to see your reaction to this story to tell me all these things came from you."

Winnie Kinslade seeing this was something that could only be resolved between Albert and his wife quickly spoke to the others.

"Well everyone, let's leave this to Mr. and Mrs. Littlejohn and make our way home."

As they went out of the front door Mrs. Kinslade could be heard reminding Mrs. Burton about the meeting in a few days time.

"I've got your address so when it's all arranged I'll send my Alan round to let you know."

They all went their separate ways. Even George saw this was something between Albert and his wife so made his way out of the house and walked up to the Portswood Hotel.

Albert was quiet for the next few minutes. He was trying to work out how he could emerge from this with any sort of credit. Ida knew about the things he and his gang could provide and the clothes on the dead girl were certainly examples of this. Slowly he looked up at his wife.

"Yes everything on that girl and what's in her purse comes from me. She was helping keep my headquarters up together, you know looking after it and keeping it clean like."

"That would be the big house in Highfield Lane then, wouldn't it?"

Albert's face clouded over. "How the hell do you know about that? I've kept it strictly to me and my gang, how bloody long have you known?"

"Since before the war, I followed you one night when you were supposed to be working late in the docks. Then, a few days later, when I knew you wouldn't be there I went back and this

120

time went inside. That's when I met this young lady," she said, tapping Janice's picture on the Echo's page.

"What I saw that day was a young and inexperienced girl putting herself up for sex with you, and goodness knows how many others, in return for money, food and clothing for herself and her family. I was really angry at first but soon saw how frightened and vulnerable she was. And now she's dead Albert so why did this happen? Why was she out in an air-raid? And just what were your long term plans for her? Tell me that my fine husband."

"Alright you know about Janice and the house, but don't judge me too quickly Ida. I admit I had some fun with her. Well I'm a bloke ain't I and we all like a bit of fun now and then. But I treated her right, even when I had to ask her to look after some of the blokes I do business with. And you don't need to look at me like that because I swear I did watch out for that girl and I did make sure she got enough of what she needed."

"Oh I see," his wife replied with sarcasm in her voice. "First off this attitude that you're a bloke so you can have a little fun is stupid, you would be quick to complain if I wanted to go and have some 'fun' wouldn't you? And if you looked after her well, why did this happen?"

Ida thrust the newspaper right up in front of Albert's face.

"All bloody right," he shouted, pushing the paper away. Me and the boys had to move our stuff out of that house and get it into a fresh hide-out that Bernard and Catherine Bumstock are letting us use. It's a secret room at the back of their cellar at the Portswood Hotel. Well, it was a big operation and I had to make sure Janice never saw what was going on. So my boys took it in turns to be with her."

Albert was big and strong. Few men ever challenged him in any way. Those foolish enough to try usually ended up with severe injuries. This was why he led his gang and his men, even George, also knew better than to do anything to annoy him. He was used to his word never being challenged in any way at all, which was why the next few seconds sent him spinning into a world that was simply alien.

Ida, who was considerably smaller than him, had drawn back her arm and with a force even she didn't know she possessed, slapped Albert round the right side of his face. The force of the blow made him stagger back and his temper exploded.

Regaining his posture he grabbed Ida and pushed her up against the wall and drew back his fist to hit her. She saw the rage in his eyes and shut her own, waiting for the blow to land. When nothing happened she opened them again and saw something she never thought she would.

Albert Littlejohn, her big strong husband and leader of the Littlejohn gang, still had a firm grip on the front of her dress. But he had put his arm down and there were tears streaming down his face. Letting her go he sobbed.

"Bloody hell mush I nearly hit you then and for a moment I wanted to kill you. But I can't. I love you and always have. I know I ain't much of a husband to you and the kids, and I did have sex with this girl. But it means nothing do it? You're the only woman for me and you must know that, wherever I go I will always come back here to you."

Ida was partially mollified, because of his admittance to what he and his gang had subjected Janice to.

"I know that Albert I always have. That's why this marriage has lasted as long as it has. I've turned a blind eye to what you do outside because I know, as you've just said, that you always come back here to me. But what you did to this poor girl has resulted in this. She's dead now and she bloody well didn't deserve it."

"I know that and I can't tell you how sorry I am. My boys should have seen she was alright and one of them should have stayed with her to make sure. There was obviously a cock up there and I'll find out why I can tell you."

Nodding her head and straightening her dress she abruptly changed the subject.

122

"And the house Albert, what about that? Why am I and the kids living in a small house like this with a tin bath and outside lavvy, when you've got that huge bloody place in a posh road in Portswood."

"Its cover Ida that's all. They are sure it's me who is behind much of the crime that goes on in this town. So I've had to throw them off the scent. If I moved all of you to a house like that the rozers would know straight away that's its phoney. After all, where would a stevedore get the money for a house like that? No I had to get cover and that house came on the market so I bought the bloody thing. And a fair old price I paid for it too.

It was fine before the war but now we have to use someplace else. Because of all the shortages and rationing if we're spotted dealing in stuff like food the bloody law and Home Guard will open fire on us if we put up a fight. And if we don't, well let's put it this way, none of us will be around for a while."

"So what precautions are you taking to see you aren't caught?" Ida demanded. "We need you here with us you know."

Albert told her about the coming meeting with the young boys from around the area.

"We'll soon have a whole lot of very eager eyes watching out for the first signs of trouble. If any do come we'll work out a way for them to get a warning to us in time. The boys will be trained to watch for any sign of coppers or ARP wardens coming here. They'll get a warning to us so we'll be ready for the raid and our Maggie can make you up to look ill like we said before. And we'll know when it's going to happen because we've got a spy in the council and he'll tip us off."

"The council, but that's impossible how on earth did you manage that?"

"Friends love, that's how. The councilor who represents Portswood ward is always informed when a raid like this is going to take place. Then, for a considerable hand out, this man gets the information to us.

His name is Teddy Wainright and I met him when he was a snotty nosed little bastard at Portswood School. Always snooping he was and trying to find out what me and the others were up to, until George threatened him with the boys toilet torture. He really whined then but I saw we could use him and his snooping ways. He got information about some of the other boys that none of us could have got. I suppose that's how he got elected into the council. So between him and our army of local boys this house will be so secure no-one will ever find anything wrong with it."

There was a disturbance outside in the street and Ida knew she had matters to attend to.

"Here is Maggie with the children, I'd better get ready to feed little Thomas. I can hear him crying from here. Maggie and the girls will have their hands full trying to wash Edwin and Charlie in the sink. Well its quiet enough now so maybe we can put them all in their own beds tonight without those bloody German planes coming over."

Reaching the door Ida turned back. "I'll always support you, whatever you do Albert. We are much better off for supplies than most other families. But if you ever even think of dumping us and going off with one of your fancy women I'll come after your bollocks with my carving knife."

Albert walked up to the Portswood Hotel with this dire warning still ringing in his head. She bloody well would too he thought to himself and smiled. Entering the public bar he joined four members of his gang at their usual table. Among these was George Harcourt. When he saw Albert arrive he immediately signaled to Bernard Bumstock behind the bar for another pint of Bitter.

Bringing this to the table he placed it in front of Albert.

"Here get this down you. It looks to me like you need it. You lot are a bit jumpy tonight so what's going on?"

Taking a long pull at the beer Albert then looked up.

"I ain't sure yet Bernard, but if it looks like trouble I'll let you and your missus know."

"Trouble what sort of trouble? Me and Catherine don't mind helping out with that room downstairs but if it makes trouble for us we could lose our license."

"What none of us need right now is any sort of panic," Albert tried to reassure him. "You and Catherine will be told about it in time for us to move our stuff out of that room. Now get back behind the bloody bar and let me talk to my men about this."

Muttering to himself, Bernard did as he was told but looked over more than once to see if he could make out what was discussed at that table in the corner.

Albert was used to this and made sure they all crowded around him to block out any chance that Bernard, or anyone else, would hear.

He whispered to them. "I'm sure George has filled you in on what's happened so I've brought the Echo for you to see. My girl Maggie bought tonight's in Bancroft's newsagents when she was out with my kids."

Then laying the paper on the table he continued,

"This girl was in my house in Highfield lane. I told all of you to keep her occupied while we moved our stuff out. So how the bloody hell did she end up getting killed when that house just up the road from here was hit and the front of it came down on top of her. Someone should have stayed at the house to keep an eye on her. I knew she might be upset with so many blokes having sex with her in one night, so she should have been kept sweet with rewards. Instead we got this."

Other drinkers now glanced over towards their table as Albert had slammed the paper down and raised his voice as he finished.

George was quick to meet the stares.

"Something wrong boys or do you simply want to mix it with any of us, because if you do all of us will oblige you."

This had the desired effect. Albert Littlejohn's men were well known and not only for their gang activities. All of them liked a fight and they were very good at it. Many men had made this mistake and ended up in hospital afterwards. So the eyes that had swung their way now reverted back and George simply nodded to Albert who wanted an answer to his question.

"Well, I'm still waiting."

Lenny Warren answered first. "Sorry boss but it couldn't be helped. I know someone should have stayed with that silly tart. But everything had to be put in that shed and it couldn't just be thrown in could it? And we needed a lot of men to get down to the river with you to meet the boat, and don't forget more of our boys were on the other side of the river unloading. They were the ones who brought it over in the boat. We just didn't have enough men to spare."

There was a menacing silence, when Albert Littlejohn was as quiet as this he was at his most dangerous. All of them could see the narrowing of their boss's eyes. His whole face had darkened and his fists were clenched. The silence lasted only for a few minutes but the tension it caused seemed to go on forever. Finally Albert spoke again.

"Ok that makes sense I suppose but it's not good at all. That bloody girl as you like to call her has been found dead in the street and the paper has her picture on the front page. That's because they and the police want to know who she is. And, more importantly, where she got the expensive clothes she was wearing and the money in her purse. This could lead straight to us and if it does we'll need to know what we're gonna do about it."

"Who is this girl and where did she get the clothes she was wearing? She'd need plenty of money and a whole load of clothing coupons to buy them wouldn't she?"

The speaker was Detective Inspector Maurice Stapleton of Portswood CID and he was now in charge of this investigation.

"I mean she's just lying there under all that rubble and she's wearing stuff that Paris models would sell their grandmother's for. So I say again who is she and where did she come from?"

Sergeant Podcove, who had worked with DI Stapleton for the past three years, now gave his report.

"We've put out an all points bulletin about this sir and we're already getting calls. Some of them are very interesting."

"Well please don't keep us in suspense Sergeant, what are these interesting calls."

"Most of them that have come in so far sir are the usual rubbish. One man said she's a film star, he knows because he's a film star too and they've been in at least two together."

"And what was his name?"

"He said it was Peter Woolworths Sir."

Laughter erupted all around the incident room and even the DI joined in.

"Well its original I suppose. But have we had anything useful?"

"Yes sir we have," the sergeant went on. "We've had a call from John Petman who's an ARP warden and he says they've been contacted by a Mrs. Saunders from Lyon Street. She's claiming this girl is her daughter."

"Does she indeed and she lives in Lyon Street you say, what number?"

"94 and I've told the ARP warden to tell her to expect a visit from us."

"Good man, that's just right so you'll come with me to see this lady. The rest of you I want out on the streets. I want information on two gangs that we know operate on both sides of this town. One is the Swaythling firm that's led by Eddie Wheeler. And the other mob is the Littlejohn Gang and they have the whole of the Portswood and Northam sides of Southampton.

Talk to your snouts because one or even both of these gangs must be tied up with this girl. Think about it, if she is local where did she get the clothes and make-up from? There's a war on gentlemen and make-up isn't in the shops any more. And from the reports so far we've been told she was also wearing silk underwear and good quality nylon stockings.

Now I know girls can't get them anymore and I've even seen my eldest girl Stephanie drawing a thin black line down the back of her legs to look like the seams of stockings."

More laughter greeted this. Several of the assembled detectives also had daughters who wanted nylon stockings. But as they weren't available they were doing the same as the DI's daughter.

"Alright get out there and get me some answers."

A few minutes later DI Stapleton and Sergeant Podcove were in a car speeding towards Lyon Street. Their conversation was interrupted by the wail of a siren warning of another raid coming in.

The young constable behind the wheel asked, "What do you want to do Sir? I can find a street shelter for all of us to get into?"

"No get on to Lyon Street then drop the sergeant and me. Once you've done that get into a shelter yourself."

"Very good sir," he answered but made sure he put his foot down to get this journey over as quickly as he could. Screeching to a halt outside number 94 Lyon Street the Sergeant and Di jumped from the car which then sped off. Constable Whitlock made a dash for his home in Belgrave Road, he was just in time to get inside the shelter that was outside his house when the first bombs started falling.

In Lyon Street Sergeant Podcove's loud knocking was at last answered and with bombs falling out of the skies and the drone of enemy aircraft filling the air the two men fell through the door nearly knocking Mrs. Saunders over.

"Bloody hell ain't it bad enough them Germans is trying to kill us without people like you barging in and knocking people over."

128

"Yes sorry about that Mrs. Saunders, that's you isn't it?"

"Yeah that's me and you must be the police. I was told you were coming but your timing is lousy."

"I tend to agree," the DI replied, "but we must work fast if we are to find out who the girl was who was crushed to death in Bevois town last night. I believe you said she was your daughter?"

Mrs. Saunders was a thin woman with equally thin greying hair. It was not easy to place her age as women in these times lived such a hard life and the lady of this house looked as though she certainly had. On hearing her daughter mentioned however the tough exterior vanished and tears welled up in her eyes.

More bombs were landing outside and the whole house shook because of it but Mrs. Saunders hardly seemed to notice.

DI Stapleton saw what was happening and spoke quietly to her.

"I know how upsetting this must be, but is there anywhere a bit safer than this where we can go to talk about it?

Shaking herself she replied, "Yeah we can go under the stairs. It's too bloody late to get down to the Anderson shelter. The bastards in them planes machine gun anyone they see outside. Even kids ain't safe."

So a few minutes later the two men and Mrs. Saunders were cramped together under the narrow stairs of this two up and two down house.

"My other two kids, a boy and a girl, is next door with Mr. and Mrs. Rockford and their three. They'll all be alright there."

So, gently now, the DI brought the conversation back around to the mystery girl.

"She's your daughter so can we start with her name please."

The elderly lady sniffed back more tears.

"Yeah her name was Janice, Janice Saunders and she was my eldest."

"I see and believe me Mrs. Saunders you do have our sympathies on your loss. But I'm afraid there is a bigger

129

mystery where Janice is concerned and we have to find out about that."

"All I knows Inspector is that my daughter is dead so she won't be coming home no more."

As gently as he could DI Stapleton went on, "I know how hard this must be for you and as I say we do sympathize. But you see your daughter was wearing expensive clothes and she had money and other items in her bag that are simply not available in this country since the war began. And even if they were, the items and the clothes would have cost a great deal of money. So did Janice have the sort of job that paid well?"

"Do me a favour will you? She was nothing short of a skivvy in a bleeding grotty café down by the docks. Paid well? Not bloody likely. The only thing that place was good for was the food she managed to get and bring here so me and my other kids didn't go hungry."

The Di's interest sharpened on this, he was speaking deceptively quietly to coax more information from her.

"That's good isn't it, it must have been a big help to you. What sort of food are we talking about?"

"Well butter for a start the little bit the bloody government lets us have is stupid. My Janice brought half a pound of it every week. And she brought tinned stuff as well, ham and luncheon meat, stuff like that."

"I see and do you have any of this in the house at the moment?"

"Yeah some in our larder and a lot more down in the shed," then suddenly suspecting this may not be legal, "it's alright ain't it mister, my Janice was a good girl, she wouldn't do nothing wrong."

"Strictly speaking Mrs. Saunders I'm afraid what you are describing is against the law. Food is so short that the rationing procedure is the only fair means we have to ensure it goes around to all of our citizens. So I will have to see what you have in the larder and also in the shed."

Entering the small and very crammed kitchen at the back of the house they were shown inside the larder. Its doors needed repair and didn't close properly so straight away the two policemen could see the assortment of tinned food that was on every shelf.

Tins of meat, peas, beans, tomatoes and even jam were there in very good quantity.

"This is a godsend to me cause I know I can feed my kids, they ain't got no dad see so money is so bloody tight," Mrs Saunders said.

"What about clothes?"

"Some, I've got a lovely dress she brought for me. When I'll ever go anywhere posh enough to wear it is something else, but you're welcome to see it if you like."

They were taking a considerable chance moving around the house with the noise of the still falling bombs rattling the beds and shaking the walls. One direct hit would have accounted for all three of them but the policemen were determined to seek answers.

Upstairs Mrs. Saunders opened the wardrobe in her bedroom. The dress she produced made both police officers blink. Both married men they knew a good quality dress when they saw one and both privately knew their wives wouldn't ever be able to afford to buy one like this. Sergeant Podcove brought out his notebook and wrote down the name of the designer.

"And your other children, did Janice bring clothes for them?"

"No she couldn't get any that would fit them so they use the handed down clothes other kids grow out of. It's ok because everyone's doing that so no kids stand out see."

Just then the all clear siren sounded.

"Good now we can go down and look inside your shed," said DI Stapleton.

Inside this ramshackle was an Alladin's cave of goods most of which were not available anywhere in this country. Besides

131

more food there were cigarettes, tobacco and even a few bottles of spirits.

"Likes me drop of gin I do, and our Janice got me that." Mrs. Saunders observed as she saw the policemen looking at these.

Outside in the road they waited for their car to return and pick them up.

"What are we going to do about all that stuff in the shed Sir? It's all contraband isn't it?" asked Sergeant Podcove.

His boss sighed.

"Of course it is and we should have taken it away. But did you see the young Saunders children as they came back from sheltering? The nipper was wearing short pants that looked as though they were held together by nothing less than a prayer and the girl wasn't much better off. No, we'll leave it because they're going to find it very hard now that Janice isn't here to help them anymore. But we will follow up on that dress and the bottles of gin. I want to know where those things came from."

"So where to now sir, here's our car now."

"It's about time, I know there's just been a raid but we need transport fast."

The car stopped and the DI noticed at once a large dent in the side of it.

"What happened Constable Whitlock? How the hell did you pick up that bloody dent?"

"Sorry sir, but when people are trying to get into shelters and the bombs are falling they don't always look where they're going. An old lady was rushing to get into one of the shelters in Belgrave Road and she didn't even see me. Stepped right out in front of the car, I had to swerve to miss her and I hit one of the lampposts."

Sighing the DI had no choice but to accept this.

"Alright Whitlock it can't be helped I suppose, but the garage won't be happy when they see it. Right, let's get moving I want to get to dock gate number 4."

"Right away sir," the young constable drove off quickly. Arriving at the dock gate he went on through and parked the police car just inside. Getting out the two detectives showed their warrant cards to the gate security and were waved straight through.

As he passed an elderly guard the DI inquired, "I believe there's a café, my sergeant and I have business there?"

"Yes that's right Inspector," the old man answered, "just up the road a bit, you can't miss it. The Tall Funnel it's called."

Thanking the man they walked up the road and almost immediately saw the café. It was set back a bit from the road and at first sight was not the place you would pick to entertain your friends or family for dinner. It looked just like a pull in café that lorry drivers used, where they could get a filling but extremely greasy fry-up.

Walking inside they were greeted by the smell of frying bacon and sausages. They were surprised at this because of the shortages, bacon especially being almost impossible to get in any sort of quantity. But they went to the counter and ordered a cup of tea each. A lot of dock workers were inside and they looked suspiciously at the two policemen. Most of them, not just Albert's gang members, pilfered as much as they could from the cargoes of ships so the police were not a welcome sight.

The young girl who served them was typical, wearing what had the appearance of make-up, but was in fact water coloured paint. Her hair was down to her shoulders and her thin dress almost transparent in the heat and steam of this place. But she looked at home here amongst so many men.

Showing their warrant cards they asked for the owner of the café.

"Oh that's Mrs. Tightwad," the girl giggled. "But don't tell her I said that. It's just our name for her because that's what she is."

The DI smiled at her.

"That may well be so but could you give me her correct name now please."

"Yeah it's Mrs. Toogood, shall I go and get her for you?"

"Yes please, what's your name by the way?"

"Gladys Crump sir."

"Very well Gladys, I may need to speak to you again before we leave."

Mrs.Toogood was nothing like the young Gladys Crump, or either of the two girls who were acting as waitresses, serving the dockers and putting up with their bawdy remarks and occasionally being pinched on their bottoms. The woman who owned the café was middle aged with jet black hair pinned back in a bun. She had a rounded figure and her legs were large. Her face was pinched and she glared at the two policemen standing at the counter.

"What do want here?" she demanded. "This is one of our busy times as you can see so please state your business and let us get on with ours."

"Our business madam is an enquiry about a young girl who we know worked for you here in this café. Her name was Janice Saunders, so what can you tell us about her?"

"Janice Saunders? I don't recall the name but wait and I'll check. Howard," she called. "Come out here for a moment will you."

From the kitchen area a rather stout man appeared. He was wearing a striped apron and was not pleased to be interrupted.

"What the do you want Mrs. Toogood? I've got loads of eggs frying back here and blokes waiting for their sandwiches."

Clearly not liking being spoken to like this by one of her employees she let it pass for now.

"These two are police and they want to know about a girl called Janice Saunders who they say worked here. Do you remember anyone like that?"

"Let me think now," the cook replied. "Oh yeah I've got it she did work here for a while helping out like. She was a willing

134

girl but not fast enough to be a proper waitress. She just helped with the orders when we was really busy."

"I see and what happened to her, did she leave or was she perhaps offered another job?" the DI asked.

"How the bleeding hell do I know she just stopped coming, all of a sudden like, and now I comes to think of it she never did collect a week's wages that she had coming. But that's what so many of these girls are like ain't it, here one minute and gone the next."

Patiently the DI asked, "But this girl must have met someone because when her body was found after one of the recent air-rids she had things with her that would have cost a lot of money. Now think, did she speak to any one man in particular while she worked in this café?"

"Good gawd mate I work in the kitchen don't I? What goes on out here ain't nothing to do with me. Ask one of the girls, they may know something about her."

Then, not bothering to be told, he turned around and vanished back into his kitchen to tend to his frying eggs.

So, turning once more to Mrs. Toogood, the DI told her, "I will need to speak to your waitresses please, this is important."

"And so is my business," she retorted, "you can see how busy we are, so if you want to speak to my girls you'll have to come back when were closed."

"No I mean now, as I have just said this is important and I will talk to your girls, either here or at Portswood police station."

Mrs. Toogood started to make a fuss but DI Stapleton knew exactly how to cut her short.

"You sell a lot of bacon sandwiches here. So where do you get your supplies from? You know of course about restrictions on foodstuffs like this don't you?"

"It's all above board," she insisted. "We get dockers in here and they're entitled to what we can get for them. Bombed every night while they're trying to work, we make sure we've got

135

something here to fill them up and, well, cheer them up as well. The sausages they get are mostly made up without much meat but my customers don't seem to notice that."

"And the bacon?" the DI would not be sidetracked from this.

"It ain't on ration is it so we get what we needs see. I told you it's all above board."

"Good, then you won't mind if we bring in the ministry of food to check that out will you?"

"No you don't have to do that," Mrs. Toogood replied hurriedly. She shouted across the crowded room. "Beryl come here for a moment, these policemen want a word with you."

Chapter Nine

The waitress who had just been called was busy serving some particularly bawdy customers whilst making sure she kept her dignity. The remarks she received from these dock workers were embarrassing to say the least, but after working here for the past year or so she was getting used to them. Groping hands she didn't like but was now quite experienced at fending them off.

Mrs. Toogood, in her impatience, hadn't exactly been subtle so now, after being called over to speak to the police officers, the cries went up straight away.

"Whoa Beryl had your hands in the till have you love?" was perhaps the least insulting one. But the waitress took no notice at all and simply made her way over to the counter.

Here the DI shouted above the noise.

"I am Detective Inspector Stapleton and this is Sergeant Podcove. We're here making enquiries about a girl who worked here recently, her name was Janice Saunders. Do you remember her?"

"I sure do, it was her picture in the paper wasn't it? She was killed in an air-raid the poor cow."

"Yes that's her, so what can you tell me about her please? But let's start with your name first."

"Beryl Martin."

"Thank you Beryl. Now how long have you worked here?"

"Just over a year now so I know most of these cretins that come in."

This was what DI Stapleton had been hoping and he was confident he could get some useful information from her.

"Yes I can believe that, so when did Janice start here?"

"About seven months ago but she was temporary like, she helped us out when we was busy like this."

"So she didn't really need the money she earned for that?"

"Eh?" Beryl blinked in astonishment. "What do you mean? Of course she needed the bloody money. No-one would work in a dump like this for nothing and they certainly wouldn't do it for pleasure. That poor cow had nothing. Even her clothes were shabby and, well, awful."

"I see, and then I believe she simply didn't turn up one day. Was there any reason for that beyond the conditions of this café?"

"Well me and Angela over there both thought about it when we was walking home, just after Janice vanished, and we both agreed that one of the men who comes in here a lot had got friendly with her. But we don't know any more than that."

"Good, we'll speak to Angela as well but right now my Sergeant is going to show you a photograph of a man and I want you to take a close look at it."

Producing the photo Sergeant Podcove held it up so Beryl could get a good look. She needed no time at all.

"Yes that's the bloke I'm telling you about, the one who got friendly with Janice."

Now back in the car with the photo in front of them the DI was satisfied with their findings. "Well that's pretty conclusive isn't it? Both of those waitresses recognized the man in this photograph."

"Yes, and it's just the person we thought it would be, Albert bloody Littlejohn."

The DI gave a decisive nod. "Now all we need to do is get evidence that he was the man who lured her away from that café and set her up, with some kind of connection to that gang of his."

"I agree with that sir but it isn't going to be easy is it? Both those waitresses said Littlejohn spoke to her a lot but most of the dockers who come into that café must have done the same thing."

"Yes but we've got to look harder at Littlejohn himself now. That girl had things she never would have even seen, not in any shop window around here. So it must have a connection with gang crime in this town. We must pull out all the stops Sergeant, beginning with regular raids on his house in Empress Road. Put that into operation as soon as we get back to the station please."

In the bar of the Portswood Hotel Albert had most of his gang around him and was outlining the situation to them.

"The police will have traced Janice by now and probably found out she worked in the Tall Funnel café. If they ain't been down there yet they soon will be. Now the girls who work there will know I took a shine to her but that's all. I'm sure there's no connection to the gang that those coppers can find out about. But if my name comes up they'll step up their watch on everything I do including raids on my family's house in Empress Road. So we need to be on our toes too."

"We all realize that boss," said Harry Small, "but if we don't know when the coppers are going to turn up at your house, how can we make sure they don't find nothing?"

"That's a good question Harry. We will have advance warning of any raid that's planned. That's not only by the law but those interfering ARP Wardens and the bleeding Home Guard. I've got a spy right inside the Council who will always know when anything is going to happen. He's the councilor for the Portswood Ward which takes in the cop shop at Portswood Junction as well as the ARP headquarters in Arnold Road opposite Ameys Laundry. Now he'll be in contact with me and will get these warnings out to us."

"Who is he then Boss?" asked Billy Marshall.

"An old school friend of mine Billy, his name is Teddy Wainright. I've already told Ida about him. We knew him as a kid when we were all at Portswod school. George wanted to teach him a lesson in the boy's toilets. But I saw a way we could use him. He was so good at snooping and found out stuff about other boys that we used to our advantage."

"Like what boss?"

"Well one of the prefects was a right bastard. If we were late he always knew and anything we did in the playground that was against the rules got reported. George was in a right rage, but even he knew you couldn't do anything to a prefect.

That's where Teddy came in. There was another boy in the year ahead of us and bloody good looking he was. Well Teddy saw something that none of us noticed and that was the looks that went between this pretty boy and the prefect. So he kept watch, and finally came to me with the story of what those two were getting up to behind the playground shed.

We was all there the next time they disappeared and watched as they got very close to one another. We jumped out and caught them with their trousers down and boy did they have red faces. Well that was the end of that prefects hold on us, we had him right where we wanted him. That's what Councilor Teddy will be doing for us now and it's going to be so important."

"But how much will he want for this help boss?"

"He'll get a cut of the proceeds like all the rest of us Billy, but believe me he'll earn it. Now has anyone any objection to this?"

"No boss," they said in unison and Albert nodded back.

After Bernard had brought another round of drinks to the table he continued making plans.

"I walked home the other night during the black out and blimey I hadn't even realized how dark it is without any street lighting. So we are going to take full advantage. Boys I want you all out, not only raiding the food warehouses but let's do a spot of house breaking as well. Get inside and find stuff we can use, ration books for a start, we can cut the coupons out and sell them on. Shops can be broke into, use you loaf and get organised. I know some of you have friends who are good at stuff like that and, providing you can trust them, bring them to me and I'll look them over. This way we can get an even bigger network going."

There was a big roar of approval before Lenny Warren voiced what all the others had been wondering.

"That's great boss, but George will want to know all about this won't he? Where is he tonight? He don't usually miss a gang meeting."

"George already knows what I'm going to say tonight, me and him have talked it over already see. But right now he's down in Bournemouth talking to a very useful contact."

Leroy Wort one of the most dangerous men in England was indeed enjoying the company of George (the cosh) Harcourt, drinking the very best Scottish Malt whisky in his luxury flat. The balcony looked out over Bournemouth beach and gave an excellent view of the swimmers and any shipping that regularly passed by.

A powerful telescope was fitted in the window and Wort used to keep an eye on the girls who used this beach for swimming and sunbathing on most days of the week during the glorious summer months. At least that's what this dangerous criminal wanted everyone who knew him to think. The truth was, however, it wasn't the girls he watched, but the young men instead in their bathers.

This was before the dark days of war. The beach now was covered with barbed wire and land mines. The pier had its middle section taken out to prevent it being used to assist an invasion of German troops. People were still about when the sun

141

shone though, and even though the beach was out of bounds Bournemouth was still a mecca for visitors, if they could get the transport to get here that was.

Leroy also used this telescope to keep watch on the many criminals who still plied their trade in the beach area. Pick pockets were busy, as were the many spivs who sold black market goods to visitors.

He was the king of crime and those who knew him were very aware of that fact. Anyone who tried to cheat him usually met very messy and painful ends. His method was to use torture to teach others not to mess with him. Men had been tied up and painfully cut with the knives he was also expert at using. He maintained this torture until his victims screamed for him to stop or to kill them to end the suffering he was inflicting.

Everyone had been shocked by the execution of a little known pick-pocket called Jerry (fingers) Malone. In the overall scheme it had to be said he was small time, and made his living solely by delving into the pockets of the many visitors to Bournemouth every year. At this he was very good indeed and the nick name of fingers was well earned.

It was said that no-one ever knew his hands were anywhere near their pockets because he had such a delicate touch. It wasn't until they wanted to make payment that people found their wallets and other personal items were no longer in their possession. Fingers, as he was more popularly called by his cohorts in crime, would have gone on happily with this trade but for just one fatal slipup.

He tried to pick the pocket of a man who was leaning on the sea wall and looking out over the water. An easy target Fingers thought and he easily removed the wallet that was carelessly in full sight in the hip pocket of the man's trousers. Just as he was turning away another hand landed on his shoulder.

"Now then Jerry that's not your wallet you've got there is it? It belongs to my colleague."

142

Spinning around Fingers looked with horror at the warrant card this man was showing him.

"Yes that's right, DS Morgan of Bournemouth CID. And allow me to introduce your victim who is the legal owner of that wallet you've just nicked."

It was his worst nightmare as the man who leaning on the wall produced a warrant card, DI Winstanley also of Bournemouth CID.

"I'm afraid you've been set up Jerry," the senior officer told him. "We've been after the pick-pocket whose made life very awkward for many of our visitors for too bloody long. We knew it must be one of a few dippers we've got here. But most of the ones we know about are already inside so that didn't leave very many for us to check out."

Being arrested was something Fingers certainly didn't want, the thought of being sent to prison held nothing but terror for him. So he made a deal with the police that he would give them information about the many criminals who operated on this part of the South Coast. And he made the huge mistake of including Leroy Wort in this.

The result being that a bent copper got word to Wort who made good his escape before the police raided his house in Hove. It took no time at all for him to figure out who grassed him up and Fingers was snatched from his grotty bedsit and brought before the king of crime.

The result was shocking, Fingers was beaten to within an inch of his life before being dragged out and taken to a point at the top of the cliffs. Here the funicular operated and Fingers was just awake enough to see it and realize what his fate was going to be.

This cliff railway was famous for the way it brought twelve people at a time either up or down the steep cliff face. It ran on rails and was operated by an engine in the top room. One operator worked here and another at the bottom to see that all was running smoothly. Cliff railways operated in other seaside towns as well and many happy holidaying families rode them, children especially were always excited to be in one and their shouts of joy as they went up or down could often be heard from a long way away.

Leroy Wort knew the West Cliff Funicular operator Wilf Townsend very well indeed, and paid him to help whenever he needed dodgy merchandise taken up or down the cliffs. This was always done at night but Wilf had the keys and he knew everything there was to know about the engine.

Plans were afoot at this time for the removal of the funicular cars to prevent their use by invading troops, since they would make the task of getting weapons and men to the top of the cliff that much easier. This did indeed take place in 1940 but at this time it was still functioning. This was all Leroy Wort needed to know.

Wilf was nervous when being asked to operate the railway on this dark night in May because he knew what it was going to be used for. He pleaded with Wort, not wanting anything to do with something this hideous.

"They'll blame me won't they? I'm the bloody operator."

"I pay you a lot of money to do what I want you to do on this railway. So get on with it and do what you're bloody well told. The law will know it's been used and why because we're gonna run it over this blabbing little creep."

Wilf was about to erupt in horror because he wasn't anywhere near as hard and ruthless as the men who were surrounding him now. He was terrified of it being found that he was responsible for setting the operating engine working and making the car do its horrible work.

"Don't wet your bloody knickers," Leroy snarled. "My men will kick the engine room door in once we've done this and we'll leave plenty of evidence that it was criminals who done it."

Fingers was begging for his life as he was lowered to a point ten feet below the funicular car. He was tied by Leroy's boys

144

who were all great climbers so the height of this cliff held no terrors. Now all standing at the top of the cliff Leroy nodded to Wilf who started the motor.

Fingers screams as the car descended towards him were terrible to behold, as was the awful crunching noise as his body was crushed beneath the car. Blood and bone were scattered on both sides of the track and now only the low humming sound of the two cars could be heard.

News of this murder filled the local newspapers for many weeks afterwards and the police did everything they could to pin the blame on the people they knew had been responsible. But Leroy and his men had wrecked the engine room after the murder and left nothing that could bring this crime home to them.

Now nearly a year on, sitting in his lounge with George Harcourt, he happily related the story of this murder.

"Squashed the little bastard real good and proper we did," he smirked then stared hard at George. "That's how we deal with anyone down here who steps out of line so make sure your Southampton lot know that."

George took a slow sip from his glass. "My boss Albert Littlejohn knows a thing or two about how to run a gang and how to keep enemies at bay. We've got two gangs in Southampton, our lot and Swaythling, under Eddie Wheeler. We don't get any trouble from them because they know our boys and what they can do."

"Yes I know about that and you should know who we have down here. You've met Salty Sam the Bournemouth knife man haven't you?"

"He came up to see us and a right hard case he is. But he and I recognized what each other has got. I think there is a mutual respect."

"So he told me. He already knew how good you are with that cosh of yours and you seemed to know about his expertise with the knife. But he's only one of us. We have them all, any crime

145

can be done with any one of them. But what we want now is to see what your lot and mine can do for one another until this war is over."

Back in Southampton the next day George was sitting with Albert in the Portswood Hotel. They had just finished another grueling day in the docks and unloaded three ships that had suffered badly at the hands of Nazi U boats and were barely still afloat. Once tied up unloading had to be done in double quick time as there was a real possibility they could sink at moorings.

It didn't help that a daylight raid then occurred and had, in fact, blown one of the ships in two. Seven dock workers were killed in that raid and morale was low as a result. Albert was on his third pint of beer and wanted some good news to raise his spirits.

"Leroy Wort and me had a good talk afterwards, you know," George told him. "He's like putty in my hands now we've got together once. He told me more about that murder we heard about, you know when that bloke was squashed underneath the cliff railway. Proud of it he was, blimey I'm bad but even I wouldn't be as inhuman as that. But he told me how our two gangs can help each other.

His lot have got contacts on the continent and even though the Nazis have occupied most countries, gangs just like us are still operating. They use the blackout like we do, but in their case it's to get small boats out crossing the channel. Bloody dangerous it is and all because of the mines that have been laid and the U-Boats patrolling all the time. But like Leroy said these French and Dutch blokes, as well as some from Belgium and Norway, ain't got nothing to lose. If they're caught they get shot like so many of their countrymen have been already. But if they make it the rewards are great. They get paid well and have the satisfaction of knowing they've put one over on the Germans.

Now they bring in stuff like spirits, fags, and clothes that they steal from fashion houses over there, ones that the occupying

Germans ain't got their hands on that is. So Salty Sam and his lot meet them at various small inlets along the coast, the stuff gets unloaded and the foreign blokes are paid.

They're willing to swap some of this stuff with us if we agree to let them in here to raid the food warehouses. They know we have all the answers where this is concerned because we unload the stuff and watch where it goes when it leaves the docks. So a straight swap is what they want and I think we should give it to them."

This was the longest speech Albert had ever heard George make and he looked hard at his second in command whilst taking a long pull at his beer,

"I like the idea of swapping stuff with them that they can't get down there and we can't get up here. But I'm dammed if I like the idea of Salty Sam coming here and working with us on the warehouses. He's too unpredictable with that knife of his and it could mean big trouble."

"Yeah I know," George agreed, "but don't forget our boys can look after themselves as well and we'll always outnumber Salty Sam's lot. We'll make sure none of his mob do anything that will bring the law down on us."

Still not satisfied Albert sat brooding for quite some time. George of course knew him well enough to know this was not the time to interrupt him. At last he looked up.

"Ok George, when do you go down there again to meet with Leroy Wort?"

"This Saturday, that's if I can get on a bloody train. They're using them for moving troops and the seats are simply all occupied. But that's the plan anyway. Bournemouth is being raided all the time too and it looks just like Southampton High Street. So many buildings have been bombed and the buses stop running when the Siren sounds. They stop at the nearest shelter so their passengers can get out and rush inside. If the shelter is full they go on to the next one. Once the buses are empty they park up until the raid is over. It makes it hard for me to reach

Leroy's flat. But don't worry I'll make it somehow and tell him we agree, right?"

Reluctantly Albert nodded in agreement as he finished his beer.

"OK George I still don't like it but I suppose we ain't got much choice. Now let's go down to the secret room and see what we've got down there at the moment."

Giving a wave to both Bernard and his wife as they walked past the bar the two men went down to the empty area on the next level. Albert surveyed the room as they made for the door to the cellar stairs.

"This is such a waste of space ain't it, all this room and just that one small bar in the corner. And as usual there ain't no-one down here. Bernard and Catherine could make something of this, if the pub survives the war of course."

"Yeah I suppose so," George was not convinced. "It suits us to have this empty though don't it. We ain't got no prying eyes watching what we're doing."

"No I don't mean that. You're right we don't want any snoopers. But this could be turned into some sort of club. You could have music down here and I bet the place would be packed."

"That's a good idea Al, but do you really think Bernard and Catherine will ever get round to anything like that?"

Albert laughed. "No of course they won't, this floor will be just as empty after the war as it is now."

Letting themselves through the door of the cellar they could hear faint voices coming from below, indistinct but audible just the same.

"There shouldn't be anyone down here, what's going on?" Albert was alarmed. "If voices carry like this any bloody copper could hear them as well, have they discovered us already?"

"That back wall is thick so it shouldn't be happening. If it is some of our lot I'll make them pipe down with my bloody cosh."

148

Once they opened the secret door the reason for this became very apparent. At least eight of the gang were there.

"Put them bottles over here and be bloody careful with them," Lenny Warren shouted. More orders were being put forward just as forcibly.

Albert had to shout louder than anyone else to get their attention.

"Look lads, I know we have to stock our stuff properly and I can see you're doing that alright, but for heaven's sake do it more quietly. George and I could hear you as soon as we started down the cellar steps and if we could then so could anyone else. This is a secret room so let's bloody well keep it that way."

"Sorry boss," Lenny said. "We'll make sure there ain't no noise anymore."

"Good, now what have we got tonight? And how have our boys fared out there?"

"We've done alright boss but old Percy Winlkeman had some trouble tonight. He was late getting the stuff down from the shed of the Highfield Road house down to the river by the Plaza cinema. We were waiting a long time for him to turn up."

"Why, what sort of trouble did the old boy have?"

"He was stopped by some of the Swaythling mob and they searched his cart, they didn't find nothing so he eventually went on his way. But he was bloody annoyed and shaken up a bit. That lot threatened him and said if they found he was helping us they'd shoot both him and his horse."

"Right, this calls for action and I mean that. I want a meeting arranged with Eddie Wheeler right away. I won't have him and his mob interfering with us or what we're doing, and they won't get away with trying to intimidate Percy."

"Ok Al," said George, "but I think you'll a have a bit of trouble with him. Our boys say they raided that food dump at the airport tonight and got away with a load of stuff. We've got butter as well as tins of meat, jam, dried eggs and milk. And, believe it or not, lots of knicker elastic.

149

But the Swaythling lot found out and they're bloody mad about it I can tell you. The airport is on their patch so they think we're taking their spoils. The airport was targeted in a raid tonight see. A lot of casualties there was. Our boys took full advantage and got into that dump without any of the soldiers what normally guard it even knowing we was there. But Eddie Wheelers lot had the same idea and they saw our boys making off with the stuff that's now here in this room."

"Ok leave Wheeler to me. Just arrange the meeting and I'll work something out. He's a hard case alright but not too bright in the brain department so I'll talk him round easy enough. Now did we have any trouble with the stuff from the house once Old Percy arrived at the river?"

"No boss," said Lenny. "But coming through that marshalling yard is getting more difficult all the time. Those old men dressed as soldiers are taking their job seriously. Old they may be but the rifles they carry are real, and for all we know they might be good at shooting the bloody things. They will if they think stuff that's supposed to be shared round is being stolen. We need some sort of diversion boss or else it won't be long before we're caught in the act like."

"I know but tomorrow night I've got a meeting arranged with a lot of the young lads from around here. They're going to act as our eyes and ears so as soon as we can get this organised the better."

There was movement outside and Albert responded immediately.

"Quiet everyone, there's someone coming. George, get ready to act if you need to and that goes for the rest of you as well."

They waited with tension running high until the voice of Pat Matthews was heard outside.

"Ok relax everyone," said Albert, "it's some of our boys, open the door."

Seven more gang members entered the room led by a jubilant Pat.

"Hey boss we've had a good night despite that air-raid. In fact that helped us a lot. Most houses were empty because everyone was down in their shelters. We've picked up loads of stuff."

Inspection of the contents of several large bags revealed the proceeds of tonight's house breaking jaunt, and amongst them were food, jewelry, a few fur coats and ration books. Albert was particularly pleased to see them.

"This is great we can charge what we like for these."

Then, noticing a few bruises and cuts on a couple of his men he spoke sharply. "What's happened to you two? Where did those injuries come from?"

"It's ok boss," one of the men replied. "Bobby and me went into the back way to a house we thought was empty. But a silly old man was sheltering in one of them new metal shelters that go indoors and of course he heard us and came looking to see what was going on. Don't worry we were both covering our faces so he won't be able to describe us.

Anyway, it was only me he saw cause Bobby heard him coming and went behind the scullery door, he let the old man go past him then jumped out and hit the old bugger over the head, Went down like a sack of spuds he did and we cleaned the house out of anything we can use. He was still breathing ok when we left so it should be alright."

"I bloody hope so," Albert was infuriated by this. "We don't want the old man to snuff it, we've got the law watching us closely enough as it is. If they link a killing to us we'll have to clear out of Southampton all together."

"Yeah but I took a look at the old man and I'm sure Bobby just put him to sleep. But more important than that boss, we found out where we can get meat from as well. They're using the old fridges near the docks to store the stuff, so we can raid that too and get some of it for ourselves."

Some of the gang were dubious about this because they knew meat had to be kept frozen or it would go bad, and more than one of them voiced this concern.

"We need somewhere where we can keep it cold don't we and we ain't got nowhere we can do that."

Albert looked at George who had already thought the same thing. "Cyril Flushy is the man who can help us there?"

There were blank stares all around the room and both Albert and George laughed openly before elaborating.

"Cyril Flushy is a small butcher who has got a shop near Kingsland Market. The shop may be small but the walk in freezer certainly ain't. Cyril will store our meat in there and get a percentage of it himself to sell in his shop."

With everything stowed safely away all of them went quietly back up the stairs. The usual precautions being taken to make sure the lower floor area was still empty before they then went on up to the public bar. Bernard met them with an anxious look before they made it to their usual table.

"There's two blokes here Albert, and they're asking for you."

Looking where Bernard was pointing Albert saw the men. They were of average height and both were wearing overcoats and trilby hats. Beneath the hems of the coats, good quality trousers could be seen.

"Alright Bernard, I think I know who they are and what they want, leave it to me please."

Albert beckoned these two over to the table. "Right, I believe you're asking for me, so what is it you want?"

The first of these, a big well-built man responded. "I'm Jo Medly and this is Mickie Flamboy. We're here on an errand for our boss, Samuel Freeman. We all come from Bournemouth so you should know who he is."

Albert looked at George who shrugged, so then turned once more to the Bournemouth man. "No, we don't know anyone by that name so who the hell is he?"

"We were told you'd say that so we're going to give you the nick-name that we all know. He's called Salty Sam the Knifeman and it's a name that's been richly earned. I don't know anyone better with a knife than him."

"Ok so what have you got to tell me?" Albert asked, and was not the least bit surprised at the answer he got.

"Our boss wants some of us to come here pretty soon and make a headquarters for our boys. We'll have transport and we'll use it to bring merchandise from our part of the world then take back what we get in exchange from you. Now we expect a big shipment to come over from France tomorrow night and we'll be here with your share the day after that, so you've two days to find our boys somewhere to sleep."

Albert decided to test them. If they were genuine they should know the answer to this. "Right we can do that but who do we report to down there when we've got any big raids planned? Who is the big boss in other words?"

"I think you already know the answer to that because your man whose sitting next to you has already met him. But just in case he hasn't told you yet I can give you his name. It's Leroy Wort and a harder man than him you'll probably never meet. So don't even think of trying to put one over on him, because if you do it will mean all out war between your boys here and ours in Bournemouth."

Refusing a drink these two men left the bar and Albert looked round at everyone. "Well that's plain enough ain't it? So we'll play it by the book to start with then see what happens after that."

Then, looking at the clock he jumped up. "Is that the time? I've got to get to this meeting and set up our lad's gangs to become lookouts for us. Where this will take us God only knows."

153

Chapter Ten

Hurrying from the pub Albert raced around to the Kinslade house in Lyon Street and was welcomed as soon as he reached the front door. Winnie was waiting for him.

"Everyone's here Mr. Littlejohn. There ain't much room in the Anderson shelter but at least its private, nosy lot of bleeders they are round here."

Going down the bottom of the garden, Albert had to squeeze his big frame into the shelter because there certainly wasn't much room inside at the moment. Jean Burton was there with her eldest son Johnnie as well as Winnie Kinslade's eldest Alan. Also present were three boys Albert had never seen before.

Jean Burton waited for Albert to make himself as comfortable as he could before observing wryly, "I know you've already met my son Johnnie Mr. Littlejohn but this is Winnie's eldest Alan, and the other three are Dennis Frampton, Ollie Wimpson and Trevor Harvey."

Albert looked at these boys and each one of them was staring back at him. It made him uncomfortable because he didn't like to be around children other than his own, boys in particular

154

seemed to always rub him I up the wrong way. They were noisy brats as far as he was concerned and he avoided any contact with them. Now these five were looking at him and waiting for him to speak.

"Ok I've been told you lot can get other lads to work for my gang and be our eyes at night when we're working like."

He was surprised to find all five burst out laughing at this and looked helplessly at Winnie Kinslade who had also squeezed into the shelter. She too was smiling. "Don't worry Mr. Littlejohn all of them know what you mean by your boys working, so just carry on and tell them what you want them to do."

Only slightly relieved but still feeling a little out of his depth, despite two of their mothers being here as well, he ploughed on.

"Right then, I know your names but where do you all come from? Alan lives here of course, and I think Johnnie is from Adelaide road?"

"Yeah that's right Mr. Littlejohn," Johnnie replied. "Denis here is from Priory Road, Ollie comes from Kent Road and Trevor lives in Belgrave Road."

"And how do you all know each other?"

"From school mostly," said Alan Kinslade. "We all went to Portswood see and a lot of our mates still do. But it's the River Itchen that brings us all together. Me and Johnnie and the Priory Road lot swim from the St Denys' end, but Ollie and Trevor with all their mates go over the railway line behind Belgrave Road and they all swim from there. But a lot of the time we see each other at Cobden Bridge, Woodmill and Mansbridge."

"I see, and what about the area around the road bridge that connects Dukes road with Adelaide and Priory Roads?"

"Piece of cake," said Alan. "Me and my two brothers go there nearly every night and I know Johnnie and his lot do as well. The rest of the boys who will work with us know the area, not as good as us but we'll soon put that right. So give us a chance Mr. Littlejohn and we'll show you what we can do?"

155

Albert quickly made up his mind.

"Alright, but there will be rules and the first of these is silence. A lot of you lads are still at school so I don't want them telling everyone in the playground where they're getting pocket money from. Secrecy in my line of work is essential."

There were nods all round as everyone agreed to this.

"You five will lead the rest and you, and only you, will report to me or any member of my gang is that clear?"

"Yes Mr. Littlejohn," they all said together.

"Right, tomorrow night you can all come to my house in Empress Road at seven-o-clock in the evening. Use the back cutways and make absolutely sure you are not seen, either arriving or leaving. Once there you will meet my second in command and he will outline what we want from all of you."

Alan, who was just that bit smarter than all the rest, now put up his hand, seeing this Albert nodded at him to ask his question.

"My boys will do whatever you want from them and it'll be exciting for all of us, but they'll still want to know how much money they're gonna get for it?"

"Hmm a businessman I see."

This was met with laughs but they were all eager to know the answer to this question.

"To start with, you five leaders will all get half a crown for every night you work. That means if you do seven nights you'll get seventeen and six each. Every one of your mates will get a shilling each for every night they work. If this is agreeable to you we'll put this into operation straight away. And remember this pay structure is only the start, do your jobs well and there will be extra rewards for you all."

A cheer went up and there was no need for Albert to worry about the boys in this shelter. But one of them, Ollie Wimpson, had his hand up and Albert thought he was going to dispute the wages he had just outlined. But Ollie had something else on his mind.

"We know who you are sir, but is your second in command a man named George Harcourt, and is he the man they call the cosh?"

Albert was startled by this, so many of Southampton's underworld knew about George and his expertise with the cosh but to have a lad who was only just out of school asking about him was unbelievable.

"What do you know about George Harcourt?" he asked sharply. "Boys of your age shouldn't know anything about people like him, so come on lad how do you know?"

Ollie had gone very red and knew he shouldn't have asked this question, but his boy's enthusiasm had got the better of him and he had simply blurted it out. Now he felt the full force of Albert's glare on him and was suddenly feeling very nervous.

"Please sir, my uncle went to school with you and Mr. Harcourt and he's told me a lot about both of you. He ain't in your gang but he do know you and he's said no-one had better upset Mr. Harcourt because if they do he'll use his cosh on them."

The other boys now stared at Ollie because he had never told any of them this. Albert still couldn't place the man he was referring to.

"I see and what is your uncles name son?"

"He's my uncle Sammy sir and his full name is...."

"Truscot," Albert interrupted, "Sammy Truscot did go to Portswood school at the same time as us but I thought he left Southampton and joined the navy, that's right isn't it?"

"Yes sir," said Ollie, "but he left the navy after only a few years because he was found pinching stuff from the Quarter Masters stores and selling it on like."

Albert surprised them by bursting out laughing. "Still up to his old tricks is he? He was good at that sort of thing even at school. Chalk, rulers and books all went missing and it drove the teachers mad because they couldn't find out who was responsible. Well now Ollie the next time you see your uncle

157

tell him I'd like a word with him please. I think he can help us a lot if we can get him to join us."

The meeting broke up at this point and five very happy boys made their separate ways home. But Albert still had business to attend to and walking down Lyon Street knew it was time to take care of Eddie Wheeler and see what the bleeder had to say for himself.

Arriving back at the Portswood hotel just as the siren began wailing he hurried inside and went straight down to the lower level where all the pubs customers had gathered to shelter from the falling bombs. Seeing his men standing together in the far corner he went across to join them.

The noise outside reached fever pitch as the drone of the aircraft and the crump of their bombs grew louder and louder. He had to shout to make himself heard above this noise but did manage to tell them all about the young lads he had just been speaking to.

"They're alright, eager little beavers in fact, but I think we can trust them all to keep a good look out for us. We can have them watching the river from Woodmill right down to Northam Bridge. The Belgrave boys know their way around on the banks of the Itchen as it runs behind their road. They cross the railway line and make their way to the river from there. They know that path like the backs of their hands so they can tip us off if any of the Wheeler Gang try to come at us that way.

The rest of the crafty little sods will watch the river from the St. Denys end, some at the road bridge and others by the Plaza. It'll take a while to work it all out but I have a good feeling about this. I never thought I would because I ain't got much time for bloody nippers. But if they do what we want from them I may well change my mind.

Now once this raid is over I want you all out so let's make sure we take full advantage of the black out and the confusion that follows a raid. Only break into houses and shops that ain't been hit. That's important because to do it when buildings have been wrecked by bombs is looked on as looting and I know that anyone caught doing that can face the death penalty."

Almost as if on cue the all clear sounded.

"Right, let's get out there boys and good luck to you all."

Once they were alone Albert and George left the pub and started walking in the direction of Portswood junction. Confusion and the aftermath of the raid were all around them and in some places they had to detour as wreckage from buildings was blocking the roads. But they carried on and finally found themselves in High Road, Swaythling.

They had passed the Newlands hotel and the Brook Inn on the way up and now went by Broadlands, Mayfield and Harefield Roads then the turn off on the right hand side that led down to Wessex Lane on the left and Woodmill on the right. Both of them were uneasy because this very definitely wasn't their territory but the domain of the Swaythling gang. They went on though and came to the Hampton Park Hotel, the pub used by Eddie Wheeler and his boys.

This pub, situated on the corner of Burgess Road, was well known in Southampton. Going into the public bar they immediately saw Eddie Wheeler sitting at a table surrounded by members of his gang.

George nudged Albert and pointed two of them out, whilst Albert acknowledged with a nod.

"Yeah I see them George, keep your eyes on them. The bloody Griffin brothers are hard cases and the back bone of this gang."

They were two of the most notorious hoodlums in this South Coast town and their reputation of beatings and general tough behavior were already legendary. George though put his hand inside his coat and felt the reassuring shape of his beloved cosh, try anything with us boys and you'll feel this landing on your skulls he thought to himself.

The Griffin brothers were staring hard at them as they approached the table, and this made even Albert feel slightly wary. Big and distinctly rough looking, both of them lived for violence and showed no mercy to any of their victims. Glancing at George it was a relief to see that his hand was not far from his cosh.

Eddie Wheeler however wasn't even looking at his two meanest gang members but at Albert himself. Enemies they may be, but a certain amount of respect was in place because both men led gangs and wanted as much from their criminal activities as possible. And Wheeler knew that Albert's gang all worked in the Docks so could get information out concerning the cargoes that were arriving in this country.

They had been in conflict since their schooldays, with Albert at Portswood School and Eddie Wheeler attending the one at Swaythling. For years the rivalry between these two schools was legendary, boys from each believing their school was better in every way from the other one. Now and again this rivalry erupted into violence as boys from both schools clashed. Only the arrival of the police stopped these fights and many of the combatants required first aid afterwards.

The situation now of course was much more serious as both gangs fiercely protected their own territory from intrusion by their rivals, which was why this meeting was now taking place.

Reaching the table Albert and George were invited to sit down and Wheeler then looked at the Griffin brothers.

"Come on you two, get our guests something to drink. It's only beer I'm afraid because there ain't no bloody whisky to be had anywhere."

This loaded statement was not lost on either Albert or George. Toby and Alfie Griffin glowered at both of the Littlejohn men and were about to refuse to get them drinks, their status in this gang was high and it was they who gave orders to others. But the one person they respected above all others was their leader Eddie Wheeler so reluctantly they made their way to the bar.

Eddie now opened the conversation.

"Well we knows why you two are here, it's because your lot have broken protocol and raided our territory. So I want to know why and what the bloody hell you're going to do about it?"

"I take it you're referring to the raid my boys made on the food warehouse at the airport the other night?" Albert enquired.

"Too bloody right I am what the fuck do you think you're doing? That's ours to raid when we like. None of your lot have got any right to come anywhere near it."

"We thought about this and all my boys agree the airport's not in either your side of town or ours. It ain't even in Southampton is it? It's half way to bloody Eastleigh. So it's fair game to whoever fancies their luck raiding it. Don't forget that place is guarded by the army and they'll shoot first and ask question later if they find anyone trying to steal stuff from there."

The Griffin brothers came back from the bar and plonked a pint of beer in front of each of the Littlejohn men. Alfie made sure it spilt when he banged it down as hard as he could in front of George. The beer spilled out over the table and George jumped back to avoid it running down over his trousers.

"Oh sorry mate," said Alfie, "my mistake like."

He received such a glare from George that did little to relieve the tension in the bar.

Eddie Wheeler didn't even notice what had happened because he was concentrating intently on Albert and what he had just said. He sputtered then and shouted.

"That ain't right and you know it. That warehouse is on airport property and that's in Wide lane. And even if it is nearly in Eastleigh it's still on our part of town. So I say again mate, what the sodden hell are you going to do about putting this right?"

Albert picked up his beer and took a long slow pull at it before carefully placing the glass back on the table.

"I don't agree with you on that and I still say the warehouse is fair game to us all. But since you made the point about not

161

having any whisky here maybe we can come to some arrangement. We'll let you have some of ours. This isn't because we think it's our duty to. Let's just say this is professional courtesy and leave it at that."

The Griffin brothers were first to react to insisting they weren't going to accept anything from their arch rivals. Toby first, followed by his brother, jumped up and shouted.

"Bloody Bevois Town pansies, they ain't gonna get away with this, let's take these two and put them out of action."

He pulled a knife from his belt and now made a lunge at George. He was soon to learn that his reputation with the cosh was well earned. George had pulled it from his pocket and now he too lunged at his enemy. His cosh caught Toby on the side of his head and sent him reeling back. This angered the Swaythling men and now all of them were on their feet menacing Albert and George. They were in a very bad position now and both of them knew it, but Albert opened his mouth and shouted, "Littlejohn Boys."

Immediately the public bar door burst open and eight of the Littlejohn gang rushed in. The Swaythling boys were caught completely by surprise but rallied quickly. A mass brawl broke out with both gangs intent on doing as much damage as they could to their rivals. George was wielding his cosh with his usual deadly accuracy and the other members of his gang were supporting him with their fists as well as an assortment of weapons that included bicycle chains, knuckle dusters, and assorted heavy metal bars.

Against them in this tussle were the Swaythling mob who also favoured bicycle chains and the more dangerous heavy wire tow ropes that were more properly used as mooring chains for small boats. Above the noise of this vicious fighting the voice of the landlord could be heard shouting for order.

"Stop this bloody fighting and take it outside, you're wrecking my bloody bar."

162

Naturally this went unheeded as the fight was now in full swing with injuries being inflicted on both sides. Albert was fighting with his opposite number Eddie Wheeler and the two of them held nothing back. Both had reputations as hard cases and tonight they were showing how correct that was, they were both bleeding from cuts and taking no notice at all. Smashing their hated enemy was the objective and both of them were doing their best to achieve it.

The Griffin brothers were in the thick of it by now and doing much damage to the Littlejohn gang members. But they fought back hard and Alfie Griffin was the first to go down under a barrage of fists and weapons. He may even have died that night if a shot hadn't suddenly rang out. The noise was so loud it stopped everyone in their tracks and all eyes went to the bar.

Standing behind it with the gun still smoking in his hand in a scene that could have come from anything in the American wild west was landlord Teddy Cockcroft. He glared at them all.

"I told you fucking lot to stop and not one of you listened did you? Well, look at my bar now. It's wrecked and every one of you had better stump up the money to have it repaired. If you don't then by God I'll shoot the bleeding lot of you."

Albert, with blood still running down his face from a bad cut above his right eye, now looked at the man who had inflicted it. Eddie Wheeler had not fared any better and he too was bleeding profusely from various cuts to his face. Then, checking his men, he was glad to see they were all still on their feet, though most of them were showing the scars of battle. This fight had been ruthless and both gangs had suffered badly. No-one got away without being injured and there would now be whole load of first aid required by both sets of gangsters.

He turned his attention to the landlord.

"Okay, you're right and we will pay our share for the damages," then after pausing to catch his breath, "we'll also see you get a good supply of spirits for the next month as well, how does that suit you?"

"Ok make sure I get both the money and the booze, and there's one more thing you and your gang can do for me and that is to stay away from this pub. I don't want to see any of you in here again is that clear?"

Albert actually managed a smile before assuring the landlord that none of his gang would ever drink in this pub again.

"But," he added, "if we do ever come here again it will to wipe out this bloody Swaythling mob and we'll come heavy handed with guns and everything else that we need to do it."

The Swaythling gang were on their feet and now shouted their own threats back at Albert and his boys, who simply gave them a combined two fingered salute before walking out the bar. The landlord came out with them to make sure they left and was told to come down to Empress Road as soon as he could.

He was given Albert's house number and strict instructions to "Come on your own or with one or more of your bar staff. I don't want to see any of the Swaythling mob with you. Do it properly and we'll pay you for our part of the damages and give you enough bottles of spirits to keep you going for some time. You'll have to make your own arrangements for getting this back to the Hampton Park Hotel and if you're stopped you'll say nothing about where the booze came from is that clear? You've seen what my boys can do when their riled so I don't need to spell this out do I?"

Back inside the bar Teddy Cockcroft told Eddie Wheeler what Albert had just said to him and added. "I want both the money and the booze so don't mess this up for me."

Eddie, whose cuts were being attended to by Teddy's wife Connie, simply nodded in agreement because he was more concerned about the rest of his gang who were looking decidedly worse for wear. Two barmaids were working amongst them and administering whatever first aid they could. The worst injuries being those inflicted on the Griffin bothers, George's cosh had connected with them both more than once and both now lay on a bench and were barely conscious.

164

Connie Cockcroft was now trying to help them but she knew it wasn't in her power to give them the help they needed. So she shouted across to her husband.

"Teddy, these two are badly hurt we'll need to get them to hospital so call an ambulance quickly."

He took one look at the brothers before going to the post office telephone that was on a table in their private living quarters. Dialing 999 he asked for an ambulance to be sent to his pub. "We've had a bit of trouble here tonight and two men are badly hurt so can you get an ambulance here as quick as you can please?"

The operator was less than sympathetic. "We'll get to you as soon as we can but there's been another raid tonight in case you didn't notice. We've got a lot of people who were injured so they come first, before thugs who got hurt fighting. I've logged your call and we'll get to you when we can."

Connie was unimpressed. "Well let's hope they're still alive by the time the ambulance does get here then because I can't guarantee that they will be."

In the Portswood Hotel the scene was very similar and Catherine Bumstock along with Helen Strapwood her barmaid, was dishing out first aid to the injured Littlejohn men.

"Men," she exclaimed angrily, "just like bloody schoolboys they are. Give them any excuse and they start fighting, well I ain't got much sympathy for them if they get hurt."

"Stop groaning," she ordered the man whose face she was tending, "that don't hurt so shut up and let me get on with cleaning this cut."

Albert, his face now cleaned up and a plaster on the cut to his forehead, was suddenly conscious of Bernard the landlord standing by his side. He turned his head. "Yeah Bernie what is it?"

"There's a bloke at the bar, says he wants to buy you a drink."

Looking over to where the Landlord was pointing Albert replied, "Ok Bernard thanks."

He walked over to the bar and took the stool next to the man he had been told about.

"Well Teddy this must be important for you to come here yourself, so what's up?"

Teddy Wainright, Conservative Councilor for the Portswod ward of Southampton was a big man who certainly liked a drink and before he even answered Albert's question he ordered a pint of beer for him. When Bernard had pulled this and placed the glass in front of the Littlejohn gang leader Teddy revealed the purpose of his visit.

"DI Maurice Stapleton is what's wrong Albert, I've just come from a meeting with him at Portswood Police Station and the news isn't very good. He's in charge of the investigation into the death of that girl who was killed a few nights ago in an air-raid. She had very expensive clothes on as well as real nylon stockings and make up, and she had money in her purse. This Di and his Sergeant, DS Podcove, have traced her family and they certainly haven't the money to buy those things.

Then there's the little matter that the clothes aren't even available in this country at the moment because of the war. So where did she get them is what they want to know. They've traced her to that grotty café in the docks, what's it called, oh yes the Tall Funnel and spoken to the owner and the two waitresses. They've told them of the blokes who spoke most to the girl when she was there and your name is top of the list. They haven't got any real evidence that the girl went off with you or whether it's you who gave her everything. But they're going to keep a close watch on you and everyone who associates with you from now on."

"How much do they know now, I mean how safe are me and my men?"

"You're alright at the moment because they don't know if it was you who whisked that girl away. They only know you took

166

a shine to her and talked to her. But I'm here tonight to warn you about a planned raid on your house."

"Raid on my house when?" Albert was alarmed. "I need plenty of warning to make sure there ain't nothing for them snooping coppers to find. My kids need to be out of the way and all."

"You'll get enough warning," Teddy assured him. "I'll make sure of that, just be sure I get my cut that's all. DI Stapleton thinks I'm the reliable bloke that I should be so he trusts me of course. But if he should ever find out that I not only know you but am keeping you informed of what the police are planning it'll be both of us who end up in bloody handcuffs."

Albert relaxed a little. "Don't worry about that, if it ever happens we'll get to you first and get you out of this town so fast the coppers won't know till you're bloody miles away."

"Well I hope it won't ever come to that because as far as I know there hasn't ever been a Southampton Councilor who was caught consorting with criminals so I don't want to be the first one on that list. No I'll look after my end so you make sure you do the same with yours."

He then looked keenly, first at Albert then the rest of his boys in the bar.

"I say you do look rather worse for wear, what on earth has happened to you all tonight?

Albert laughed. "It's the old joke ain't it, you should see the other bloke, or in this case the other gang. Me and my boys had a disagreement with the Swaythling mob tonight and we showed them who really runs this town. They'll try to fight back but I'm not worried about that because we've got a system that we're just putting into place that will give us fair warning if Eddie Wheelers lot try to creep up on us."

"But there's only a few of you here tonight, and I know the docks is closed down again because of all the bomb damage. So where are your boys now?"

167

"Oh they're all out, visiting different places. You know, houses, shops, factories, to see if they can take anything that will be of use to us. We're getting very good at it now because the blackout makes our job so much easier, which reminds me. You'll have to excuse me Teddy because some of the boys will soon be back so George and me need to be there to meet them."

In Bournemouth another meeting was taking place between the gangster Salty Sam the knifeman and the even more dangerous Leroy Wort. Sitting in his flat Wort wanted to know how things stood.

"So what's happening in Southampton now, are your boys ready to move up there?"

"Yes they are," Salty Sam replied. "And they'll be taking a lot of the spirits and fags that came into Lulworth Cove last night. We want perishable stuff like butter, eggs and the powdered stuff as well. They've even got things like knicker elastic that women need and can't get at the moment. Littlejohn has meat stored away up there too so we'll get our cut of that as well."

"Ok but make sure we do. Make contact with the man they call the cosh, you've met him before haven't you?"

"Yes I bloody well have," Salty Sam assured him, "and a right hard case he is as well. Don't get on the wrong side of him or he flashes that sodding cosh."

"Hmm yes I've heard that but when he's with me he flashes something else."

Salty Sam was the only man in Bournemouth that Wort would say that to and he knew it wouldn't go any further. Salty himself knew exactly what Leroy meant and would of course keep it to himself. But being a very masculine man whose sexual desires were all directed at women he simply couldn't understand how a hard case like Leroy Wort could go with other men. But he made sure his contempt for this never showed when he was talking to the king of the Bournemouth crime scenes.

He, as well as most others down here, still remembered the horrific funicular murder of Jerry Fingers Malone. A hard case and soulless criminal he may be but he still shuddered as he thought of that car going over Malone's body and crushing it. Now Leroy was talking again.

"We want our share of everything the Southampton mob can get to us and we make sure they get their share of what comes in here from the continent. I know there's supposed to be honour among thieves but both of us know that's a load of bollocks. But with this deal we have to make them sweet so let's do it right. Who are you sending up there?"

"Well besides me I'm taking Richie Halliday, he's a fighter if ever I saw one and will take on anyone who dares to try and put one over on him. Then I'll have little Victor Warrendor, a right little weasel as you know but he's shrewd as well. Light fingered of course and I'll be watching him for that, but he can smell a deal a mile away, and he's always around to see it through. He'll watch that Southampton mob and report to me if he even gets the slightest whiff of treachery. Finally I'm taking Pat Morello and his boys. Four in all and you know what they do for us down here?"

Wort smiled evilly at this.

"Yes I do, he and his boys do the protection racket down here. So I'm assuming you want him to do the same in Southampton?"

"Yes that's the plan, Littlejohn and his mob don't do that and they're missing out on a lot of money. We'll alter that and share the proceeds with them. They'll have to make sure we don't get any trouble from the mob that operates on the other side of the town."

"Hmm yes George Harcourt said something about a lot of schoolboys being brought in to keep a watch out for any sort of trouble along those lines. Find out about that and get the details back to me Salty, it sounds like a good idea and one we can use down here as well. And while I'm on the subject, if you take Pat

169

Morello and his boys with you, who does the protection racket here in Bournemouth?"

With a sinister smile of his own Salty reassured him. "Don't worry about that. Pat has a very good second in command. Davie Silver is as good as Morello himself and has at least six boys working with him. Our shop keepers won't get away with anything I can tell you."

In Southampton, at exactly the same time, Albert Littlejohn was talking to George Harcourt.

Chapter Eleven

"Tomorrow night George I want all five of those nippers back at my house in Empress Road but it'll have to as early as possible cause I've been tipped off about a raid. Who have we got to be shagging in the spare back bedroom?"

"It's Billy Marshalls turn," George answered, "but we'll need him for the food dump job in our old warehouse. The Home Guard have stepped up their patrols. Billy can get in through that small opening right at the back of the building, the one that's almost underground. He goes through like a little dog and once in he can get what we need and pass it out to our boys who'll be waiting outside. We'll have some of the lads acting as decoys to keep those old men busy and they'll do it properly so none of them get shot."

"Right that sounds good. And they know what's needed for our business? I must say it's picking up nicely now, especially when we bring in that lot from Bournemouth."

"All in hand Al don't worry about that. Our lot will be helping themselves from houses and shops and doing bloody well. We'll have all we need for this week by this time tomorrow. Now I've told Willy Ford that he's the one to be caught in bed with one of the street girls when the house raid is on, so when is it exactly?"

"Teddy Wainright said tomorrow night so make sure Willy has a girl picked out and is in my house with her no later than six-o-clock. I want them both bollock naked in the single bed when the cops burst in."

"He ain't that happy about it Al. Oh the shagging bit is okay but if he gets sent down for having a go at the cops' as he knows we want him too, it means at least six weeks in clink. He and his missus ain't going to like that at all."

"Too bloody bad," said Albert, "both of them get looked after by us, all members of this gang and their families do. If he's got to cool his heels in clink for a few weeks it ain't much to have to pay is it. And don't forget his reputation in the docks will go up as well, caught with his pants down in bed with a naked woman."

"How long have we got to keep this up Al? The bloody coppers ain't stupid and our blokes using your back room as a brothel ain't gonna keep them from looking a damn sight closer next time they come."

"Not much longer," Albert reassured him. "Sam Clifford and two more of our neighbours lads have almost finished digging out the ground in our shed. It's falling down and isn't used, because of that the coppers ain't even given it a glance. Well, as soon as the boards and the damp proofing have been done we'll start putting the stock that we sell from here down in there. It's foolproof because only people we know will benefit from what we sell. They won't need coupons for it either, they'll want to keep quiet about it."

"Yeah well we've almost finished moving stuff from the Highfield Road house. Old Percy Winkleman is bloody good at moving it down to the river by the Plaza. I suppose you won't be using the shed at that house any more once we've got everything out and down to the secret room in the Portswood Hotel?"

"Why not?" Albert asked him. "I've only used that house as a luxury before. It's so much posher than my home in Empress Road. But think about it George. All them houses in Highfield Lane are huge and only people with lots of money can afford to live there. Well, our boys are really good at house breaking now, so let's get some of them paying a visit to some of those properties. It'll be a laugh as well as a profitable venture. The coppers are going to be out looking for burglars ain't they. But they simply won't twig it's someone who lives there whose behind the burglaries."

George didn't need to think about that for very long before bursting into a loud laugh.

"Bloody hell Al, that's brilliant. The stupid coppers will be running round in circles and they won't find out a thing. The posh sods in Highfield aren't gunna know what's hit them."

"I want that house taken apart when we strike tomorrow night," Detective Inspector Stapleton told the assembly of police officers who were listening intently.

They were in the incident room at Portswood police station and the air was electric. Everyone knew their boss wanted to clear up the case of the mystery girl that was still getting a mention in the local paper. Many people were dying every day in the air raids, but none of them wore clothes that couldn't be bought anywhere in England. The police knew she must be implicated in the black market activities that were starting to become a real nuisance in Southampton.

"It's the Littlejohn Gang, I'm sure of that," the DI repeated, "but we haven't a shred of evidence to pull them in. So let's get out there and raid his house again. This time I want the place torn apart. If there's contraband in that house I want it found. Sergeant Podcove will lead the raid so follow his orders and go in hard and fast. We will catch them unawares because the raid is only known about in this room."

173

Later in the DIs office Sergeant Podcove challenged him on this.

"Is this true Gov, that no-one but us knows about the coming raid? I've carried out two already and I swear Littlejohn has been tipped off each time."

"Yes I know and believe me sergeant I am concerned about that. How the blazes does he know? Where is he getting his information from? If we could answer those questions I'm sure we'd have that crook and all his gang by the short and curlies."

"Yes I agree Gov, so we need to find out who, besides us, has advance information about our activities."

"Hmm, yes that's right of course but the list is small. The ARP wardens and the Home Guard are always told and they help us out a great deal. But apart from them it's only the council and let's face it sergeant, if we can't trust them who the bloody hell can we trust?"

This was not the only meeting taking place in Southampton today. The Swaythling Gang were all in the Hampton Park Hotel and Edie Wheeler was holding what was effectively a council of war. All of his gang was present, with the exception of the two Griffin brothers. They had been taken by ambulance to the Royal South Hants Hospital where they both needed treatment for the wounds inflicted by George Harcourt's cosh.

Both were being kept in for the next few days before they would be allowed to go home. And even then they would have to take things easier until they got their strength back. This, of course, was not going down well with Eddie Wheeler. These two brothers were the back bone of his mob and to have them sidelined by another gang was something he was finding extremely hard to take.

"That Bevois town lot needs to be brought down and bloody permanently. They've made us look like a right bunch of pansies and they did it here in our local."

He banged his fist down on the table in frustration and all of his men knew just how angry he was.

"They've got such an advantage over us, Littlejohn and most of his gang work in the docks and he's got his fingers into all the dodgy deals that go on in there. I know he's giving Teddy Cockcroft a lot of booze and they'll be some for us as well, but I want more boys, I want that mob put out of business. We are going to raid their territory and strike hard and fast so they won't know what's bloody well hit them.

We can follow the railway line down to St. Denys station and wait for them there under that road bridge. We know they're getting stuff from somewhere and bringing it by boat to that spot. So that's where we'll strike. Hard and fast and I don't expect to see a single one of them still standing when this is over."

The next night five excited young boys sat in the front room of the Littlejohn House in Empress Road. They had met up early and arrived together, coming in through the back cutways so as not to be seen. Ida and Maggie gave them some lemonade to drink.

"Go into the front room boys, my husband will be with you soon," and all of them hurried to do as she told them.

Now with Albert and George in attendance all of them were a little bit frightened as well. The very presence of a man like George Harcourt was intimidating to boys of their age. Johnnie Burton and Alan Kinslade as the oldest made sure they stayed close to the younger boys. All of them were now riveting their attention on the commanding figure of Albert Littlejohn.

"Right now you two," he said indicating Johnnie and Alan. "I want you to organize the groups of boys and where they will work please. I want names and numbers and these will be given to our banker whose name is Ginger Strangemore.

Just you two will go and see him and collect the wages for that week. You will keep records of how many lads have

175

worked and on what nights. These you will give to Ginger every Friday night, is that clearly understood."

"Yes Sir," they both replied in unison.

"Right I want a rundown of what territory you will all be watching and how you intend to get warnings to us, you first Johnnie."

"Me and my friends will be at Northam Mr. Littlejohn, if anyone we don't know comes through there and makes their way to the part around the Plaza we'll get the message to you fast. There will be boys under the road bridge on the other side of the river and it will be Alan here in charge of them. Me and him will work out a code we can use with torches to let each other know when any sort of trouble is brewing and they will make sure you gets the tip off bloody quick like."

"Ok and Ollie I think it is and Dennis will be part of that set up will they?"

"Yeah a lot of their boys will be with us at both those spots, but some will stay and help out in and around St Deny's like. They'll spot anyone coming at you from places like Belmont Road, down St. Deny's Road or over Cobden Bridge."

"Right, and do you know who it is you're looking for who could be a threat to us?" Albert asked and was surprised by the prompt reply.

Alan Kinslade spoke up.

"Well Sir we all know the Swaythling lot cause we went to Portswood while the kids from Swaythling went to that poncy Swaythling School. We hated them and they hated us. But we always knew where they was and kept a watch to make sure none of them came into our part of Southampton or anywhere near our school. We kept such a close eye that we knew their dads by sight as well. We know what Eddie Wheeler looks like and the Griffin Brothers. They've got nippers who are just as bad as their dads and we've had a lot of fights with them, so we'll know if any of that lot move against you from more than one spot.

And we'll keep watch for police too. Some of our boys will be hiding in the gents toilets by the tram shed entrance where they can watch the cop shop next door. Any big lot of coppers coming out of there and moving towards you they'll send a runner ahead to tip you off."

Albert was starting to see how useful these young but enthusiastic lads were going to be to him and he turned his attention to the one who so far had not said a word.

"Trevor Harvey isn't it from Belgrave Road? What can you tell me about your part in all of this?"

Going slightly red, as he was quite shy underneath his tough exterior, he quietly answered.

"We're railway boys Mr. Littlejohn as well as knowing all the roads around Portswod up to and just beyond Portswood junction. We goes to the flicks at the Palladium a lot and Portswood School as well."

"Good but what is it about the railway? You said you're railway boys, what does that mean?"

Trevor relaxed a little and gave a grin.

"The London line runs behind our road sir and all of us make short work of the fence that's supposed to keep us off railway property. We goes over the line and makes our way round the sewage works till we comes to our special part of the bank of the River Itchen. We swims from there and believe me, we knows every bit of the ground on that side of the tracks. We can go right up to where we can see the old ruined boathouse at Woodmill, and anyone coming down river by boat will have to start from there. We can also walk the track up to the bridge over the line in Woodmill Lane. Again we can keep watch for anyone coming from that direction. We can see Swaythling Station from there too."

"Very impressive young man but how do intend to get a warning to us if and when you have something to report?"

"We'll use our raft sir and a good one it is too. One of our boys is in the Scouts see and he's shown us how to build one

177

proper like. It goes good with the current going down river and we uses paddles to get up again against it. We've even got a sail we can use when the wind is in the right direction."

Albert looked at George and they both laughed as they remembered their own boyhood efforts at raft building. They looked sturdy enough when on the bank, but once out in the water with at least six on board the same thing happened every time. The rafts broke apart dumping everyone into the water. So the ability to swim with your clothes on, especially in such a swift running river as the Itchen, was not just essential but vital.

Albert now said as much to Trevor and asked about his lads and their swimming abilities in just such a situation as this.

"The current is so strong and clothes drag you down so are you going to be ok if anything happens to your raft?"

"Yes sir we can all swim with our clothes on and we do it all the time from our place on the bank. And besides one of my lot is a Scout and they know all about building a sturdy raft."

"Alright all of you that's it for tonight," Albert concluded, "except I want the two older boys to stay for a few more minutes please. The rest of you can make your way out and go back on your way home. Go through the back just as you came in. But I think my daughter Maggie has some lemonade and biscuits waiting for you in the kitchen."

When the three who had just been dismissed had rushed enthusiastically out to the kitchen Albert faced Johnnie Burton and Alan Kinslade.

"Now you two when you have something to tell either me or George here you are to go to the side door of the Portswood Hotel. Once there you will give two knocks followed by three more. The door will be opened by the landlord or his wife. They'll show you into their private rooms and then one of us will come and talk to you.

But make sure when you're out there that you and the rest of the boys are not put in any sort of danger. Be particularly careful in and around Bevois Park Marshalling yard. The Home Guard

178

soldiers carry rifles and may shoot if they think any sort of looting is going on. Keep a sharp watch for them at all times. What's funny young Alan? What I'm telling you is very important."

"Yes sir I know but you see we do this sort of thing all the time and my brothers and me like, are really good at it. See, we have such a lot of fun letting grown- ups see us when we're somewhere we shouldn't be. Then we run off and hide. And we can get in to small places that big blokes like you haven't a hope of doing. We can watch them searching all over the place and it's such a laugh. So we can do that with them old soldiers in the Marshaling yard. When you and your men are taking stuff from the river to that room at the pub we will make all sorts of noise and even let ourselves be seen. So those old blokes will be looking all over the yard for us and won't even notice what else is going on."

"Hmm I'm beginning to see what your mother meant when she suggested this. It's a very good plan, but I say again watch yourselves. Those old men, as you call them, are trained soldiers and they can shoot. So if you let yourselves be seen don't do it anywhere they can get off a shot at you is that clear?"

Alan was grinning from ear to ear.

"Yes sir, but me and my lot can run faster than any of them old soldiers, we'll be gone out of sight before they can even aim their rifles."

Sighing now Albert and George let them go and get their lemonade and biscuits, before quickly getting down to the next more pressing concern.

"The coppers will be here soon George so are we ready for them?"

Almost," George answered. "Your wife is in bed and your Maggie has done a really good job with her make-up. Blimey, she looks as though she's going to peg out at any minute. She looks so awful that even that hard bastard Sergeant Podcove won't want to disturb her."

179

"Yes Maggie is a genius when it comes to make-up and my Ida is a very good actress. So what are we hiding in her bed tonight?"

"Bottles of whiskey, gin and brandy down the bottom of the mattress, all well covered and wrapped up so there ain't going to be any rattling of glass if they do move the bed. Then on top of that we've got clothes, including nylon stockings, elastic, ration books and a lot of tinned meat. We haven't brought as much to the house as usual because the shed is almost ready and then everything will be well hidden in there. Your kiddies room is clear tonight so the cops can take it apart if they want and they won't find a bloody thing."

"Ok but why almost ready, what ain't right yet?"

"It's Willy Ford Al, he ain't here yet and the bloody times getting on."

"Ain't here," Albert exploded. "He's been told what time he's supposed to be here so where the hell is he? If he lets us down he's going to regret it George. One thing I won't tolerate, someone not doing what their bloody well supposed to be doing and letting the whole gang down. We ain't got much time so get someone out and round to his house. If he's there drag him out and carry the bleeder here if he won't come willingly."

Just then there was a commotion at the front door and Albert quickly strode down the passage and threw it open.

Willy Ford was trying to pacify a young woman who was clearly not happy at all.

"No I don't want to do this," she was shouting and tried to pull away from Willy. Taking this all in at a single glance Albert grabbed the girl and simply yanked her inside. Willy quickly followed and the front door was then slammed shut. Pulling the girl through the passage then up the stairs Albert got her into the small back bedroom with George standing close by.

"Now girl what's all this? You do this sort of thing all the time so why are you making such a fuss?"

Although Albert was quite frightening, the girl, whose name was Mary, stood her ground.

"I don't like this mister and I ain't been doing it long. I only got involved because my family needs money but sleeping with blokes like this that I don't even know is horrible so I ain't going to do no more see."

The fear was reflected in her eyes and was made even worse when she saw that Willy Ford was already stripped down to his underwear and was about to take that off as well.

"No I ain't doing this," she screamed, "let me out of here I'm going home."

Albert gripped her by her shoulders and spoke very loudly. "Look girl we haven't got time for this. You don't have to have sex with Willy here but just take off your bloody clothes and get into bed with him. Coppers are on their way to this house as I speak and we want you to be found naked in that bed with him. That's all you have to do and you'll be well paid for it.

"No I ain't going to I'm getting out of here."

Albert simply looked round at George who nodded and went out of the room. Mary was openly crying and looking longingly at the door when it opened again and George came back in. But he was not alone. He had gone out to the back cutway where he knew some of the gang were hiding. Waiting for the police to raid the house and then go away when they found nothing to incriminate their leader. Then operations inside the broken down shed could get underway once again.

Two of these men were now following him into that small back bedroom and George nodded to the girl.

"We need this silly girls clothes off because she needs to be in that bed in the nude with Willy here when the coppers get here. We ain't got much time so get to work and strip the sodden girl."

They moved so quickly that Mary had no chance of putting up a fight. She was held in a grip of iron as her dress was unzipped and pulled from her body, quickly followed by her underwear. Now naked she was pushed to the bed and ordered to get in. She did as she was told because she was embarrassed to be seen naked by so many men and the bed at least allowed her to cover herself. Willy got in beside her and then all hell broke loose downstairs.

The front door knocker was banged loudly. "Police, open up," they shouted through the letterbox.

Albert went down the stairs and walked slowly and calmly to the door.

"Good evening officers, what can I do for you?"

Sergeant Podcove was in front and shoved a piece of paper at Albert.

"Police sir, I have a warrant here to search these premises so stand aside please."

Albert barely even glanced at the warrant as at six burley police officers barged past him and entered his home. The ground floor rooms were searched and nothing was overlooked. The furniture was checked to see if anything was hidden inside, even the kitchen didn't escape this close scrutiny. The gas cooker and copper were inspected as was the old mangle. Bowls and cardboard boxes that were in use for storage were tipped out and sifted through.

Maggie clicked her tongue in disapproval at the mess these men were making. "Isn't it bad enough me mum is ill upstairs without you bastards making her kitchen into a tip. Get out of here and let me clean up your mess."

"Just doing our jobs miss," said Sergeant Podcove. "We are in our rights to search if we suspect contraband is being hidden."

"Oh piss off and get your ugly face out of here before I pick some of this up and bloody chuck it at you."

The sergeant looked sternly at her for a moment as he decided what he should do about this. The girl was not only swearing at the police she had now uttered a threat against them. This was an arrestable offence, but he was here on more important business.

"Mind what you say to us young lady or I promise you'll find yourself in a whole lot of trouble."

He thought this would be enough to frighten her and was shocked when she simply poked her tongue out at him. She pushed him to one side and started clearing up, not even bothering to look at him or any of the other officers as she did so.

Like father like daughter the sergeant thought to himself but left her to it and led his men up the stairs.

"I want this floor taken apart," he said to them as they reached the top floor. "Leave nothing unturned, if there's something in this house that we can get Littlejohn for I want it found. What the bloody hell is that noise?"

The loud scream had come from the back bedroom so the sergeant led his men up there and they burst through the door. The sight that met their eyes was that of a young woman, who was obviously naked, trying to push an equally naked man away from her. But, confined to the bed, she was losing this battle and realizing this had started to scream.

"No, no, get off me. I don't want to have sex with a dirty old man like you. Get off."

Willy Ford was completely out of his depth by now as this certainly wasn't going to plan. The girl should just be here for sex, all done for the benefit of the police to put them off the scent of anything the gang had hidden in the house. But this stupid girl was acting as though he was trying to rape her.

"Shut up you stupid cow," he raged. "I ain't going to shag you, bloody hell I'm old enough to be your father. Just keep quiet and do what you're told and nothing will happen to you."

That's when the door burst open and Willy found himself dragged from the bed and thrown to the floor.

"Hold this bastard until we calm the young lady," Sergeant Podcove yelled, then went over to the bed where Mary was now covering herself with the bedclothes.

"Are you alright Miss?" he asked gently. "Has this man violated your body in any way?"

Crying openly now Mary replied. "No, but he was going to and I told him and them other blokes that I didn't want to do it."

"What other blokes Miss?"

"The man who lives here and that other creep with him, they was the ones who...."

She stopped abruptly at this point as she caught sight of George Harcourt standing out in the passage. He was making sure the cosh that he had partly drawn from his pocket was clearly visible to her. That, and the look he was giving her, was enough to convey the message she had already said far too much. Any more and she would be facing injury or worse from George. She may not like what she had been brought to this house to do, but she knew the reputation of the Littlejohn gang and George the Cosh especially.

So she changed direction rapidly. "Well, what I mean is I did come here for sex, but I got frightened see and well, it made everyone mad like."

"Miss, what is your name?" the sergeant asked.

"Mary sir, Mary Simpson."

"Alright Mary but be careful what you are saying. Are you willing to charge this man with attempted rape, because that's what it looked like to us as we burst in. You were fighting him off and screaming the place down as you did so?"

"No see I ain't done nothink like this before and I thought it would be a good way of making some money. But I didn't like it and wanted it to stop, I just want to go home now please."

"Yes I can see that but I'm afraid this is a little more serious and you will have to come to the police station and make a statement. You see, if you changed your mind and told this man that, then by forcing you to go on with it that constitutes rape and that is a very serious charge."

"Oh no, I don't want to do that," she wailed, "I have to get home see because me mum will worry if I don't. She ain't very

184

well and she worries all the time in the air-raids. I'm all she's got, so I must go to her."

She then received a glare from Sergeant Podcove that frightened her every bit as much as the obvious threat from George Harcourt. It seemed that no matter what she did she was still facing trouble.

Then the police officer relented. "Alright Miss we can't make you lay a charge against this man, but remember this. When you sell your body for money that is against the law and if we come across you again in similar circumstances I can assure you we will arrest you. Now get dressed and get out of this house because you are obstructing us from performing our duty."

Mary needed no second telling and hurriedly threw her clothes on and dashed from the room. Almost tripping up as she ran down the stairs she reached the front door but George Harcourt loomed out of the darkness.

Grabbing her by her shoulders he snarled, "You did right to shut up about what was really going on there girl, but mind you keep your trap shut about it. If I find you've talked to anyone I'll come and find you. Wherever you are I will find you and then I'll shut your mouth for good."

"Please mister," she begged, "I won't say anything I just want to go home let me go please."

"Alright, you can go and take this with you. But remember what I said, keep your bloody mouth shut about what went on in this house and where the contents of that bag came from."

She simply nodded her head in agreement then rushed through the front door and disappeared down the road and out of view. Albert's attention was divided between this and keeping an eye on what was going on upstairs.

"What have we given her George?"

"Stockings, some make-up for herself and food for her family, and we've given her the usual fee as well."

"Good, she was panicking and I don't like that so can we trust her now to keep her bloody mouth shut, including where she got the things like stockings and make-up?"

"I've just told what she can expect from me if she does blab," said George. "And she knows I mean it I'm quite sure of that. She'll keep quiet or we'll deal with her."

There was quite a commotion on the stairs then as three burley policemen started dragging a hand cuffed Willy Ford down with them.

"Get these cuffs off of me you bastards," he was shouting. "I ain't done nothing wrong and that tart told you that, we didn't do nothing so what the fuck are you arresting me for? Ow."

One of the police officers had had enough and head butted him, out of sight of his superior. This drew blood both from Willy and the officer. Wiping this off his forehead the PC seemed unperturbed.

"Resisting arrest and assaulting a police officer in the performance of his duty. You really shouldn't try violence like this when all we wanted to do was have a quiet talk with you."

As he was dragged through the door Willy was heard shouting all the way to the Black Maria.

"This is a setup, why can't I get dressed? I'm still in the bloody nude. Perverts thats what the bloody lot of you are."

His voice faded away as the door of the police car slammed shut and Willy was driven off to Portswood police Station.

Albert and George had watched the whole thing unfold, even the attack on Willy by the PC, but neither of them were going to say anything about it. They wanted him arrested because that was always their plan. Events may not have gone quite to plan on this occasion but it took some of the attention away from the other bedroom and this had been a very useful tactic, until now.

Tonight though Sergeant Podcove was more determined. "Right men, let's take these bedrooms apart. I want everything up here searched including the attic, get up there and don't miss a bloody thing."

186

Chapter Twelve

"Is that attic clear of everything George? You heard what the bloody sergeant just said. They're determined to find contraband."

"If they even find any rat shit up there Al I won't be pleased. Don't worry, Harry Pinshoe has done a great job and he's now waiting to move into the old shed in the garden. They can look all they want but I tell you even the keenest eyes won't spot that the wall between the attic here and in Benny Prendergast's next door is false."

"Well I hope that's right," said Albert. "As you say Harry Pinshoe is a bloody genius where brickwork is concerned. That wall looks solid doesn't it and will stand up to scrutiny."

"That's the beauty of it Al, Sergeant bloody Podcove will know that the houses in this road should have attics without separate adjoining walls. So they can all go into each other's lofts if they want to. He'll be mighty suspicions of the fact there's been a new dividing wall put in between this house and the Prendergast's next door."

The police party had by now found the ladder used for getting into the loft and brought it into the house. It had been propped just inside the old shed that was in such a state of disrepair the police officer who had been sent for the ladder pulled it out without giving the shed another thought.

So, once the ladder was brought in and set up in the spare bedroom Sergeant Podcove, armed with a very powerful torch, led his men up into the darkness of the loft. Strong boards had been put down to give a solid floor to walk on, and this simply heightened the sergeant's suspicion. Why else would they go to all this trouble if not to use the place for storage?

He hauled himself through the narrow opening and now, with three of his officers assisting, the loft was carefully inspected. After an exhausting half an hour they did indeed have something to show for it, two sweet wrappers, a rat's nest next to the water tank and several dinky toys that had belonged to Albert when he was a boy.

"This is impossible," the sergeant shouted, his anger and frustration getting the better of him. "There should be contraband up here and why is there a dividing wall? The rest of the houses in this road have an open walk through. Let's have a closer look at that wall. It can't be right can it? PC Offenbright, you know a lot about the building trade, what do you make of this?"

"I should hope I do sergeant, I was a bricky before I joined the force."

Then, going over to this new wall, he shone his torch on it and pushed in various places to see if there was any give. He also checked for openings that men could crawl through. Finally he looked up.

"I can't see anything wrong here sergeant, this is a very smart piece of bricklaying. The wall is solid."

Back down in the small back bedroom the sergeant's anger was boiling over.

"Right, there's illegal contraband in this house somewhere. I bloody well know there is because all my senses are telling me. So, that only leaves the main bedroom for us to search and I want it done properly. They usually fob us off with her being ill

188

but not this time. Take the bloody room apart as well as the bed. Have we searched the kid's room yet?"

"Yes sarg, the kids are away at their aunties tonight so we were able to search the room properly and we did look inside the bed. The mattress isn't open so nothing can be put inside it, but we took it off the bed anyway and gave it a bloody good shake. There was nothing in there or anywhere else in that room."

"Right, so if there is anything to find it's in that main bedroom so let's get in there."

They went down the passage and pushed open the door. There were two people in here, Ida Littlejohn in the big double bed and her daughter Maggie sitting beside it. The girl looked scornfully at the police contingent, who were not overjoyed to see her again, and shouted at them.

"So, not content with making an awful mess in our kitchen you're now going to disturb my mum. Can't you see how ill she is, get out of here."

Sergeant Podcove didn't say anything for a moment because he was transfixed at Mrs. Littlejohn. Maggie always did a good job with the make-up but this time she had surpassed herself, and made her mum truly look as though she was at deaths door. And Ida herself was playing her part to perfection, continually groaning as if in a lot of pain. Never-the-less he knew why he and his men were here and what he had to do now.

"I can see that miss, but my men and I are here on legal police business and I suspect that stolen articles are hidden somewhere in this room, so we are going to search it."

Then, turning to his men he instructed them to get on with the search. They responded well and looked everywhere, including under the bed, they even tipped the up the chamber pot to see if anything was hidden inside. Thankfully for all concerned the pot was empty at the time. Maggie sat fuming as this search continued and boiled over when they disturbed her mother and started to poke at the mattress on the bed.

Ida gave a very genuine shriek as this was happening and Maggie, who was as startled by it as the police, now erupted in fury.

"Leave her alone you bastards, I've told you she's dying so you try and help that along by shaking her about like this. Get out and fuck the lot of you," she screamed.

Sergeant Podcove was shocked that a young girl like this even knew swear words like that, but he stood his ground.

"I've been very tolerant with you up until now miss but swearing at the police and interfering with our duty is against the law, so if you persist with this I will have no alternative but to arrest you."

"Good," she shouted, "so I'll give you a reason to do that you fucking pig."

She then picked up the broom that was lying on the floor and swung it at the sergeant. He saw it coming just in time to duck out the way then his men pounced on Maggie. This prevented her from mounting another attack, and a struggle broke out with Maggie fighting and swearing at the police as they tried to subdue her, until it was interrupted by Albert.

"Take your filthy hands off of my daughter, what the bloody hell do you think you're doing? She's only a girl and it takes three grown men to hold her does it? Let her go now or my men and I will fight the whole bloody lot of you."

"Is that a threat then Littlejohn?" asked the sergeant. "I can and will arrest you for it if you attempt any violence against any of us. We are here on police business and your daughter is being particularly offensive to us. Even resorting to violence herself by attacking us with a broom, she is now coming with us to answer a charge of attacking police officers in the line of their duty."

"Bollocks to both of those," Albert retorted. "My daughter was trying to protect her seriously ill mother from the unwanted interference you and your men were putting her through. And I don't give a damn about your bloody search warrant. My wife is dying and needs complete rest, peace and quiet, so get the fuck out of this room now, or the whole of this town will be reading about this in the echo tomorrow."

There was a complete stand off as the Sergeant and Albert stood glaring at each other. Finally the police officer broke the silence.

"I could arrest you right now Littlejohn for the threats you have just made, but we both know because of your work in the docks you are protected from that. But we also know crime inside Southampton docks is rampant and I'm bloody sure you're up to your neck in that. So we'll be keeping after you and we will get all your bloody thugs. Your time is limited Littlejohn, we'll not stop till we nail the whole bloody lot of you."

Despite what he had just said the sergeant was very reluctant to leave it at that, despite Ida's apparent condition making matters complicated and hindering his search. Suddenly though the wail of the siren broke out announcing yet another raid on the town, it now appeared everything was going against him tonight.

"Right you lot get out of here," Albert snapped at him. "I hope you lot cop a bomb on your way back to Portswood nick."

"Just like that young girl who was killed in raid a few days ago then," the sergeant answered. "I think you know the one. She was wearing things that could only have come from a black market racket. The like of which I'm sure you and your mob are running. But, like I said, we're after you and closing in."

Albert was shaken by the mention of Janice Saunders. He had put her to the back of his mind so to have this thrown at him was not good at all. But he rallied quickly.

"I don't know what you're bloody talking about copper, but it ain't only you who are closing in mate. The bleeding Germans are and all. So I say again, get out of this house and let me get my sick wife and our daughter down to the shelter."

191

Reluctantly the sergeant knew he had no choice but to get his men out and into a shelter themselves, so they made a dash for the big ones in the neighboring roads. After three attempts one was found with enough room for all of them to be admitted.

By this time the bombs were falling, so the Sergeant was struggling to make himself heard.

"When this lot is over I want two of you back in Empress Road and you're to go into the house next door to the Littlejohn family. Go up into the loft and inspect the whole place. Look for any sign of contraband that could have been stored there."

"You think they're using that one to throw us off the scent sergeant?" PC Offenbright asked.

"Yes I do constable. Why else would they have built that dividing wall? I want that loft next door to number 94 Empress Road gone over with a bloody sight more than just a fine tooth comb."

In the Anderson shelter in his back garden Albert was talking to his wife and daughter.

"Well done both of you tonight. Maggie that make-up job was beautiful and it really made your mum look as though she was at deaths door."

"Thanks dad, I like doing it. Mum is great, sitting so still while it all goes on, and ain't she good when the coppers come bursting in? Blimey if I didn't know better I would think she was dying as well."

"Yes Albert your daughter is a very talented girl, and once this bloody war is over, I'm going to talk to Gerry Ramshot about her," said Ida.

"Who the bleeding hell is he?" Albert demanded.

"He's an old friend of mine from school days and he now works at the Grand Theater, you know the one down by the Hants and Dorset bus station, near the fountain in front of the rose gardens and the Civic Centre. He's a make-up artist to the stars who perform there and he knows a lot of them very well indeed. I think he'll take our Maggie on as an apprentice. If he does and she sticks at it well a bloody good life is in front of her I can tell you. Good God that was too close for sodding comfort."

A bomb had landed very close and shook the ground under the Anderson Shelter which set the whole structure shaking. Maggie screamed in fear and Ida was also very frightened indeed.

"Hold on for Christ's sake," Albert shouted. "We're alright I think, that one must have landed out in Bevois valley. Now get hold of yourselves. The Germans still haven't managed to hurt any of us. I just hope it hasn't hit the Portswood Hotel that's all."

More and more bombs fell that night and the Littlejohn family sat through it all, the children with their auntie's family in Dukes Road, and their parents and eldest in their garden in Empress Road. Under the Road bridge leading from Dukes Road into Adelaide Road Alan Kinslade was holding onto his younger brothers and quietly singing to them as explosions and fire from the incendiaries erupted all around them. He knew that the targets for these were the railway line and the Marshalling yard, as well as Northam Bridge. The people of Southampton endured it as they did almost every night and simply waited for the all clear to sound.

The raid did lesson in intensity and they could finally manage to have a proper conversation. Albert was talking to his daughter.

"Now I know you don't like the bloody coppers Maggie, especially when they're making a mess of our house. But you must curb your temper. If you threaten them, much less clout them with a bloody broom stick, they will arrest you and bring a very serious charge against you. This is war my love and they ain't got no patience for anything like that. So shout all you want, but please don't hit the bleeders."

This broke a lot of the tension and all three of them burst out laughing. Ida did admit she was getting a bit fed up with the way things were going.

"I don't mind the make-up going on and having to act as though I'm really ill, but lying on top of all them bloody bottles and the other things you lot stuff inside our mattress is no joke I can tell you. It's not like I can grab a drink myself is it. When is it going to stop Albert?"

"Very soon my love," Albert reassured her. "Harry Pinshoe is ready to finish the underground storage space in the old shed in our garden. He's a genius at it and I have the greatest confidence in him. He's even going to make sure the shed don't fall down by strengthening it from the inside. But outside it will still look completely ramshackle. The beauty of that love is that you and our girls can serve the neighbours with food and stuff that they can't get anywhere else from inside the shed."

The all clear finally sounded and Albert set off out. He first went up to the top of Dukes Road and was relieved to find the Portswood Hotel still there, completely undamaged. But further down Bevois valley two houses and one shop had been hit and the damage was horrible to behold. He collected his three younger daughters and sons from his sister's house and was told they had come through the air raid alright.

"They was scared of course but they're little fighters all of them."

He looked down at the sleeping form of his youngest son Thomas and his sister was full of praise. "And this little one, slept right through it he did, just like his dad see."

Now, sitting in the bar of the Portswood Hotel with George Harcourt, he was in earnest conversation over gang matters.

"We'll need to be downstairs soon George because our boys will have been busy during the air raid. A lot of stuff should be coming through the railway yard up to the secret rom."

"Some of it already has Al," George told him, "but we have had a bit of trouble."

"Trouble, what sort of trouble?" Albert demanded, "have any of our boys been caught?"

"No they ain't but there was a problem at the old warehouse in Empress Road tonight."

Albert sighed. "Alright tell me about it George, what the bleeding hell happened there?"

"Well you know what the plan was Al. Young Billy Marshall was going in through the back of the warehouse through that tunnel in the back wall, then he would get his hands on anything that we can use and pass it out. Well, it started alright. Billy got in there without any trouble at all. We've got fags as well as butter, lard, tins of dried eggs, milk, ham and luncheon meat, even some parachute silk, and would you believe it a bag full of knicker elastic. Well it was going too good I suppose because our boys stopped watching for trouble and just went on putting all of the stuff into the sacks they had with them.

Then we got done by bleeding Home Guard shining their torches at us when the air raid was over, accusing us of looting. Said our crime was against the very nature of the country and we was taking food out of other people's mouths. I didn't even have time to get my cosh out, they was gunna unmask our boys but young Billy saved us. Whacked one guy over the head and grabbed his rifle then pointed it at the other old boy. Pat Matthews hit him with a straight right to the jaw. Left both of them unconscious in their long johns and we now have two uniforms."

"And the rifles?" Albert enquired, "What about them, did we take those as well?"

"We thought about that but decided it's too bloody risky. The coppers would be out in force if weapons were stolen from the Home Guard. So they left those with the two old boys."

"Good, that was the right thing to do, where are they now are they here?"

"All down in the secret room Al and they've been told to wait there until you arrive because I knew you'd want to talk to them."

Albert thought to himself for a few minutes.

"You know George, taking them uniforms was a smart thing to do because we won't sell them on. We can use the bloody things ourselves. Two of our boys can wear them can't they, so no-one will question them when they're out at night?"

Georges considered this new development.

"Yeah that's right, why the bloody hell didn't I think of that? No-one's going to challenge a Home Guard soldier are they? But they all carry rifles Al, and we didn't take the ones from the old boys our lads knocked out. They only took the uniforms. So where are we gonna get rifles for our boys to carry?"

"Have you seen the toy guns that some young nippers play cowboys and Indians with?" Albert asked with a smile now lighting up his face. "Very realistic some of them are, and in the dark whose going to know they aren't the real thing. Most boys have pistols with caps of course, but a lot of them like to be the same as their cowboy heroes so they carry rifles as well."

"I like this idea Al, but where are we gonna get these toy guns? Your two nippers, well three now with the new one, ain't old enough to be playing with guns yet are they?"

"No, you're right there George," Albert agreed, "but remember we now have a whole lot of lads of various ages working for us as lookouts, and I'm sure some of them will be able to supply us with what we need. I'll speak with them as soon as I can."

Suddenly all hell was let loose. Some of the gang came running up from the cellar over to the table where Albert and George were sitting. Pat Matthews sat down to catch his breath.

"We've just had a message from a lad called Alan Kinslade. He arrived at the side door of the pub and Bernard went and answered his loud knock. He's told us more Home Guard soldiers and the cops are heading here and they look as though

196

they mean business. They were all hiding in the Marshalling yard, but they saw a lot of activity coming from the direction of Northam Bridge. He got a coded message from the group down there, from his opposite number, a boy called Johnnie Burton.

One of his boys was in the water, swimming up the river against the current. He could have sprinted it I guess but they was worried about getting spotted if they came up alongside the railway track. And those kids love the water see. But the boy delivered his message alright and it don't sound bloody good."

"Where is Alan Kinslade now? Albert demanded, "Is he in the secret room as well?"

"No he just brought the boy who had swum up from Northam and then went back. I think they're going to set up as decoys when the coppers and soldiers get here. I just hope they all know what they're bloody doing that's all."

"We need to keep a sharp look out tonight because we know there's been a wave of crime during and after the last air-raid," Di Stapleton said to his men as they prepared to set out for the raid on the Marshalling yards at Bevois Park, and the surrounding areas, including St Deny's railway station.

"We know robberies have taken place, and one of these was at the food warehouse in Empress Road. Two Home Guard soldiers were knocked out when they caught a gang of men stealing from there. They were left tied up in their underwear so we know that two uniforms have been taken and what they will be used for I have no doubt we will soon find out. Sergeant Podcove will now fill you all in on what we know so far and what he and his men have been busy doing this evening, Sergeant," he said, turning to him.

"Thank you Sir," he said as he turned to face the room. "Me and my men turned over the house of Albert Littlejohn who lives, as no doubt all of you know, in Empress road. We found nothing at all that would incriminate him, which means he's got a scheme to keep ahead of us and it's very frustrating I can assure you."

"Have we got anything to go on about where his information is coming from Sergeant?" a young DC asked. "I mean if you didn't find anything at all he must have had time to hide his stolen goods mustn't he?"

He got a very searching look from Sergeant Podcove and for a few moments thought he had said something wrong.

"What's your name Son. You haven't been with us very long have you?"

"No sergeant I've just been promoted to CID. My name is DC Arrowsmith."

"Well DC Arrowsmith, well done lad, you've worked that out alright, yes," he went on, once more addressing the whole room. "This young DC has got it right. We are looking into the fact that someone is tipping Littlejohn off about when and where we are going to raid him. We don't know who this is yet, but one thing we do know is that Littlejohn's lot are up to their necks in the crime that takes place in this town, and we are going to nail the bastard before long."

After the briefing was dismissed DI Stapleton met with Sergeant Podcove in his office and asked for the results of the latest raid on the Littlejohn house.

"Clean as a bloody whistle again guv, though I didn't get as far with the search as I would have liked," the sergeant gloomily responded. "Nothing in that sodding house that didn't have a right to be there, and the daughter, Maggie her name is, gave us a right hard time and even went for us with a broom when we wanted to search her parent's bedroom thoroughly."

The DI picked up on this at once and wanted more details. "Why did she do that? he demanded. "What possible reason could a young girl have for attacking the police when they have a legal right to carry out a search. When did this attack happen, downstairs or in the bedroom?"

"She shouted at us downstairs because we made a mess in the kitchen. Well, we get that sort of thing all the time don't we, so I just warned her to keep her mouth shut and get out of our way and left it at that, but upstairs when we started on the main bedroom the girl went berserk and that's when she picked up the bloody broom."

"Yes, but why sergeant? What provoked her into an action like that?"

"She was saying that her mum was ill and we should leave her in peace. I said we had a duty to search but I must say Sir, Mrs. Littlejohn did look very ill and we couldn't really disturb her. But I was going to arrest that girl for attacking us in the manner that she did but Littlejohn himself came charging in demanding we leave both his wife and daughter alone. I would have arrested him if he caused us any trouble but the siren went and we all had to run for shelter."

"You did search the attic of course?"

"Yes sir we certainly did, and found that the Littlejohn attic has a new wall built between their house and the one next door. That's suspicious enough in itself, though we didn't find anything at all up there, in either one. I sent two of my men to search that attic once the raid was over but apart from the usual junk you find in places like that they found nothing out of the ordinary."

The DI was silent for some minutes after this and just stood looking out of his office window.

"Because Mrs. Littlejohn was so ill you didn't actually check the bed she was lying in?"

"No Sir.I was going to, she is always in that bed when we raid but it's like I say, she was so ill looking this time and groaning something chronic. To start pulling the bed apart, well it would have been a terrible thing to do."

"Ida Littlejohn," said Inspector Stapleton quietly. "I knew her a few years ago and she was something of an actress then. Not exactly Greta Garbo or Bette Davis of course. Nothing big time but she did appear in amateur productions and had a good reputation. Playing the part of a lady who is at deaths door would be a walk over for her. Next time we enter that house I will be there and we will pull that bloody bed apart because I believe it was stuffed full of contraband."

As they approached Northam Bridge the whole police contingent were primed for the search ahead. Extra Home Guard soldiers had been brought in to help and a police launch was standing by to ferry them up the river, and stop any other boats that might be out on the water in order to search them.

The orders were to keep watch on the Plaza cinema, to see if anyone tried to take to the water from there, as well as all roads leading to this part of Northam. Satisfying himself that his men were in place the DI and his sergeant went aboard the police launch. Speaking to the inspector in charge of the boat he asked if anything had moved out on the water so far this evening.

"Not a thing sir, even if a duck had been out there we would have seen it. There's a boat moored over by the side of the Plaza but we've had a look at that and it's clean."

What the river police had not seen, however, was the very small head of a young lad as he swam up to the other end to report what was going on at Northam. Little Tommy Maynard was one of only two boys who owned a pair of swimming trunks and he was battling the strong current of the River Itchen.

Exhausted when he finally made it, he was pulled from the water by Alan Kinslade and his two brothers. They asked what the situation was further down the river.

"The rozzers are everywhere now it's even worse than we thought earlier. Johnnie Burton said to get a message about it to Mr. Littlejohn. He needs to know what he's got to do about it see."

"Alright nipper, wait here with my brothers while I run up to the pub and find out."

Alan ran off immediately and was soon pounding on the side door of the Portswood hotel for the second time that night.

Catherine Bumstock opened it and looked at the boy standing there bedraggled in his wet trousers, socks and shoes.

"Please missus I need to speak to Mr. Littlejohn quick."

Just then the man himself appeared and the landlady, with a last look at the lad, went back into the bar. Alan quickly gave Albert the message from Johnnie Burton and asked what they should all do now the police were everywhere.

"Keep out of sight and get a message back here if anything gets out of hand. And tell my men they must ignore old Percy Winkleman tonight. Get one of the boys over there to tell the old man just to unload his cartful of metal and then head for home. He's to keep whatever he's carrying for us and store it at his house tonight. Then tell my men to use the boat to simply come up the river, have you got all that?"

"Yes Sir," Alan said and made to run back to the bridge, but Albert stopped him.

"Get that message to the boy who swam up and send him back again then get back here as fast as you can."

Racing back Alan was soon with his equally wet brothers and the boy from the Northam end. Giving him Albert's message Alan asked if the boy would be alright swimming back.

"Course I will, I go with the current in that direction, piece of cake it is." With that he splashed back into the water and was soon out of sight.

Alan spoke to his brothers, telling them to wait here for him as he once more raced back to the pub. Here he was told to use all the boys he could muster and make a right nuisance of themselves in the marshaling yard.

"There are extra men on guard in there tonight and they're all on the lookout for trouble. So be careful. Just let them hear you moving about but don't get caught if you can help it. Have them run around chasing shadows if you can alright?"

He was met with a big grin from Alan. "This is what we're waiting for Mr. Littlejohn. We can make a noise then vanish into

201

places them old soldiers won't even know about. Don't worry, we're all up for this."

As he dashed off George Harcourt joined Albert. "He sounds cocky enough to pull this off but what if any of them do get caught?"

"I don't think there's anything to worry too much about in that direction George, after all they're only kids and they'll be treated like that won't they. All that will happen is they get a telling off for being in the yard and sent home with a clip round the ear or being put across the knee of one of the soldiers and getting their backsides tanned. Every one of them will simply laugh that off and be back here again tomorrow to do it all over again."

At that precise moment Percy Winkleman turned up and so did Albert's boys who, with the police watching intently, made their way to the boat. DI Stapleton whispered to sergeant Podcove.

"Now we've got them, let's just see what they put into that boat then see if they can explain their way out of this. I think we'll be feeling some collars tonight."

Chapter Thirteen

Pat Matthews and Lenny Warren were leading the rest of their men on the way to the boat to meet up with old Percy Winlkeman as usual. Suddenly a young lad who had been lurking in the darkness stepped out in front of them.

"Hello I'm Johnnie Burton and I've got an urgent message for you from Mr. Littlejohn".

"Johnnie Burton?" said Pat. "Are you Phil Burton's boy?"

"Yeah and now I'm working for Mr. Littlejohn, just like my dad did before he got killed."

"Alright son we're all sorry about that, we knew your dad well and liked him. So what have you got to tell me?"

"There's a big police and Home Guard raid on in this area tonight so I'm going to meet old Mr. Winkleman and tell him to keep the things he usually passes to you. He's to unload all the metal stuff as usual and then turn for home. You should get in the boat and set off upstream. But there's a police launch watching and they'll stop you. Mr. Littlejohn wants you to say that you always go home this way because it's quicker and safer than the roads, especially when there's a raid on."

"Ok Johnnie we'll do that, and thanks for the warning."

Pat stood and watched as the young boy ran off, simply melting away into the darkness.

"Look at that," he said to Lenny Warren. "One minute he was there and now he's gone. This black-out really is useful to us ain't it?"

Johnnie knew he had to intercept Percy before he took the little road that led down to the river bank, but first tore across Northam Bridge. Three of his boys were stationed along its length, clinging to the outside of the bridges parapet so as to be out of sight of everyone else crossing it.

Johnnie stopped and spoke to each of them in turn.

"Any sign of them yet?"

"Loads of bleeding bobbies Johnnie," one of them piped up, "but I got one of them with my catapult, hit him right good and proper on the head I did."

Johnnie was instantly alarmed.

"You daft sod, what happened? Did they see you?"

"Na course they didn't. Had a good look and did a lot of shouting but I was down, nearly in the water, and in this dark they never had a chance of seeing me did they?"

"Alright you cheeky blighter," Johnnie scolded him. "Get back across the bridge and meet up with the others and this time I want you in the water properly, all of you."

Reaching the last of his boys on the far side of the bridge he gave him the same instructions then sprinted back across ahead of them and down the steps to the side road. He was just in the nick of time as he could make out the familiar sound of echoing hooves.

Johnnie stationed himself in the road so as to give himself a good chance of stopping Percy Winkleman. It very nearly went wrong because Percy didn't see the boy standing in his path but Major certainly did. The old horse reared up and snorted in fear and Percy had a devil of a job bringing him back under control.

He glared at Johnnie.

"What the bleedin' hell do you think you're doing boy, standing in the road like that. You scared my horse and he could have killed you. I've a good mind to take your trousers down and lay my belt across the back of your arse."

"I'm sorry Mr. Winkleman but I had to stop you. There are a load of coppers here tonight and Mr. Littlejohn says for you to just turn around and go home. Keep his stuff in your cart and he'll make arrangements to get it from you tomorrow."

"Well that's alright then I suppose," the old man replied, "but don't you ever stand in front of a horse like that again."

With this he shook up the reins and shouted,

"On Major, come on then early finish tonight, let's get you home for your oats."

As the horse and cart disappeared into the darkness Johnnie ran back and called his boys together. Up at the Bevois Valley end by the road bridge Alan Kinslade was giving an earnest pep talk to his troops, where tonight he would be ably assisted by Denis Frampton, Ollie Wimpson and Trevor Harvey.

"Right you lot we want everyone in that marshalling yard. It's really dark cause there ain't no moon tonight, so we can lose ourselves in there. My brothers and me know our way around so keep us in sight and dodge when any of them Home Guard blokes or coppers get too close. We have to distract them so they won't go anywhere near the Portswood Hotel, at least not the back of it. That's our job see, to protect that pub and make sure the secret room ain't found."

Johnnie and his lads gazed through the darkness and could just about make out the Littlejohn men as they made their way to the small boat they used to carry them up the river to the road bridge. But this evening it was being done without any cargo.

The inspector on the Police launch whispered to DI Stapleton.

"This lot look as though they're up to no good. We'll let them get out onto the water then race out and stop them. A search of that boat should prove very interesting indeed."

They watched as Pat Matthews and the rest boarded the boat and pushed off. Once free of the bank they started the motor and began the slow journey up the river.

"Just a little bit further then we'll have them," said the launch inspector, "What he bloody hell is all that noise?"

A search light was swung round and quickly picked out all of the boys under Johnnie Burton's direction, gleefully jumping fully clothed into the water. Heads were bobbing around all over the place and the police knew they had to put a stop to this right away. A loud hailer was soon in use.

"This is the police, what do you boys think you're doing? You know swimming here is not allowed, all of you should be home and in bed by now. Get out of the water at once or the whole lot of you will be taken to the police station and severely dealt with.

Johnnie wasn't going to be deterred by this.

"Ok, let's give them a bit of cheek before we get out the water and scatter. Mr. Littlejohn's men are out in the middle of the river now so we need to give them time to make it up to Bevois."

"Yeah you'll have to catch us first," they taunted the police boat with much merriment. As the launch began to bear down on them they swam to the bank and got out of the water as quickly as they could, all making a fine sight as they ran off in different directions with their clothes soaking wet.

Turning the launch the inspector shouted out in frustration. "Forget the kids we'll never find them now. Let's get after that boat, if there's anything hidden we want to see it."

With its engines roaring the launch raced upstream and came to a halt at the bank, just as the Littlejohn men arrived. As they started to get out they found themselves surrounded by police.

"Stay where you are this is a police stop and we want to see what you've got in that boat of yours."

Pat Mathews answered. "We've no objection to you looking into our boat, but what you think you're going to find I don't

206

bloody know, this is just a small motor launch that's seen better days, but please help yourselves."

The police did just that and looked into every nook and cranny of the small boat. But Albert had so drummed into them the importance of removing everything when unloading that their boat was clean and passed the inspection with flying colours.

DI Stapleton watched all this with growing frustration.

"So why are you men out in this boat tonight, it's pitch dark and you could be in a collision with any other craft that happens to be out there."

Lenny Warren answered this time.

"Look, we're all dockers and we've just worked through another bloody raid. We're tired out and want to get home as quick as we can. So this is the fastest way for us to get up the river to our homes."

The DI was in two minds on how to handle this. He knew of course another raid had just occurred and Southampton had been badly hit again, which meant the docks had certainly suffered more bomb damage. The men who worked there had to face this danger all the time, which made them heroes in many respects.

But his natural instincts were also telling him these men were crooks and he didn't believe a word of what he had just been told. But he couldn't disprove it either so with anger rising he had to concede.

"I think you're all up to your necks in crime and black market activities and I'm going to catch you with some gear soon. But right now just get out of my sight."

As they trudged off into Dukes road, on their way to the Portswood Hotel, the DI turned to his sergeant. "Guilty as sin the lot of them and we can't prove it can we? Right then, somewhere in that marshalling yard there must be a place where they store their stolen goods. So let's get organised."

They made the short journey up to the shunter's hut and met with the Home Guard soldiers who were equally as determined it seemed.

"Somewhere in here there's a stash of contraband and I want it found. Take the yard apart, move anything that will move, get into places you haven't even tried to look into before. But get me some results.

Just then a small rock hit the side of the hut and the DI shouted "What the bloody hell was that?"

"Intruders sir, I know they come here a lot but we've yet to get our hands on them or even find out who they are. But they've never done anything like this before," said the Lance Corporal in charge tonight.

Suddenly a hail of more small stones began flying through the air towards them.

"This looks like the work of more kids," DI Stapleton yelled as another stone just missed his head. "Probably the same ones, spread out and round the little sods up. We'll tan their hides before we send them home."

"But why are they doing this sir"? asked Sergeant Podcove. "This doesn't make sense, boys in the water with all their clothes on, now this over here. What is going on?"

All eyes were now on the DI, as well as dodging the stones that were coming at them. He thought for just a moment.

"It's a diversion isn't it? Why were those boys in the water at this time of night. They do it during daytime, though they shouldn't because of the strong current at this point in the river. Now we've got more kids diverting our attention in this marshaling yard. Right, round every one of them up. I want some answers and those nippers are going to give them to me."

Alan Kinslade was hiding with his brothers beside him and all of them were busy with their catapults. In between firing stones at the police he instructed Dennis Frampton and Ollie Wimpson.

"Take your lot and evacuate into the yard. There are small places we can get into that grown- ups cant. Hide under the trucks, not inside them cause that's where they'll look. Be careful though and make sure none of you are caught. Have your smaller kids watch my two brothers, they'll show them how to get right up behind the axles of the trucks. Because of their small size they can get higher than the axles themselves so they can't get hurt even if the truck gets moved. Just make sure they hold on tight and don't make a sound."

Dennis and Ollie selected three of their smaller boys each to go with Barry Kinslade, who was eleven years old and his younger brother Michael who was eight. They quickly found their way to the lines of empty trucks that were standing quietly waiting for the next day where they would be coupled to a steam engine and taken to various locations to be loaded with all sorts of goods. Barry, as the oldest, took charge of this small group once they reached the side of these big trucks.

"Make sure you let these old blokes know you're here by making a noise see, then duck under the trucks quick. Watch what my brother Michael does once he's underneath then all of you can try it."

With that the youngest of the Kinslade brothers ducked beneath a truck and squirmed his way onto the axle. Reaching up from there he managed to push one of the floor boards of the truck so he had a hand hold. Once this was done he pulled himself clear of the axle, and even though the watching boys knew he was there, none of them could see him. A practice session then took place for the others who were new to this, so they could manage to do it.

This took a little time and a few cuts and bruises, but soon all eight boys had the ability to become completely invisible. Now Barry Kinslade got them down again.

"Right lads let's let the old buggers know we're here."

A volley of small stones then went flying through the air with precision and hit the police and the Home Guard soldiers.

"Catch these bloody little trespassers," the DI shouted.

There was a whole load of activity as the police and Home Guard looked under and inside all the trucks as well as any places where rubbish and discarded sleepers were piled up. But not one boy was found as even the older ones who were with Alan Kinslade didn't give their position away.

Not until the searching soldiers and police had reached the blocks at the end of the railway lines, just inside the fence that separated the yard from Empress Road, was the search called off. Alan Kinslade had already whistled the signal for everyone to withdraw so the yard was empty and DI Stapleton was not a happy man.

He glared at both the Lance Corporal and his own Sergeant and shouted.

"Nothing, that's what you're telling me? Bloody nothing. You've torn this place apart and not even caught the nippers who were taking the piss out of you."

He spread out his hands. "Look at these, go on have a damn good look, what do you see?"

All he got was a whole set of confused looks so he told them what it meant in no uncertain terms.

"They're bloody empty aren't they? That's the result of tonight's raids, sod all. Well it's not good enough and I won't have it."

Dismissing the Home Guard soldiers and the police launch he went out into Dukes Road with his sergeant and soon pushed open the door of the public bar of the Portswood hotel.

He glared across the room and quickly spotted Albert Littlejohn and his boys sitting at their usual table. Striding over he addressed Albert.

"Alright Littlejohn, we know you and this bloody lot are up to your necks in the crime wave that Southampton's having to put up with at the moment. It's not just the Germans that are making life hard for everyone here is it? Well your days are numbered mister, believe that because I won't stop hounding you, and I will have the cuffs on you eventually."

Albert looked steadily back at this angry policeman before responding politely.

"Good evening inspector, can I get you and your sergeant here a drink?"

"No you can't, I wouldn't drink with low life like you. Keep your bloody drinks. Next time you see me it will be inside a police cell and it's you who will be facing charges. You will be sent to prison where you belong for a great many years."

With that the two police officers stormed out of the pub.

"Well that was all very polite wasn't it?" said Albert. "It's a bloody good job neither of them coppers looked under the table."

A chorus of laughter greeted this statement because concealed under the table were several cuts of prime lamb that Pat Matthews and Lenny Warren, along with the rest of their group, had smuggled under their clothes even when they were being quizzed by the police.

Albert enquired about this and how it had been done. Pat Matthews took the lead here."

"You was right boss, it is the King Brothers who run this meat racket inside the docks. Four of them there are, and they're known simply as the Kingers. They work with bandy legs Sid Smugeley and between them they gets away with meat for all of their families every week. And a nice little racket it is too. They don't touch a bloody thing all week but on Fridays they grab a whole lamb carcass and take it behind the sheds.

There, bandy leg Sid cuts it up. He used to be a butcher so he knows how to do it. Then the Kingers as well as bandy put the cuts of the meat inside their clothes. They wear coats just like these ones they gave to us. The meat hangs down inside it but can't be seen from outside. They then put a whole leg of lamb into one of their bags see.

Once they get to the dock gate the one whose got that is first to reach the gate house. The guard, old Steve Westerbrook, says he needs to see inside the bag. Well of course, as soon as he opens it he sees the leg of lamb inside so he says he's going to have to confiscate it but let's all the others go through.

Everyone's happy see, they gets their families Sunday joints and the old guard gets his leg of lamb as well. It's worked a treat for a long time and now we're in on it as well."

"Good, but what do we need to give the Kingers and bandy legs Smugeley in return for this?"

"Fags and the odd bottle of spirits boss, give them that and they'll be quite happy."

"Hmm yes but we'll give them something for their wives and daughters as well I think," said Albert. "Let's keep them sweet boys."

Bernard the landlord came to the table to report that two boys were here to see him and one of them was soaking wet. Going to the side door Albert saw both Johnnie Burton, who was indeed standing in soaking wet clothes, and the grinning Alan Kinslade. He spoke to Johnnie first.

"Your mum isn't going to be very happy when she sees you is she?"

"It's ok Mr. Littlejohn I'll tell her I had to dive in the water to avoid the bombs cause I couldn't get into a shelter in time."

"Well that's crafty enough, ok," Albert mused. "Right boys I want a full report from you both about tonight's activities. I know everything worked out as we wanted it to and nothing was found by the law. I'm pleased with you both and want you to keep up the things you did tonight for at least another two weeks. That way the law and the ARP wardens, as well as the Home Guard, will think you're just a bunch of troublesome kids who are out causing mischief every night. They'll try to grab you so be very careful. Now I need to speak to the boy who leads his group from Belgrave Road, what's his name again?"

"Trevor Harvey sir, and he's here now."

212

Johnnie stood aside so Albert could see Trevor standing a little way back in the darkness.

"Oh I didn't see you there, come closer son so I can talk to you properly."

Trevor shuffled forward, his clothes also wet and making a slushing sound as he moved.

"You and your lads all live in and around Belgrave Road lad, that's right isn't it?"

"Yes sir."

"How much do you know about the Swaythling boys and, more importantly to us, their dads?"

A grin now spread across the face of Trevor Harvey.

"As I've said before sir we know them very well and we've had lots of fights with them. They're led by the Griffin boys whose dads are in the Swaythling gang. Crap they are at fighting and we lick them every time we meet."

Albert was unable to hide a smile at this.

"That's great Trevor but what I want from you and your boys now is Information about that senior Swaythling gang. I know they will soon try to attack us and take over our end of town. Like you we can lick them in a fair fight, but not if they jump us when we least expect it. Now how will you go about a job like that?"

Trevor didn't even hesitate.

"Mr. Littlejohn, that's easy, me and my boys can use the railway to keep a watch on High Road and anyone coming there from the flower roads. We can go right up to the bridge over Woodmill Lane and even on up to Swaythling station."

"I don't like the sound of that lad. I don't want any of you run down by trains. It's very dangerous being anywhere near a railway line."

"It's ok sir we know the dangers and we don't actually walk on the line. There's plenty of room to walk beside the tracks so even if a train does come it goes right on past us. When we cross the line to go to our favourite swimming place over the other

213

side we make sure there ain't nothing coming from either direction before we cross."

"Well make sure you do and if you see any of that mob coming in this direction get a runner started to reach us here as quickly as you can."

"That's easy and all, we'll have contacts with Alan here from Adelaide Road as well as Dennis Frampton's Priory Road lot, and Ollie Wimpson's Kent Road boys. Between us we'll make sure you know when any trouble is going to happen from Swaythling. And if they tries to come down the river me and my boys will be watching from over the railway line at our swimming place. We can see right up to Woodmill from that bank and if we sees a boat with any of the Swaythling men in it we'll launch our raft blooming quick and get down to you before they does."

Albert was even more impressed with this network of young lads he had created.

"Alright that's great and Alan there's work for your lot as well."

Bringing out a drawing he gave this to him and explained. "This is a very good picture of a man who is coming here to join up with us. He and his men come from Bournemouth and he's been told to come to the Plaza cinema. He's due there tomorrow night so when you or any of your boys spot him, you and you alone are to approach him.

He is a very dangerous man Alan so let him know who you are straight away, tell him you have a message from me and then give him this. That's all I want you to do as far as he is concerned. Then keep up your swimming and things because the law is likely to be watching for this, so have you got that straight? It's very important lad because it's your safety I am concerned about."

"I'll be ok Mr. Littlejohn and my boys and I will do a good job for you again, leave this to us sir we won't let you down."

"No I'm sure you won't, now have you got something you all want to give to me?"

He was met with three grinning faces and all of them had a sheet of paper. On these were the names of all the boys who had been involved in the night's activities and Albert scanned it.

"That's a lot of you isn't it, but you all did what you were asked. I will now give this to our banker Ginger Strangemore. He will meet all five leaders and give you payment both for yourselves and the rest of your lads. Well done tonight all of you. Now get off home, and you two get out of those wet clothes."

He could hear them still laughing as they walked off and the darkness swallowed them up. He thought back nostalgically to his own childhood when he and his friends did exactly the same thing and also got lectured about getting wet.

In Bournemouth a meeting was taking place between Salty Sam and Leroy Wort. They were in Wort's flat and the atmosphere was not good.

"So when are you going to Southampton and how many of your boys are you taking with you?" Wort asked.

Salty Sam took his time answering this. Although he knew Leroy very well indeed he still didn't really trust him. His reputation stood for all who knew him to see, and the murder on the funicular railway was still very much in the minds of the entire Bournemouth criminal fraternity. None of them were squeamish about murder and most had committed it on more than one occasion. But the horror of that particular one said all that was needed about the man who had carried it out. Eventually though Salty Sam broke the silence.

"I'm taking five with me and the ones who I'll rely on the most will be Pat Morello and Davie Silver."

"Yes of course you've told me that already ain't you and I think it's a good choice. They're the best we've got down here running the protection racket so will you have them doing that in Southampton?"

"That's the idea, because as organised as the Littlejohn gang are, none of them work that particular racket, so we'll do it for them and split the proceeds."

"Hmm, we'll make sure we get more than our share because it's your boys who will be doing what is necessary in that line," said Leroy. "Get yourselves sorted out up there then let me know. I'll come and meet you and Littlejohn in that pub again, the Horse and Groom in East Street. You know the one with those stuffed bears in the bar. Make sure you and Littlejohn as well as George Harcourt are there to meet with me."

Giving one of his evil smiles Salty Sam answered him. "Yeah ok Leroy and I'll have Pat Morello with me as well. By that time he'll have had a good look around what's left of the shops and pubs in Southampton so he'll be able to tell us all how he's going to work the protection racket."

"Good and I want no interference from the Littlejohn gang with this, other than to add some muscle when Morello and Silver need it. Make sure they know this is our racket, all they are doing is assisting us."

Salty Sam had already been thinking this through. "Littlejohn himself is going to get us work in Southampton docks with them. It won't be any trouble because we know a bit about the way stevedores work. And with so many men being killed in the raids more men are always needed to get the ships unloaded. So Pat and his boys can get to work in the small café called the Tall Funnel. Always packed it is so the woman who runs it must be making a packet. Well not for much longer she ain't because we will take our share of the profits or else that little place will go up in flames and it won't be caused by no German bomb."

"I like the sound of that but what about pubs, are there any still in business round the dock areas?"

"We've looked up five pubs in that part of the town and the two oldest are the Duke Of Wellington in Bugle Street and the Red Lion at the bottom end of the High Street. Then there's the Lord Louis Mountbatton. We'll certainly target them. But we want the ones the dockers use the most and they are, The Grapes in Oxford street and at the Town Quay is the best known pub in that area, the Platform Tavern. A lot of very tough men use those pubs but Pat and Davie have ways of making even the toughest see sense when it comes to their health."

"I'm quite sure they do" Leroy mused. "So when are you all going to get to Southampton?"

"We go tomorrow. I don't know what arrangements Littlejohn has made for our accommodation but we have a meeting set up with him and some of his gang for tomorrow night. It's by a cinema called the Plaza and that's by the side of the River Itchen at one end of a bridge, Northam I think it is. It's all going according to plan at the moment Leroy so I don't expect any sort of trouble."

Bright and early the next morning old Percy Winkleman was surprised by a loud banging on the door of his small bungalow and this brought him rapidly out of the deep sleep he had been enjoying. Sitting up in bed and rubbing his eyes he couldn't work out who the bloody hell could be knocking him up at this time. He got out of bed, opened his window, then leaned out and shouted.

"I don't know who you are but I ain't up yet so piss off and let me get back to bed."

"It's me Percy, Albert Littlejohn, so come on. Open up and let us in. We ain't got much time because we need to be at work soon."

As the cogs in his brain began comprehending this message he realized who his early visitor was and, more importantly, why he was here.

"Oh sorry Albert, wait a bit and I'll let you in."

Then, dragging on his old and tattered trousers, he stumbled to his front door and threw it open. Standing on his doorstep were Albert, George Harcourt and Pat Mathews. These three came swiftly inside the bungalow and wrinkled their noses at the smell that hit them. Percy wasn't the cleanest of people and his home certainly reflected that. They therefore turned down the offer of a cup of tea.

Albert was keen to get started.

"We've managed to borrow the lorry that's outside Percy so we need what's in your cart that we couldn't take from you last night."

"Oh yes of course Albert, that nipper you sent to warn me off nearly spoiled everything. Stood in the middle of the bloody road and nearly gave poor old Major and me heart attacks. Threatened to tan his backside for him I did."

All three men smirked at this but Albert defused the situation.

"Be fair Percy that was Phil Burton's boy Johnnie and he was acting under orders from me. It was vital that he stopped you before you got under the bridge because it was crawling with bloody coppers there and they were checking everything and everyone who came anywhere near. We didn't want you being seen down there otherwise they would be suspicious of you too.

Young Johnnies method of stopping you may have been a bit extreme but he actually did a very good job last night so he didn't really deserve a tanned backside. Now Percy let's get started shall we and get our stuff out of that cart of yours."

Chapter Fourteen

Percy led the way out to the stable in his big yard. Major was taking no notice whatsoever of this interruption to his normal morning routine. He was eating from his hay net and was very content to do so. Percy spoke strongly to him.

"Get out of the way Major, can't you see these men need to get to my cart."

Albert and the rest were amused to note the old horse still took no notice but simply went on eating his hay, and the oats he was always given as well. Pushing on past him they came to the cart which looked empty now, but Percy quickly pulled open the secret hiding place beneath the floor and revealed what was stored there.

"That's all the booze what you had in that big house Albert," he said, "but there's a lot of stuff here your men have found."

This was very true and as the unloading took place Albert watched keenly to see just what they had got for him. Underneath the floor of that cart were the proceeds of burglaries from other houses in Highfield Lane. He saw at once that the previous nights activities by members of the Littlejohn gang had produced wonderful results. There were at least five fur coats, jewelry and a big haul of watches. Some of these were cheap imitations but others were high class, expensive ones that would fetch a very good price when they were offered for onward sale.

"Right, get this lot boxed up and out into the back of the lorry, we need to be on our way as quickly as we can."

George and Pat went out to attend to this whilst Albert stayed with Percy.

"Thanks for this old man," he said, pushing a bottle of fine malt whiskey into his hands. "This is for you because you did just what I needed last night. Keep a good look out tonight though in case the bloody law is about. Oh and watch for any lads who may need to flag you down."

Percy could see the funny side of it now and grinned. "Thanks Albert, I'll enjoy this, and don't worry. Me and old Major will be watching all the way when we comes in sight of Northam Bridge tonight."

Now in the lorry George wanted to know exactly how they were going to work this next bit.

"It's daylight after all, so we ain't got no cover for what we're carrying into the Portswood Hotel have we? We'd best go round to the road bridge at the bottom of Dukes Road and get through the fence there with this lot."

"For Christ's sake George think about it will you. Yes, it's daylight and that marshalling yard is busy with bloody shunting and coupling up the freight trains. There are shunters working in there and all sorts of eyes can see what's going on. We'd stand out like a bloody sore thumb. No, we'll simply pull up in front of the Portswod Hotel and unload our stuff out on the street. Then we'll carry inside, just like regular deliverymen. All we've got to do then is get it down to the secret room."

"Bloody hell that's risky ain't it?" George objected, and Pat Matthews was nodding his agreement.

"Not a bit of it. Lorries, horses and carts are all over the place every day delivering all sorts of stuff. No-one will give us a second look as we appear to be doing the same thing."

George and Pat remained unconvinced but both of them knew better than to argue with Albert. So, with great misgivings, they pulled up outside the pub. Once the unloading began, however, they came to see the wisdom of their boss. People were about alright, climbing over the rubble from the shattered buildings after last night's raid. But their attention was solely on where they were going and the safest way to get there. Men delivering items to a pub before they were even open was way down on their list of priorities.

Bernard had been surprised to see them at first when he answered their knocking, but quickly realized the purpose of the visit. Someone else was less impressed though and Bernard had to call out to his wife.

"Catherine come and get Saber here and shut him in with you. I can't make myself heard above his bloody barking."

The dog in question was a large Alsatian who was not used to men coming into the pub at this time of day and loudly voiced his disapproval. Catherine Bumstock now came through from the living quarters and summed up the situation straight away.

"Saber, stop that noise at once. Get in here now."

Big and fierce as his breed was, Saber knew better than to ignore a command from his mistress. So with a last departing growl at Albert, Pat and George, he followed her back into the private part of the pub.

Bernard went with them down to the secret room, each of them carrying a box, and once inside the contents were removed and placed with the rest of their stolen property. Albert took a good look around.

"Well there's enough here to keep us going for a long time. These watches will go very well. Some of them are going to fetch a good price. I want our men to be wearing some every time they go out. They can have at least four each to sell."

"And we won't expect them to have any left when they come back at nights will we?" George interrupted making as if he was reaching for his cosh. But he was having a rare light hearted moment which drew chuckles from everyone at the implied consequences. Woe betide any poor gang members who were unable to sell every single one of their watches.

221

Albert had a little chuckle himself. "No, it will be great if they can sell all the time, but they're bloody dockers George, not salesmen, so I think we'll accept whatever they can do ok?"

Bernard, who had been quiet until now spoke up.

"Alright Albert this is all going swell, but you said something about these blokes from Bournemouth coming here to stay and my missus is giving me a bloody hard time about that. She says they'll have to pay the going rate for their rooms and if they cause any trouble they'll be out on their ears. And you know my Catherine, she don't make idle threats."

"No I know she doesn't," Albert agreed, "but don't worry about this. Those Bournemouth men will be under my watchful eye and my men will take care of any unacceptable behavior. We have our reputation to keep up in this town. We won't let anyone from outside come and muck that up."

George was now back in full menacing mode and agreed, assuring Bernard that he and his wife had nothing to worry about.

"Those blokes know about me and my cosh and what I am capable of doing with it, and I ain't the only one who can look after myself in this gang. We've got many hard cases working with us and they'll make sure our visitors don't make any trouble, either for you or us."

"Right let's get going now," said Albert. "We've got to get that lorry back and then we need to get to work. So long Bernard, we'll see you tonight and we'll be here when the Bournemouth lot arrives."

Once the Public Bar door closed behind them Catherine Bumstock came back and confronted her husband.

"I heard all of that Bernard and I hope Albert bloody Littlejohn and that odious George Harcourt know what they're talking about. It may be only four blokes coming from Bournemouth, but I heard Littlejohn telling his men about them the other night. They're bad news and could very well bring a whole load of trouble to this pub."

222

"Not now Catherine, please," Bernard pleaded. "I know Albert and his boys better than you do and believe me they certainly can take care of any trouble that threatens them. These Bournemouth blokes will find that out soon enough. Now I've got cellar work I need to get on with."

In Lyon Street, the Anderson Shelter in the garden of the Kinslade home, five boys had met up and were earnestly talking together. Alan Kinslade had been joined by Johnnie Burton, Dennis Frampton, Ollie Wimpson and Trevor Harvey and he was going through their plans for that night.

"We all have work to do because the men from Bournemouth are coming here and I think you have a job to do with that ain't you Johnnie?"

"Yeah, Mr. Littlejohn has given me a letter that I've got to give to the bloke what's in charge of that lot. He's called Salty Sam the Bournemouth Knifeman and I've been told just to say who I am and then give him the letter. Then I've got to skidaddle pretty damn quick like."

"And what then?" asked Alan, "What are your group supposed to do for the rest of the night?"

"The same as last night really, keep a watch for the rozzers and make sure old Percy Winkleman gets his stuff in the boat and see it's shoved off with the Bournemouth blokes in there as well. Then, if that all goes ok, me and my lads with Dennis and Ollie here, we'll all be in the water just like we was last night. We have to make it look like we does this most nights just for fun see. But tonight I've told everyone to bring swimming trunks with them if they've got any, otherwise they'll have to swim in their underwear. Most of us, including me, got a bloody good hiding from our mums when we got home with our clothes soaking wet."

There was laughter all round at this, as Trevor agreed with Johnnie.

"Yeah not half, blimey my bum still hurts after the way my mum hit it last night."

Alan now outlined the job he and Trevor Harvey would be taking on and it was an important one.

"We've had a message from Ronnie Marsh who lives in Mayfield Road now. He don't like it there. Mainly because it means he's got to go to Swaythling School instead of with the rest of his mates at Portswood. Well that's working out super for us because he hears things about the Swaythling mob from there. The Griffin boys and some of the others talk about what that crowd of blokes is planning to do and the loud mouthed sods are planning a raid on Mr. Littlejohn's gang. So, me and Trevor will be spreading our boys out tonight and for the next week until the Swaythling gang make their move. Then we've got to act quick to let Mr. Littlejohn know.

We've also got to keep up with our job in that marshalling yard, especially tonight when there's going to be stuff brought from the Northam side that's got to be put into the secret room. We've got to way lay them old soldiers and lead them away from the area around the entrance."

"Have you told him about this yet?" asked Trevor. "About the Swaythling lot I mean, we ought to warn him so he can get ready."

"Not yet," Alan replied, "but we will tonight. Once those Bournemouth blokes are in the pub with Mr. Littlejohn and the stuff from old Percy is in the secret room. Me and Johnnie here will go to the side door of the Portswood Hotel, and meet with Mr. Ginger Strangemore. He'll have our list of names what was working last night and he'll give us the money to pay them with. So all five of us will meet here again at this time tomorrow night and we'll give you the the money to pay your boys."

In the Docks, that were still smouldering from yet another raid the night before, Albert, George, Pat Matthews and Billy Marshall had huge cups of tea and were tucking into bacon

224

sandwiches in the Tall Funnel café, the bacon having been smuggled in during the raid. As she served them Beryl Martin had stared nervously at Albert in particular.

George picked up on this immediately. "What you looking at girl? Speak up or this will soon make an appearance."

As he said this he parted his working jacket to reveal the deadly cosh sitting in the inside pocket. Though frightened by this, because even she had heard of Georges reputation with this weapon, she showed straight away that she was made of sterner stuff.

"Don't you wave that bloody thing at me mister. I know about you but I ain't scared. My boyfriend is big enough to sort you out if you threaten me."

Albert quickly saw the funny side of that and it was he who defused this awkward situation.

"Calm down girl, Beryl isn't it? George don't mean you no harm, but we need to know why you are staring so hard at me. Don't be scared just tell me please."

"Well we've had the police here nosing around, asking about Janice Saunders who was killed a couple of weeks ago in an air raid. They wanted to know what me and the other waitress knew about her. Well I told them Janice worked part time here and that some of the men took a fancy to her. They showed me a picture of someone they thought might have been closer to her than all the rest and, well mister, it was one of you."

Immediately alert, Albert spoke sternly.

"And what did you tell them about me Beryl, speak up because I need to know, this is important girl."

"I only said you was sweet on her, because that's all I knew. She never said anything about you so I couldn't tell that Inspector nothing more than that, that's all that happened mister I swear."

"Alright Beryl calm down, I believe you and you did well. Now I did know Janice and we helped each other out a lot, but I never lifted a finger against her and I wasn't responsible for her

225

being out in the street like that when she was killed. You must believe that because it's important."

Beryl was scared because all the men at this table were now looking straight at her, and she knew that if she did anything wrong she would certainly need more than her boyfriend to get her out of it.

"Yes I suppose but I ain't certain am I? Like I said I never knew what Janice was doing or who she was seeing when she wasn't here. But the papers said she had clothes and stuff she would never have had the money to buy. That's right mister because she was always shabbily dressed when she worked here with us."

Beryl didn't know how Albert was going to take this, so as the silence lengthened she felt a tightness in her stomach. Fear was creeping up on her and her legs started to shake. She really only knew Albert and the other men at this table because they used this café a lot. But she had also heard of his reputation outside the docks, the presence of George Harcourt and his cosh bringing this home with terrible effect.

But when Albert spoke again she was taken completely by surprise. "Do you like working here Beryl?" I mean really like it?"

She took her time answering because he had thrown her right off balance. Finally she responded.

"Well, not a lot no. I have to put up with so much from all these blokes in here and sometimes when I gets home my backside is all bruised where I've been pinched such a lot. I fend off most of it but I can't avoid it all. The money here is lousy as well, so no mister I don't like it, but I do it because I needs the money. Me and my boyfriend want to get married after the war so I'm trying to save up for that."

"Where is your boyfriend now Beryl, is he in the services?"

Beryl answered with a sniff and he could tell this was making her upset.

226

"Yes he's been away for such a long time and I don't even know where he is. He's in the army that's all I knows so when I'll see him again I don't bloody well know."

"Well how would you like to give your notice in and come and work for me? I can offer you much more money that you're getting here and other things besides. Take your time thinking about it but let me know as soon as you can."

Beryl stared at him for a moment, her mind in a whirl. She couldn't take in what was being said to her. She knew these dock workers well enough but surely none of them were in a position to offer her a job. But suddenly her mind clicked into gear.

"Ere it's not what that poor cow Janice did is it? I don't want to end up like her, dead in the bloody street mister."

"Keep your voice down Beryl," said Albert sternly and George was glaring at her as well. They quickly glanced around the café to check if this had been overheard, but luckily the usual noise the dock workers made had drowned it out.

Albert spoke quietly now, "Janice ran out for reasons of her own. My boys and me did nothing to cause it. It was very sad and we all felt that too. But as I've just said, think about what I've offered you and then get back to me. You can speak to me in here and give me your answer, and if you want the job we can take it from there."

The rest of that day was turmoil as more German aircraft came over and blasted Southampton, including, of course, the docks. Men they had seen drinking tea and eating bacon sandwiches only that morning now lay dead under piles of rubble as more sheds were hit. But the unloading of two ships that had limped in that morning and managed to escape further damage in this raid went ahead. The foreman in charge spoke to Albert as this was taking place.

"Six dead already and more planes coming over, bloody hell duck," he shouted as another bomb landed sending debris flying into the air. As they all regained their feet they could see at least three pairs of legs under what was left of one of the dockside cranes, and inside the cab the driver had also been killed.

"How the hell can we carry on working the docks when we're losing men like this?" the foreman asked. "We're losing so many of our blokes and their ain't any we can get to take over their jobs. I know women are doing the work of men in factories and out on the land, and some of them are driving buses and ambulances, but in here it's a man's world and nothing will ever change that."

"Look I've got some of my friends coming here from Bournemouth to stay for a while," Albert told him. "They haven't done this sort of work before, but they can pick it up quick enough. They're all good workers and will be glad of the opportunity."

"They're coming here, from a place like Bournemouth, here to this hell hole that's being bombed flat every night. Are they mad or are they running away from something else?" the foreman asked incredulously.

"They've all got friends and family here and they want to spend some time with them. It's no bloody good sitting down there and worrying is it? They need to see for themselves whether the people who mean so much to them are alright."

Albert was still getting a very suspicious glare from his foreman who remained unconvinced.

"And what do they do for a living these friends of yours? I know we need men in here but not just anyone."

"They're labourers and bricklayers mostly but at least three of them have done this sort of work before," Albert explained. "And two of them were called up, but got injured duing the early part of the war so they were invalided out of the army. They can still work though and I will guarantee all of them."

"And how many are we talking about?" the foreman, Joe Humphrey's, demanded.

"Five in all and I expect them to arrive here this evening, we're putting them up at the Portswood Hotel."

"Right then bring them all with you tomorrow and I'll give them a good look over. I'm not promising anything at this stage mind, but if they're okay then we'll take them on."

Albert told the rest of them that evening as they all sat in the Portswood Hotel. "The Bournemouth lot are due in an hour's time so we need to be ready for them. How many are out at the moment on our business?"

"Just four so far," said George, "and all of them are raiding houses in Highfield Lane. At least they will be as soon as the next bloody raid starts."

Before Albert could answer this the wail of the siren sounded and all of them got up to go to the lower level to shelter from the falling bombs. Albert had made sure his family had everything they needed and knew his wife and eldest daughter would get them safely inside their Anderson Shelter.

But he, like so many others in this situation, had that nagging doubt about a direct hit on a shelter. If this happened then no-one inside stood any chance of escape. So he stood with the rest and listened to the huge bangs of bombs hitting the ground all around them.

Under the road bridge at the bottom end of Dukes Road, Alan Kinslade, along with Dennis Frampton and Ollie Wimpson, also waited as the air raid went on. The younger boys who were with them, including Alan's young brothers, got as close to them as they could. Little mischievous monkeys they may be, but these were real bombs coming out of the sky and they would kill anyone who got hit.

Alan and the other two did their best to reassure the young ones.

"It's ok kids this will soon be over and we're alright under here. Once it is we've got more work to do making a nuisance of ourselves in the marshalling yard. We've got to make sure those old soldiers don't see anything again."

Johnnie Burton and Trevor Harvey together with their little gangs were also waiting out the raid, all of them hiding by the

Plaza cinema. For them it was Northam Bridge that provided shelter and they had a good view of what was happening. Especially when incendiary bombs contacted with the ground, the erupting flames from these was an awesome sight to behold as well as a sad one as more of their home town was being destroyed.

Once the all clear sounded though Johnnie gave an order, "Right you lot let's get our clothes off and get ready to go into the water. Remember, we wants a lot of noise as we do it cause we want folks to see us, especially any coppers or Home Guard blokes."

There followed a rustling as all ten boys stripped down to either their underwear or swimming trunks. Taking no notice of the chill in the air, and showing no concern about the temperature of the water, all of them took up a stance overlooking the water from the Plaza. There they stood, getting very strange looks from people who happened to be coming down the path after leaving the safety of the air-raid shelters, until Johnnie tensed up.

He was standing beside Trevor Harvey and told him, "get everyone ready to go in Trevor, as soon as I get back I want all of us in the water."

"Yeah ok but where are you going now?"

"I'll tell you later," Johnnie replied abruptly before he disappeared into the darkness.

Salty Sam and the rest of the men he had brought with him had also come out from the shelter they managed to get into. They had arrived in Southampton some two hours previously having managed to get onto a train from Bournemouth to Southampton Central station. Moving on up the hill they had observed the devastation that was Southampton High Street and wondered how anyone could have survived destruction on such a large scale as this.

But Salty Sam had more pressing concerns and set about finding the whereabouts of Northam Bridge and the Plaza cinema. Now approaching it in the dark he made out the cinema and knew the bridge must be nearby so stopped and waited for some form of contact.

Pat Morello, standing with him whispered, "What now Sam, who are we waiting for?"

"I'm not sure yet Pat, but we're in the right place I do know that. What the bloody hell is this?"

He was genuinely startled and had instinctively drawn one of his knives. The messenger he was expecting certainly wasn't one like this. Emerging from the pitch darkness was a boy of about 15 and he was wearing nothing but a pair of navy blue swimming trunks.

"What the bloody hell is going on?" Salty shouted as he slipped his knife back inside his coat.

Johnnie Burton, keeping his nerve, quietly replied. "Excuse me sir, but I have a note here from Mr. Littlejohn, he's told me to make sure I gives it to you."

Salty Sam had recovered quickly and was right back on his game.

"I see and how do you know I am the man you have to give this note to?"

"Well you are known as the Bournemouth knife man see, and that's quite an impressive weapon mister. I seen a picture of you too so I would know you when you came here."

Then without giving Salty a chance to say anymore Johnnie pressed the note into his hand and once more disappeared into the darkness.

For once the usually sneering Salty Sam was dumbfounded and at a loss for words.

"Well I don't know what to make of that," he said eventually and Pat Morello agreed with him.

"We know we'll be picked up from here don't we so what does that bloody note say?"

Salty didn't reply straightaway because he was still reading Albert's note. "We've got to meet some of the Littlejohn gang

231

who should be here any minute now, then all of us have to wait for an old bloke called Percy Winkleman whose a rag and bone man."

"What the bleeding hell for?" Pat demanded, but before Salty could answer all hell broke out around them. There were splashes and loud laughter as the whole group of boys lowered themselves down the sides of the bridge and dropped into the water.

They swam around making even more noise, aimed at attracting attention to themselves, and this certainly worked. From the darkness came three police officers, two ARP wardens and two Home Guard soldiers. The police sounded their whistles and shouted.

"It's the same lot as last night so round the little buggers up. We can catch them and find out what the sodding hell they think they're doing."

Saying this and doing it were quite different things though. They were all excellent swimmers and none of the adults were wearing suitable clothing so they decided to wait until the boys grew tired and came out of the river of their own accord.

Which meant none of these men even noticed Salty Sam and his boys as they waited for the contact. Alert as they all were it was Pat Morello who first heard, above the shouting of the police and home guard, the clip clop of horses hooves and he pointed this out to Salty.

"This sounds like the old rag and bone man we've been told about coming now."

Immediately Salty Sam and his men found themselves surrounded by five of the Littlejohn gang, who had all been waiting in the shadows for old Percy to arrive. They had kept a very keen eye on the men from Bournemouth and didn't like what they were seeing.

"Rum looking bloody lot I must say," Lenny Warren had observed to Pat Matthews. "Especially those two standing with the big bloke who I suppose is this Salty Sam we've been told to look out for."

"Yes you're right Lenny. That's him alright, Albert showed me the picture of him he had painted and there's no mistake, that's Salty Sam the Bournemouth knifeman."

"How good is he with a knife then?"

"Bloody good, George Harcourt has said. He has killed a lot of people without any show of mercy if they cross him in any way. He even knifed one bloke right in front of the poor sods wife. There was blood all over the small living room in their house. And not content with that he then dragged the blokes wife upstairs and made her perform sex acts on him before he simply walked out of the house. No, he's bad news, and looking at the others he's brought with him none of them are much bloody better. But here's Percy so let's go and make contact with them."

Now they stood with these gangsters from the sea side town and after identifying themselves Pat outlined the plan.

"Old Percy Winkleman is nearly here so once he turns in all of us will walk on the outside of his cart because he hasn't had a chance to do the metal drop yet. Once we're there we simply mingle with the others who are bringing metal objects to be used in the war effort. We stick with Percy until he's finished unloading, then walk beside the cart again as he takes it on to the boat. Once there we unload our stuff from the compartment underneath the floorboards of Percy's cart, put it in the boat and make for the road bridge further up the river.

We have nippers over there who will be making a nuisance of themselves in the marshalling yard and distracting the Home Guard soldiers. That gives us the chance to get through the yard and up to the secret room where all of our stuff is kept. So stick with us all the way and we won't have any trouble."

Not only were Salty Sam and his boys not used to taking orders like this but they all just looked at each other with the same thought. What on earth had they been dropped into by

233

their boss. The Littlejohn gang had a tough reputation but what an unconventional way of working, old rag and bone men, relying on gangs of nippers, taking the boat to go just a short distance up river. But they were strangers here so would have to do what they were told, for now anyway. Let's see how this plays out. So Salty simply nodded and then both saw and heard the rumble of Percy's old cart.

He turned in off the little side road and pulling Major up, looked around for Albert's men as he did every time he came here. But when he saw the others, who he certainly didn't recognize, he panicked and made to turn Major to make his escape.

Pat Matthews came out from the dark and shouted to him. "It's alright old man we know who these men are and Albert is expecting them. Just do everything as normal and it will be ok."

Percy though wasn't so sure. He wasn't happy because he had usually dropped his metal off by now hated his routine being altered in any way. Now that he had a good view of the Bournemouth men he didn't like what he was seeing. He leaned down and said quietly to Pat.

"Are you sure young Albert knows what he's bleeding doing, this lot are bad news and I knows what I'm talking about."

"Yes Percy, he does know what he's doing and these men are here for a reason. Now move old Major on and we'll walk beside the cart."

Later on once in the boat the Bournemouth men were looking around to make out as much as they could of where they were going. But with the black-out in force there wasn't much to see. So, as the boat grounded further up by the road bridge they all jumped out and started to pick up the goods that had been loaded from old Percy's cart.

Tonight these included alcohol as well as other things taken from the well to do houses in and around Highfield Lane. There was even a vacuum cleaner that had been stolen from one house and Salty Sam observed. "Well I've bloody well seen it all now, where the hell did your lot get that?"

"All will be revealed soon."

"Ok but it better be quick cause we all want to know what our cut will be once we get started in this town. What the blazes is all that noise, what's going on over there?"

He was referring to the yells of the Home Guard soldiers as they tried to get their hands on the small invaders in the marshalling yard. But Alan Kinslade and the rest were doing their usual fine job of distracting and leading these elderly men away from the side of the yard where the Littlejohn men, with their Bournemouth counterparts, would very soon be making their way through to the secret room.

All of these, with arms full of stolen property, did indeed make their way across this yard. The yells were still audible, but faded as the search for the boys took them ever nearer to the far side.

As they reached the entrance door of the secret room at the back of the Portswood Hotel, Salty and his men watched Pat Matthews knock.

"It's us, and we've brought plenty of stuff, including the men from Bournemouth, so open up and let us in."

Chapter Fifteen

Salty Sam and his men were fascinated as they watched a seemingly solid wall begin to open up right before them. Following Pat Matthews and his men they were even more surprised by the contents of this room. Everything imaginable was stored here from alcohol to shoe leather and it reminded Salty of a Christmas bazaar he had once seen as a small boy. Albert Littlejohn and George Harcourt were standing waiting for him as their men worked all around them. Goods were stacked in the right places and they made sure nothing that could get broken was stored carelessly, alcohol especially coming into this category.

Albert now came forward.

"Welcome to Southampton again Sam, and who are these men you've bought with you?"

Salty Sam shook hands with him.

"These are my best men for what we think is needed here Littlejohn, and they're led by Pat Morello and his sidekick Mickie Trumpforth."

Both Albert and George looked at these men, and the other two who hadn't been introduced, and neither of them liked what they saw. But Salty, seeming not to notice this, just carried on.

"Bloody good at what they do they are, and completely reliable."

"I see and just what is it they do?" Albert wanted to know.

"Protection," Salty replied looking him straight in the eye. "There's a lot of pubs and shops that ain't been hit by bombs here and we think they need protecting from bad blokes who might try to take advantage of them. For a price, we make sure that don't happen."

"Yes I can see that might be something that could work here, but what is the price you would want from them?"

"Half their weekly takings is what we want, and for that they won't be bothered by anyone else, we'll make sure of that."

"And if they don't want your help?" asked George. "What then? Half their weekly takings will cripple most of the small shop keepers."

Salty Sam gave a smile that could only be described as pure evil.

"That's where Pat and Mickie come in with their boys, they have methods to make shop keepers see things our way and co-operate with us."

The silence that greeted this statement lasted for at least a minute while Albert and George took it all in. Finally Albert spoke directly to Salty, ignoring the rest of his men. He made sure the tone of his voice backed up what he was saying.

"My men and I do two things here Sam, working in the docks and helping ourselves to a better way of life by what we do in our spare time. But so far this has only resulted in the accidental death of one young lorry driver, just before the war started. What I think you are proposing could open up a whole load more trouble. Southampton is a port with many tough characters living here. They won't simply give in to the demands you are likely to be making. They'll fight, you can bet on that, and my boys will have to wade in with you to get the better of them.

Now, as I understood it, your reason for coming here is to help us with what we do, and exchange items that are beneficial

237

for both us. There has been no mention of anything like a protection racket."

"No your right," said Salty Sam, "but Leroy Wort and I see things different. He's coming here in a couple of days and we'll meet in that pub again, the Horse and Groom. He'll tell you what he expects to happen here now we're involved as well."

George Harcourt was glaring at Pat Morello, who sneered at him.

"What are you staring at duckie? Fancy a snog with me do you?"

All the Littlejohn gang stopped working at once and looked straight at George Harcourt. They couldn't believe what they had just heard and were now watching to see what his reaction would be. There was a look of thunder on his face and his hand reached inside his jacket. Then, as his cosh came into view, he gave a roar and lunged at the Bournemouth man.

He very nearly made it and the fate of Pat Morello would certainly have been sealed if he had. But Albert, as well as Salty Sam and the rest of the Bournemouth men, rushed to get between them and George found himself pinned, his cosh arm useless now.

"Calm down George," Albert shouted. "I'm sure this bloke was only joking he didn't mean anything by what he just said. Did you?"

The question was directed at Pat Morello, who was now standing watching George very carefully.

"Blimey mate, can't you take a bloody joke? You was staring at me so I called you a queer, it didn't mean nothing."

George disentangled himself from the men who were holding him back.

"A joke was it? Well as you just saw I didn't think it was very funny. No-one says things like that to me Morello, not if they want to keep healthy. So you just bloody well remember that."

He pushed his cosh back into his pocket and the tension in the room eased considerably.

Albert now explained that Salty and his men would be staying in this pub while they were in Southampton and he, along with George Harcourt, left the secret room and started to make their way up to the public bar to introduce them to Bernard and Catherine Bumstock. The Littlejohn men went back to work, proud of George for the way he had stood up for himself. By openly implying he was a homosexual Pat had certainly risked getting his head bashed in by the king of the cosh himself.

But as the door closed behind his leader and the Bournemouth men, one of Albert's boys stood staring very intently at it. He alone now in this room knew there was a lot of truth in the accusation that had just been leveled at George Harcourt. Pat Morello was in fact only making a sneering joke, he had no idea it was true. But young Billy Marshall was reliving the night in Highfield Lane when George, with the threat of his cosh, had sexually assaulted him.

Shocked and degraded by the attack, although nothing like it had happened since, the memory still burned inside his head. He gave no outward sign of this, however, talking normally to George and obeying any orders he gave about gang matters. But he secretly longed to deliver some form of payback.

"Are you gonna stand there all night Billy? We've got work to do here so come and give us a bloody hand."

He quickly snapped out of these thoughts and went to help the others.

Upstairs in the public bar Albert and George were ordering drinks and also introducing the men from Bournemouth. Bernard wasn't very happy to have these men staying at his pub, but none-the-less greeted them as every good landlord should and shook hands with each one of them."

"Welcome to the Portswood Hotel gents. My wife is getting your rooms ready now and she'll be down in a moment, now what can I get you all to drink?"

They ordered pints all round.

" I'll get these Bernard and we'd like some whisky to go with them."

"I ain't got much of that left Albert," the Landlord replied in a low voice so as not to be overheard by the rest of his customers. He had told them all he was completely out of whiskey.

"Why?" asked Albert in the firm voice he always used when he wasn't happy about something and insisted on a straight answer. "We gave you enough just a couple of weeks ago to keep you going for at least three weeks. So why are you telling me you ain't got much left?"

"Because you didn't just supply us with whisky Albert, but you and that mob of yours have drunk most of it as well."

The booming voice of Catherine Bumstock sounded from behind them. She had just come back into the bar and overheard what Albert said.

"So, to keep our bargain going we will need more bottles, not just whiskey but, rum, vodka and gin as well."

Albert was silent for a moment, highly aware that Salty Sam and his lot were taking in this particular exchange with interest. Holding his temper was going to be of extreme importance. So, instead of getting angry, he smiled.

"Yes, I'll have to stamp on my boys. They do drink a lot of spirits don't they? Alright, make me a list, and we'll give you and Bernard whatever you need. Now, here are our friends from Bournemouth who are going to be staying here so over to you Catherine."

She studied a piece of paper in her hand. "Yes, which one are you then?" staring straight at Salty Sam.

"Sam Freeman Missus but everyone calls me Salty Sam so I'm used to that."

240

"Well Mr. Freeman," Catherine replied, taking no notice of this, "I see your name is at the top of the list so you must be the leader of this group."

She got a nod of the head from Sam so carried on.

"I've got three rooms ready for you. Yours is the single at the top of the stairs and the other two, one on each side of the corridor, are to be shared between the other four men. The bathroom is further down and you'll all have to share that. Now, we don't usually let rooms out here and we're only doing it now to help Albert out. But there are rules, and if any of you break them then you'll find yourselves thrown out on the street.

We don't want booze in the rooms and certainly no noise at night. My husband and I work late every day and we're up bloody early in the morning to get it all done. No women in the rooms at any time, that's certainly one thing I won't tolerate, not under my roof. You'll have your meals with us. Now, you can enjoy your drinks and go to your rooms when you're ready. And Bernard, there is whisky in the cupboard in the cellar, so bring a bottle up here for these men please."

Pat Morello was the first to comment. "Blimey Littlejohn, are all of the women in this town like her? She seems like a bloody dragon to me."

"There's a war on and things are not good for any of us. Catherine Bumstock is a no nonsense woman yes, but she's a great gal when you get to know her. She means what she said though about ignoring her rules so don't do it. We had a hell of a job persuading Catherine to take you in so if she throws you out we don't know anywhere else you can stay."

Just then Bernard arrived carrying a tray covered with a dishcloth. On this were seven glasses containing generous tots of Bells whisky.

"Keep these out of sight if you can Albert, I don't want the rest of our regulars to see it. Oh and by the way, here's the bill."

Outside in the marshalling yard Alan Kinslade and the boys working with him tonight were having the time of their lives as they led the Home Guard soldiers on another unsuccessful chase. The younger boys had learned quickly from young Barry and Michael Kinslade the art of allowing themselves to be seen, then darting away and hiding right behind the axles of the stationary trucks. More than once these boys were within inches of the soldiers.

The dimmed down torches still would have located the hiding boys if their beams had actually fallen on any of them. But if they did start to get a little too close for comfort, Alan Kinslade along with Dennis Frampton and Ollie Wimpson, were busy with their catapults sending missiles that just missed these elderly men.

"You little bleeders," they roared out.

One of them was looking down when a small stone spun off the side of the truck he was examining, narrowly missing his head.

"I'll tan your bloody asses for you if I get my hands on you."

Alan kept the barrage up until he was sure that the Littlejohn men, along with the strangers who had arrived with them tonight, were inside the Portswood Hotel. Then, he sent out a quiet whistle that all the younger boys could hear.

They immediately made their way, easily avoiding the still searching and cursing soldiers, over to meet up with the three older boys.

"Ok everyone that was great, we can go home now," Alan said to them. "And all of you will be getting paid for this on Saturday, I've got all your names and I'll be giving them to Mr. Littlejohn tomorrow night."

They quickly dispersed, going their own way home and smiling broadly at the prospect of the wages they would soon be getting for their work tonight.

Down the Northam end Johnnie Burton and Trevor Harvey were still in the water with another little group of keen nippers, leading the police on a merry dance as they attempted to get them out and arresting as many of them as they could get their hands on.

But Johnnie, having satisfied himself that they had done enough for this evening, quietly gave the order.

"Pass the word, dive dive dive."

Once this was circulated all little swimmers dived under the surface and made for the bank. There they emerged from the water, covered by darkness, and gathered up their clothing before disappearing into the night. Each time this would be carefully and strategically hidden in one of the bushes on the path in a different place to the night before.

What a sight they were. People making their way home after the recent air-raid were startled to see these bedraggled boys, clutching their clothes and running past them. Each one of these lads was also contemplating what they were going to do with the wages they would be getting.

It seemed to be another triumphant night for the Littlejohn gang, very important as they wanted to appear an efficient and professional organization to their new colleagues from Bournemouth who were accompanying them. One thing did go wrong though, and unfortunately this was going to cause quite a problem.

Albert was alone now with his men. Salty Sam and the rest of the Bournemouth lot were upstairs with Catherine Bumstock, being shown their rooms. So he glared at Harry Small, who had just joined them, and demanded to know what he meant by the message he had just given.

"What do you mean Harry, we're in the shite, why are we?"

"We couldn't help it boss," Harry nervously answered, "but we had no bleeding choice did we?"

"Make sense," Albert demanded. "What the hell are you talking about?"

"Well me, Jamie Weston and Mark Purser was breaking into houses at the upper end of Highfield Lane. Done alright we did and got a lot of good stuff. That's all down in the secret room. But we was just coming out of the gate of a big house when a bloody torch was flashed on us and an ARP Warden shouted. Wanted to know who we were and why we were there cause he knew we didn't live there like. Well we knew if he got too close and looked into the bags we was carrying the game would have been up for us. We knew other Wardens was about and all this bloke had to do was blow on his whistle and we would have been done for. We wasn't having any of that were we, so both Jamie and Mark dropped their bags and went for the warden.

He was an old bloke but blimey he put up a fight I can tell you. It took all three of us in the end to knock the bleeder out. Well we was just going to run off and leave the old boy there see, because it wouldn't be long before his mates found him and got the old sod home. But Mark wanted to have a look at him, thought we had hurt him a bit too much.

There was a lot of blood coming from the wound in his head. One of us cracked him one, but we never meant to really hurt the bloke. We didn't know what to do about it but we soon heard people coming so we made ourselves scarce. I don't know how bad that old bloke was, but before we got back here an ambulance raced past us. This one came from the direction of Highfield Lane so it don't look good boss."

There was complete silence around the table. Albert looked at George who shook his head in return.

Finally Albert spoke. "This sounds serious. We need to find out about it bloody quick. If that warden is badly hurt it will set the coppers off and make them up their patrols in that area. It will put a stop to the raids on the houses in Highfield Lane and Bassett, but that can't be helped at the moment. We need information and the only bloke I can think of to get it for us is Councilor Teddy Wainright. I will get a message to him tomorrow; we have a way of communicating if an emergency does crop up. I'll ask him to find out what's happening with this and how bad that warden is hurt. But in the meantime we keep a low profile is that understood?"

It was then that Ginger Strangemore, the gangs banker, entered the bar and joined them. Sitting down and accepting a drink he looked up at Albert.

"I've brought the list of proceeds for the past week and if you inspect them you'll notice in the expenses column there's the record of money being paid out to all these nippers who are now working for us. And there's a lot of them Albert. I know we ain't paying them much each, but when you add up the number claiming their wages it is a tidy little sum."

Albert was not concerned by this.

"Yes I know that Ginger, but they're a good group of boys and all of them are doing a perfect job for us. They're worth whatever we're paying them and you'll get another claim tomorrow for the work they've all done tonight."

Being a banker for the gang Ginger had grown used to viewing this job in the same way as his legitimate counterparts who worked in real banks. He tended to see any money paid out to people who helped the gang in any way as coming out of his own pocket.

Albert of course knew this and slapped Ginger on his knee.

"Cheer up, they're only kids but we've already seen what a great help they are to us, so stop grumbling and give me the money so I can pass it on to their leaders."

Ginger was still unhappy. "Caution must be recognized. Money has a way of disappearing quickly if it's not looked after properly."

He quickly produced another shorter list.

"And who are these men who are joining us from Bournemouth? What are they here for and how much are we supposed to pay them?"

"You'll pay us in full for all the things we do for this gang," a stern voice came from behind Ginger's chair and swinging round he came face to face with Salty Sam and his men, who had come back into the bar unnoticed.

Albert quickly intervened.

"Ginger, these are our new allies from Bournemouth who will be helping us to make even more money, so that should make you a lot happier shouldn't it?"

Ginger wasn't happy at all as he gazed disapprovingly at the men who were all now glaring back at him.

"I see, but what's this about them making more money for us. I don't like the sound of this, are they joining our organization?"

Salty Sam was losing patience and answered before Albert had the chance.

"The gang's banker? You must be because you talk like one. Well, me and my boys are going to swap stuff with Albert's, but we're also going to add to the rackets that their gang are pulling in this town. It will bring in plenty of extra revenue. So when it comes to pay out time you make sure we gets what we've earned, or else," he ended menacingly.

Ginger may be a banker and not so involved in the criminal acts of his counterparts. But he was also a docker and one who had been involved in many a skirmish about stolen bounty over the years. Now, this man from Bournemouth was standing in his gangs favorite pub and actually threatening him. His reaction was rapid as he jumped from his chair and, grabbing the front of Salty's shirt, drew back his fist to hit him.

"I don't cheat no-one you bastard," he roared "You'll get you're bloody money but any more talk like that to me and I'll do my bloody best to knock you back from where you come from."

The Bournemouth men rushed forward to help Salty out, because he had been taken by surprise he hadn't had the chance to reach his knife. This of course brought the Littlejohn men to their feet as well and a fight was just about to break out, one which would have been brutal with injuries likely on both sides.

It was prevented by the loud voice of Catherine Bumstock who had come rushing out from behind the bar and now stood between the two lots of men.

"I won't have any bloody fighting in this bar so if you want to do it then get outside the whole lot of you. Albert Littlejohn, you know my rules about this so sort it out and make sure we don't have no more of it. Otherwise you and your lot can find somewhere else to drink, and another store room."

This would pose real problems and Albert knew he had to respond so his was the voice that was next heard.

"Right Sam, your lot over the other side of the bar and you and me over here, we've got some talking to do."

As the two sides retreated to opposite ends and more drinks were brought to both, Albert said quietly to George.

"Watch that lot and make sure they don't cause any more trouble in here, we can't afford to lose the use of that room."

He got a nod from Georg which was all that was needed to show that the message had been received and would be acted upon if necessary.

Albert now sat at another table with Salty Sam and the two of them waited until Bernard had placed full pints of beer in front of them. Then Salty began the conversation.

"That banker is a hard case. I thought blokes like him were wimps who only thought about ledgers. He nearly bloody well choked me."

Albert thought back to some other times Ginger had been involved in fights.

"Our banker works alongside us in the docks here and is as good at looking after himself as any one of us. It's a cut throat job in there, cargoes come in and are pilfered all the time. There are smaller gangs who just work the docks and fight anyone who tries to get their hands on cargoes they think are their personal property.

Ginger has fought off more than his share of blokes who tried cutting us out of what we get for ourselves. One mob in there you will meet tomorrow and from them you'll see for yourselves what I'm talking about. The Kinger brothers run the meat racket and they rule. So when meat cargoes come off they get in before anyone else can take their share of it."

"So where do you get your meat from then?" Salty demanded. "That's one of the things we want, Meat is so strictly rationed now so we want more of it for back home."

"You'll get it," Albert replied sharply, "but I want you to see the sort of things dockers do to get stuff out past the gate security officers. We don't do that, but we know where meat is stored in refrigerated warehouses and my boys know a thing or two about helping themselves to stocks of it."

"So they nick whole carcasses do they and what then? Have you got your own fridges to store it in?"

"In a way yes. We have a butcher who we supply with meat and he keeps ours for us in his big walk in. And that's another thing you'll see tomorrow when we take you to meet him. But for now I want you and your boys to go to work in the morning with us. We'll pick you up here at six thirty, so be ready."

"How bad is the warden?" Di Stapleton asked. He was in his office at Portswood Police Station with Sergeant Podcove.

"We don't know yet sir, but it's pretty bad. He's been beaten up and has got a serious head wound. He's in intensive care at the Borough Hospital. We've got Pc Willis there to get a message back to us as soon as there's any news."

"And where exactly did this attack take place?" the DI asked.

"Right at the top end of Highfield Lane sir, just before it meets the common. With no street lights it's really dark there but this warden must have seen something we think and simply performed his duty in challenging anyone he thought was up to no good."

"What are we basing this on?"

"The houses were empty at the time of this attack sir, we know that because the occupants were in the shelters. But we've now had a chance to talk to some of them, especially the owners of the house where this all occurred. They did a quick check and I've got a list here."

He handed the DI a piece of paper with all the things that had been discovered as missing from this one house.

Scanning this quickly the senior officer came to an immediate conclusion.

"All saleable isn't it, the sort of things the Littlejohn gang would go for, or anyone else working the black market racket. I take it a more thorough search of this house is now taking place?"

"Yes sir, that and the surrounding houses as well. You know the reports we already have of break ins in that area, this looks like a continuation of that particular crime wave."

"Yes we do have a long list of burglaries from houses in Highfield Lane, prosperous people living there and a lot of valuable items have gone missing. How many arrests have we made in connection with this?"

"None as yet sir, because we're up against men who know their business, and with the black-out in place all the cards are stacked in their favour."

The Di was silent for a moment because inside he was fuming. He knew what his sergeant was saying was true and that his men were doing their best to stop the crime in this town from escalating any further. Then before he could say any more there was a tap on his door.

A young PC came in and handed the DI a small piece of paper.

"We've just received this from PC Willis sir at the hospital."

"Thank you constable," then as the door shut behind the PC he read the message.

He looked up with a very serious look upon his face.

"It's a bloody sight more serious now Sergeant, the warden has just died so we've got a murder enquiry on our hands."

Then he leaped into action.

"I want that crime scene gone over with a fine tooth comb. Take the damn paving stones up if necessary. I want forensic up there without any delay."

His sergeant rushed for the office door but he thought of something else,

"And get me a meeting with councilor Wainright. Make it top priority, I'm going to go personally to the Littlejohn house in Empress Road with a team and this time we'll take that house apart."

Early next morning a rickety van pulled up in front of the Portswood Hotel. The driver sounded his horn which brought Salty Sam and his boys out of the pub and into the back of what was an already crowded vehicle. Albert and some of his gang were already inside and the van's springs began to groan as it was driven away down Bevois valley on its way to the docks.

Albert was sat in the front and turned round.

"Good morning Sam glad to see all of you were ready when we arrived."

"Didn't have much choice did we?" Salty replied. "That bloody landlady is a right tarter, almost kicked us out of your rooms she did. Though we got a good breakfast, she made no secret of the fact she wanted us out of the pub."

There was some laughter from the Littlejohn gang over this, all of them knew Catherine Bumstock very well indeed and what she was capable of when she's not happy. They sat huddled together in the van as it made its careful way, through the damaged streets to Dock Gate Ten. Getting no resistance from the gate security they went on until they came to a stop by the foremen's office.

Here, all of them piled out and went to where they were needed for the day's work, but Albert took Salty Sam and his boys in to meet Joe Humphreys.

He took his time looking them over.

"Well I can't say I'm not pleased to see you because I certainly am. We're seriously short of men to keep these docks working. I will start you today and I'll be keeping a good watch to see how you cope. Then, looking at Salty, he continued.

"Albert tells me your men are mostly labourers but at least two of you have done this sort of work before. Is that true and if so where did you do it?"

Albert had prepared him so Salty was ready for this question and answered without any hesitation at all. One of his boys had gone to sea before the war and had first gone through ten weeks of training on an old sailing schooner called the Vindicatrix that had been moved from its berth at Gravesend in Kent to a canal by the side of the River Severn in Gloucestershire in a small place called Sharpness.

Sam explained further.

"Two of us worked for a time in Sharpness. That dock is a lot smaller and only had cargo ships coming in and out. But the principle of the work is the same as you do here."

Joe had never even heard of Sharpness, let alone the docks there, and couldn't really dispute what he was being told. So he dismissed them with another warning that he would be watching for some time to make sure they really did know what they were doing.

As they walked away Albert emphasized the importance of this. He means what he's just said Salty so make sure you watch us all the time and do exactly the same. We'll help you all we can but you need to help yourselves as much as possible. At dinner time I'm going to introduce you to the Kingers, remember I told you they have the meat racket cornered in the docks. They're a tough bunch so go careful when you're talking to them and don't go waving one of your knives around.

Three of them are brothers but they also have a shady character who we know as bandy leg Joe. They're just one of the groups in here who are experts at getting stuff out and making sure their families are taken care of, they sell on what's over.

251

Now we have rackets going on in here as well, but most of what we do is done outside after dark."

The morning was very busy and it was all Albert could do to keep his eyes on the Bournemouth men. But Salty seemed to either know what he was doing, or was able to pick it up very quickly, and made sure the rest of his men followed suit. Joe Humphrey's appeared satisfied that he had some more men he could rely on to keep this busy dock ticking over as it should, despite all of the trouble coming from Germany.

After dinner Albert took Salty Sam to meet Sydney King, the eldest of the brothers and head of the Kingers mob. A thick set man with bulging muscles and a no nonsense look, he clearly didn't like what Albert was telling him.

Sydney looked him up and down.

"From Bournemouth are you, well what the bleeding hell are you doing here mate? We've got this dock sewn up and we don't want no strangers coming in here trying to break into what we do. This is our town mate, we gets what we want from it."

Salty quickly eyed him up before, with a speed that was almost impossible to anticipate, he had the right arm of Sydney King twisted up his back and in his own right hand a knife appeared. This he just touched against Kings throat before quietly speaking into his ear.

"I know what you do King and as far as I'm concerned you're welcome to it. Getting small amounts of meat out of this dock is fine, but it's small time. We're here for the bigger game. But, from now on you and your group will let us know when a meat boat has come in and just what the cargo is. Then we'll want a share of the cuts you steal. Your operation is going to increase and it's more than just joints of meat you're going to smuggle out. How well do you know the guard on the gate and how much can you trust him?"

"Let go of my bloody arm and I'll tell you," King said through gritted teeth. Aggrieved at how he had been overcome in front of his colleagues he longed to connect with a solid

252

punch as soon as he was free but he was also curious to see if all this could benefit him in some way.

"I can't talk when you're nearly tearing it off. And get that bloody knife away from my throat."

Salty released his hold and slid the knife back inside his coat. "That's better, now then Mr. King start talking."

Chapter Sixteen

Rubbing his right arm after Salty released him Sidney King was a little shaken up.

"Bloody hell mate, you don't have to be that rough. You could have cut my throat then as well as breaking my sodding arm."

"Yes I could, and now you know me and my men mean business. So, I asked you a question about the guards on the gate."

"Yeah well we have an arrangement in place. They know what we're doing and they turn a blind eye as long as they get their share of what we take."

"Alright then so speak to them about us and what we want from here, they will still get their share and it will be larger than they're getting now. Make them see that, it's important."

Sidney King looked first at Salty Sam then at his men who were standing behind. He could also see Albert Littlejohn and George Harcourt, which meant his gang was involved, so there was nothing he could do to stop this invasion into his private meat snatching racket.

Grudgingly he replied. "Ok I ain't got much choice here have I? But I don't like the way some of your men are looking at me.

I don't want any of my brothers or bandy leg hurt in any way. We only take what we want for our families see. We ain't into big time crime."

"Very good," Salty replied. "We need to see our families don't go without. Especially in these hard times of war, but we want to increase the output of what you do. So it's simple, we know you take one carcass and then cut it up into joint size pieces. So in future you'll double that and cut one up for us as well. But make sure we can get our share out of the dock gates. Do that Mr. King and you as well as your brothers and this bandy bloke will not only stay healthy but your wages will increase quite a lot because we will pay you for what you do for us."

Satisfied with this good start Salty Sam was now eager to find more opportunities.

"Well that's one thing done," he said to Albert. "Now how many other blokes in here are working the rackets?"

Albert was amused by this. To be honest it was probably more difficult to find anyone who wasn't working one.

"Just about everyone, oh not big time of course but nearly every bloke goes home with something tucked away at the bottom of their bags, and some have false bottoms and get a lot of stuff out that way. But as for organised crime, no there isn't anything like that in here."

"Not at present perhaps but that can change. I think Pat Morello wants to start showing what he can do before this shift ends today."

He didn't have time to say anymore as the wail of the siren announced another German raid and all hell was about to be let loose around them.

Joe Humphreys yelled for everyone to take cover, "The bastards are heading straight for us."

Albert and Salty dashed to join the others just as three German planes came roaring in. They dropped their bombs as they passed over and the explosions sent everything in the vicinity flying into the air. One of the bombs hit the cargo ship that was being unloaded and from where they were, the Littlejohn men as well as those from Bournemouth saw the explosion as deck cargo was destroyed.

More alarming than that was the sight of some of the ship's crew as their bodies were sent flying into the air, to come back down and land with an awful sound on the dockside. Looking at these mangled bodies Albert quietly said to himself.

"The poor bastards they never stood a bloody chance, where the hell are our guns? We should be shooting back at those murdering bloody Jerry's."

As if in response to this the anti aircraft guns that were on the old walls did indeed open up and the air was soon filled with the noise and smell of gunpowder.

George was crouching next to Albert.

"Watch out this one's coming straight at us."

They all looked to where he was pointing and saw the German plane screaming in to where they were with machine guns blazing. Bullets started to hit the ground all around them and they saw more of their friends and fellow workers mown down by this murderess fire.

With the ground now covered in wreckage, bodies and blood on the ground this made for a very grim sight. The German plane had turned and was starting to come in again when the guns from the old walls again opened up. This time though their aim was true and the plane screaming in at them, again firing its guns as it came, was suddenly hit and it exploded in spectacular fashion before crashing into the waters of the dock.

"Well that's one of the bastards we don't have to worry about no more," said Albert triumphantly, and he could hear some cheers ringing out all around the docks. The wreckage was sinking fast, the German cross on its wings being the last things left visible above the water. But, as it too disappeared, the body of one of the crew floated to the surface.

256

The all clear sounded and men came out of hiding to survey the devastation around them. The cargo ship was now on fire so hoses were brought out to fight this. Men were racing to help injured colleagues and start the clearing up once again. As the fire raged in the stricken ship Albert and the rest were doing all they could to put it out. The heat was almost unbearable but they had to get as close as they could to make any sort of progress. Water poured in and they began to make some headway. The noise from this fire and all around them on the dockside almost made them miss a small cry for help.

"What was that?" Albert yelled. "I thought a heard a shout."

They stopped for a moment, but hearing nothing were about to wade in once more with their hoses when it came again.

"Help me please, I'm stuck in here."

"The galley," said Billy Marshall, "It's coming from there."

They were near the after end of the ship so this was nearby. Making their way through thick smoke that was still filling the air around, they came to the door and tried to open it.

"The bloody things stuck," George shouted. "That bomb has bent it out of shape."

"Well there's someone in there who needs our help," said Albert. "We need to find another way in, come on follow me."

He led them around the top deck to the crew's accommodation alleyway. This led into their mess and from there a way into the galley. The sight that greeted them was something from a horror film. The German bomb had indeed twisted the door to the poop deck completely out of shape, but the explosion ripped into the galley as well.

The result of this being that the mangled body of the ships cook was now lying on the deck, minus one of his legs and half of his right arm. The mess that had once been this man's face left no doubt at all that he was dead. The second cook was dead as well, though his body was at least not so horribly maimed.

Looking away from these two bodies Albert yelled at them, "Someone's alive in here so where the hell is he?"

Then the small voice they had heard from outside came again. "I'm here sir, please can you help me?"

The voice came from under the sink, or what was left of it amongst the twisted pipes and other remains. Closer inspection however revealed a young boy's leg.

"Christ there's a kid under there, come on let's move this bloody wreckage and get him out."

For the next twenty minutes they worked themselves to a standstill until eventually they managed to, very carefully, lift the boy out. He was a sorry sight with cuts all over his body, his clothes had almost been blown from him and Albert suspected at least some of his bones must be broken. Gently he spoke to him.

"It's alright now son you're safe. So what's your name?"

"Michael sir," he weakly replied, "Michael Roberts."

"Alright Michael we're going to get you some help as quickly as we can, what do you do on this ship?"

"I'm the galley boy sir, and that was my boss, the ships cook."

Looking at the horrible remains of this man Michael now burst into tears.

"He was a mean old bugger and was always shouting at me, but he taught me a lot about cooking, oh blimey look at him now."

"Don't look son," Albert told him, then turned to George, "We need something to carry him on, we don't know how bad he's hurt but we have to get him off this ship."

Billy then came back with a stretcher he had found in the ships first aid room.

"This should be ok boss. We can get him off on it."

"Great Billy, well done, now let's get Michael onto it and get the hell off this ship with him."

Carrying the stretcher they made their hazardous way through the still burning ship, dodging the jets of water that were being trained onto the flames, until coming to the gangway when they finally got him onto dry land.

Looking around they saw Joe Humphreys and shouted to him. He came running over and at once saw the pathetic sight of the partly clothed and injured boy.

"Whose this?" he shouted, and when informed he was the galley boy from the ship, Joe made arrangements for one of the doctors who were busy with the injured dock workers, to come and take a look at him.

There was no time for Albert and the others to dwell on this. As he was carried away they turned their attention to the shouting that was coming from their fellow dock workers, also with them was the imposing figure of Pat Morello.

"What the hell is going on here? Albert demanded. "Find out George, quick before something else goes wrong."

George set off to investigate and quickly returned.

"There's going to be a lynching Al unless the bloody army get here in time to stop it. That German body we saw that came floating up from the wreck of the plane wasn't a dead one. He's badly hurt but still alive. Once they got the sod out of the water a lot of our blokes saw it. They've just been bombed by that bastard's plane and a lot of their mates are either dead or wounded because of it. They want to string him up from one of the surviving cranes and I don't bloody well blame them."

Albert now walked over to this baying mob and took in the scene straight away. Two ARP wardens were trying to hold back this crowd of dockers shouting.

"Get back, this man is now a prisoner of war and as such is under our protection until the army arrives here to formerly take him prisoner. Any of you harming him will be in very serious trouble."

This of course had no effect at all and the mob began closing in on the two wardens. Albert had no love at all for anyone German, especially one who had been involved in the carnage that had just hit the docks and the ship in its berth. So his natural instinct was to turn his back and walk away. But there was something that was causing him to see red.

At the centre of the mob calling for the Germans blood was Pat Morello. No-one had noticed him slip away as they left the ship carrying the injured galley boy. Now he was in his element inciting violence. He had a knife in his hand and was urging the crowd into even greater desire to hang this German airman from the crane.

"That's it boys string the swine up and before you do that let's castrate the bastard."

There were shouts of agreement at this and, despite the warden's efforts, they reached the helpless man and started tearing his hated uniform off.

George had now joined both Albert and Salty Sam and the three of them watched this display of open hatred with mixed feelings. Not one of them had any pity for the German, but they did worry over the antics of Morello.

The German's uniform was in tatters and Morello was moving in with an evil look in his eyes and his knife quivering in his hand. That he had a blood lust was all too plain to see. He actually got to the side of the now terrified airman when a shot rang out.

"Get away from that man or we shoot to kill," came the voice of Captain Eric Osborne. He had arrived with three men, one a sergeant and the other two both corporals. Quickly summoned from their base at the Bargate as soon as the German airman had been taken from the water and found to be alive, they were here to formerly take charge of him for interrogation before sending him on to a prisoner of war camp.

Seeing the fate about to befall the stricken man he ordered some shots to be fired to bring these dock workers under control. For all but one of them it did, and they backed off quickly to allow the army men to do their duty. But Pat Morello still stood close to his enemy with his knife in plain view.

Now he snarled. "If all you bloody cowards are going to let these fucking soldiers rob you of taking revenge against a bloody German then watch what one man from Bournemouth can do. We ain't cowards down there so watch this."

He then lunged at the airman with the intent of carrying out his threat to castrate the man. He never made it though because as fast as he moved sergeant John Morgan was quicker. Without waiting for orders from his Captain he moved swiftly and coming up behind Morello hit him over the back of his head with the butt of his rifle. Pat Morello went down unconscious and was dragged away from the German.

Now, when the airman was safely in the army jeep with a British uniform jacket covering his exposed genitals, Captain Osborne looked down at the still unmoving form of Pat Morello.

"We should arrest this fellow and take him with us. What he was about to do was barbaric, and why was he carrying a knife?"

Surprisingly it was Albert and not Salty who answered first, having thought quickly.

"He has no love for anyone from Germany sir. His whole family got wiped out in a raid on Bournemouth just a few months ago. He has carried that knife ever since for just this reason. He always hopes to get the chance for revenge."

"I see," the Captain replied. "Well I'm sorry to hear about his family, but this sort of thing is taking place all the time across the British Isles. What if everyone acted in this way, we would be no better that any of our enemies. Alright, get him to the first aid room if you have one but if we are called here again and he starts trouble like this it will be the Guard House for him."

The Army Jeep then drove off with the German now looking distinctly relieved, a spell in an English prisoner of war camp being preferable to losing his manhood.

Pat Morello was taken to the first aid room and Salty Sam went with him. Albert and the rest were about to go back to work, doing what they could to clear up after the raid along with the much more gruesome task of finding body parts of men they had known who had literally been blown to pieces.

261

He was stopped though by Joe Humphreys. "Just a minute Littlejohn I want a word please."

Turning Albert saw the look on his foreman's face and knew this wasn't going to be good. But he went with him and entered the office. Now, standing in front of the big desk, Joe's first words took him completely by surprise.

"A young boy arrived at the gate and handed in a note addressed to you. He told the guards on duty that it is very important that this gets to you. So here it is."

Albert at once recognized the hand writing of councilor Teddy Wainright. He drew in his breath because to send a note in this way meant it was very important so he couldn't wait to read it. But Joe Humphreys was speaking again and this time Albert knew what was coming.

"That display out there with the German and the threat made against him was disgusting. I saw the whole thing and I didn't like it one bit. That man," he glanced down at his list, "Pat Morello meant what he said. He incited everyone to close on that helpless man. But Morello wasn't going to stop was he? I know a bloody knifeman when I see one and that is what that crook certainly is.

Fortunately the army responded to the phone message I sent and they handled the whole thing brilliantly. But let's make this very clear. Morello is out of this dock. The gate guards have already been told that he is not welcome in here ever again. And we will be watching the rest of his mates from Bournemouth and if any of them step out of line then out they go as well."

Rejoining the rest Albert was still fuming about it himself and told George Harcourt.

"We need to speak to Salty Sam about this tonight, but right now I need to see what Teddy Wainright has taken such a chance for by sending me this note."

Albert tore open the small envelope and read the message with growing concern.

"Albert, I have found this boy Alan Kinslade who I know is working for you. I have told him to make sure this reaches you without delay.

I have just come from a meeting with DI Stapleton at Portswood Police Station. He has told me, amongst other things, he knows someone is tipping you off when a raid on your family home is imminent. He doesn't however have any idea that the person he is talking about is me. But I will have to be more careful now.

The warden your men beat up last night has since died and this has been elevated to a murder enquiry. He's pulling out all the stops to find the killers and still has you at the top of his list of suspects. Men are crawling all over the front of that house where the warden was found and of course he knows there are items stolen from not only that one but several neighbouring properties.

It's these he particularly wishes to get his hands on so a surprise raid on your house is going to take place tonight. The DI himself will lead it, so please ensure sure they don't find anything."

Albert stared at this for a few minutes then sprang into action. Running to the dock gate he found, as anticipated, that Alan Kinslade was still there waiting for any response. He quickly took the boy to one side, out of earshot of the security guards.

"Well done Alan, this message is important. Now I want you to go to my house in Empress Road, you know which one it is?"

"Yes Mr. Littlejohn."

"Take this note and show it to my wife, tell her she is to carry out the usual plan for anything like this, have you got that? It's very important."

"Yes sir, you can rely on me. I'll make sure Mrs. Littlejohn gets your message."

"Good lad, so get off now and go straight to my house."

He stood for a few moments watching Alan sprint away from the dock gates. The situation was critical. If this went wrong it could be the end of the Littlejohn gang and almost certainly the hangman's rope for him.

There wasn't time to dwell on this. He was needed back where the bombed ship was still burning and there was much clearing up still to do, fighting the fire and trying to keep the ship afloat. The docks fire brigade was coping as best they could, but with so many buildings in Southampton being set alight by incendiary bombs the regular fire brigade were at full stretch, so couldn't attend this one.

Joe Humphreys was directing every man who was still on his feet to fight the fires and help pull bodies from the rubble of dock buildings. This work went on for hours but eventually some sort of order was restored and most of the fires, including the bombed ship, were brought under control.

It was time for the weary men to make their way home, but before he did Albert called into the first aid room. He glared at Pat Morello, who was now fully conscious and sitting up. He had a bandage round his head but was otherwise back to his old self. Salty Sam had come in behind him and now went over to his man. A whispered conversation took place between them and Albert could see that Salty was as angry about Morello's actions with the German airman as he was. But he kept out of this because he knew he would be talking about it later with Salty.

He turned his attention to the boy who was still lying on a bed, he had been patched up and was now wearing clothes that although too big for him, at least covered him up and allowed him to keep his dignity.

Going over to him Albert spoke softly.

"Well Michael how are you feeling now? You look a lot better than when we brought you in here earlier on."

A small smile crossed the boys face at seeing Albert.

"I'm feeling a bit better now sir and I want to thank you and the other men who got me off the ship."

264

"It was our pleasure son. You're far too young to die in a fire like that. Now where are your relatives? You do have some I hope."

"Only an uncle sir and he lives in London."

"I see," said Albert who now turned to the doctor. "What is the position with young Michael here doctor? His ship obviously isn't going anywhere, other than dry dock and he needs to recover from his injuries."

"Yes of course you're right, Littlejohn isn't it? Michael has told us how you and your men rescued him from the wreckage of that ship's galley. Now we have patched up the cuts and bruises he has suffered, but he has cracked bones in both arms that will take time to mend properly. He needs care and we are trying to get a hospital bed for him. We have found him some clothes. His own were in tatters and have been thrown away. They are far too big for him as you can see but they're better than nothing."

"Does it have to be hospital?" Albert asked. "Surely he will be better off being looked after by local women, and I know the best one to do the job. My wife has nursing experience and my eldest daughter will be able to help her as well. Give the boy to me and I'll do the rest."

The doctor mused over this for some minutes. "It's very irregular, but the lad's injuries aren't that bad and we do need every hospital bed we can get for the many casualties we receive. So alright, let's have your name and address and your wife's name as well and then you can take him home with you.

We will contact his relative in London who we hope will come down to find him. You will hear from us as soon as we've done that. And if this boy does get any worse get in touch with us or the nearest hospital straight away, is that clear?"

"Yes it is doc."

Albert now looked back towards the bed.

"Alright Michael, can you walk or do I have to carry you?"

Cut, scrazed, bruised and frightened half to death, Michael Roberts was however, a tough boy who had run the streets of London's East End, before going to Sea School and then into the Merchant Navy. He had looked after himself against some of the toughest boys around and done so with courage and determination. So he now looked back at Albert Littlejohn and stuck out his chin.

"I ain't hurt that much am I? The doctor just said so didn't he? Anyway I don't need him or anyone else telling me whether I can walk or not, of course I can."

With that he jumped to his feet and made to walk from the first aid room. It was a show of determination that, had it worked, would have been very impressive. But as soon as he took his first steps he tripped over the legs of the trousers that were several sizes too big for him. He would have fallen but for the shout of "Catch him" from the doctor. Albert saw the danger and acted with speed, darting forwards and catching Michael before he completely lost his balance. He gently but firmly placed the boy back on his feet.

"Well done," the doctor said. "If he had hit the floor it would have done him no good at all. Some of the bones in his arms are already cracked and falling on them would have caused so much more damage. This is one thing you and your wife will have to be aware of."

"Yes I can see that doc, don't worry both my wife Ida and our eldest daughter Maggie will watch out for that."

Then again, turning to Michael, "Right son, let's get them pants tied up a bit so your feet are clear, otherwise you'll go arse over head again when you start walking."

Ida Littlejohn was working hard with Maggie and her three younger daughters in the back garden shed of the house in Empress Road. Here they were stacking everything that had been brought to the house on old Percy Winkleman's cart.

The specially constructed store room under the floor of their old garden shed had been cleverly done by Sam Clifford. With an opening just big enough for Ida and the girls to go through and a small set of steps leading down to the floor, when closed the door simply melted into the shed floor and was invisible to the naked eye. The floor too had been cleverly strengthened so it wouldn't actually collapse.

Ida and Maggie told the younger girls to put everything where it would be easy to find later on in the evening once the shed was turned into a shop for their neighbours to use. They would be down in the room and have lists passed to them which they would need to make-up really quickly and pass the items back up to Ida and Maggie. Were this to become too slow then queues could form which would draw attention to their garden.

So work on this was well underway when they were interrupted.

"Ida, I need you here for a moment."

"That's your father, take over here Maggie and finish getting everything ready please. I'll go and see what your dad wants."

Hurrying into the house through the back door Ida was taken completely by surprise because her husband wasn't alone. Standing in their small back kitchen was this boy of about sixteen wearing clothes that were far too big for him and standing awkwardly as a result of this. His face was creased up in pain, and he also had an apprehensive look.

"We don't have much time love," said Albert. "I know we're going to be raided again tonight and a Detective Inspector is going to lead it this time. So is everything out of the house now? It's very important."

Ida was still looking suspiciously at Michael.

"Our three boys are with your sister in Dukes Road again so I'll just run down and tell Maggie to speed things up a bit. Everything we had in the house is in the shed so there won't be anything for the coppers to find, no matter who the bloody hell is in charge. And when I get back you can tell me who this lad is and why you've brought him here."

She ran back to the shed and quickly got them organized. Maggie would finish up there then go to the house while Ida joined the younger girls under the shed floor to make sure everyone was absolutely quiet. Maggie assured her she knew what to do and Ida was confident, so returned to the kitchen.

"Alright then Albert, I'm listening. Who is this boy and why have you brought him here?"

He told her about the bomb hitting the ship and how Michael had been trapped under the galley sink.

"It took us bloody ages to get him out and the fire was still burning so we knew we had to free him and get him off of that ship. Then we left him in the first aid room while we fought the fire on the ship and tried to sort through all the wreckage from the Jerry bombs. A lot more of our men died today love, and it wasn't a pretty sight. Well once we were finished for the day I went to see how young Michael was. He's pretty shaken up and some of the bones in his arms are cracked. Well they didn't have room for him in any of our hospitals so I got permission to bring him home with me. He needs care love and I think you and Maggie, between you, can give that to him."

Ida looked at Michael for a long time and he began to squirm, believing this to be a look of contempt at him invading her home. He was just about to say that he would rather leave now and go back to the first aid room at the docks.

"You look as if you need more than just care son," said Ida. "A bath first then we'll see where we can find to make up a bed for you. And those bloody clothes will have to go as well, they're miles too big and you look ridiculous."

She turned to Albert. "Mrs. Brighthouse over the road has a boy, Eric. He's about the same size and age as Michael here. As soon as I get a chance I'll talk to her. She's sure to have some clothes Eric doesn't wear much that she can pass on to us. If not, she knows many other women who should be able to rally to this cause, but right now, Michael when did you last eat?"

Taken by surprise at the kindness Mrs. Littlejohn was now showing him he stuttered.

"Umm well we had our dinner at twelve o clock today Missus, but I ain't had nothink since then because the ship got blown up see."

"Yes I think I do."

Ida pulled out one of the kitchen chairs and told him to sit down while she got some leftover stew from their evening meal. Michael's eyes came out on stalks when the plate was placed in front of him. It was filled with lean meat and plenty of vegetables that even on a merchant ship were very hard to get. He fell on it and started to clear the plate and Albert, watching him, spoke quietly to his wife.

"At the rate he's going we should have an empty plate, and a bloody good job too. There's stuff in that stew that any copper would love to see when they come round here. They'd have us by the short and curlies straight away because in that one plate there's more that our ration for the whole week."

Ida agreed and had to smile.

"Yes you're right. I'd forgotten about that left over stew. It would have been found and queried. I think I'm warming to this lad already."

Just then Maggie came into the kitchen and told her mother that everything was ready in the shed and she could go down there whenever she was ready. Then she noticed Michael.

"Who the hell is he and what is he doing here?"

"I haven't time to tell you that now Maggie," her mother replied as she made for the back door. "But make sure once he's finished the plate and stewpot are washed up before the raid."

"But what do I do with him then?" Maggie shouted.

"Get him upstairs into the boy's room and into their bed. Just tell the bloody coppers who he is and why he's here. Your dad will give you the details."

With that she disappeared from sight and entered the rickety old shed. Maggie may have been young but genuinely enjoyed taking charge of the others and the responsibilities her mother gave her. She was not about to be upstaged by the presence of this older lad and was determined to show him who was boss, snatching away the empty plate without glancing at him and clanging the pots around in the sink as she washed up.

Albert returned from checking on Ida and the others and he got Michael upstairs and into the bedroom before sitting down with his daughter.

"He needs help Maggie. Not just with his injuries, which in fact aren't all that serious. But he was caught in the blast that wrecked the ships galley and trapped for a while before we heard him call for help. He saw terrible things. The ships cook and the second cook were killed right there and its bound to have an effect on him for some time to come."

Maggie now felt a bit sorry for him.

"Don't worry dad, he did look ill didn't he? Me and mum will look after him alright."

Before Albert could answer there came a loud knocking on the front door and a voice roared.

"Open Up this is the police. Open the door at once or we'll force it."

Chapter Seventeen

In the incident room of Portswood police station DI Stapleton addressed the assembly of uniformed officers who were going to be taking part in tonight's raid.

"Search everywhere, especially the bedroom of Mrs. Littlejohn. I'm not convinced she's as ill as we've been led to believe. Move her if you must and turn that bed upside down. We've got medical staff with us who can verify her condition. If anything but fluff is found in the mattress then we can pull Albert Littlejohn in and throw him where he belongs, inside one of our cells."

Just then a constable entered the room and strode over to the DI.

"Excuse me sir but this message has been received from forensics." The desk sergeant said "you should see it without delay."

Taking the sheet of paper and thanking the constable the DI quickly read it. A slow smile crossed his face as he turned to Sergeant Podcove.

"My office, please sergeant. We have a breakthrough in the ARP warden murder. Things are starting to look up at last."

Once inside and out of earshot of everyone in the incident room DI Stapleton showed his sergeant the forensic message.

"Fingerprints at the murder scene have been matched to one John Penfold, who has previous convictions for robbery in London's East End. A prolific burglar he left London suddenly just before the outbreak of war. He apparently said something in a pub and upset a pair of twins, well known thugs who operate in that area. Knowing he was in deadly danger escape was the only option. He works in the docks and probably knows the members of the Littlejohn gang. That he was present where robberies were being committed gives us the reason we need to pick him up."

"Do we think he had anything to do with the beating of the warden sir?" asked Sergeant Podcove.

"Regretfully no sergeant, they've sent his records through and there's no record of his ever resorting to violence. No I don't think he had anything to do with that. But he was there Podcove, he may have some useful information. We can find out who he is working with. We have to get down to Empress Road as quickly as possible but put out all points bulletin and circulate Penfold's description.

Now, standing at the front of the door of Albert's house, the warning had been issued and the men gathered around the DI were ready to force entry if necessary. The door opened and the face of Maggie Littlejohn peered out at them.

"Oh it's you lot again is it?" she glared at Sergeant Podcove and then at his superior officer. "And who the bloody hell is this then PC forty nine?"

Ignoring this insult DI Stapleton simply replied, "Police miss and we have a warrant to search this house. My name and rank is Detective Inspector Stapleton of Portswood CID."

Producing his warrant card to back this up he pushed on past Maggie and entered the house.

She followed behind determined to let them know how she felt about this unwelcome visit.

"If I knew you lot would be turning up here tonight I'd have saved you the trouble of wrecking our kitchen again. I could

272

have just thrown all our food on the floor. To give these clods of yours a hand see."

DI Stapleton shouted to his men.

"Look everywhere, and you in the kitchen I want to know exactly how much food is in the cupboards. Look at labels and check every single thing."

Turning to Maggie his tone changed. "Now then miss, Maggie Littlejohn isn't it?"

"Yeah copper but you know that already don't you?"

"Yes I do and I have reports on you of attempted violence against police officers in this house."

Maggie started to argue but he cut her short.

"No don't interrupt just listen for once because what I've got to say to you is very important. You are very young but we can prosecute you without either of your parents being involved. And to be taken into custody, especially in times of war like this, will have lasting effects on your future life. We know you're old enough to go out working and I believe you do have a job, is that right?"

Preening herself now she cockily answered.

"Yes I do work you nosy sod and I've got a bloody good job. I work in the Grand Theatre."

"Really well that's impressive miss and what do you do there?"

His tone had softened and Maggie fell headlong into his trap without even realising what was happening.

"I've got an apprenticeship with the make-up artist Gerry Ramshot. He knows my mum and she told him I was good enough to work in that trade."

"Well that is impressive, so you're good at make-up then? Good enough in fact to make a perfectly healthy woman look so ill she is already at deaths door."

Too late Maggie saw the trap she had fallen into and started to panic.

"You can't accuse me of anything like that you bastard, I'm a good girl and I ain't done nothink like you're talking about."

"Well let's go and put that to the test shall we?" turning to sergeant Podcove, "Miss nothing sergeant, keep the men at it."

He and Maggie then mounted the stairs, the small children's bedrooms were now being thoroughly searched.

"Rest of the children not here tonight?" DI Stapleton observed.

"No they are round at their auntie's house in Dukes Road, they like's going there because they play with all their cousins. And they don't have to see their home being invaded by bloody flat footed coppers."

"Well my dear we only invade, as you say, the houses of people we believe are breaking the laws of this country. The young lad in bed, who is he and what is he doing here?"

Maggie had no answer to this really.

"My dad brought him home, he was on a ship what got blown up, you'll have to ask dad about that."

DI Stapleton chose to accept this for now and they came to the door of her parent's bedroom where four police officers and some medical staff were already waiting outside.

"What the hell is this lot doing here?" Maggie demanded. "Don't they know my mum is ill, get them out the bleeding way now."

DI Stapleton was quietly amused by this outburst because he expected it. He had already let Maggie know he suspected her of using make-up artistry on her mother and now she was in panic because she knew her work was about to be exposed.

"Alright everyone, let's get this door open."

One of the burly police officers put his shoulder to the door and it flew open. The DI was first to enter the room but the scene that greeted him was not what he was expecting and his face fell. The bed was neatly made up and empty. There was no sign of the very ill Ida Littlejohn.

Whirling round on a now grinning Maggie, he demanded to know what was going on.

"Alright, don't bloody shout. If you'd asked me before forcing your way in here I'd have told you. Me mam is staying with relatives for the next few days. Because she is really ill and needs the rest and a change from all of the bloody bombing."

"Where do these relatives live? We must check this out properly."

"I don't know do I? It's somewhere in Kent I think. My dad will know but we don't ever go to see them."

"And where is your father at the moment, as if I didn't know."

"Well if you already know why the sodding hell are you asking me for?"

"I won't tell you again girl," the DI was rapidly becoming impatient. "You will answer my questions or pay the penalty for it, now where is your father?"

"Why don't you try the Portswood Hotel? That's where he nearly always is at this time of night."

With his temper about to explode he rounded on the uniformed officers. "Alright, don't just stand there. Take that bed to pieces if you have to, I want evidence so find me some."

With that he stormed out of the room and went in search of his sergeant and found him in the kitchen.

"There's nothing here sir, we've been through everything. Nothing in those cupboards comes from the black market. In fact there's hardly anything in there. It's just like so many other homes."

"Yes and that's what's wrong here Podcove, this family is on the take. I know they are but this house is just too sparse? They're hiding something and we need to find it. Have we searched the attic and back room properly?"

"Yes sir and like all the other rooms both are clear of any sign of contraband."

"Right that leaves the garden then."

275

They went outside to join several police officers who were going over every stretch of this small back garden which was, in fact, little more than a back yard. The only building of any sort, apart from the outside lavatory, was the ramshackle shed.

"What's in here?" the DI demanded. "Has this been searched?"

"There's not much point sir," the sergeant replied. "As you can see it's only a quirk of fate that's stopping the whole thing from falling down."

"Never-the-less let's take a look inside."

The two of them gingerly opened the sagging door and stepped inside the musty smelling shed. It was damp because of the leak in the roof. Seeing a few old tools and some parts of a bicycle, it didn't need an expert to conclude that nothing of any consequence was being kept here.

Standing in the middle of the floor the DI was very angry.

"It's the work of that bloody informer who's tipping Littlejohn off every time we are going to raid him. He's up to his neck in the crime scene in Southampton and I won't rest until I nail the bastard. Come on, let's finish off here then you and me are going for a pint in the Portswood Hotel."

Coming out of the shed they were met by a motor cycle cop who handed the DI a note. Reading it swiftly he looked up at Sergeant Podcove.

"Well the night isn't a complete waste, this is a note telling me we have picked up John Penfold and he's now in custody at the station. Come on, I can't wait to see Littlejohn's face when we tell him this."

As the sound of voices faded Ida Littlejohn, with her three youngest daughters, cautiously opened the hidden door to the underground storeroom. They had been down there the whole time and heard everything that was said.

"Alright, we'll just wait until were sure it's safe and then start bringing things up to sell to our neighbours."

"Will the shed be alright mummy?" asked Jean Littlejohn, the next eldest of Ida's daughters. "It looks so rickety none of us ever go inside it."

Smiling at this Ida replied. "Your dad knows a lot of very clever men Jean and Mr. Clifford is one of them. He is a good builder and the room under the floor is all his work. He has put spars in place inside this shed to strengthen it and a door in the side that is not noticeable unless you know it's there. Now our neighbours can come and buy things from us they can't get anywhere else. They can come through the hedge of our garden and into this shed from there. So come on, let's get this place looking like a shop shall we."

In the public bar of the Portswood Hotel Albert and his men were settling down to an evening of beer drinking, the more they could consume the better chance they had of putting the horrors of today's raid out of their minds. Salty Sam was there with his boys as well and Albert looked at Pat Morello.

"What the bleeding hell has happened to you?"

Morello had a large bruise across his forehead and it looked nasty.

"None of your bloody business," he growled before finishing his beer and leaving the bar to go upstairs to his room.

Albert fired Salty Sam a questioning look.

"We went into that cafe in the docks, what's it called? Oh the Tall Funnel. Well we was delayed by Pat still being held in the first aid room, though all he had was a bump on the back of his head. When we got to the cafe they was just about to close up. The waitresses had gone home and the owner was behind the counter. She wasn't pleased to see us and it showed. Moaned about us holding her up and what a bloody nuisance we were.

For Pat this was the perfect time to start his protection racket. We was the only customers in the place so he went and had a chat with the owner. Told her who he was and what he and his boys could do for her, for a price of course.

277

Well the bloody woman just looked at him for moment before she reached under her counter. Then she brought out an Irish shillelagh and before Pat had a chance to dodge she belted him with the sodding thing. Accusing us of being crooks she did and said she wasn't going to pay a thing, threatened to get her brothers over from Ireland to do us. Then she threw us out, you should have warned us about that bossy tart Littlejohn."

Salty Sam took out a knife and ran his finger along the sharp blade before waving it a couple of times then replacing it. It was obvious his pride was dented and he did not take too kindly to being threatened in this manner. Albert was trying not to laugh and only just managed to keep a straight face.

"Well if that's the best your boy can do in the protection racket Salty, I must say I'm not impressed. Mrs.Toogood is a tough cookie but she has to be. The men who use her place would take advantage if they got the chance. She makes sure they never do. Well, tell him I hope he does better from tomorrow onwards."

There was more than a touch of sarcasm here, but before Salty could answer the door opened and DI Stapleton and Sergeant Podcove strode in purposefully. They reached the bar and ordered drinks and then the DI walked straight up to Albert's table.

"We've just been turning your house over Littlejohn, and as usual you've been tipped off. We found nothing incriminating and we know it's because you've got it all spirited away somewhere."

"Well if you found nothing it must mean there ain't nothing for you to find copper, so why don't you go and bother someone else for a change and give me and my family a rest."

"If I thought there was even the slightest chance that was correct I would indeed move my enquiries elsewhere. But let's not kid ourselves. You and your friends are thieves. We know it and you know it, so we will be on your case until you make the slip we know you will eventually. Oh and by the way do you know a man named John Penfold?"

The question took Albert completely by surprise and he wasn't quick enough to prevent a look of alarm from spreading across his face. Up to that point it had just been the same old routine and he had really been switched off and on autopilot. Now though the police officer had his full attention and he recovered quickly.

"John Penfold, yeah I know him, he works with us in the docks. So why are you asking me about him?"

"Because we both know he isn't just a dock worker now is he? He's a professional house breaker and we have him in custody. His fingerprints were found at the scene of a crime. I take it you have heard about the murder of an ARP Warden in Highfield Lane. Penfold's prints prove he was there when that happened so we'll be asking him about that and who else was there. He'll talk alright I'm sure. He'll want to save his own neck won't he? In case you've forgotten the penalty for murder is death by hanging. Enjoy your beer Littlejohn, it may be the last you'll ever get."

He quickly glanced around the table.

"And who are this motley lot, we haven't seen any of them here before, are they with you?"

Salty Sam answered before Albert could say a word. "Good evening inspector, my name is Samual Freeman and I am currently visiting this town. I hope to do business here in the future, when this awful war is over of course."

"I see sir and what is your line of business please?"

"Horse and cattle feed inspector, we wish to start up a factory producing this necessary food supply as soon as we can. It's so important for our animal friends to be looked after properly isn't it?"

DI Stapleton fixed Salty Sam with a look of deep suspicion. He didn't believe a word of what he had just been told but had no reason to argue about it. He then surveyed the rest of Salty's

279

men and the hackles went up on the back of his neck. He knew villains when he saw them and was certainly looking at some now.

"Well I wish you luck Mr. Freeman. I have a feeling we will be meeting again very soon."

He quickly turned his attention back to Albert.

"Well, we must be on our way. We have a murder suspect to interview, good evening."

He could sense the unease that Albert had displayed and felt he had finally managed to put one over on him. As he and Sergeant Podcove walked to the door the DI quietly instructed him.

"Keep this new lot under observation. They're no more into animal feed than we are, so I want to know the real reason they're here."

Once more alone in the bar Albert turned to George.

"You heard what that bloody copper said, how reliable is Penfold, will he talk?"

George had been very quiet up until now.

"I don't think he will Al. We don't know as much about him as we'd like, but he's from London and he knows how to look after himself. He won't bother about a spell in clink, but the hangman's rope is something else.

Albert was about to erupt but George continued.

"I've spoken to our boys who were involved in beating up that warden and they all say Penfold stood back and never laid a finger on him. But of course if the law can prove he was there when it happened they'll still charge him with complicity to murder, which is just as serious as the murder charge itself. But, from what I know of the man so far, he's great at getting himself out of situations like this. As I say, prison won't bother him. He'll simply say it was a coincidence that he was breaking into a house in that vicinity at the same time as our boys were fighting with the warden."

"Will he give descriptions of the men he saw beating up the warden?" Albert demanded and he was surprised by Georges answer.

"Oh I expect so, but I'm sure he'll describe men who look nothing at all like our boys."

This calmed both Albert and Salty Sam, so all of them took the DI's advice and got back to enjoying their beer.

In the back shed of the Littlejohn home business had been brisk, so many of their trusted neighbours coming in with lists of stuff they needed to buy. Ida was serving and her daughters Jean, Doris and Angela were down in the underground store room handing things up to their mother. This went on for just under two hours and when the last of the customers had been served Ida herself came down into the store room.

"Well done girls, let's get this place tidied up then we can go indoors and have some supper."

"What shall we bring up for that mummy?" Angela asked.

"Oh I think we can bring two tins of salmon don't you and some of that nice new bread."

So, it was an excited crowd that locked up the shed and went up to the back kitchen. Maggie was waiting for them and after noticing there were no more customers had put the kettle on. She had also brought in the tin bath from the garden and put the copper on to boil, which Ida quickly spotted.

"This is for that poor boy upstairs is it?"

"Yes mum," Maggie answered, trying to sound completely disinterested, and not looking up. She usually helped with all the baths but seeing to this strange older lad would definitely be her mum's job, not hers. The salmon was very quickly consumed and the younger girls sent to their rooms to read or play. Ida then filled the tin bath with hot water from the copper and made sure it wasn't too hot.

Michael was none too keen on the idea of undressing in front of a strange woman but she spoke firmly in a manner that reminded him of his aunt in London, whenever she wanted him to do something he didn't want to. Stressing the need to clean up his injuries and change his bandages she finally managed to convince him.

After taking off the makeshift clothes she could see his underwear was in tatters and on view now were all of the bruises and cuts that the bomb blast had inflicted upon him. Ida shouted up to Maggie.

"Run across the road to Mrs. Panshackle, I've asked her to round up a full set of young men's clothes for Michael here, and if I know her she will already have done that."

She eased him into the bath but as the water touched his body he cried out in pain.

"It will be alright in a minute, just sit still and let the water do its work." Ida tried to reassure him. "And don't use your arms as you have damage to some of the bones."

She proceeded to bath the whole of his body with sunlight soap including his hair and as he was being dried Maggie returned, carrying the clothes that Mrs. Panshackle had easily gathered. Seeing Michael stood there with nothing but the towel round him she stopped suddenly put the clothes down and shuffled awkwardly back towards the door.

"She said the ladies in the road were only too pleased to help mum, when they was told what has happened to umm … Michael. Most of them have got sons his age and size so these clothes should fit okay like."

With that she turned and disappeared. Ida smiled because she knew her neighbour would indeed rise to a challenge like this. So Michael was allowed to pull on the underclothing first before, with Ida's help, putting on the shirt and trousers. The shoes he was given were a bit on the large size but once he had them on and was fully dressed he looked just as he really was, a handsome sixteen year old boy.

Maggie was back, lurking by the door and now she looked at him.

"Not bad I suppose, actually you're cute, I could fancy you myself."

With that she was off again leaving him bright red, but before he could even think of an answer the house resounded to noise. The young boys as well as their father had arrived and the Littlejohn household was complete.

The boys fell on what was left of the salmon in the parlour, and Maggie attended to the needs of baby Thomas. The noise level rose as the boys argued with their sisters over who should have first go at the toys. Albert came into the kitchen and looked at the clean now smartly dressed boy who he had pulled from the wreckage of the galley of his ship such a short time ago.

"Hey this can't be the same lad I brought home with me today. The one wearing clothes that were far too big and wasn't very clean because he had just been blown up. So who on earth is this young man?"

Michael grinned at him.

"It's me sir, your wife has give me a bath and she got me some nice clothes to wear and all."

"Yes I can see that and very smart you look as well. So all we need to do now is get this bath out to the drain in the garden and tip the water away."

By the time this was done, with Albert at one end and Ida the other, and the bath placed back on the outside wall there came another commotion from inside the house. The boys had burst into the kitchen and were loudly demanding to know who this strange older boy was.

Ida managed to quieten them a little before explaining.

"This is Michael and he has been through a very bad experience, his ship was hit by a German bomb and he was hurt in the explosion. He is going to stay with us until we can make contact with his relatives in London. We have made up a bed for him in your room so you can get to know him very quickly can't you?"

This had the effect of bringing out hero worship in both the Littlejohn boys.

"Coo you was blown up by the Jerry's, what was it like, was you hurt? I bet you was." said Edwin as he stared at Michael with a new found admiration.

Albert now intervened and took both his sons in hand.

"Alright nippers let Michael get his breath before you bombard him with questions. I'm sure you want to have time to play before bedtime so off you both go."

Now alone in the kitchen Albert finally got the chance to speak to Ida about the evenings trade in the shed.

"Is the security still working alright? That blasted copper Stapleton is sniffing around all the more now that warden died. How was it here when he came?"

"Well to answer your first question, security is just fine. Only the people we know in this road, or friends of theirs that they bring, are being served. All your gang's wives are known to us so the same thing applies to them. As for the police raid, Maggie can tell you more about that than me, though when that inspector and his sergeant came into the shed the girls and I heard everything they said. It was all I could do to stop the girls laughing. Those coppers had no clue we were right there under their bloody feet."

"Yes but what did they say Ida, about me I mean?"

"Watch yourself Albert. He's after you because he knows you and your boys are up to no good. He's going to keep coming, he said as much to that sergeant of his. Then he was given a note about one of your boys being arrested and I don't like the sound of that, is it as bad as I think?"

"No it's the Londoner John Penfold who they've got and he won't grass us up. He's a hard case crook Ida. He'll keep quiet about our gang activities."

He turned his attention once more to Michael and called him back in so he could find out a bit more.

"You live with your parents I expect but what part of London is your home in?"

"Nah I ain't got no mum and dad. They was both killed in a train crash when I was still a baby. I've been brought up by my aunty Mavis and uncle Benny. They live in the East End of London and they know who runs the crime there. Maybe they could even help you Mr. Littlejohn."

"Yes I dare say but now I need to know where they live so we can let them know what's happened to you and where you are. So take this piece of paper and pencil and write down their address for us."

Later when all of the children, including Michael, were in bed Albert looked at this London address.

"This is a well-known hot bed of crime in the capital, we'll need to contact this uncle Benny of his as soon as we can. They need to know the boy is alive for one thing because it's certainly possible they know what's happened to his ship. So get me some more paper Ida please, and I'll get a letter off to them straight away."

At Portswood police station things were getting very heated. Inspector Stapleton and Sergeant Podcove were sitting on one side of a rickety oak table and on the other side, flanked by a constable, sat John Penfold.

"Come on Penfold we know you were there. Your bloody prints were all over that crime scene so come on tell us what we want to know. You're facing the drop if you don't, make no mistake about that."

"What for pinching a few items from them posh bleeders in Bassett, do me a favour copper I wasn't born yesterday."

"Okay then, an ARP warden was beaten up so badly that he died Penfold. You're right, we're not talking about petty thieving here. It's murder and you were there so you are implicated."

"Have you ever heard of the word co-incidence inspector? Yeah I was there and saw it all. I come out of a house right next door to where the fight was going on. I'd done alright there and got some good stuff but blimey I ain't into violence and when I saw what was happening I run off as fast as I could. Dropped the swag I had with me and all so I come out of it with nothink, now I gets picked up by you lot, well sod the bloody lot of you."

Inwardly the inspector groaned, he had already been told that stolen items had been found near the murder scene, now this thief was telling him it was he who had dropped them as he ran off.

Bringing the interview to a conclusion he had Penfold returned to his cell, then went back to his office with the sergeant.

"We both know not only was he involved with that murder but he was there working for Albert Littlejohn."

"Yes we know it sir but how the hell do we prove it? We need information and even our snouts aren't telling us anything useful."

"Get to work on uncovering the swine who is tipping Littlejohn off about our raids. It has to be someone inside, a bent policeman is all we need right now. Unmask whoever it is and we've got Littlejohn right where we want him."

At the same time as this meeting was taking place news was coming through on the BBC about a very significant event half way round the world that was to make a huge difference in this war. The American Navy installation at Pearl Harbour had been attacked by the Japanese with great loss of life and so many of its war ships sunk. This was to bring America into the war on the Allies side and also bring American GI's over to this country.

They would bring many things with them that Albert and other black marketers could sell. This was to open up many more opportunities but Albert himself didn't have a chance to think this over properly because a message had just been brought to him that Alan Kinslade needed to speak to him urgently.

Rushing round to the Kinslade house Alan met him in the Anderson shelter and he had Johnnie Burton there with him.

"Well what is it boys? It must be important for you to call me out."

"It's the Swaythling gang Mr. Littlejohn. We've found out they're going to move against you tomorrow night so we'll all have to keep a sharp look out for you."

Chapter Eighteen

Albert was alert to this straight away and demanded to know how the boys had found out.

"From Trevor Harvey's Belgrave boys sir," said Johnnie. "They've been listening to what that Griffin lot have been saying. Remember what Trevor said about one of the Belgrave boys' families moving to Mayfield Road, he had to transfer to Swaythling School from Portswood. Well he's been keeping them up to date about what them Griffin boys are talking about. They ain't got the sense to keep things secret see, so we knows what their grown up brothers and the rest of the Swaythling Gang are planning."

"Right and what precisely has this boy told you about their plans for tomorrow?"

"They're coming in force Mr. Littlejohn, some by boat and some by road. They want to catch you off guard and then, well they want to beat you all up sir."

"Yes I'm sure they do. Alright lads you're all needed tomorrow. I want to know that you are out watching and that you can get a warning to us once the Swaythling gang start to move."

"That's already been talked about sir," said Johnnie. "And I can tell you that Alan and me, with our group will be watching the roads from the Northam end and the Dukes Road Bridge. Anyone coming that way will be spotted, and a warning sent to you. Denis Frampton, Ollie Wimpson and of course Trevor Harvey with their boys will be all along the river bank and the railway line, they'll have their raft in the water and sail it down river blooming quick once they spot anyone from Swaythling in either or both of those places."

Albert now relaxed a little as he looked at the two eager faces in front of him.

"Well done both of you. Pull this off and get warnings through before Eddie Wheeler and his lot get anywhere near us and you'll all get extra money for it. Well done again boys and thank you."

Walking back he decided to go for a quick pint in the Portswood Hotel as he knew at least some of his gang would be there, along with Salty Sam. He saw George Harcourt straight away and went to join him at his table.

"I've just come from a meeting with Alan Kinslade and Johnnie Burton George. They've told me the Wheelers gang is going to stage a surprise attack on us tomorrow night. I've made sure they both know to get a warning about it through to us so we can be ready for them when they come. This is the big one George, we need to show that lot there's only one gang in this town who are any good and that's us."

George sipped his beer before he answered, and when he did there came a wicked grin spreading across his face.

"Good let the bastards come Al, we need some action don't we? And that lot is going to provide it. I'll get everyone up from downstairs so you can tell them about this. Have we heard any news about John Penfold yet?"

"No, but if he had talked that bloody inspector Stapleton would have come steaming round here with arrest warrants, you can bet on that. No it's as I thought, he won't drop us in it."

George went down to the secret room and came back with most of the Littlejohn men. Among these were Billy Marshall, Lenny Warren and Pat Matthews.

Albert addressed them all and outlined once again the threat emanating from Eddie Wheeler and his gang.

"I know I can trust all of you to pass on this message to the rest of our men. Make sure they know about it and are here in force tomorrow evening. We'll give the folks of Southampton a night off from having their houses burgled and put all of our energy into wiping out the Swaythling gang."

"And does this apply to my men and me?" came the voice of Salty Sam from behind them. "We can handle ourselves in a rumble like this and we have done many times before."

Albert turned round and looked at him.

"Yes I dare say you have but this fight is personal. We don't like that mob and they don't like us. So now they've decided to strike at us it gives us the right to defend ourselves and inflict some damage on them while we do it."

"There's only one man in Bournemouth who's more powerful than me and that man is Leroy Wort," said Salty Sam gazing intently at Albert. "All the rest of the crime scene is under the control of my men. It wasn't always like this, we had to fight to get the supremacy we now enjoy. What I'm saying Littlejohn is that my men are pros at this sort of thing and I can back them any time in this kind of fight. Besides, Pat Morello needs a confidence booster after that cafe woman walloped him with that shillelagh. He's a good man and a fight like this will bring out the best in him."

Albert thought this over.

"Alright Sam you're on, all your lot can join us, but we don't want to kill any of the Swaythling mob, just beat the crap out of them and let them know they are second best to us."

Pat Morello was feeling very down. He knew he had made a very big mistake in not properly estimating what a woman like Mrs. Toogood was capable of. He thought the female sex were weak and every single one of them would wilt under the not so thinly veiled threats he made about what would a happen to their businesses if they didn't cede to his demands.

He had found out very quickly and painfully that some ladies were very capable of protecting themselves and this one had made him look like a fool. He told himself it wouldn't ever happen again, from now on he would be the one doing the bashing.

The man himself now appeared back in the bar and accepted a drink from George before facing Albert.

"I may of made a bloody fool of myself twice today, but no-one regrets that more than me. Tomorrow me and my hand-picked boys will be paying a few visits to pubs and shops in this town. We'll use that as practice for the evening's events. We won't let you down, on that you can depend."

Albert accepted this without any problem at all and said. "Yes I think we all realize that Morello. You are the same as us and a set-back the like of which you suffered today should spark you and make you more determined. I look forward to hearing a report of how you get on before we tackle the Swaythling mob."

The next day brought some relief to the docks as no German aircraft came over so the job of clearing up and unloading went ahead much unhindered. But in town peace was most certainly not forthcoming. Pat Morello was good to his word and, along with his next most trusted thug Mickie Trumpforth, was spreading terror to local shop owners and pub landlords. Mickie had come in place of Davie Silver as he was needed in Bournemouth to keep the protection racket going down there. Starting at the Platform Tavern he and Trumpforth, flanked by their two mates who were both simply muscle with very little brain, were talking to landlord Neville Sampson.

"Nice little pub you've got here," said Morello.

Neville did not like the look of him. "Yeah and that's how we want to keep it."

"Well that's understandable and me and my boys here are the ones who are going to help you to do that. You must get a lot of dodgy customers who can cause a lot of damage. So we are here for you if and when that happens. We come and sort out any trouble see so you can just get on and run this nice little pub without any worry."

"That sounds good mate, but how much will this help of yours cost me?"

"Well since we will be in partnership so to speak how about half of your weekly takings?"

"I thought so, a bloody protection racket. Well I can answer that very simply. Piss off mate and take these prats with you."

Sampson had been around for a long time and had mixed with some of the toughest men in the dock area of Southampton for all of his adult life. But he was not prepared for the speed and ferocity of the attack that came from these Bournemouth men.

Pat Morello grabbed the front of his shirt and hauled him over the bar, where Mickie Trumpforth joined in and they both waded into the now helpless man. Morello had produced a pair of knuckle dusters and Trumpforth a lethal looking knife. Between them they made a considerable mess, the knuckle dusters causing cuts to the face while Trumpforth's knife was busy slashing at the landlords body.

He was soon covered in blood which spilled onto the floor. While this was going on the other two were doing as much damage as they could to the glasses and much of the stock as well. Once it was over the bar looked as if it had been hit by an enemy bomb. Glasses, bottles of beer and stout as well as some wine were smashed, their contents soaking into the sawdust that covered the floor.

Neville Sampson was also a very sorry sight, blood was covering his face and dripping off his chin so that the white shirt he was wearing had changed colour and was now bright red. At this point his wife came running in and, seeing her husband lying on the floor in a pool of his own blood, she screamed.

"Oh my God what's happened? Are you alright Neville?"

Pat Morello found this extremely amusing and laughed in Mrs. Sampson's face.

"No luv of course he ain't alright. We have just been teaching him some manners and letting him know he shouldn't try to disobey us."

"But I don't understand. Why have you done this and wrecked our pub? Who the hell are you you bastards?"

"We're friends missus, friends who will stop anyone else from doing anything like this in your nice little pub. All you have to do is pay us what we ask every month and you'll stay nice and safe."

"We don't need no protection racket, I've got lots of friends in this town who can take care of a little bastard like you. Get the bloody hell out of here and don't come back."

Neville's cry of "watch him Sylvia" came too late and she quickly found herself in an iron grip with the tip of Morello's knife to her throat.

"Now then lady, me and my men come from Bournemouth and there are a lot more like us down there. Any more threats from you and this pub will go up in flames. We know how to do that properly. You'll pay us every month or it won't be a bloody German bomb that burns this place down."

Shivering with fright now she could feel the evil that was coming from this man who had hold of her. She knew at this point that she and her husband were helpless, and resigned herself to having to find the money each month to pay these gangsters off.

Morello left the pub with an evil grin on his face.

"One down Mickie and we did good, those two stooges of yours are great at wrecking places ain't they?"

"Yeah Pat they are and both have done time for it as well, that's all they are good for."

293

"That's ok, just smash everything that you see and it's job done. So now we'll go and have our next drink in that pub where the crew of the Titanic had their drinks before it sailed. It's the Grapes in Oxford Street."

Over the next few hours in a merry little wrecking spree the Grapes as well as the Cork and Bottle, The Duke of Wellington, and the Red Lion all experienced the Morello treatment. Although in the case of the last two, which are the oldest pubs in Southampton, the landlords had agreed more readily than either of the other three.

Both of these ancient public houses were famous for their history and the Red Lion was where the conspirators for the assignation of King Henry 5th were tried and convicted. They were executed outside the Bargate and the pub now has memorabilia about this famous case inside. Having survived through all sorts of trauma in Southampton over the centuries, to have them destroyed by a group of ruthless thugs from Bournemouth was simply out of the question.

Standing in the sunshine outside the Red Lion they were satisfied with their work. Here they had threatened not just the landlord and his wife but their teenage son with unspeakable violence. The boy, Robert, was just seventeen and rebellious so a group of men threatening his parents was too much for him to ignore.

He had lunged at Morello and actually got in two punches before Mickie Trumpforth grabbed him and hauled him off. Then, with his parents watching, Robert was held by the two mindless thugs while Morello rained punches on him. He was beaten to within an inch of his life and dropped to the floor as soon as he was released where his screaming mother had rushed to help him. All that was on Pat Morellos mind was the fact that he was hungry.

"I need some grub Mickie so let's find somewhere to eat."

"That's easy Pat," Trumpforth told him, "just the other side of that castle thing, what is it they call it? Oh yeah the Bargate, there's a Lyons eating place, we can go in there."

It was crowded as usual, everyone hoping that Lyons had enough today to go round. There was a strict rule that people would only be served once they reached the head of the queue. No pushing in was tolerated because it simply wasn't fair. But Pat Morello wasn't going to wait. He always thought he was too important so queuing was for other people, not him. In this mood he bypassed the queue, which at this time of day was right back to the door, and marched to the front. Here he elbowed an elderly couple out of his way and demanded to be served.

There came an outcry from the other people waiting behind and violence was quickly looming. The manager came out and tried to calm things down.

"Take it easy everyone, I'm sure this is simply a misunderstanding," then he turned to Morello.

"There is a queue sir and we do have rules. Kindly take your place at the back and wait your turn like everyone else."

Morello was furious and reached inside his coat for his knife. The manager's life really was in danger at this point because the blood lust was once more coming to the surface and consuming him. It was Trumpforth who saw the danger and grabbed Pat by the arm to drag him away.

"Not in here Pat with all these bloody witnesses, Christ with this lot against us we wouldn't stand a bloody chance. Besides we don't want any of them knowing who we are or why we're here."

This made sense but as they left the jeers of the people in the queue made Morello even more dangerous. He was red in the face.

"Alright Mickie but we'll be back, I want that bleeding manager and I'm going to teach the swine a lesson."

After the air-raid, that came as soon as darkness fell that night, the ARP wardens were to find the body of a man lying in the street merely yards from Lyons. Turning the body over both of them recoiled at the state of it. The man had not just been beaten, his life had been taken from him in the cruelest and most inhuman way.

One of the wardens, Arthur Turnbull, managed to recognise the man, although his face was so disfigured it was a miracle that he managed this.

"Bloody hell I think this is Walter Simpson, he's the manager of Lyons. And I think I know who done this. A bloke with three others came in at lunch time today and tried to bypass the queue. He pushed an old couple, who were first, out of the way and demanded to be served.

Walter Simpson came out and calmed the situation because the rest of the queue was going to take matters into their own hands. Well, he told this bloke to go to the back and wait his turn like everyone else. The bloke nearly went ballistic and put his hand inside his jacket. I didn't see what he was reaching for but I'll bet it was a bloody knife. One of the blokes stopped him but I saw the look on the bleeders face, he was fuming and kept glaring back at Walter. I'll bet my life on the fact he's the bastard whose done this."

Morello himself was back at the Portswood Hotel up in his room, washing off the blood of the man he had just killed. He had waited, in the shadow of the car park at the back of Lyons, until the manager called goodnight to the cleaners who were now at work inside and made his way over to his car. He never got there.

He tried to fend off this attacker and was slashed twice in his right arm. Then making a break for freedom he ran for his life. Morello was much faster though and once out in the High Street he set upon the now helpless manager of the Lyons eating house. The attack was ferocious and this time there was no-one there to stop this ruthless man. Again and again the knife flashed and knuckle dusters were once more being used.

When he finally ceased and looked down at the wreck he had made of a fellow human being Morello's only comment was.

"That'll teach you to speak to me like you did today you bastard, no-one does that to Pat Morello and gets away with it."

Now he was attempting to clean himself up before joining the others downstairs to finalise their plans for the coming fight with the Swaythling gang. He had stripped off all of the blood soaked clothes and bagged them up, they would be thrown in the river at the first opportunity.

Now washing the blood from his body, his room resembled a slaughter house rather than a pub bedroom. But he cleaned everything before going down to the bar. He had been in this situation before so knew exactly what to do. Once satisfied he simply and calmly walked down to the bar to join all of the others.

No-one paid him much attention with the exception of Mickie Trumpforth. He saw the look on Morello's face and noted that he had changed his clothes, which could only mean that he had been to carry out his threat against the manager of Lyons. Another bloke in hospital now, he thought, but when the news of the murder and its ferocity broke the next day even this hardened gangster was going to be shocked by it.

Albert was outlining plans for this evenings fight and had delegated his forces to deal with the impending threat.

"Some of you will be with George under the road bridge at the bottom end of Duke's Road. You will watch for whoever comes that way. The rest of you will be with me in the marshaling yard. Our job will be to welcome any of the Swaythling lot who attempt to travel either by the railway or boat from Woodmill."

Billy Marshall spoke up.

"But what about the bloody Home Guard blokes who guard that yard every night? They're not going to miss a lot of us suddenly turning up in there are they?"

"No Billy they ain't, that's why we're going to pay them a little visit in that old hut of theirs. When this all this breaks out those two old codgers will both be sleeping peacefully, Georges cosh will see to that."

"And me with my boys, where do you want us?" asked Salty Sam.

"Play it as you see it, watch how things are going and wade in when and where ever you think you're needed."

There came an interruption as Albert was told that a man had turned up from London and was waiting at his Empress Road house to speak to him. Walking round to his home Albert wondered who this man could possibly be. Entering his house he was introduced to Benny Motson.

"I've come down from London because my missus and me were told about our nephews ship being blown up in the docks down here. We've got our own phone you see so the shipping line called us. What they didn't tell us and young Michael just has, is how you and your men rescued him from the wreckage of the galley and how much you and your family have looked after him."

"It was the least we could do," Albert assured him. "The poor lad was trapped in that burning galley. We had to get him out of there."

"Yes but you opened your home to him. My wife and I are extremely grateful to you and your family for this. I would like to leave him with you for a few more days as I don't think he's up to traveling at the moment."

"Of course you can he can stay as long as it's necessary."

The conversation then took a rather unexpected turn.

"You're Albert Littlejohn aren't you? We've heard of you in London. It may interest you to know that you and I are in the same line of business. We too operate a black market racket and we do it on a much larger scale than you can down here. We know who else in the south of the country is doing this besides us. And we keep an eye on everything that's going on.

298

We operate in London's East End are we are led by a pair of twins who no-one gives any trouble to, not if they want to stay healthy that is. Now we have more man power and clout than any other gang in the country. For what you have already done for us, if you and your boys are ever in trouble that you can't handle yourselves give me a ring on this number."

He handed Albert a piece of paper then continued.

"Because of this war you may have to wait a time before you can get through, but keep on trying and like I've said we'll come in force."

Albert thanked him and invited Benny to join him and his boys for a drink, also mentioning they had a bit of business coming up this evening with a rival gang.

Benny laughed, "This sounds just up my street, but I have to get back to London as soon as possible tonight. I'll just go up and say goodbye to Michael and tell him he'll soon be coming home to live with his Aunty and me again. I'll be in touch about that when it can be arranged."

Once back in the Portswood Hotel Albert knew it was time for them to get organized.

"Right, get ready. As soon as our young nippers tip us off about the Wheeler lot being on the move then we will give them a very warm welcome."

Johnnie Burton and Alan Kinslade had their mini troops in hiding along Portswood Road. Just past the Brook Inn at the bottom corner of Sirdar Road was a metal works. Trevor Harvey and his Belgrave boys often played in here, though they weren't supposed to. Tonight though they were ably backed up by Dennis Frampton and his Priory road lot and strategically stationed along the river bank and railway line. Dennis' group were in hiding by the side of the railway line where they could see right all the way up to Swaythling Station.

They knew it was most likely the Wheelers boys would come from the road bridge in Woodmill Lane so special attention was being directed there. If any of the men they were watching for turned up a runner was already in place to rush the information to Trevor who was watching the salt water side of Woodmill along with many eager little helpers. They could see right up the path from their swimming spot and their raft was already in the water so at the sign of trouble it would be launched and the information quickly relayed to Albert.

That just left Ollie Wimpson and his Kent Road accomplices. They were down the Northam end by the bridge. It wasn't really feasible that any of the Wheeler lot would come that way but they wanted it covered just in case.

The first warning message came from three boys who were concealed along High Road and could see the Hampton Park pub. A large group of men suddenly came out and started making their way towards Portswood. This had to be the Swaythling mob.

A runner was sent with this information and Johnnie Burton waited just long enough to get a look at these men before he sent not one but three further runners to get a warning to Albert. One thing that was apparent was there weren't as many men in this group as he had been told to expect so he whispered to Alan.

"There ain't so many here, which means some of them are going a different way, I hope Trevor and Dennis are alert."

They were indeed, both boys also had some of the Swaythling mob firmly in their sights. Men had been spotted climbing over the wall of the bridge and jumping down on to the narrow track that ran alongside of the tracks. Hiding among the long grass on the opposite side of this Dennis and his eagle eyed little companions watched as the men stared to walk slowly towards St Deny's Station. A runner was swiftly dispatched with this information for Trevor.

He and his little Belgrave Road helpers had also just spotted men from Swaythling, this time pulling a rowing boat heading towards the salt water side of Woodmill. So with the information from Dennis as well he directed operations to launch their raft. Once this was done Trevor and three of his boys jumped aboard.

Swiftly hoisting the sail they knelt and began to use the paddles as well. Carried by the current and with the wind hitting the sail the raft soon picked up speed. With all four of them paddling away furiously the water raced over the surface of the raft, soaking the boys from the waist down. This made no difference to any of them and they soon reached the road bridge at Dukes Road.

Shouting for the others to beech the raft further down out of sight Trevor jumped off and swam the last few yards to the bank, then ran to the side door of the Portswood Hotel to give this information to Albert.

Having just received the information about the men coming by road from Johnie Burton, Albert now looked at an out of breath Trevor as he stood dripping water on to the small step outside. He listened carefully then thanked him.

"All of you have done bloody well tonight so you will be handsomely rewarded. But get off now and get into some dry clothes."

Grinning at this Trevor replied. "Thanks Mr. Littlejohn but it's good for us to get one over on that Griffin lot. It's well worth a soaking and the good hiding I'll probably get from me mam."

Ollie Wimpson and his group were still keeping watch on Northam Bridge and so far had nothing to report. But they would stay on duty for a little bit longer to make sure. It looked as though their swimmer wasn't going to be needed tonight.

Inside the Portswood Hotel Albert was quickly organising his troops. The public bar was crowded as his gang had been joined by the Kinger brothers and some more of their friends. Each and every one of whom enjoyed a good fight.

"First of all I want those two old codgers from the Home Guard put out of action. They're not to be harmed mind you just put to sleep for a while. Then I want a lot of you hiding in the marshalling yard. Some of the Swaythling lot are coming by road so will come here first.

Bernard will tell them we're down by the water's edge waiting for a shipment, or something like that. So they'll come on down and we'll be waiting for them. The ones following the railway line will go through St Deny's Station and come into the marshalling yard from there.

I hope none of the porters are daft enough to challenge them because if they do they'll get hurt. Therefore I want enough of you watching the station and getting the jump on them. That leaves the daft sods in the boat. Well they're coming by water so I want them ending up in it. We'll get the better of them, then put them back in the boat and push them off into the river."

"Let them get away boss?" Billy Marshall enquired.

"No Billy, for one thing the current here is very strong and will carry their boat a long way down river, and the Swaythling boys will be too busy bailing their boat to get to the bank because we'll have punched a couple of holes in it."

There was a round of laughter before everyone moved off into their allotted places. First though Billy Marshall and Harry Small made their quiet way to the old shunter's hut in the marshalling yard. This was to have been the job of George Harcourt and his cosh, to put the two Home Guard soldiers out of action. But Harry Small had a cousin who was a chemist and had managed to get hold of some chloroform.

So Billy and Harry now took up positions on either side of the door, before banging on it. The two Home Guard Soldiers inside raced out to see what this commotion was about and soon found themselves held from behind while rags filled with chloroform were pressed against their nose and mouths. Both of these men fell to the ground deeply unconscious and were dragged back inside the hut. Then, at a sign from Billy, Albert's men took up their positions inside the marshalling yard.

Eddie Wheeler and his group had reached the Portswood Hotel. Going inside he quickly looked around for any sign of the

Littlejohn gang. Seeing none he walked to the bar and confronted Bernard Bumstock.

"Where are they then?" he snarled.

"Where are who, and while we're at it, who are you lot and what do you want here?"

"We've come to pay a little visit to the Littlejohn outfit. We owe them a bloody good thumping, and if you don't help us out with information this pub is going to be changed a lot. My boys can be very destructive at times, just as much as all what happened in town today that everyone is talking about."

"Don't you threaten me you creep," shouted Bernard, "Get out of here the lot of you, if you want the Littlejohn boys they're probably out by the river somewhere waiting for things to arrive. So get out of my pub now."

"Well thanks for telling us that landlord, but we ain't in no hurry to leave see. I think we'll have a pint each before we start."

"You'll get fuck all in this pub now or at any other time, I've asked you nicely to leave now I'm telling you, get the hell out of my pub."

"Fighting words ain't they boys, but you ain't no fighter I can tell," Wheeler smirked to his group before returning his gaze to Bernard.

"And whose going to help you chuck us out, not these locals. None of them look ready for a fight either."

"We are," came the booming voice of Catherine Bumstock. She was standing at the end of the bar holding a wicked looking and very stout walking stick in one hand. With her other she was holding on fast to the collar of their German Shepherd dog. He knew something was not right and was snarling ominously as he eyed up the Wheeler group.

Swinging back round, Wheeler noticed Bernard had armed himself too. In his case with a twin barrelled shotgun. The fact that he had no ammunition for the gun was not a serious problem because Eddie Wheeler wasn't to know that. Just the sight of this weapon pointing at them, plus Catherine and her walking stick along with the snarling dog that was straining at the lead in his efforts to get at them, made Wheeler's men decide to move very quickly towards the door.

"Well boys we lost that one, but when the rest of us get here we move down to the river and teach this bloody Portswood lot a lesson they won't easily forget."

With that this group made their way down the side of the pub, ready to cross the marshalling yard. Here they would wait until they could see the rest of their boys coming, before launching what they believed would be a surprise attack on their rivals. Albert and his group though had already spotted them and were ready for a counter attack they knew would go in their favour.

Everything was looking good but unbeknown to Albert trouble was brewing elsewhere due to a late night meeting at Portswood police station.

Chapter Nineteen

The incident room at Portswood police station had been a busy place of late but tonight was especially so. DI Stapleton was addressing a room full of CID officers. He pointed at a blown up photograph.

"This, gentlemen, is the battered and bloodied body of the manager of Lyons in the High Street. And I have to say this is the worst case of violence inflicted upon an individual that I have seen. We believe only one man was responsible for this and we need to have him in our cells quickly."

"Do we have any leads on him yet sir?" asked one of the listening officers.

"Oh it's better than that because of reports of an incident that took place in Lyons yesterday lunchtime. Four men barged in taking no notice of the long queue and went straight to the front. After demanding to be served the manager was called and told these men to wait their turn. Three of them started to turn away but the one in the lead made an attempt to attack the manager. He moved forward whilst putting his hand inside his jacket where we believe he had a knife. It was seen by at least two people but their descriptions vary somewhat. This attack was prevented by one of others in this group who pulled this man away telling him not to start anything where there were so many witnesses.

A lot of the people we have spoken to already say they heard this man utter evil threats against the manager. Last night I think that same man waited outside Lyons for an opportunity then viciously attacked him. We know a knife was used, and we have information now that knuckle dusters featured as well."

There was a shocked silence whilst the officers took in this appalling information, until a young DC spoke up.

"What do we know about the man who did this sir?"

The DI looked at this young constable and noted he was very keen. This was something he liked to see in his officers.

"We have more than that son because we think we know exactly who he is. Two days ago Sergeant Podcove and I were in the Portswood Hotel talking to Albert Littlejohn. We had turned his house over again and found nothing, so it was more anger than anything else that made me go in there to confront him. He, of course, wasn't even phased. He knew he had got one over on us again.

But there were men in there with him that night that I had never seen before. And a right lot of villains they looked as well. They were led by a man who said his name was Samuel Freeman from Bournemouth and he and his team were there to look for suitable places to open an animal foods factory. Complete nonsense of course because I knew I was looking at a right nasty piece of work. But looking back on it now I remember one of the men standing behind him and this one made my skin crawl. More importantly than that though the description we have of the man who started the trouble in Lyons fits this particular man."

There was a very definite stirring of interest and suggestions were soon being made about what they should do in order to find and arrest this man.

Holding up his hand or silence the DI continued.

"We know this blighter fits the description alright but we still don't have any evidence so we're going to raid the Portswood Hotel and surrounding areas very carefully indeed. We need something that ties this man to this particular murder, so let's get down there and make a start."

They piled out and soon several police cars were speeding they're way down to Bevois Valley. Screeching to a stop outside the Portswood Hotel, however, they were confronted by a mass brawl that was taking place behind the pub and the noise from this was deafening.

Albert has bided his time until all three groups of men from the Swaythling gang were within a few yards of where he and his men were hiding. The group that had walked down by the side of the railway were led by the Griffin brothers. And as they made the platform of St Deny's Station and started walking along it they had been confronted by Rupert Longstirip who was a porter. He demanded to know who these men were and where they had come from.

"Here you can't just come walking through here you know. This is railway property, British Rail. Members of the public are not allowed to walk by the side of the tracks nor enter a station in this way. I shall have to report you for this."

He got no further as the largest of the Griffin boys strode up to him and gripped the front of his uniform.

"Now you listen to me Mr. Porter," Griffin told him, "we go where we want, when we want, and no little company official is going to stop us. So get back inside before you get really badly hurt."

Thoroughly shaken up now Rupert Longstirip did as he was told and the Swaythling boys moved on, stopping under the road bridge at the bottom end of Dukes Road. Looking towards the river they checked to see that the boat party were making their way towards them. When these two groups met up Kenny Hoare, who was leading the boat lot, asked if there was any sign of the Littlejohn gang anywhere near the river.

"It don't make no sense," said Kenny, "some of those bastards should be active down here, they are always loading stuff onto their boat so where the bloody hell are they?"

"They must be around," "somewhere," the Griffin boys replied one after the other. "So let's move on in and scare the bastards out into the open."

This whole group now forged ahead together, making for the marshalling yard but watching them coming were Albert and George.

"Wait just a bit longer, until Wheelers group meets this lot, and then make sure our men know what to do." Albert hissed at him.

"Don't worry about that, all of our boys and the others who are here to help us know exactly what's required. Once you shout they'll bound into action."

Albert nodded in agreement and watched as Eddie Wheeler met up with the rest of his gang. Then, as they started to make their way into the marshalling yard Albert placed his hands around his mouth and shouted.

"Littlejohn Gang!"

From the St Deny's side of the road bridge, from concealment amongst the wrecks of the old wooden boats on the Itchen shoreline, and from inside the marshalling yard, Albert and his troops came at the Swaythling lot from three sides. With shouts curdling the air they fell on their enemies and a bitter fight ensued. The Swaythling mob, although out flanked and taken by surprise by the turn of events, none-the-less quickly rallied because all of them were seasoned pub fighters.

Fists, chains, knuckle dusters and an assortment of other weapons were now brought into the fight and men from both sides fell. But Albert's boys held all the aces with the Kingers and their group along with Salty Sam and his, outnumbering and outfighting Eddie Wheeler and his mob.

Fighting with Salty Sam was Pat Morello, a natural thug with a very definite blood lust, using both his knife and

308

knuckledusters to awful effect. Salty Sam put his blades to good use, whilst George Harcourt, of course, was wielding his cosh and taking out more than one of the opposition.

On the fringe of the fight some of Albert's men were rounding up some of the fallen Swaythling lot. At least twelve of them were put into a rowing boat that now had three holes punched into it and they were pushed off into the current and taken downstream as the boat slowly took in water. Other Swaythling men were simply dragged to the water's edge and pushed in.

Albert, with blood running from a cut above his right eye, was savouring the way this fight was now going but it was interrupted very suddenly by the sound of police whistles.

As soon as the police car arrived outside the Portswood Hotel the noise from the battle going on behind was so loud it couldn't be ignored. DI Stapleton made a quick decision. Sending two of his men inside the pub with orders to search the room of Pat Morello, he made a dash with the rest of his team to break up whatever was going on outside. With whistles sounding they swooped on what was fast becoming a massacre.

Albert's men now outnumbered the Swaythling lot and the sheer weight of numbers was becoming apparent. More of Eddie Wheelers men had ended up in the water which was now red in places. The Griffin brothers were standing firm and gave a good account of themselves until George Harcourt waded into them with his cosh. Eddie Wheeler was facing Salty Sam, who had his trusty knife in hand and was about to use it with his usual deadly effect. This could have caused Wheeler to lose his life or be very badly maimed. He was saved by the interruption of police officers who were now rushing amongst them with truncheons drawn ready for action.

This ended the fight there and then and DI Stapleton took charge. Sending his men to pull the Swaythling lot out of the water he saw to his satisfaction that the rowing boat, packed with twelve more of the Swaythling mob had been stopped by a

309

police launch. This was probably just as well as it was already half full of water and very unstable indeed. Now, with all of the combatants rounded up including the ones from the rowing boat, ambulances were called and the more badly wounded from both sides were taken off to hospital.

Albert and Eddie Wheeler were the first to be spoken to by DI Stapleton who demanded to know just what was going on here.

"This is a private fight between men from different areas of Southampton," Albert told him and was backed up by Wheeler. "Yeah that's right copper, this is a private fight and nothing to do with anyone else, not even your lot."

"That's as maybe," the DI then beckoned to Salty Sam to come and join this discussion. Deciding upon a subtle approach he started by asking the gangster from Bournemouth how his search for premises to open his animal food factory was coming along.

"Found any likely places for it yet have you?"

With blood running down his face from a head wound sustained when a piece of metal hit him on his right hand side, he wasn't really expecting this.

"Nothing yet, but we'll keep looking."

"Will you really? We both know this is a load of bullshit really don't we? You're no more looking to open a factory in this town than I am. You're here for a very different reason and we are watching you closely. But tonight we want to talk to one of your men who we think can help with our enquiries."

Salty replied carefully with a sullen look on his face.

"Oh yeah and which one is that then. We ain't been here for more than a couple of days so how can any of us help you?"

Without answering DI Stapleton produced a blown up photograph that had even Salty retching as he looked at it. Both Albert and Eddie Wheeler turned away, their stomachs heaving.

"Not a very nice photo is it?" But this is why my men and I are here tonight. The manager of Lyons in the High Street, he

310

was a decent hard working man who earlier that day got threatened outside his shop. This has been testified to by several of the people who were in the queue, all of whom have made statements.

Now when I saw this I remembered the first time I saw you in the Portswood Hotel. I didn't believe your story about the animal food factory because I know villains when I see them. The descriptions we have about the trouble maker in Lyons matched one of your men to a tee. We contacted Bournemouth CID about this and they have positively identified the man we want in connection with this vile murder. His name is Pat Morello and he's here somewhere."

There was an interruption at this point as one of the police officers, sent into the Portswood Hotel to search Morello's room, returned bringing a large bag with him.

"I think you need to see this sir."

DI Stapleton saw immediately what he meant for the bag contained some heavily blood stained clothing.

"Where did you find this?"

"In Morello's room sir."

"Right get most of this lot into the black Marias when they get here, but I want some of you with me. Morello is here and we need to find him."

Mickie Trumpforth was standing with George Harcourt.

"If any of those coppers gets hold of Morello it will mean big trouble for all of us. So where the hell can we hide him?"

George knew they needed to act swiftly.

"Where is the mad bastard? We need to get him out of sight and there's only one place we can put him."

"I'll get him just wait a minute."

It was less than that before Mickie returned dragging a very disgruntled Pat Morello.

"What the bleeding hell is this all about? You wanna be careful or I'll do you right now and all. I ain't afraid of a few bloody coppers either."

311

He soon found himself in the vice like grip of George Harcourt.

"I don't care what you think you mad swine. You killed that manager of Lyons and we're just getting details of how bad the beating was. This is putting police attention onto us. We don't want your sort of madness in this town so you're going back to where ever you bloody well came from. But first we have to make sure the coppers don't get hold of you. They've just found the blood soaked clothes you was wearing when you committed that murder, you were stupid enough to leave them up in your room."

Morello then felt the end of George's cosh pressed against the side of his face and received a chilling warning.

"Every one of our boys is capable of the sort of violence that you seem to thrive upon. But they know how to control it. Me on the other hand, well I'm like you and I get a thrill when I'm bashing some poor sods head in. So you move with me right now or I'll be happy to give you a demonstration."

This wasn't strictly true but Morello wasn't to know that. He therefore let George and Mickie Trumpforth lead him to the back of the Portswood Hotel where George opened the door to the secret room and pushed Morello inside.

"Stay in here and keep bloody quiet until we come back in."

Then as he went to go outside again he turned back and glared at Morello.

"And keep you're thieving hands off all this merchandise. We know exactly what's in here and if any of it is missing when we come back then God help you."

It was to be a long time before they did return. Albert and Salty Sam were missing when he returned and there was no time to work out where they had gone before two police constables appeared on either side.

"Nice of you to show up Harcourt, we've been looking for you so now you can come and join your boss in the Maria out in Dukes Road."

He was led out after being frisked and having his beloved cosh taken away, then thrown into the back of the black Maria where he saw Albert, Salty Sam and some of the rest of the Littlejohn Gang, including Billy Marshall. All of them were displaying their battle scars and bleeding.

"What about Morello?" Albert whispered to him.

George tried to reassure him that they wouldn't get their hands on this man because he had hidden him away. He then glared at Salty Sam.

"This swine brought the mad murdering bastard here to cause all this trouble."

"Don't you turn on me for this," Salty shouted. "Morello is a good man to have around but he does have a very nasty temper."

"A nasty temper, is that you call it? Well I'm telling you he should be admitted to a bloody lunatic asylum."

Salty went ballistic, reaching for his knife which was no longer there, having been taken away by the police. The two men tried to get at each other and a fight would have ensued but for the intervention of Albert.

"Stop that you stupid idiots. We're in the back of a police wagon so how far do you two think you would have got, fighting in here. Now where is he? You sure the coppers have not got their hands on him?"

"No, his mate Mickie Trumpforth came hurrying up to me and between us we got the murdering pig into the secret room at the Portswood Hotel. I've told the bastard to stay in there until we get back and I've also warned him that we know everything that's in there so we'd better not find anything missing when we check."

It was now Albert's turn to glare at Salty Sam.

"Right that's it for you lot up here. You're trouble and you're bringing it down on us. Every bleeding copper in town is going to be on the lookout for him. We've got to get him out of here somehow and send the swine back to Bournemouth where he belongs."

313

"Just like that is it. One of my boys loses his head and you're kicking the rest of us out?"

"Too bloody right we are. We never wanted you here in the first place and now even less. We'll beat this bit of trouble alright because a brawl only means a slap on the wrist. But tomorrow night George and I will meet with Leroy Wort in the Horse and Groom and I'll be telling him the same bloody thing I've just told you."

At this point they all arrived at Portswood police station and were ushered inside. There were skirmishes while this was taking place because the Swaythling mob tried to restart the fight that had brought all of them here in the first place, the Griffin brothers being particularly aggressive until stopped by overwhelming numbers of police officers.

All of them were pushed into cells, but it wasn't long before Albert, George and Salty Sam were escorted to an interview room where DI Stapleton and Sergeant Podcove were waiting. The DI stared intently at each of them in turn.

"Well Littlejohn, it's nice to see you here as our guest, if only for a short time. There will be fines for tonight's little fracas, but I'm sure that won't bother you at all now will it? You're getting off lightly because you're needed in the docks tomorrow and that is why you will spend just the one night in the cells here. We don't want the kind of brawls that you and the Wheeler gang were engaged in tonight taking place in this town. Oh we know you need to show how hard you and your men are, but not out in the open. And you can thank your lucky stars that the two Home Guard soldiers who your men put to sleep have recovered and are none the worse because of it."

He then turned his attention to Salty Sam and his voice hardened.

"As for you my fine friend Mr. Freeman, you're not even from this town, so why would you be involved in a skirmish like that?"

He quickly raised his voice.

314

"Where is the mobster Pat Morello? We know he's with you and he is now wanted for murder. And a particularly vicious one at that, we've searched his room at the Portswood Hotel and found this."

A constable came forward carrying the sack. Di Stapleton took it and opened the top.

"Look inside Mr Freeman and see what your henchman is capable of."

Salty did as he was asked and even though he was a tough gangster who relished violence, he recoiled slightly at the state of the clothing inside.

"Yes not a pretty sight is it, clothing so soaked in blood that it defies explanation how they came to be in this state."

He then produced a photograph before carrying on.

"Not that is until you see how badly hurt the victim of this crime was. This sack was found in Morello's room along with these." He now produced the knife and knuckle dusters. "These were also recovered from the bastard's room and we will soon have evidence that the blood matches that of the murdered victim. We won't tolerate violence such as this happening in our town Freeman, so I say again, where is Morello?"

Salty Sam was conscious of everyone looking at him, both police and Littlejohn gang members. His normally calm, smooth talking and sneering manner had temporarily deserted him and he had no idea what to say in response. He was not a very good liar and was sure the police would soon trip him up and obtain the information they required.

Albert knew Morello's hiding place must not be revealed. If the police found out about the secret room then they would also uncover all the merchandise hidden in it. That would be a disaster for the Littlejohn gang and for Bernard and Catherine Bumstock.

Salty Sam finally spoke up.

"Morello was with us when the fight started but none of us have seen him since. If your lot didn't find him when you dropped on to us and broke up the fight, then he must have seen you coming and scarpered."

"If he has then he won't get far," the DI insisted. "We've already got the bus and rail stations covered so he only needs to turn up at either of those and we will grab him."

Albert and his men were then ushered out and returned to the cells and the DI gave instructions to Sergeant Podcove.

"Give them breakfast early because they need to be at work in the docks before seven."

He quickly recognised the look the sergeant always used when he didn't agree with his superior officer.

"I know, they're crooks, the bloody lot of them, but by day they keep the docks working and now it's even more important than ever."

Eddie Wheeler, along with the Griffin boys, was now being brought in.

"Well I haven't had the dubious pleasure of making your acquaintance before, though of course we know all about you and your gang. So what was all this fighting about tonight?"

Sullenly Wheeler answered. "Look mate that was a private fight between two rival lots of blokes who don't like each other very much. It ain't nothing to do with anyone else, not even the bloody police."

The Di gazed steadily back at Wheeler, then at the Griffin brothers, all of whom were sporting injuries sustained in the fight.

"Well by the look of you your gang lost didn't they? To answer your comments I can tell you that what happened tonight was a breach of the peace as well as a public outrage, and I am well within my rights to hold the lot of you for an appearance at Southampton magistrate's court in the morning."

"Hey hang on a bloody minute that Littlejohn gang was just as involved as we were so are they going to be up in court for it?"

"No, as we have found out that it was your lot that started it

316

and the Littlejohn gang were protecting themselves as a result."

There was silence before Wheeler replied.

"Look Inspector none of my boys are angels I know that, but we do know what's going on in this town."

"And what's that?"

For the next few minutes the Inspector held his breath as the information he had been searching for was delivered by Eddie Wheeler.

"We've been around in Swaythling for as long as Littlejohn's lot in Portswood. We go back to school days. We know Littlejohn and Harcourt were there at the same time and one other I have a feeling you might be interested in. His name is Teddy Wainright and we all know he's the councillor for the Portswood Ward.

Well me and my boys keep an eye on that lot, just as we know they do on us. But the Griffin brothers here can tell you something else I'm sure will interest you."

DI Stapleton now eyed the two thugs and invited them to tell him what they knew.

"We know what pub Littlejohn's lot hang out in and we have both seen that creep Wainright going in there and talking to Littlejohn and Harcourt."

The hair on the back of the DIs neck stood out as he took in this information. He had for so long wanted to know how Littlejohn was alerted to raids on his home. Now these two brothers were telling him that one man he trusted above all others was perhaps the very one he was looking for in connection with this. It made perfect sense. He always discussed raids with Councillor Wainright before they were executed, without ever dreaming this information was being passed on to Littlejohn.

This still seemed unbelievable. So he questioned the Griffin brothers a lot more and found out not only had they seen the councillor drinking with Littlejohn, but they also had times and dates when these visits occurred. A quick check with police records showed that each of the councillor's visits to the Portswood Hotel coincided with plans for raids on Littlejohn's home. It wasn't conclusive evidence of course but certainly warranted deeper investigation.

Sending the Swaythling lot back to their cells he talked to Sergeant Podcove about the whole situation.

"Release both lots of thugs we've got in the cells tomorrow morning, but make sure the Littlejohn lot are well clear before you release the Swaythling contingent. The last thing we need now is for both sides to meet out in the street and start bloody fighting again."

He then moved onto the situation regarding Councillor Wainright. Outlining what the Griffin brothers had told him he asked his sergeant for his thoughts on the matter.

"This takes some believing sir, the councillor has always been invited here to be told what we are planning. I can't believe he went and revealed our plans to those bloody gangsters."

"I know I can't believe it either but those Griffin brothers certainly do and they've given us dates when Wainright and Littlejohn have met up. And they tally sergeant, so we have to take action bloody quickly. Get out a warrant for the councillors arrest, we need to grill him over this. I want him here in this station by no later than tomorrow morning."

Sergeant Podcove knew why his superior officer was getting so worked up. He not only trusted the councillor completely, but had always thought of him as a friend. That was the reason he never even considered this man as being the one responsible for the leakage of confidential information.

With plans in place for his arrest the DI signed off and went home. He never dreamt that the PC who said goodnight to him as he left the station would be the one to thwart his plans altogether. PC Norman Pussyfoot was in the pay of Albert's gang and lost no time at all sending a warning that Councillor Wainright was now in danger of arrest and exposure.

It was Bernard Bumstock who took the phone call and he was

somewhat at a loss to know what to do about it. After all, Albert and George were at that moment locked in a cell at the police station. He called Catherine over to discuss the situation.

"Albert can't do nothing about this can he because the coppers have got him and George, as well as some of their boys locked up for the night. We need to do something to help but I don't know what."

Catherine was made of sterner stuff.

"Pull yourself together you great toad, Albert always said if a situation like this comes up we need to alert the councillor without delay. And he's left a phone number for us to do that."

Going to the till she reached over the back of it and pulled out a small piece of paper, then dialed the number that was scribbled there. Eventually it was answered.

"Hello, is that Councillor Wainright?"

"Yes it is I'm rather busy at the moment in the middle of my dinner so what is this about?" came the disgruntled reply.

"This is Catherine Bumstock of the Portswood Hotel councillor. I'm sorry I've interrupted but you must get yourself over here at once. My husband and I are acting for Albert Littlejohn and we've just been tipped off that the police want to interview you about the information they believe you have been passing on to Albert."

There came the sound of someone chocking down the other end of the phone until the councillor managed to compose himself enough to answer.

"Oh I say this is quite terrible, how have they got onto me? I will be ruined I'll be thrown out of the council and probably locked up in prison."

"All the more reason to get out of your house and over to this pub without any more delay, goodbye councillor we'll expect you here in the next half an hour."

In fact it only took him twenty minutes and when Catherine explained that a warrant had already been issued for his arrest he went to pieces.

"Oh my God what can I do? Prison will be the death of me and my name will be forever dragged in the mud."

"Well there's nothing we can do about your name, but I believe we can keep you out of prison. Firstly take your stuff up to the high attic room. It's not used for anything more than storing things we no longer need. There's not much room in there but you'll just have to make do."

The councillor quickly did as he was told and Catherine turned to her husband.

"Alright we carry on as usual tonight and hope that Albert and his boys get out of the cells and call in here before they go to work."

Chapter Twenty

Emerging into the sunshine outside Portswood police station, Albert and his boys made straight for the Portswood Hotel. They knew they wouldn't have long because they had to be at the docks very soon. But after the comings and goings of last night every one of them needed a drink, no matter how early in the day it was.

They hammered on the public bar door and even though it was just after six in the morning the door was opened and Bernard Bumstock let them in. He went behind his bar and quickly filled enough glasses with beer for all of them. While he was doing this Catherine came up to Albert and spoke in a quiet voice.

"I've taken some food down to that odious man who's been in the secret room all night. All I got from him was a lot of abuse, so I want him out of here as soon as. I have also taken one breakfast up to the small attic room."

Albert looked sharply at her.

"Who's staying up there? I thought you never let that room."

"We don't, but this was an emergency."

Within minutes Albert came charging up the stairs and hammered on the attic room door.

"Who's there?" came the nervous reply.

"Teddy it's me, open the door I need to speak to you."

The door was cautiously opened and the frightened face of Councilor Teddy Wainright peered out. Seeing it was indeed Albert standing outside he was relieved and opened the door more fully.

Albert lost no time coming to the point.

"Alright Teddy, Catherine has told me what's happened and we need to get you out of Southampton as quickly as that can be arranged."

"Yes that would be splendid but how can we do it?"

Albert thought long and hard.

"I do have contacts in the docks and I'll be talking to them today. You must stay here and keep your head down."

"Yes yes I know that but how on earth did that police inspector find out it's been me who's tipping you off about his raids on your house?"

"I've been thinking about that and I think I know who has done this. But now isn't the time for that. The Echo will have the story by now and a whole lot of bloody coppers will be out searching for you. So stay low here today and I'll be back to see you tonight, with good news I hope."

Returning downstairs the others were quickly informed about this new development, and it was Billy Marshall who reacted first.

"How the hell did they find out about Teddy Wainright? We've kept him right out of anything to do with the gang. I can't see how they've got on to him."

"Eddie bloody Wheeler is the answer to that Billy," said Albert. "We were interviewed first this morning and I saw Wheeler and the Griffin brothers waiting to take their turn after us. They were standing outside the cell and the look Wheeler gave me was a right smirk. We gave his gang a good hiding last night and I think that was his way of saying ok you beat us, but now we're going to drop you lot right in it."

"Teddy didn't have anything to do with them did he?" asked George.

"No but he often came here to talk to me, and I think some of the members of that blasted Swaythling mob saw him. Now they've simply put two and two together."

"Well what can we do about it? DI Stapleton has been trying to find out how you get your warnings for ages. Now he has this information he'll turn this town upside down looking for Teddy."

"Yes so I'm going to talk to Bobby Artole today to see if he'll use his boat to get Teddy out of the country."

"He'll charge a bloody lot for that though won't he?"

"Yes George you're right but we must pay whatever he asks. Stapleton must never get his hands on Teddy Wainwright."

Then Albert turned to Salty Sam. "Now what about that murdering swine of yours who we've got locked up downstairs. He's got to be taken well outside of Southampton. The police are out in force looking for him as well."

"Alright, what he did to that manager was slightly excessive and out of line and he's going to pay for it. But we'll be meeting Leroy Wort in the Horse and Groom tonight and it is he who will decide Morello's fate."

With that they finished up their beers and headed off for work. Albert and the rest were busy all day so it was late afternoon before he finally managed to talk to Bobby Artole. Explaining the need to get the councilor out of the country Albert stressed the importance of the whole thing.

"We can't let the cops get him Bobby. A bent councilor, they'll throw the bloody book at him. We must get him away and I mean out of the country."

Bobby was an old hand at this game and had used his small motorboat for all sorts of dodgy dealings in the past.

"That's as maybe Albert but I don't think, even you, realize how dangerous it is to try and cross the channel at the moment.

And if we make it where is this councilor bloke going to live? Does he know anyone in France?"

"Don't worry about that Bobby, Teddy Wainright knows his way around France and he knows a lot of people there who will help him. Just get him there and he'll do the rest."

"Get him there you say, haven't I just told you how risky that is?"

"Yes I know that, but you've got across and back before so I'm sure you can do it now."

"Yes that's true but you must realize that I have to charge high for a job like this. Even if I get this geezer over, we still have to be careful not to be seen by the Germans who are occupying France. They are more of a threat than the French you see."

With a sigh Albert asked, "How much?" and was staggered at the reply.

"Two hundred quid I can't do it for less."

"Bloody hell Bobby I only want to hire you and your boat, I don't want to buy the bloody thing."

"Listen I'm the one who's taking risks here and I have overheads. Bloody petrol for a start," but Albert was ready for that one.

"I know how hard it is to get petrol at the moment and what you have to pay for it. But me and my men can take care of that. We have supplies of petrol and we'll fill your boats tanks up before you set off."

Bobby was only slightly mollified by this.

"Ok then but petrol or no petrol the price is still two hundred quid."

So the deal was struck and early the same evening, just after dark, Albert and George met with Bobby at the place where he moored his boat. This was down at the town quay and they had a nervous little trip getting Teddy Wainright there without him being spotted.

Despite Bobby's fretting and anxiety to get going, Albert took time to shake his hand and say goodbye properly.

"Good luck Teddy, thanks for all the help you've given us. Are you sure you can meet up with the people you know in France without coming across German soldiers or the bloody Gestapo?"

"Yes I know my way around there as well as I do in this country, many of the outlying farms know me and will hide me until this war is over. Good luck to you and your boys Albert and thanks for helping me."

Albert and George stood in the darkness and watched Bobby's boat move out and fade from view.

"Well that's that," said Albert. "Now let's get to the Horse and Groom and meet up with Leroy Wort."

Albert had picked up an Echo along the way and was finding plenty of interest as they walked down East Street.

"Let's see what Wort makes of this paper shall we? Because both the story of the murder by mad Pat Morello and Councilor Teddy Wainright being wanted by the police for complicity in crime, have both headlined."

"Well we'll soon know," said George as the Horse and Groom pub loomed out of the darkness.

Going into the lounge bar they almost collided with one of the stuffed bears. But, recovering quickly, they made their way over to the same corner table where Wort and Salty Sam were waiting for them. Not even bothering to order drinks Albert started straight away.

"What do you think of this then Wort," at the same time slapping the evening's local paper down onto the table in front of the Bournemouth crime king. Not used to being addressed this bluntly he, none the less, took his time and drank some of his beer before casually picked up the Echo to look at the screaming headlines.

"Well now it makes a change to see something reported that's not war related does it not?"

325

"That's hardly the bleeding point is it," Albert stormed. "Alright the missing councilor is down to us, our cock up but we've already taken care of it. Your man Morello has been a disaster since day one and we've run out of patience."

Salty Sam now intervened.

"We've made sure the coppers here have got him because he got us kicked out of the Portswood Hotel. That bloody landlady said she will not tolerate any of us animals in her pub for a moment more. Now I don't appreciate being called an animal and it was all I could do to keep my hands off of her. But then I realized it was all down to Morello. So I made arrangement for a boat to be waiting to take him down the river to where that big cinema is. I told him he would be met there and got out of town."

"The Plaza you mean at the end of Northam Bridge?"Albert asked.

"Yeah that's the place. Well a reception committee was waiting because I tipped off that copper who was interviewing all of us last night. He and a lot more coppers were waiting and pounced on Morello as soon as he got out of the boat. He put up quite a fight and two or three of them were hurt but they got the cuffs on him and he's now in a cell at the same police station we were at."

"So you see Littlejohn we sort our own problems out," said Leroy Wort. "So now that's taken care of we can get down to business about the next stage of our joint venture in this town of yours."

"No we bloody well can't," said Albert. "Morello and his thugs caused so much damage in small shops and some of the most well known pubs here that the law is out in force to protect them. Your lot have caused nothing but trouble, do what you bloody well like in Bournemouth but get the hell out of Southampton."

The atmosphere became highly charged. It was as if they were in a film and the sound had just failed, because despite the

326

noise from the other drinkers in both the lounge and public bars, at that small table in the corner there was nothing but silence. Four men glared at each other and not a word was uttered.

Salty Sam's hand went to his pocket where his knife was once more to be found. And at the same time George reached into his jacket pocket and made contact with his cosh. This moment, like something frozen in time, lasted for just a few seconds but it seemed like an eternity with plenty of menace.

Finally and perhaps surprisingly Leroy Wort diffused the situation.

"Alright have it your way, we will go back to Bournemouth. It's just a pity this hasn't worked out."

Then, getting up, he beckoned to Salty Sam and made to leave the pub. As a final gesture he patted George on the shoulder and quietly said. "I'll miss you George."

Albert, who didn't understand homosexuality at all, would normally have been a little disgusted at the look that passed between these two men. But tonight he had other things on his mind. Once they were alone George went up to the bar and bought two pints of beer and coming back to the table put one of these in front of Albert. He didn't even notice and made no move to pick the glass up and drink from it. Instead he was staring into space and it was George who finally broke the silence.

"For Christ's sake Albert, what's wrong? We've got our way and got rid of Salty Sam and his thugs. Our town is ours again now ain't it?"

"It was too easy," Albert mused. "Wort is a crime king and he always gets his own way. Now we told him to get the hell out of our town and he's just said ok and walked away. No George we haven't heard the last of this. We're going to have to keep a sharp lookout from now on. They may strike back next week or lie low for months and months until they think we have forgotten about them, but we must never forget and always be on our guard."

327

Albert's words proved to be prophetic and it was indeed some time before they would encounter their foes from down the coast, in fact three years would pass by. The war was progressing and had turned in favour of the allies. As had been expected the fateful events across the Atlantic in Pearl Harbour had an enormous impact. The presence of American GI's were a delight to children everywhere as they were more than generous with supplies of gum but it also afforded more opportunities for black market activity.

Albert and his boys were of course at the thick of it in the docks. The Americans brought different things like cakes over and some of these found their way into the back garden shed shop. The Battle of Britain was won and the Blitz receeded. Though there were still air raids these did not occur on a nightly basis and were more spread out. The German Luftwaffe simply did not have enough aircraft left to sustain the attacks at this level.

The children were growing up, little Thomas Nevan was walking about getting into all sorts of mischief whilst Maggie was now out at work full time and taking on even more responsibilities when at home to help out her mother.

Hitler had one more deadly weapon up his sleeve that he was now unleashing on this country. Doodlebugs were what they were known as but they were in effect pilotless planes, once their engines cut out they crashed to the ground where they exploded with devastating effect. None of this bothered Albert however, as long as his family was safe that was all he worried about.

In 1944 came preparations for the D-Day landings and much of the build up to that took place in Southampton. The docks were a thriving place with all sorts of craft moored ready for the big invasion that was fast approaching, There were landing craft, destroyers laden with things like the wonderful Baillie bridges, and also a floating dock which could be put together so that tanks and lorry's could simply be loaded onto it and then driven from the ships to the beaches. It was hoped that this big push should bring about the end of this war very quickly indeed.

Many girls were tearful because they had married American GIs and would now have to wait to see if they survived this invasion. Children, both boys and girls, were not so happy either as their supply of gum would go along with these troops. The threat from the air may have been less than in times before but the Channel was still full of German ships and U boats, as well as all the mines floating about.

Albert and all the dock workers were particularly busy at this time right up until the flotilla set sail for the beaches of Normandy. From there the quest to liberate Europe was on and the allies began marching towards Berlin. It seemed indeed as if the war would be coming to an end soon and times were looking up. Although ironically some of the opportunities that Albert and his men were taking advantage of would also be closed to them once the war ended.

From time to time came reminders of the events that had transpired with the rival gang from Bournemouth, none more so than when the papers were full of the trial at the Old Bailey of a gangster, one Pat Morello. It was a clear case as the police had found the blood stained clothing in his room at the Portswood Hotel, and both the knife and knuckledusters found with them covered with Morello's finger prints.

The judge, summing up before the jury left to consider their verdict, said this was the most vicious crime he had ever seen and urged the jury to come to the correct decision. This they did, in no time at all returning with a guilty verdict. The judge then had the black cap placed on his head before he sentenced Morello to death.

Albert looked up from the paper. "Well that's one of the Bournemouth lot we won't ever have to worry about. Let them hang the bastard and we'll all celebrate."

He often thought it strange that they had never heard anything more from Leroy Wort or Salty Sam. Indeed over three years had passed since the day they just walked away. A few weeks later Albert was told by Bernard that a man had called and wanted to speak with him.

"It's one of them blokes from Bournemouth who stayed here when that murdering bastard who they hanged killed that Lyon's manager."

"Where is he?"

"In the Private bar but I don't think it's safe for you to talk to him in there."

"No it won't be but that big empty space downstairs will do nicely, send him down Bernard and I'll join him soon, incidentally while we're on the subject what do you and Catherine plan to do with all that space down there once this bloody war is over?"

"She's still got some idea of making it into a club Albert. You know she loves jazz so that's what she wants to put on. She even has a name in mind for it. One of her favourite dogs is a Golden Retriever and she says it could be called the Yellow Dog jazz club. It won't ever happen of course but I just agree with her for the moment, it keeps the peace see."

A few moments later Albert went down the stairs to the bottom floor of the pub and found the man who had come to see him waiting there. He stared for a moment because he couldn't believe his eyes.

"Yeah I know you didn't expect to see me again but I have to tell you something so here I am."

"Mickie Trumpforth, you worked with Morello while you were here. So why are you back now? Is this some sort of message from Leroy Wort?"

"No it ain't a message but it is about him and what he's planning to do in a very short time from now. I worked with Morello for a long time and I ain't no bloody saint, but that last murder he did sickened me and I ain't been the same man since.

330

Oh I know he's been hanged for it but I want out, so I'm going up north where I've got friends and relatives. But Salty Sam and Leroy Wort are still mad at you for kicking them out of Southampton. Everyone sees this as an opportunity, and they had one foot in. They have never forgiven you but Leroy is so patient. He will wait and wait then strike when he thinks you are not expecting it.

They're getting a lot of blokes together and they aim to come in force and slaughter you and your gang and in the process take over here. They'll negotiate with the other Swaythling gang and if they don't join Wort and Salty then they'll be wiped out as well. Be warned, they'll come armed with guns and each and every one of them won't be afraid to use them."

Albert was silent for a moment then he looked closely at Mickie.

"How do I know this is true, and if it is why are you here warning us?"

"I told you it was that last murder and the way the Bournemouth lot took it. They simply turned Morello in and hung him out to dry. That was that as far as they were concerned. But not me, it's made me look at myself and I don't like what I see so as I said I'm getting out. You can believe me or not but I know what I'm talking about. So if you've got any sense you'll start doing something about it. Anyway I've told you and now I'm getting out of here."

As he prepared to leave Albert asked him one more question.

"If you can't tell us when they're coming can you at least tell us how?"

"Eh, what do you mean how? I don't understand."

Patiently Albert explained, "Will they come by train or rail Mickie, we need to know that much at least."

"Oh they won't come on the train cause they're still running full all the time, no they've got enough cars and petrol so they'll come by road, through the New Forest and into Southampton from there."

"Right Mickie thanks, I appreciate you taking the time to warn us about this, good luck with getting up north."

"Thanks Mr. Littlejohn and good luck to you as well."

As he was leaving Albert called after him, "On your way out Mickie will you ask George Harcourt to come down and join me please."

A few moments later George appeared and one look at his friend and leader told him all was not well.

"What the hell's wrong Al?"

As swiftly as he could Albert told George all that Mickie Trumpforth had told him and now both men knew they were in for the fight of their lives if they were to repel this threat and make sure the town stayed theirs.

"You say they'll all be armed with guns Al, which means we're stuffed don't it? We've only got a couple of guns between us."

"Hmm yes I know that George so we need help, and I think I know how to get it, leave this to me for now and I'll get onto it bloody quick."

Just a few hours later Albert was in the telephone box that was situated on the corner of Dukes Road. Here he carefully examined the crumpled piece of paper in his hand and slowly dialed the number. He had put three pennies in the slot and as soon as the phone was picked up at the other end, pressed button A so that he was connected. It was a ladies voice on the other end.

"Hello who is this please?"

"This is Albert Littlejohn in Southampton and I would like to speak to Benny Motson please."

The lady on the other end of the phone took few seconds to work out who this was.

"Oh yes the man who helped our nephew Michael when his ship was bombed. Well it's nice to speak to you and to thank you for what you and your men did for Michael that day. Hold on a second and I'll get my husband."

332

It was a couple of minutes before the phone was picked up again at the other end.

"Littlejohn it's good to hear from you but if I'm right this means you're in some sort of trouble and need our help."

"Yes I'm afraid so Benny, it's quite serious. My gang and I are soon to be attacked by a large mob from Bournemouth. They will be led by a man named Leroy Wort and his sidekick Salty Sam the Bournemouth knifeman. We kicked them out of Southampton three years ago now but now we've been warned that they're getting a lot of men together to wipe us out."

"Like the elephant that never forgets I see, and how are they going to do this?"

Albert told him what Trumpforth had said about this mob being armed with guns. "We ain't got no guns here so I don't see how we can protect ourselves from a threat like this. I wondered if you could help us to get some?"

"Yes that's not a problem but just getting guns isn't the answer to this so phone again at this time tomorrow and I'll tell you what we can and will do to help you."

Albert relayed this message to the rest of his gang in the Portswod Hotel that evening.

"This sounds good Al especially if they can get some guns for us."

"I think they're going to do more than that George, don't be surprised if a whole lot of them turn up here in Southampton to join us in this fight to the death with Leroy Wort, Salty Sam and the rest of their boys."

Later that evening Albert spoke to Bernard and Catherine Bumstock.

"I know you two have helped us a lot while this war has been going on, but what we're facing now is far more serious than anything me and my gang have dealt with before. That Bournemouth mob are coming, this time armed with guns, and their aim is to wipe us out completely."

Catherine was shocked. "What kill you all you mean?"

333

"Yes, that's what tends to happen when guns are involved."

Albert had felt a bit more confident since speaking to Benny, enough to even be able to joke about the situation.

"Bloody hell Albert what can me and Bernard do to help?"

"Two things, first of all a lot of men I think will be coming down from London to join us for this fight. If you can squeeze them in here for as long as they need to stay that will be a great help. And secondly, Bernard, I'm sending four of my boys down to Bournemouth to keep an eye out for that mob. We need to know when they're on the move. Once they have information they will phone here and send the warning. It's bloody important that message gets to me as soon as you hear it."

Bernard didn't even flinch. "Ok Albert you know you can rely on me."

"And don't worry about accommodation," said Catherine, "if these men are coming here to help you then we will fit them in somewhere. Some of them may have to sleep on the floor but that's better than nothing."

So the scene was set and early next morning Albert was once more putting pennies into the slot of the same phone box. He soon found himself talking again to Benny Motson.

"Ah good morning Littlejohn, well since we talked yesterday I have spoken to our crime lords up here. They wanted to know why we should help you and I told them of the debt I owe you where my nephew Michael is concerned. They are now ready willing and able to come down and assist in your fight with these hoodlums from Bournemouth.

So, I'm on my way down there later today and I'll be bringing ten of our best boys with me. They love a fight and each one of them is handy with a gun. We'll also bring more guns for you and your boys to use. Now then two questions for you. Where will me and my boys stay while we're down there, and when is this Bournemouth lot expected to move? I need answers to these before I can commit from this end."

334

"To answer the first one I've already spoken to the landlady of the Portswood Hotel and she is going to put all of you up. It will be a crush but she'll fit you in somewhere. And as for the other question we don't know when that lot will move but I'm sending four of my men down there to keep watch where both Leroy Wort and Salty Sam hang out. They'll be under strict orders to phone the pub when they see any large movements and they'll know bloody Salty Sam as soon as they see him."

"That sounds about right," said Benny, "Ok we'll be down there with you later on today so I'll see you then."

Albert has already dispatched Lenny Warren, Pat Matthews, Harry Small and Ned Smallbridge to Bournemouth, with strict instructions.

"It's bloody vital we know when that lot are starting out, so find somewhere to stay down there. It won't be easy because they've been bombed the same way we have, but you're sure to find a B&B somewhere. I'm sending four of you so you can work in shifts, two watching and two getting some sleep. So once you see that mob starting to make a move get to the nearest phone and let Bernard know."

Now waiting in the Portswood Hotel for their friends from London to arrive Albert was being told of some more setbacks to their gang activities.

"It's Cyril Flushy Al," said George. "His butcher shop was hit by one of those doodlebugs and he was inside at the time. The whole shop was destroyed and they're still looking for what's left of Cyril."

"Damn, he was a good bloke and very helpful to us. We'll miss the old bugger in more ways than one. His help with storing our meat in his freezer was great. But we've got more important things to worry about at the moment."

"Yes I know," George hesitated, "but there's one more thing."

Albert looked sternly at his second in command.

335

"It's old Percy Winkleman, he and his faithful old horse were also caught by the blast from one of those deadly things and both of them are dead as well."

This came as a shock to all of them. Percy was well liked, the whole gang had a genuine affection for him. Even George appeared to be a bit down upon hearing this news. But there wasn't really time to take it in, before Albert could comment on this there came the sound of cars drawing up outside.

Eleven men came into the bar and it was very clear these were serious criminals. Benny Motson was leading them and Albert got up to greet him. Shaking hands they went to the bar and Bennyy was introduced to Bernard and Catherine Bumstock.

"Welcome to the Portswood Hotel sir," Catherine greeted him. "My husband and I will try to make you and your men as comfortable as we can, though with so many of you I'm afraid there will be a lot of doubling up."

"That's alright Catherine these men are used to roughing it I can assure you," said Albert. "But it's just ten to put up here. Benny will be staying with me and my family in Empress Road."

Once all the London men had been served with drinks and shown to their rooms Albert made his way home with Bennyy Motson. Ida Littlejohn had welcomed him into the house and now Maggie was getting him some supper. When it arrived Benny was surprised to see red salmon sandwiches along with big pickled onions on his plate.

"You live alright down here then don't you?"

"Yes Mr. Motson, my husband and his gang make sure that we, along with many of our neighbours, do not go without food supplies," said Ida. "The shops often run out and families go hungry as a result, but not us."

"Then it's just as well we have come down to see that he and his men aren't wiped out by this threat from Bournemouth. I haven't forgotten how both of you, along with your children, welcomed and looked after my nephew when he was hurt after his ship got hit by a German bomb. The boy means so much to me and my wife. If it hadn't been for you young Michel would have died, as the galley was already on fire when they dragged him out. Then you looked after him until he was fit enough to return to London and live with us again."

"It was a pleasure," said Ida. "He's such a nice well mannered young man and it was lovely having him here for a while. Where is he now, still in London with you?"

"No he's back at sea but we're not so worried now as we were before. The U boat threat seems to be all but over, as is this war."

Maggie overheard this conversation as she started washing up and cast her mind back to the time when Michael had stayed in the house. She knew she hadn't been very welcoming and felt a little guilty but she had been very young then. Things would be different now, she had always wondered what happened to him and was glad he was doing alright.

Benny finished his supper and was shown where he would be sleeping. He and Albert were going to be making plenty of plans the next day. Sure enough after work all members of the Littlejohn gang were gathered in the downstairs room below the public and private bars of the Portswood Hotel. They had taken over the small bar in the corner, so each one of them had a drink as they listened to Benny Motson.

He was stood in the centre of the room surrounded by his own London men and on the floor was a very sturdy box. It was unusual for Albert not to be in command at a meeting but in this case he was quite happy to stand aside.

"Now then boys as you can see my men are ready to step into this fight you are about to be engaged in and support you. But make no mistake, what you will face will be something none of you have ever been involved in before. I know, from what Albert here has told me, that each of you is good in a fight.

337

Well that's fine, but you were using your fists then, or maybe a cosh or two," he said as he glanced at George who acknowledged him with a nod.

"And you had other weapons to help you," Benny continued. "This time it's far worse than that. You will be up against a very determined gang of tough men who are intent on trying to wipe you out and take over the crime scene in this town. And they'll all be armed with guns. Now my men and me have been in this sort of situation many times before and we've always held our own against other gangs.

London is a mecca for crime so to be able to survive up there it's not only necessary to handle a gun, but have the bottle to use one. This box contains sixteen guns. Now, we're going to hand some out to you so take one and be prepared to use it. We haven't time to train you because this fight is almost upon us so the training will be on the job when this all kicks off.

Albert and I have studied the terrain of the New Forest and we think the best place to set up an ambush is between the village of Ashurst and the town of Lyndhurst. There's a long stretch of road and we can be ready on both sides. Now, when you see them coming wait until I fire the first shot then open up with everything we've got.

Aim at the tyres to stop the cars and force the men to get out. When they do, aim to bring them down fast. And one more thing," he stressed as the Littlejohn gang were being handed guns by the London team, "it's vital none of you lose your bottle once the shooting starts. If you do then the Bournemouth lot will gain the advantage. Remember they're coming here to try and kill all of you so let's make sure we kill them first."

All of the Littlejohn gang responded by cheering. When peace was restored everyone could hear the telephone ringing in the public bar.

Chapter Twenty One

Bernard answered the phone and heard the excited voice of Lenny Warren down the other end of the crackly line.

"Bernard," he shouted, "can you get Albert it's bloody urgent."

Albert took the phone. "Hello Lenny, what have you got for me?"

"They're moving Albert, all of us have seen what's happening and I can tell you that Leroy Wort and that bloody Salty Sam are leading the whole thing. They're coming in a procession of cars. We got to the train station and saw them set off."

"Right Lenny thanks for this, are all four of you at the station now?"

"Yes and there's a train leaving for Southampton in ten minutes time, we'll all be on that."

"Right there will be a car waiting for you and it will bring you to the village of Ashurst. The car will be parked there with the rest of ours. Then, all of you walk down the road until you see me waving to you, have you got that?"

"Yes and we'll do as you say," shouted Lenny before ringing off.

Albert went back downstairs to report to everyone what was going on.

"The Bournemouth mob is on its way so we need to do the same. Have you all got guns? Bring the spares for the other boys to have when we meet them."

There was a chorus of cheers as each member of the Littlejohn gang raised their gun into the air. Benny Motson and his London men also indicated they were ready for the coming fight so this combined army came up into the public bar, left the pub and started walking towards Portswood Junction.

Coming to the Gordon Arms they turned into Gordon Avenue. Here, the London boys had parked all their cars and now everyone piled into these. Just one was told not go with the rest and that was Billy Marshall who was instructed to drive to Southampton Central Railway Station to pick up Lenny Warren and the other three from the Bournemouth train. Then to drive down to Ashurst and park with the rest of the cars in front of the row of shops where there was a space.

"Walk on down the road, but watch out for me Billy," Albert told him. "I will see you coming and will wave, so when you see that run over as quickly as you can and join us."

Now sitting in the front seat of the lead car next to Benny Motson, who was driving, Albert admitted he was concerned about his gang.

"My boys are all fired up for this but none of them have used a gun before so I hope they don't lose their bottle once the shooting starts."

"I've had time to look them over, and I can tell you I like the look of them. I'll fight with you all any time so don't worry about that."

Coming to the small but tranquil village of Ashurst they all pulled into the spaces outside the shops then got out of the cars. It was mid morning and some of the curtains in the big houses opposite the shops were twitching as people looked out, surprised to see so many cars arriving and parking up near their homes. They also didn't like the sight of so many tough, intimidating looking men.

This of course didn't bother Albert or any of the others one single bit as they made their way towards the bridge over the railway line. Here it curved and led to the long stretch of forest road leading on up to the larger town of Lyndhurst. They walked down this for a short distance before splitting up and taking cover in the trees on either side. Benny Motson went with his boys on one side while Albert, with his, occupied the other. George Harcourt reminded all of them that they had to wait for the first shot to be fired by Mostson before any of them opened up.

The next three quarters of an hour were sheer tension as they waited for the sound of cars. The road at present was deserted save for a few ponies walking across it on their way to graze. But, after half an hour, George nudged Albert.

"Someone's coming from that village. It should be Billy Marshall with the rest of our boys."

It was indeed and Albert stood up and signalled. Billy Marshall saw him and rushed with the others to join the rest of the gang in hiding on the right hand side of the deserted road. They were given guns and told to wait until they heard the first shot fired by Benny Motson. Then, as Albert put it, "We open up on those bastards from Bournemouth and make sure it's them who are wiped out, not us."

For the next half an hour they waited and watched the ponies grazing and, to the delight of some of them, a small herd of deer appeared and went across the road. Then, in the distance, came the unmistakable sound of many car engines.

Albert tensed and whispered, "here it is boys so let's get ready to blast them."

The cars appeared and came on at a reasonable speed and as they reached the spot where the reception committee was waiting a single shot rent the air.

"Right lads let them have it," Albert shouted.

Standing up he pointed his gun at the road and opened fire. Shots now rang out from both sides and the gangsters in the leading cars suffered badly. Many were killed while others were badly injured. In the rear cars however, men were pouring out and they started to return the fire. The air was thick with both noise and smoke from the guns and many more of the Bournemouth crowd got hit. They didn't have the advantage of cover that their enemies were enjoying.

Albert watched as the battle progressed, then at last he got the chance to take the shot he most wanted to fire. Salty Sam poked his head up to get a clearer view and Albert squeezed his trigger. The bullet hit Sam squarely in the center of his forehead and his lifeless body fell to the ground.

The battle was going well and so far none of the Littlejohn Gang had been hit. The London boys were also still intact. But, out on the road, there were bodies lying all over the place. George Harcourt was enjoying himself hugely, normally using a cosh in any sort of fight he was finding the gun did so much more damage to his enemies. If the shot was good they would go straight down and stay down.

So George was getting reckless, poking his head up and shouting insults at the Bournemouth lot as he sent more bullets flying in their direction. Watching this was Billy Marshall, and in that moment the hatred he had always felt towards George after being raped by him in the Highfield Road house back in 1940 rose to the surface.

He had never got over the humiliation of that day because he was a young man who loved women. So to have a man forcing him to strip naked and then doing unspeakable things to his body was something that had burned right into his soul. He had never let George see how much he loathed him so the cosh had no idea of the danger he was in at that moment. Billy was suddenly not in the trees in the New Forest but back in that house where the atrocity took place.

Having enjoyed wonderful sex with the girl Albert kept at the house, he came out of the room to be threatened by the most famous cosh in Southampton, then forced into a bedroom on the other side of the landing and given the choice. Strip and give in or suffer the cosh. He saw again his own clothes strewn across the floor and suddenly felt the pressure of the man who had been on top of him.

It was all too much and Billy could no longer control his temper. Right in his line of fire was the man who had done all that to him and Billy knew this was his chance to get his revenge. So, with the gunfight raging all around him, he took aim and fired.

The bullet hit George Harcourt squarely in the centre of his chest. He looked up and saw Billy's face behind the gun and, with a look of total amazement and shock, sank slowly to the ground. He was dead before he hit it and Billy quietly said to himself, *'That's got you back you bastard. Now you won't be taking advantage of any more young men.'*

Albert was firing at a steady rate, as were the London boys on the other side of the road, the noise of this battle shattering the usually peaceful scene in this beautiful forest setting. So much so that the people of Ashurst had come out of their houses to try and find out what was going on. Many of them believing that German troops had landed in a last desperate attempt to salvage the war and our army were fighting against them.

Suddenly however, from one of the shops, came an excited shout.

"It's over, the wars over. The Germans have surrendered."

All too soon this message was relayed everywhere so now people did not find it odd to hear so much noise. Hitler was dead and the war was over. All over the country people were reacting to having to be quiet for so long by making as much noise as possible, with children encouraged to run up and down the streets banging pans. A lot more noise was going to be made on this historic day of May 8th 1945.

On the road however this news certainly hadn't reached any of the combatants, but this battle was rapidly reaching its conclusion. Many of the Bournemouth men now lay dead and it was clear they had lost, so the firing ceased. With silence descending one sound became very audible, that of the last car in the convoy revving its engine as it turned in the road to speed off.

They let it go because Albert wanted to make sure that the biggest threats to him and his gang were lying amongst the dead. He looked around and soon found Salty Sam's body. The bullet wound in this man's forehead and the amount of blood that it had caused meant he wouldn't ever be threatening anyone ever again. But search as he could there was no sign of Leroy Wort.

Benny Motson now took charge and had all the dead bodies put back inside the cars. Even though the tyres had been shot out, he had them driven under the cover of the trees.

"This will hide them for a while at least and it will give us the time we need to get away. Your men can come in our cars and we'll drop them off in Southampton before we go back to London."

Albert hardly acknowledged this though as he was gazing down at the dead body of George Harcourt.

"We've been together for more years than I can remember. How the hell am I going to run this gang without you?"

Benny was sympathetic but also determined to put an end to this conflict and get them out as quickly as he could. He spoke gently.

"I know how you feel and it's a bastard to lose someone who means a lot to you. But his body must be put with the rest and you can be assured that all of your men except him have survived."

Albert looked down upon the still form of his friend.

"Ok but give me a few minutes first."

Then, standing alone, he addressed him one last time. "Goodbye George, somehow this gang has got to go on but without you and I haven't a bloody clue how it can. But one thing I am promising you is that the people who are responsible for this ain't going to get away with it."

He had no idea of course that the bullet that had killed his friend had been fired by one of his own men.

Benny Motson now joined him.

"Shall we leave his body here with the rest?"

"No, he goes back to Southampton with us. At least with the rest of my men, but I need to borrow one of your cars."

"Why?"

"The leader of the Bournemouth mob got away and he's the bastard I want, so I'm going after him. If I survive this we'll get it back to you as soon as we can."

"Don't bother about that we can manage without it. Get your boys back home before we high tail it back to London. Anyway only three of our cars actually belong to us. We, shall we say, borrowed the rest. You can have one of those and do whatever you want with it afterwards."

He suddenly looked up. "What the bloody hell is all that noise?"

It was coming from Ashurst and getting louder by the minute. Cries of "We've won, we've beaten the German's," were renting the air as was the sound of children who had been given plenty of pots and pans to make a noise with and they needed no persuasion to comply.

"Good God, the bloody wars over at last," said Benny Motson as he looked down the road. "We'll need to get going there's a mob of people coming this way and they'll block the roads."

So, shaking hands with Albert he wished him luck then got everyone back in the cars. His parting shot made everyone laugh.

"At least the bloody coppers will get held up if they're on the way to find out about the shooting in this peaceful forest."

345

Albert now sat in the car and tried to get his nerves under control. He knew what lay ahead and wanted to get on with it. But, as Benny Motson had pointed out, this quiet road was now full of people as crowds from Lyndhurst were out and about celebrating the wonderful news of the end of the Second World War.

He started the engine and slowly edged his way through people as they banged on the windows and gave him the victory V sign. It took some while before he could see a clear road ahead but quickly put his foot down and raced along the now open road.

Bournemouth was the same as every other town and city in Great Britain on this day with streets thronged with people dancing and singing at the wonderful news. Albert had to slow almost to a stop to get through and many more Victory sings were directed at him. He had to remember George's description of the way to Leroy Wort's flat but his memory was good and he finally stopped outside the building.

However repeated banging on the door of the flat brought nothing but silence from inside. So Albert left and started walking towards the highest part of the cliffs. He could see the rails of the funicular railway in the distance, the cars having been taken away back in 1940 in case of invasion by German troops. As he stared at it he suddenly noticed a lone figure gazing out to sea.

His walk turned into a rapid sprint because this was indeed the figure of Leroy Wort so he reached into his pocket and pulled out a gun. This was the same one they had taken from Philip Burton all those years ago and now Albert was going to put it to good use.

He almost made it to him without being noticed, and now shouted at him. "Wort, turn around you bastard I've to come to finish you."

Spinning round the king of Bournemouth crime saw the threat and acted swiftly to counter it. Without a word he too pulled his gun and two shots blasted out.

Wort's bullet hit Albert high up on his right shoulder and sent him spinning backwards to land on his back. He was in pain but still alive and after a time managed to get to his feet. Of Wort there was no sign at all. So Albert walked to the edge of the cliffs thinking he may have gone over the edge. But there was still no sign with no body lying on the beach below.

He was really angry believing his quarry had once more eluded him when something attracted his attention. All was not well on the rails of the funicular railway and the reason for this was the dead body of Leroy Wort.

Albert's bullet had hit him on the left side of his chest and entered his heart, bringing instant death. It had also sent him reeling backwards where he had fallen off the cliff down onto the rails. Albert looked down at him, with blood still running along his arm from the wound in his shoulder and quietly said 'Good riddance you filthy swine' before turning to make his way back to the car.

There was an irony here that was missed completely by Albert and that was the position of Wort's body on those railway lines. Back in 1940 he had horribly murdered the pick pocket Fingers Malone by having him tied to the rails then sending one of the cars down to crush him. It was such a terrible crime that it raised much concern and was still being talked about today. Now it was Wort's body lying there in exactly the same position as his pathetic murder victim's had been nearly five years before and it seemed like justice had now come full circle.

Albert's last act before making his slow return to Southampton was to get rid of the gun he used to kill Leroy Wort. This was thrown from the cliffs into the sea and as he watched it disappear he knew that it was the end, not just of the war, but of his life in this country. He started his car knowing he would have to first explain things to his wife then avoid capture by DI Stapleton.

As he drove he thought to himself 'This is another job for Bobby Artole.'

Epilogue

Whilst the end of the war was reason for much rejoicing, this did however create problems for DI Stapleton and his men. Having received reports of gunshots being fired in the New Forest, together with eyewitness accounts of the battle that was raging there, he had brought his team together and made what he hoped would be a very quick dash to the reported scene.

With so many people dancing in the streets and bonfires made up of the hated blackout curtains starting up all over the place, it took considerably longer for him to reach the spot just past the village of Ashurst. When he did get there he was met by Inspector Wallford of Lyndhurst Constabulary who led the Southampton party over to the wrecked cars still amongst the trees. "This is how we found them, and we make it eleven men dead."

DI Stapleton and Sergeant Podcove grimly surveyed the scene and soon came upon a face that both of them recognized.

"Well we've seen this fellow before," the DI said, "and we know a lot about him now. We first came across him in Southampton when he came out with that cock and bull story about being there looking for suitable premises to open an animal feed business. We've checked up on him of course and he's a well-known criminal from Bournemouth. Now this gives us a lead to Albert Littlejohn and his gang, because this man was with them in the Portswood Hotel that day. We can follow it up and finally get our hands on Littlejohn. If we can pin murder on him it will get rid of him for good because he'll be for the drop."

The DI didn't realise just how close he had come because another car had passed theirs as they travelled in opposite directions. Albert, edging his way through ever increasing throngs of people on his way back to Southampton, whilst the police cars were doing the very same thing as they tried to make headway towards the crime scene.

Upon reaching his home town he made a diversion to the doctor who was always on hand when first aid was needed, even though he had long since been struck off the medical registry. He looked closely at Albert's shoulder.

"Well the bullet isn't in the wound but you've lost a lot of blood. You need to be in bed for the next few days."

"No I can't do that doc, I have to be out of the country as soon as I can arrange it. Just put a bandage on it so it stops the bleeding."

His next call was to the home of Alan Kinslade whom he found in the company of Johnnie Burton. Both boys were shocked at his appearance, he had lost so much blood the colour had drained from his face and the newly applied bandage on his shoulder was already red.

"Don't worry about me. I'm only here to bring your wages for the brilliant job you all did, warning us of the coming of that Swaythling mob. Now those for you both and the other three leaders are in this envelope and the rest of your boys can be paid out from what's in this big envelope. Now two things have happened, the end of the war and probably the end of my gang. So I want you all to retire from the work you've done for us. Enjoy the rest of your youth and just do the things boys are supposed to do."

Then as he left he turned back, "And when you go swimming, take your ruddy clothes off first."

The grins he got in response told him they would take no notice of this piece of advice. Now he needed to contact Bobby Artole before making his way back to the house in Empress Road and speaking with Ida.

He found Bobby at the Town Quay doing odd jobs to his boat and when he saw Albert he exploded.

"Bloody hell mate what the hell has happened to you. You look as if you're at deaths door."

"It's just a shoulder wound and I need to be out of this country bloody smartly, can you take me to France in a couple of days time?"

"Do you think you'll last that long? I tell you mate, you do look awful."

"Bobby can you take me or not, I need to know."

"Relax Albert, I'll take you but where do you want to land over there?"

"The same place where you dropped Teddy Wainright, I've already got a message to him telling him I'm coming so he'll be there to meet me."

The deal was quickly done so Albert headed home.

Ida screamed when she saw him and Maggie also looked shocked at her father's appearance. He calmed them both down assuring them that he would get medical help when he arrived at his chosen destination.

"I have to get out of the country Ida, there's been a gunfight in the New Forest and a lot of blokes have been killed. It won't take bloody DI Stapleton long to put me and my gang in the frame for it. Now the boys are all coming here tomorrow to move this furniture and all of yours and the kid's things because you're all moving."

"Moving?" Ida gave an incredulous gasp. "What do you mean we're moving? And where to I should like to know?"

"The house in Highfield Lane Ida, I want you and our kids to live there now. It's been empty for some time. I did offer one of the girls from the café in the docks the job of moving in to look after the place but she turned me down, said her boyfriend wouldn't like it. So all of you are moving in tomorrow, get packing quickly."

"Just like that?" Ida protested. "It's nowhere near as simple as that, how are we supposed to be able to move into such an expensive property? The houses there must cost a bloody fortune and we ain't got anywhere near enough to even rent."

Albert went to one of the drawers in the old sideboard and after rummaging around for a few moments came out with a brown buff envelope.

351

"It's all in here love, the deeds of that house and other things that will back you up if and when the bloody coppers start sniffing around. See, I knew I couldn't just hand the house over to you because of the law in this country, that no-one can gain from the proceeds of crime. So I've used my knowledge of the crime scene here and have come up with Cyril Marlow. He's the best forger in this country and this envelope contains a great sample of his work. The house is in your name, it always was, and the money to buy it has come from the legacy of one your rich but eccentric relatives."

"But I ain't got no rich relatives, eccentric or otherwise."

Albert simply smiled back at her.

"You have now. Cyril Marlow has created one and given her a birth certificate and identity card. I tell you Ida the man's a bloody genius. All the proof you need is here so all you have to do is move. The neighbours there will be curious so if any of them get too nosy you simply tell them your husband was killed in the war. The kids will be fine. They can go to my old school, Portswood Secondary Modern. Even young Thomas can start now in the infants."

"This is all very well Albert. But when will we get to see you again? The children need their father."

"I can't answer that at the moment Ida, but I won't be that far away and I will be in touch with you all, if only by letter."

The next day saw the Littlejohn family moving out and it brought all the neighbours out to watch. But once completed the younger children were rushing around the house and the garden because they couldn't believe they were going to be living in this big, comfortable house that even had an indoor bathroom with a toilet. This was sheer luxury for them.

As they were settling in DI Stapleton was in his office at Portswood Police Station.

"We've got enough to bring the members of the Littlejohn gang in Sergeant. But all we can really prove is that they were there. We've nothing to say any one of them killed any of the men we found in those cars. And we haven't got Albert Littlejohn have we?"

"No sir but we just found out his family have moved from Empress Road. The whole house as well as that rickety old shed is clear and empty."

"Well I suppose we've smashed their gang. We've found the body of George Harcourt. He's the one piece of evidence we do have because the cause of death is a bullet to the chest. But as for the rest of the gang all we can charge them with is disturbing the peace of the forest."

The irony of this was not lost on him and he allowed himself a chuckle.

"Once that message came out of Downing Street about the end of the war so many grown-ups and kids were out celebrating there wasn't really any peace to disturb. They made a damn sight more noise than any gunfight."

"So what do we do sir?" asked the sergeant. "Round up all of the remaining members of Littlejohn's gang and charge them with affray with a deadly weapon. It won't stand up in court but it may put the fear of Christ up all of them."

DI Stapleton closed the drawer he had been clearing. "I'll leave that decision to you Sergeant. Either way it won't involve me anymore because as from a few moments ago I am retired."

Ida quickly settled into the house in Highfield Lane and looked back over all of her time with Albert. It may have been quite dodgy at times but the way he beat the coppers all the time was exciting. She looked out of the window and watched her three boys busily kicking a football around the big garden. At least they didn't really know what their father had done so none of them would try to copy him. She'd made quite sure of that.

What she failed to notice was the fact it was only her two eldest boys playing with the football. Her youngest son, Thomas Evan Littlejohn was standing on his own in a world of his own. Even though such a young child, he had somehow watched his dad

353

and knew he had been a crook, and it excited him. Unlike his brothers, his father's spirit was inside him and growing all the time. How could Ida or anybody else know that this innocent looking boy was in fact someone who was quite literally born to be evil.